PRAISE FOR
DOCTOR WITCH

"In *Doctor Witch*, Frank Edwards performs true literary sorcery: he delivers a wickedly suspenseful novel that also has enormous heart and many comedic moments. These characters and their harrowing adventures will stay with you long after you've read the last sentence. A very fine new book from a writer of many gifts."

—CHRISTINE SNEED, author of *The Virginity of Famous Men* and *Please Be Advised: A Novel in Memos*

"*Doctor Witch* is a fast-paced, suspenseful thriller written by an author who knows how to craft a spellbinding story. The plot could be straight out of a James Bond movie, but with Frank Edwards's own unique twists and turns. This stand-alone third in the Jack Forester series is a can't-put-down tale that will keep you on the edge of your seat until the end."

—KAREN SHUGHART, author of the Edmund DeCleryk mystery series

"There's far more going on at New Canterbury Medical Center than meets the eye. A megalomaniac who runs a floating nation has the facility in his crosshairs, a beautiful impostor stalks the halls, and a creepy serial killer lurks nearby, too. Frank J. Edwards's imagination fills the pages with so many twists, turns, and evil plots—good luck putting it down and turning in for the night! A great novel."

—MATT BARROWS, coauthor of *Muddy the Water*

"In his latest in the Jack Forester series, Edwards draws on his own medical and combat experience to deliver a gripping thriller. Losing his job as director of the university's medical center, Dr. Forester struggles to overcome life-threatening obstacles placed in his way by an international conglomerate. Edwards skillfully casts new light on key events in earlier books (including the death of Forester's wife) while priming the reader to anticipate future developments."

—RAY COLLINS, author of *Setup* and *Motive for Murder*

DOCTOR WITCH

Doctor Witch

by Frank J. Edwards

© Copyright 2025 Frank J. Edwards

ISBN 979-8-88824-617-7

All rights reserved. No part of this publication may be reproduced, stored in a retrieval system, or transmitted in any form or by any means—electronic, mechanical, photocopy, recording, or any other—except for brief quotations in printed reviews, without the prior written permission of the author.

This is a work of fiction. All the characters in this book are fictitious, and any resemblance to actual persons, living or dead, is purely coincidental. The names, incidents, dialogue, and opinions expressed are products of the author's imagination and are not to be construed as real.

Cover art and design by Lauren Sheldon

Published by

3705 Shore Drive
Virginia Beach, VA 23455
800-435-4811
www.koehlerbooks.com

A JACK FORESTER THRILLER

DOCTOR WITCH

FRANK J. EDWARDS

VIRGINIA BEACH
CAPE CHARLES

This book wouldn't have been possible without the support, encouragement, and close advice of Mary Ann.

CHAPTER ONE

OCTOBER 2018

Dr. Jack Forester had been lying awake, eyes open in the darkness, when the bedroom door creaked open and there came the rustle of small feet on the carpet.

"Julia," he said.

"I had a bad dream, Daddy," said the four-year-old.

He lifted her. She was still so light. The clock said four thirty. He smoothed her hair, fragrant with baby shampoo. "Everything's okay," he said.

"I thought someone was hiding in the closet."

"Would you like me to check it again?"

"No," she said. "I know there's nothing really there. Can I stay here?"

"Of course." He slid the covers over her.

"Why don't I remember what Mommy looked like?"

He inhaled slowly. She'd asked this once before, a few months ago. "Because you were very young," he said. "That's why you have her picture in your room, to look at whenever you want."

"I know, but it won't stick. When I close my eyes and think about her, all I see is either Aunt Zoë or Kaitlyn."

Not surprising. There were family resemblances, especially in his niece Kaitlyn's profile. "You should go back to sleep now," he said. "I've got to get up in a little while and I'll try not to wake you."

"Why do you work so much?" she said. "Do you love it?"

"Not as much as I love you."

"Why don't you retire? Then you could stay home. Susan's grandfather retired, but she says he goes golfing all the time."

"I won't be able to do that for quite a while."

"Like when you're a grandfather?"

"Like then, maybe," he said. He tried to imagine her all grown up, married, moved away, children of her own. What would she remember of her childhood? He hoped it wouldn't be of the hours she spent wondering when he would come home.

Sighing, she settled in and her breathing grew regular. He wouldn't mind dozing off himself, but that was unlikely to happen. Those two scotches and the sleeping pill that used to keep him down till five thirty hadn't worked again. He should return to exercising in the evenings after work, even if he felt exhausted. He should push through the fatigue instead of ending up in these predawn hours feeling suspended between the past and present, sorting through uncomfortable memories. An odd image came to him of an old man scrubbing dirty socks on a washboard, rinsing them again and again, waiting for the sun to bleach them clean. In any case, the sooner day broke, the better.

The psychiatric literature says that intense grief reactions following the death of a spouse may take six months or even a year to lift. But Zellie's car accident had happened three years ago, and the pain at times was still as raw and paralyzing as the day he got the phone call. He knew the reason for this. Though he wasn't in the car with her, he felt responsible for what had happened. He hadn't shared this sense of responsibility with anyone yet. He knew that keeping it to himself was in some ways cowardly, but he wasn't sure that sharing would help. More than that, sharing it would force him to cross a line in his mind, beyond which lay something that seemed even more unbearable. So he existed and waited and remembered, letting his life's compass shrink into the elements that mattered most to him—his daughter and his work—and trying to take care of those things the best he could.

The sudden chirping of his cell phone on the nightstand startled him. Its screen glowed, casting a greenish light on the ceiling. The sound was that of an incoming text.

Julia stirred. "Don't they ever leave you alone, Daddy?" she mumbled.

That could have only been a phrase she'd picked up from Zoë, the aunt who had been living with them since shortly after his wife's death, an addition to his household that made a semblance of normal life possible. He sighed and reached for the phone. When he saw who the sender was, his eyes widened. It was Jan Cummings, the university president. He sat up. This was unprecedented. She had never texted him before—and certainly never at such an unusual time. Looks like he wasn't the only insomniac in New Canterbury this morning. The message was brief and coldly succinct.

Jack—Critical situation involving the med center. Urgent meeting in my conference room at 11:30 a.m. Say nothing till then. Text back to acknowledge.

Blinking, he read it over several times before thumbing a response: *I'll be there.*

Julia was sitting up now too and staring at him, her face pale in the screen's light. "What's the matter, Daddy?"

CHAPTER TWO

In the predawn darkness, Jack eased out of his driveway and headed toward the distant lights of New Canterbury down in the valley, coasting much of the way. He crossed over the Seneca River Bridge, where the countryside ended and the city began. Reaching his fifth-floor office at the medical center by six o'clock, he brewed himself a mug of coffee and took it to a window from which he could look out over the sprawling complex—the two clinical towers, the nursing school, the medical school, and the original hospital building. The original hospital building was three stories tall with granite front steps, limestone pillars, and a cupola on top, and it now housed the library, boardroom, research labs, and classrooms. A helicopter was approaching the brightly lit helipad above the new emergency department, and he could hear the muted whopping of rotor blades.

His pulse quickened at the sound. There was a time not long ago when he'd have been in the critical care bay awaiting its arrival, poised to do whatever was needed to save a life. After graduating from medical school here at New Canterbury, he'd completed an emergency medicine residency in California, then returned and soon became the ER director, even managing to convince most people to stop calling it the ER and use the more comprehensive term "ED." Within a few years, he had done what few thought possible, jumping through a myriad of hoops to start an accredited emergency medicine residency program. He'd worked hard, treated people well, taught enthusiastically, and never refused taking on more responsibilities. His rise through the ranks had been swift. Several years ago when in his early forties, a few months before his wife's fatal accident, he'd accepted the post of medical center dean. Early on, he'd continued to pull occasional shifts in the ED, but there were not enough hours in the day nor days in the week, and after Zellie's death, needing to spend as much time as possible with his daughter, he'd taken himself off the clinical schedule.

The medivac chopper landed, its whirling blades shimmering in the lights. He knew that the patient on board would be well cared for by his former colleagues in the ED. There were times, though, when he missed simply caring for patients. It was a more black-and-white life. You identify the problem in front of you, then act. Period. His only patient now, however, was the medical center itself—a demanding beast with countless moving parts. Despite the frustrations, he loved the work he was doing now, and he loved this place. It was home, and it helped keep him whole.

So, what in God's name was Jan Cummings talking about—a crisis at the medical center? He had his finger on the center's pulse as good as anyone and was unaware of any brewing critical situations. Finishing the coffee, he went to his computer and scanned his inbox for suggestions of something awry.

Nothing. No clues. He would have to wait.

At eleven fifteen, Jack slipped out of a meeting and headed outside, taking the footbridge over Bracken Avenue to the main campus of New Canterbury University, a sprawl of neo-Georgian buildings nestled in a curve of the Seneca River. Dodging undergraduates on skateboards and bicycles, he passed through the main quad, the lawns and brick paths thick with fallen leaves still soggy from last night's rain. The sky was gray, the air cold. At the Hawthorne Building, he rode the elevator to the fourth floor and opened the door to Jan Cummings's conference room. It was 11:25. He was five minutes early.

The only person there was Martin F. Bentley, the university provost, seated at the long cherrywood table and fixated on his phone. Bentley glanced up, wearing his usual stone-faced expression. "You're in the right place, Forester," he said. "She's running late." He returned to his phone.

A stocky man with sagging jowls, the provost was one of the few senior figures across the university with whom Jack had never been able to strike a cordial relationship over the years. Bentley made no bones about the fact he didn't think physicians made good administrators, and on a personal level, he hadn't been in favor of Jack becoming the med center dean at such a relatively young age.

"Morning, Martin," Jack said, as he pulled out a chair.

Bentley responded with a grunt and a shrug of his eyebrows. The room was warm, but the provost was wearing a tweed jacket over a shirt, tie, and yellow waistcoat. Beads of perspiration glinted through his thin reddish comb-over.

"What exactly is going on?" Jack said. "Jan mentioned a crisis."

Bentley sighed and set his phone on the table. "What's going on is a shitstorm, Forester. A category five shitstorm."

"Involving the medical center?"

"Yes."

"For how long?"

"For the past several days."

"Several days?" Jack felt his face growing warm. "Why am I just hearing about it?"

"There was no need to involve you."

"What?"

"You know, Forester, we haven't seen much of you on the main campus lately. You've missed the last few board meetings."

Jack's jaws tightened. "If this concerns the med center, where's Jason?" he shot back. Jason Everts was the medical center CEO, the business counterpart to Jack's academic role as dean.

"It hasn't been announced yet, so this is between you and me, but

Everts walked the plank this morning. He was suspended."

Jack stared, a tingle spreading over his scalp. "Suspended? Why?"

Bentley held up his hand. "I'm deferring any further explanation till the boss arrives. If it were up to me, you wouldn't be at this meeting. This is top-layer decision-making territory. You're an academic."

"You know what I think?" Jack said, swallowing. *Don't do it, Jack*, he said to himself.

"No," said Bentley. "What do you think?"

"That I'm tired of your condescending *bullshit*."

Bentley's eyebrows levitated toward his receding hairline.

At that moment the door sprang open, and Jan Cummings strode in carrying a coffee cup and a folder. Closing the door with a backward jab of her foot, she halted, looking at them. "Am I interrupting something?" she said.

Bentley cleared his throat. "Nothing of consequence. Dr. Forester was just exercising his First Amendment rights."

Obviously deciding not to pursue the matter, she dropped the folder on the table, took a sip of coffee, and glanced out the windows. "Nothing but clouds," she said. "Every damn day. Western New York is the dreariest place on the planet." She sagged rather than slid into the chair at the head of the table.

Ever since Jan Cummings had assumed the leadership role at New Canterbury University last year, Jack had never seen her anything but relaxed and elegant, always ready for a publicity photo or a press conference. Today she looked like someone who'd spent the night in her office. "Your years in California spoiled you, Jan," Bentley said, unctuously. "But you bring an inner sunshine with you."

"I'm in no mood," she said, cutting him off. "Have you given Jack any information yet?"

"Just about Everts's suspension. I thought that everything else best come from you."

She fixed Jack with a stare, her hazel eyes intense and bloodshot. Then she looked away and drew in a deep breath. "I've been in many unexpected situations. But nothing like this before. What I'm about to tell you needs to stay confidential until I say otherwise. Do you understand?"

He folded his hands and nodded.

She leaned forward. "Okay. Five days ago, I received a call from J.P. Morgan telling me that the hospital's primary disbursement account was overdrawn. Which made absolutely no sense. Last week's financial report showed the medical center having over ninety days of operating cash on hand."

Jack frowned. "Sounds like a mistake on the bank's end."

"Not hardly," said Bentley. "They've got the best—"

"I thought you wanted me to talk," she snapped, interrupting the provost.

"Please go on," Bentley said, reddening.

"Thank you," she said, looking back at Jack. "So I reached out to our comptroller, Judy Marsh, who was equally perplexed, to put it mildly. I could hear her jaw drop from the other side of the campus. Obviously, something very weird was going on, so we immediately called in a team of forensic accountants from Manhattan and they're still sorting through the mess. But so far it looks like a perfect storm of accounting errors has accumulated undetected over the past several years."

"Several years?" said Jack, his heart pounding. "What sort of errors?"

"There's quite a laundry list. They include overreporting of collections, underreporting of accounts payable, and worst of all, a failure to properly bill and collect hundreds of thousands of patient accounts. Hundreds of fucking thousands of patient accounts." She paused and took another sip of coffee. "Excuse my goddamn French."

Jack sagged back. "And no one noticed this until now?"

The provost hooked a finger in his shirt collar and twisted his neck. "We all trusted Ms. Marsh's reports, Forester. Obviously, we were getting corrupted information."

Jan set down her coffee cup with a bang. "And to be fair, she may have been getting corrupted information too. Our accounting software is ancient. The only thing we know for certain is that the med center is on the verge of bankruptcy."

Jack looked up at the ceiling and shook his head. This was some kind of joke.

"May I speak?" said Bentley.

Jan sighed. "Knock yourself out."

"That's why Jason Everts isn't here, Forester," he said. "The financials of the medical center were within his and Judy Marsh's sphere of responsibility. Both were put on administrative leave this morning."

Jack straightened. "They're taking a fall even before you know why this happened?"

"Don't look so surprised," Bentley replied. "It's standard procedure. This is what happens when a fecal typhoon makes landfall."

There came a loud knocking on the door. It opened and Jan's administrative assistant, a black-haired woman named Tulip, peered in.

Jan pushed back and rose to her feet. "This had better be important."

The assistant met her halfway and whispered in Jan's ear. Jan went visibly rigid and swung around to Jack and Bentley. "Back in a minute. Stay exactly where you are."

Swiveling his chair toward the window, Bentley made an exaggerated sigh. "What now? Listen, Forester, you're lucky your bailiwick is academics. You'll likely escape the scaffold."

Jack swallowed against the dryness in his throat. "What about you? Isn't this within your sphere of responsibility as provost?"

Bentley sniffed. "The plane I fly goes above the storm clouds. And I'm an old shitstorm survivor."

"This whole thing seems crazy," Jack said. "Why would a series of mistakes go unnoticed? Could the software have been tampered with externally?"

"The accountants say no. We may have old accounting software, but our firewall is first-rate. State-of-the-art. No evidence it was breached. Whatever happened came from inside. The real question of whether it was accidental or intentional remains to be seen."

Jack didn't know Judy Marsh well, but she seemed like a good person. The door swished open and Jan reentered. Her face had gone pale and her eyes were glistening. Lowering herself into the chair in slow motion, she reached for a tissue.

"Jan?" said Bentley.

She blew her nose and shook her head.

Jack leaned toward her, the back of his neck tingling. "What's happened?"

Jan took up another tissue. "Judy Marsh is dead. She was in a car crash. Less than an hour ago."

Bentley made a whistling sound. Jack closed his eyes, battered by a wave of shock. News of accidents reawakened memories.

"Her car went through a guardrail on the Seneca River Bridge," Jan said in a thin voice. "She was on the way home after leaving here." She paused and swallowed. "A witness told police that it looked like she kept swerving until her car rolled over the edge. It's seventy-five feet down."

"I hate to seem callous," said Bentley. "One must wonder if this might be an admission of responsibility."

Jan turned to him, her eyes widening. "Or it could have been the horror of seeing her reputation destroyed. Or a seizure or something. The least we can do is withhold judgment until we know more."

"Of course. I agree," Bentley mumbled.

"I put in a call to Jason Everts to let him know and make sure he's all right," she added. "He is, but this brings up another issue." She turned to Jack and frowned. "Are you all right, Jack?"

He folded his hands and cleared his throat. "Yes."

She went on. "With Jason gone, we need an interim med center CEO for the time being. I know you've got the confidence of the medical staff, Jack. That will be crucial for morale in the coming days. Would you be willing?"

He released a breath. "Would I be willing to be both dean and CEO?"

"Only the interim CEO," said Bentley. "You'd be a placeholder, a figurehead. Consider it a little window dressing on your CV."

"You don't have to be so cynical about it," Jan said, turning to Jack again. "It would be one less thing I have to worry about. We'd appreciate your help. Martin will give you any support you need."

I'd rather do without that, Jack thought, then he said, "If it helps, I'll accept."

Jan glanced away and dabbed at her eyes again. "Thank you. Sorry. I keep seeing her car on that ridiculous bridge. But we must put our heads down and keep moving forward or this debacle will drown the entire university in a sea of red ink."

She gathered herself. Opening the folder in front of her, she removed two sheets of paper and slid one each to Jack and Bentley. "Here's the latest interim report from Brink and Waterborne, the forensic accountants. The medical center is 226 million underwater and it's likely to get worse. That's over a quarter of the hospital's entire annual gross revenue. As you both know, the university's endowment never recovered from the recession of '08. We can only draw operating cash from it for several weeks. Building it up was one of the reasons they recruited me in the first place. But that takes time."

"Obviously, we'll need to begin searching for outside help," said Bentley. "As soon as possible."

She sniffed. "What the hell do you think I've been doing these past three days? Practicing the cello? I've pleaded with the governor twice, and I've spoken with every contact I could find at the federal level. I've called several dozen commercial lenders. So far the only thing I've received is some guarded sympathy. Everyone is appalled that we let something like this happen. We look like imbeciles."

"I might have an idea," said Jack.

Bentley snorted. "Know some good loan sharks, Forester?"

Jan Cummings glanced nervously at her watch. "It's almost time," she said.

"Time for what?" Bentley said.

"To explore what may be our only viable remaining option."

"Which is?" said Bentley.

She folded her hands and eyed each of them in turn. "That the university sell the medical center."

Jack stared back, his neck tightening.

"Hmmm," said Bentley, thoughtfully. "You're suggesting we divest ourselves of the whole kit and caboodle—the hospital, the medical school, the labs, the training programs?"

"Yes, as a single package," she said, drawing in a deep breath before continuing. "I have made inquiries."

Jack shook his head. He felt as if his chair was sitting on a trapdoor that might suddenly open.

Jan leaned forward and jabbed the table with her red-nailed index finger. "There are four healthcare consortiums in the nation with sufficient resources, but only one is interested. I assume you both are familiar with Health Wealth Associates?"

This could not be. Jack inwardly groaned. The very thought was like fingernails on a blackboard.

"Of course," said Bentley. "In point of fact, HWA expressed interest in buying the medical center a few years before you arrived, Jan. They'd love a foothold in the Northeast. But we declined at the time. I believe, Forester, you were one of the naysayers."

"I definitely was." He turned to Jan. "HWA bragged about us being one of their targeted acquisitions in the *Journal of Health Economics* without bothering to tell us first."

"They're aggressive," she said. "I'll give them that."

"Cutthroat is the word," said Jack.

"So, they're still in the market?" Bentley asked.

"Very definitely." She glanced at her watch again. "Martin, I apologize for not letting you in on this aspect of the situation yet, but things have been moving very fast. After I spoke to you last evening, I had a long conversation with Dr. Lawrence Haines, the CEO of HWA, and he agreed to fly up this morning from North Carolina." She leaned back and folded her arms across her chest. "He's in the next room waiting to talk."

"Jesus no," Jack said.

She shot him a hard look. "Don't *Jesus no*, me. Nothing is worse than the university going bankrupt and the hospital closing."

"Jan, this is brilliant," Bentley said, beaming. "I'm glad you jumped ahead."

"We're going to at least hear his proposal. And Jack, despite your obviously negative feelings, I'm counting on you to be a good team player. If this goes through, I'm sure he will want you to stay as dean. That's already been discussed."

Jack took a deep breath and felt the trapdoor crack open.

CHAPTER THREE

A few minutes later, Tulip ushered a tall man into the conference room. He wasn't just tall. He was gargantuan. His eyebrows jutted like ledges over a pair of caves, out of which stared two intense gray eyes. In that article where HWA had expressed interest in buying them several years ago, Jack remembered reading that Haines was from rural North Carolina, had been a six-foot-eleven basketball star at Duke, got an MD from Stanford, and did an internal medicine residency at Boston University while earning an MBA at Harvard. He'd founded HWA on a shoestring twenty years ago and built it into one of the nation's largest healthcare networks, mainly operating in the South and Southeast. He was also an accomplished pilot who flew the company jet and kept a helicopter in his backyard.

As they shook hands, Jack felt as if his own was being swallowed by a whale.

The meeting lasted an hour. After Haines departed, Jan, Bentley, and Jack reconvened in Jan's office. Jack still felt the pressure of Haines's parting handshake.

"Okay, gentlemen," she said. "Before I present this to the board, I want your opinions. Martin, you first."

Bentley tapped his lower lip and smiled. "I think we've just been thrown the mother of all lifelines. Kudos to you, Jan. Kudos. HWA's offer will relieve our unexpected debt load and bolster our endowment. It's true that the university will no longer be able to boast of having its own hospital and medical school, but the med center was never a profit center. Plus, he believes that his contacts in DC can help lubricate the regulatory approval process. I'm in. A hundred percent."

Jack had been watching Jan's face, which had remained neutral. She swung her gaze toward him. "And you? You stayed awfully quiet throughout."

"As a mouse," said Bentley.

Jack inhaled and forced his muscles to relax. "But I was listening," he said. "And this is what I heard. HWA will turn the research labs into nursing home beds. HWA will outsource half our administrative jobs to their central office. HWA will increase the number of medical students while lowering admission standards. HWA will raise tuition, slash the faculty, move many classes online, give up the non-primary care residency programs and—"

Bentley made a chopping motion with his hand. "Forester, we both heard it all too. I think Dr. Haines is a refreshing fountain of cost-saving ideas. What's your point?"

Jack swallowed back his burgeoning anger, trying to keep his voice even. "My point is that we are one of the finest small-city academic medical centers in the country. We've had a Nobel Prize winner on our faculty. We draw great med student and residency applicants, and we consistently punch above our weight in NIH grants. That'll all vanish. A hundred and twenty-five years of history up in smoke. Not to mention that he'll cut the workforce by about nine hundred jobs."

"But it won't affect you," Bentley said, a bushy eyebrow rising sarcastically. "As Dr. Haines mentioned, you can stay as dean. If anything, your job would be even easier. I should have thought you'd appreciate that."

"Jack, you can slap him if you like," Jan said, grimly.

"Only kidding," said Bentley.

Jack looked away, gathering his thoughts before responding. "I'd like to propose an alternative."

"This is no time for frivolous brainstorming," Bentley said.

Jan held up her hand. "What are you proposing, Jack? Please make it brief."

Jack nodded and described meeting someone at a conference in San Diego several months ago, a venture capitalist who had sought him out to discuss partnering in the creation of a genomic research center powered by artificial intelligence at New Canterbury. It would be similar to the one at the University of Leiden in the Netherlands, which was turning out great work and finding financial success.

"Interesting," said Jan. "Who was he?"

"Damian Falconi. He and I've exchanged emails and talked about meeting after the first of the year."

She smiled. "Yes, Damian Falconi. I crossed paths with him a few times on the West Coast. Impressive individual." She glanced at Bentley. "I don't know if you've heard of him, but Falconi runs a venture group out of Oakland that wields something like fifty billion dollars. Jack, let's hear more."

"I'm sure you're familiar with the fact that genomic medicine aims to fix the root cause of diseases by resetting DNA base sequences at the gene level. The surface has barely been scratched. The idea would be to create a research center here that laser-focuses on genomic treatments using the full power of AI. We'd be among the first to take up the challenge in earnest. We're talking about expanding our workforce, about generating local high-tech spin-off businesses, about building something instead of selling out."

Bentley sighed and glanced toward the ceiling. "Why would anyone pour millions into such an enterprise here in New Canterbury? Last time I drove down to Manhattan, it took me twenty minutes just to reach the bleeping interstate."

Jack nodded. "I asked Falconi the same question. He said that being off the beaten trail means fewer political hurdles and more tax breaks. It doesn't matter where something like this is based. All that's needed is a high-quality academic research infrastructure and fiber optic broadband, and we've got both."

Bentley's color was darkening. "Forester, if this is such a golden opportunity, why didn't you bring it forward earlier?"

"That's a fair question," said Jan.

Jack's face warmed. "Because I had no idea our finances were about to collapse." Though this was true, Jack had to admit to himself that he'd let things languish.

"So now the beast is stirring," Bentley said. "At a minute to midnight."

"This is intriguing, nevertheless," Jan said, drumming her nails. "Falconi's group certainly has deep enough pockets to stabilize our situation. No question. Lord knows I'd rather see progress than dissolution. The question is whether it could patch the hull before we slip beneath the waves."

Jack leaned toward her. "What have we got to lose by giving it a try?"

"Everything," hissed Bentley. "Arranging a deal could take months. Dr. Haines said he'd sign a letter of agreement tomorrow. This could scare him away."

"Highly unlikely," said Jan, drumming her nails. "I thought we were going to have to put a drool bucket in front of him."

"Exactly," said Bentley. "I doubt he'd take kindly to this, Forester. If this falls through and we end up selling to HWA, you could likely kiss your chance of staying on here goodbye."

"I understand the implications," Jack said.

Jan turned to him. "When did you last communicate with Falconi?"

"Several weeks ago."

"Okay," she said, pressing her palms onto the table and rising to her feet. "I'd be willing to give us two weeks to come up with the outline of a deal with him. That's all the time we can afford. Are you up to this, Jack?"

He nodded. "Absolutely."

"I want progress reports twice a day," she said, reaching out and shaking his hand. "In the meantime, we need to tell the troops something about this whole situation. I'm going to release a memo today. It will simply state that unexpected financial issues have arisen, more to follow, etc. In the meantime, we'll start drawing up a strategy for public relations in the event we must take HWA's offer."

"I've got a bad feeling," said Bentley. "A bird in the hand is worth two in the bush. A lot can happen in two weeks, and we'll be dipping into the endowment even to wait that long. But it's your call, Jan. You'll have to answer to the board."

"That's right," she said, taking a navy-blue overcoat from a hanger on the wall. "It's my call. I'm going to go talk with the chairman of the trustees right now. Martin, please contact Dr. Haines. Tell him we are giving his offer all due consideration and will have a decision within two weeks."

"May I tell him why the delay?"

"No. That's none of his business. Jack, I'm eager to speak to Falconi too. Get him here. Whatever it takes. And say a prayer for the family of Judy Marsh," she added. "Goddamn this business." She marched out.

"If you have a minute, Forester," said Bentley. He strode close. They were about the same six-foot height. "I know you're aware that I opposed your appointment to the deanship."

"Well aware."

"I didn't like the idea of a convicted juvenile delinquent running a med school."

"I was a kid, Martin, and I paid my debt."

"Be that as it may, if this idea of yours causes Health Wealth Associates to withdraw its offer and ends up going nowhere, Doctor, not only will you be on Mr. Haines's shit list, you may go from being one of the youngest medical school deans in the country to . . ." The provost's face twitched.

"To what?" Jack retorted, clenching his jaw.

Bentley sniffed. "To a middle-aged burger-flipper."

The door opened and Tulip appeared. "Oh good, you're still here, Dr. Forester," she said. "Your assistant is on the line. You left your cell phone back in your office. The high school has been trying to reach you. Here's the number. Something urgent about your niece, Kaitlyn. You can use my phone."

He thanked her and stared down at the slip of paper she'd handed him, wondering what else would fall out of the clouds today.

CHAPTER FOUR

Jack had been serving as his sixteen-year-old niece Kaitlyn's temporary guardian for the past three months, since the end of summer. Kaitlyn had gotten into a fight at school that morning and the other student's mother was demanding to talk with him. Was there any chance he could come to the school? Thanks to the morning's schedule reshuffle, he had a small window of time, if now would work. It would, so he got his car and drove across town.

Fifteen minutes after leaving Jan Cummings's office, he was jogging up the high school's front steps, his mind preoccupied with thoughts of how to best make urgent contact with Damien Falconi. The security guard checked his name and waved him inside.

He was no stranger here, though it had been twenty-seven years since he'd last set foot in this building as a high school senior. He slowed upon entering, gobsmacked by the eerie lack of change—the same fluorescent lights and buffer swirls on the speckled linoleum floor, the sound of lockers slamming and voices echoing, the smell of gymnasium and disinfectant. He turned a familiar corner, and there it was, exactly as he remembered, two doors down on the right: the guidance counselor's office.

In the reception area, a young secretary smiled, her earrings swaying like tiny wind chimes. Identifying herself as the one who'd called, she thanked him profusely and pointed toward the inner office, where his presence was expected. He hadn't gotten halfway there, however, when the door flew open and a woman strode out, charging by him without a word or a glance.

The secretary sprang to her feet. "Ms. Greer—is everything all right?" No response, just the retort of heels receding down the hallway.

Out of the inner office came a Black man with graying hair who gave Jack an apologetic look and a sigh. He extended his hand and introduced himself as Jim Brady, the guidance counselor. His face seemed familiar, but Jack couldn't place him. He explained that the angry woman was the other student's mother, the one who'd demanded to talk with him.

"Unfortunately, she took offense when I explained the rules of engagement," Brady said. "I hate to have wasted your time, Doctor. But as long as you're here, come on in and let me explain what happened this morning."

"Is Kaitlyn here?" Jack said.

"No, she's back in class now."

The office looked much as Jack remembered from over two decades ago. He took the chair nearest the dusty curtainless window overlooking the Seneca River. Brady began describing what had transpired. It seemed that Kaitlyn's friend, Aishia Almasi, an Iraqi girl who wears the hijab, was getting teased to the point of cruelty that morning. Kaitlyn went up to the ringleader, Conrad Greer—who's a foot taller than her—and gave him a shove. Unfortunately, Conrad tripped and banged his head on the floor. He was in the ED with a concussion and ten stitches.

As Jack's eyes widened, Brady held up his hand reassuringly. "His brain scan was normal. They're just going to watch him overnight."

At that moment there came a loud rapping on the door, giving Jack déjà vu of the interruption not long ago in Jan Cummings's conference room. The door flew open, and Ms. Greer marched in, holding her purse like a breastplate. Jack rose. The secretary was standing behind her in the doorway, raising her eyebrows in exasperation. She eased the door shut while the angry mother dropped into a chair. Nonplussed, Brady thanked her for returning and made introductions.

"I know who he is," Ms. Greer blurted. "What I don't know is why a *doctor* would bring someone as vicious as that girl into this school."

Brady folded his arms across his chest. "As I said, Ms. Greer—we need to talk this through calmly."

Her face went even more florid. "Don't you dare patronize me. She could have killed my son."

"I was just telling Dr. Forester that I spoke to the physician caring for Conrad and—"

Her body stiffened. "You talked to his doctor without my permission?"

"No confidential details were shared. But his situation is reassuring."

"You call a concussion *reassuring*?" She swung around and leveled her eyes at Jack, pupils wide. "Your niece has a history of violence. Her background is common knowledge. I'm holding you responsible."

Jack cleared his throat. "Respectfully, Ms. Greer, I am not aware of any such history. I'm not sure what common knowledge you mean."

"The fact that her mother got thrown into jail somewhere out in Ohio and that the girl is uncontrollable."

"I hear your anger, but please let me set the record straight," Jack said. "Her stepmother is in a court-mandated inpatient rehabilitation program in Dayton, not prison."

Ms. Greer sniffed. "What's the difference? The point is that she's here in New Canterbury because they couldn't handle her."

"Again, that's not the case. Kaitlyn is with us because we're her closest family, and this was the best option while her stepmother gets treatment, which will be finished in just a couple of weeks."

"But you're a widower, I know that much. Who takes care of her when you're working?"

"The same person who cares for my daughter, Ms. Greer. My wife's retired aunt lives with us."

Brady leaned forward. "Her name is Zoë Andersen, Ms. Greer. I met her when Kaitlyn enrolled. Seems a very responsible soul."

Ms. Greer squinted dismissively. "What about those jailhouse tattoos on her wrists? It means she's either murdered someone or been raped. You can look it up yourself."

"My niece has never been arrested or assaulted. I'm certain she's never been in jail."

"Ms. Greer." Brady said. "Those tattoos can also mean that a person's lost a loved one. Kaitlyn told me that she got one for her real mother and one for her father."

Jack looked at Brady, feeling a sense of surprise tinged with guilt. That was news to him. He'd never asked Kaitlyn about them, had just made assumptions about rebelliousness.

"I'm not going to argue with the two of you against me," she said, her nostrils flaring. "I want her expelled and you should call the police."

"I agree that your son's injury shouldn't have happened," Brady said. "But it was an accident. Kaitlyn didn't intend to hurt him, and she was quite upset about what ended up happening. Neither she, nor Conrad, meet criteria for being expelled. We have a policy about fighting. For a first event, unless something egregious happened—which was not the case here—the student is assigned community service." He glanced at Jack. "Kaitlyn is already aware of that. We have a policy for bullying behavior too. And Conrad—"

She shot to her feet. "My son is lying in the hospital and you talk about bullying?"

"Ms. Greer—"

"*Community service!*" Her voice oozed scorn. "If something happens to him, you won't know what hit you."

The door slammed behind her, rattling the frosted glass.

Brady sighed. "Wow. I apologize again, Doctor. I didn't know it was going to go like this. It's unfortunate that false rumors about Kaitlyn are circulating, but I guess it's not surprising in a small community like ours. Conrad's not a bad kid. I suspect he was partly showing off for Kaitlyn's benefit. Bad decision." He leaned back in his chair. "Dr. Forester, you probably don't recall, but my wife was a patient of yours in the ER about six years ago."

That's where he'd seen him before.

"I wouldn't expect you to remember," Brady continued. "She had stage-four ovarian cancer and things had started going downhill real fast. We hadn't accepted the inevitable yet. She was in terrible pain that night. You got her feeling better and facilitated our hookup with hospice. You had a great bedside manner." He sighed deeply. "We were grateful."

Images crystallized in Jack's mind. A lovely woman in her mid-fifties lying on the stretcher, face taut with agony; Jim Brady standing by the stretcher, gripping the rails as if his own life depended on it. "Yes," he said. "I do remember that. It's good to see you again."

Brady glanced down at his hands and then back up at Jack. "I've thought of that night often. Your empathy meant a lot. When I knew you were coming over today, someone mentioned that you'd attended this high school, so I looked in the records and sure enough." Then Brady's face twitched. He looked away, his eyes growing distant as if embarrassed.

Jack read his thoughts. "If you saw my history, you'll know I went through a rough patch."

Brady met his eyes and smiled. "But you sure came through it well, Doctor. You're an inspiration. You honor your alma mater. Maybe you could come talk to our future health care professionals club sometime."

"I would like that," Jack said.

"I understand you're the dean now. Do you still see patients?"

Jack shifted. "I don't, no."

"That's a loss. Not to pry, but I was surprised when Ms. Greer mentioned you were a widower yourself."

Jack's scalp tingled. He looked out at the river and said, "We lost my wife Zellie three years ago."

Brady nodded and pursed his lips sympathetically. "So, we're fellow travelers down that sad road. You have my sincere condolences."

"And mine to you," Jack said, still looking outside. The river was churning fast and muddy thanks to recent heavy rains. The water must be scouring the bottom, grinding stones to sand and gravel. He suddenly recalled his need to get in touch with Damien Falconi. It couldn't wait. And he had other duties this afternoon. He had to leave here.

"Is everything okay, Doctor?" said Brady.

Jack glanced up at the wall clock. "Just running short of time."

"Of course. Forgive me. I've been rambling. But listen, do you have another couple of minutes to talk about your niece? I've actually been meaning to reach out to you. I'll get to the point."

"A couple of minutes is about all I can spare."

"Okay. Here's the deal. Kaitlyn's doing extremely well here academically. I spoke with her old guidance counselor, and that was far from the case in Dayton. She was barely scraping by and there was concern about depression and disengagement. You know all this, I'm sure. It sounds like the situation with her stepmother was, to be blunt, very toxic."

"It wasn't ideal," Jack said. "But her stepmother has been getting extensive treatment and hopefully that will right the ship."

"Hopefully, yes," Brady said, frowning. "But I hate to think of a window of opportunity for Kaitlyn closing. She's thriving now. I'm talking valedictorian potential. Forgive me if I'm overstepping my bounds . . . but have you thought about her staying to finish high school in New Canterbury?"

Jack glanced at the clock again. "That subject hasn't been discussed, no. As far as I know, she's looking forward to returning home."

"I see," Brady said, clearing his throat. "Something else too. I also coach the varsity baseball team. One day I happened to see Kaitlyn playing catch in gym and was impressed. So, I had her give me some pitches. Your niece has a seriously good throwing arm, one of the best I've ever seen—boy or girl. But she has never *once* participated in any school athletics back in Ohio. She tells me her father used to play professional baseball before he died. Was he your brother?"

"No. He was my wife's younger brother. He spent a couple of seasons pitching with the triple-A team in Dayton."

Brady leaned closer. "Here's the thing. We took the varsity baseball team coed last year, and I have no doubt Kaitlyn would make it this spring. A success like that could make a huge difference for the rest of her life."

Jack remembered when Kaitlyn first arrived back in August, Zoë eagerly driving out to Ohio to pick her up. Kindhearted Zoë, who'd never had any children of her own. But he'd had no idea how much Kaitlyn now resembled Zellie in facial features and mannerisms, and how that tended to rekindle his grief every time he saw her.

He met Brady's gaze. "I understand what you're saying, but the plan is for her to return home when her stepmother is out of treatment. That's in about two weeks. I don't see how we can alter that." Brady was about to say more when Jack looked again at the clock and stood, holding out his hand. "And I really must go, Mr. Brady. Genuinely nice to see you again."

It was the end of third period. Kaitlyn Andersen and her friend Aishia were waiting near Mr. Brady's office when Uncle Jack emerged and strode down the hallway away from where they stood.

Aishia nudged her. "Say something. He doesn't know we're here."

Watching him recede, Kaitlyn hesitated. "Maybe this isn't such a good idea."

"I thought you wanted to ask him about doing your community service at the hospital. If you don't call to him, I will."

"No," Kaitlyn said, grabbing Aisha's arm. "He's busy. Obviously. Don't. I mean it."

Aishia fingered the edge of the hijab covering her black hair.

"This isn't like you. I'm supposed to be the shy one."

"As if," Kaitlyn said. Compared to Aishia, who had moved to New Canterbury from New Jersey so her father could manage a convenience store, Kaitlyn was the more reserved. Some of the kids might tease her about hiding behind a hajib, but there was nothing subservient about Aishia.

Uncle Jack turned the corner and was gone. Kaitlyn couldn't hear his footfalls anymore.

"I'll do it at home. He may not even want to talk. Like I said, he doesn't like me anyway. We'd better get to class."

"Why do you keep saying he doesn't like you?"

They walked. "Because he acts like I'm not even on the same planet. He never talks to me. Never."

"Maybe he's stupid. Some doctors are, you know."

They passed a group of senior boys going in the other direction, friends of Conrad. One of them made a farting sound and the others laughed.

"Speaking of stupid, there sure are a lot of redneck a-holes in this school," Aishia said, lowering her voice. "I wish I were back in Newark. But then I wouldn't have met you. It's so sad you're leaving. It's not fair."

"We'll stay friends," Kaitlyn said. "You're going to come visit me."

"Sure," said Aishia.

"I'm serious."

"How did you come up with that hospital volunteer idea?" Aishia said.

"I saw a poster about it in the cafeteria."

"If it was me, I'd take detention so I could sit and read and not have to go home to all my brothers. You want to talk about a-holes."

"I'm sure they love you," Kaitlyn said.

"They love to remind me I'm not one of them. What's so great about having a penis, anyway?"

CHAPTER FIVE

Late that afternoon, Jack was at his desk, the light dying outside, when he heard something thud against the window. He rose to see. All afternoon between meetings he'd been trying to reach Damien Falconi. No one would say for certain where he was. Possibly attending a conference in Greenland, or maybe flying back from a meeting in Ecuador, or perhaps hiking in Spain. There on the weathered limestone sill lay a bird, either stunned or dead. Its wings twitched, and its beak opened and closed once like the jaws of a hemostat. With some difficulty, he opened the ancient window and brought the bird inside. It was a female cardinal, eyes wide open, not moving now. It was almost weightless in his palm. He thought he could detect it shivering, but that might have been imagination.

Back on his desk, his cell phone began chiming. Bringing the bird with him, he rushed over. The caller identified herself as Sylvia, an assistant to Mr. Falconi, who was unable to return the call himself.

"How is it we could help you, Dr. Forester?"

Without going into detail concerning the financial dilemma, Jack launched into a brief description of the project, mentioning Falconi's previous interest in developing a genomic research center at New Canterbury.

"I'm sure he will be very pleased to talk with you, Doctor," she said.

"How soon might I speak with him?" Jack said, trying to tone down the eagerness in his voice. "The situation is time sensitive." The bird was still not moving.

"Could you clarify what you mean by time sensitive? Are we talking hours, days, weeks?"

Seconds, Jack thought. "Definitely not weeks or days," he said. "The sooner the better. He'll understand when we talk."

"Got you. I'll reach right out and make sure he gets the message. Is this your best number?"

Jack had no sooner hung up than the voice of his administrative assistant, Tré Tannino, crackled over the intercom. "Dr. Dugan is here, chief."

"Send him in." Jack laid the bird on his desk.

Tré, a thin young man in a dark suit, swung open the door and in marched Hal Dugan, a silver-haired portly man in his early sixties. They shook hands. Dugan had been chairman of the psych department since Jack's days here as a medical student.

"Sir, I'll be leaving in about ten minutes," Tré said. "Would you like me to turn on the overhead lights?"

"No, don't bother. I'll see you tomorrow."

"You like working in the dusk now?" Dugan said, settling into a chair.

"It snuck up," said Jack, switching on his green-shaded desk lamp.

Dugan wagged his brows. "Strange how night does that. Listen, I got that mass email from Jan Cummings this afternoon. Unexpected financial issues. Jason out. You named the interim CEO. What the devil is going on? Why is the window open?"

"Would you like a drink?" Jack said. He removed a bottle of scotch and two glasses from the bottom drawer.

Dugan smiled. "Well, this is a first."

Jack poured and handed him a glass.

"This reminds me of when old dean Gavin was sitting where you are," Dugan said.

"Except his poison was sherry. You've upped the ante, bless you." He raised his glass. "To Jim Gavin."

Jack followed suit.

"Let me guess," Dugan said. "You're not at liberty to discuss what's going on. Bullshit. We've known each other too long. Spill the beans."

Jack swirled the whiskey. "You didn't hear this from me," he said, then briefly summarized the crisis.

Dugan went pale. "Jesus," he said. "And no one saw it coming?"

"Unbelievably, no."

"Does Judy Marsh's tragic accident factor into this?"

"Unknown. I hope not."

Dugan drained his glass. "Wouldn't it be nice if it were the fault of that prick of a provost, Bentley?"

Jack smiled. "I'm afraid he's coated in Teflon."

"What the hell are they going to do?"

Jack sighed deeply. "Good question. The easiest option is to sell the med center to Health Wealth Associates."

"Health Wealth Associates! HWA is to medicine what Burger King is to cuisine. Say you're kidding."

"I'm not. Dr. Lawrence Haines, their CEO, flew up here from North Carolina this morning on his private jet. He's already put an offer on the table."

"For the love of God! Lawrence Haines—I've heard of that guy. He's a damn shark. Lawrence Haines, please no."

"I agree, which is why I'm working on a long-shot alternative." He described his plan.

Dugan beamed and pumped his fist. "Yes, Jack! That would be brilliant. I must say that it's good to see you stirring into action again. It's been a while since you've thrown off sparks. Which brings me to why I'm here. I've got three things to discuss. But the first one is the fact you've been avoiding me."

Jack felt his face warm.

"We made a deal," Dugan pressed on. "You were having trouble with a prolonged grief reaction. You wanted to talk to somebody. I suggested one of our young therapists, but you said you felt most comfortable with me. I said fine, but that we'd need to meet at least every two weeks."

"Hal, there's been a lot on my plate."

"Don't want to hear it. When I call to schedule something, your assistant—what's his name, Trent?—waffles for you."

"Tré."

"He looks more eccentric every time I see him. Don't you find his appearance distracting? What do they call that hairdo?"

"A man bun, I think."

"He looks like something out of medieval Japan. And he's got a tattoo of wings on the back of his neck."

"He's very good at the job."

"I would hope. So how are you feeling? With regard to the grief, not this financial apocalypse."

Jack inhaled sharply. "Pretty much the same. It's never far below the surface."

"Any thoughts of self-harm?"

"As I've said many times, I'd never do that to my daughter."

"Do you still think about it?"

"Who doesn't?"

"Why do I always get the feeling you're not telling me something?"

Jack leaned back, his thoughts slipping away. He pictured that Saturday afternoon three Februaries ago. Julia was fourteen months old and napping in her crib. Zellie decided to go food shopping. He was going through the motions of tying a trout fly, but mainly thinking about issues at the medical center. She handed him the baby monitor, kissed him goodbye, then a few moments later she called to him from the kitchen. Her car wouldn't start. Could she take his? Of course. She yelled thanks. He heard the door shut. When he remembered a quarter hour later what he should have told her, it was too late. He had been meaning to get his vehicle checked by a mechanic. Something wasn't right. He looked down at the bird lying on its side, inert, eyes already turning dull.

"That's what I mean," Dugan said, shaking his head. "You disappear somewhere. Who's your friend?" He nodded at the creature. "Is that why the window's open?"

"It flew into the glass."

"Listen, Jack, let's try you on another antidepressant."

"No."

"I swear to God, I'll never take on another physician as a patient. How's your sleep?"

"I'm taking Ambien occasionally."

"How often is *occasionally*? Be honest."

"Every other night or so."

"That's more than occasionally. If you want me to continue prescribing it, keep touching bases. As promised."

"Fair enough."

"Jack, you do not deal well with loss. I believe that situation partly stems from the fact you lost both your parents when you were, what, fifteen?"

"Yes."

"That's a tender age. It's no wonder you went wild for a few years. We need to talk more about that."

"Not today."

"Not today, not today." Dugan raised his arms. "One of the reasons people stay in a state of grief is because they fear the potential of future losses." Dugan glanced at the bird. "And now you're about to lose the medical center. But it's a good sign that you're going to do something about it. A great sign."

"Fearing future losses? I'm not sure that makes sense to me."

"I'll take another finger of that," Dugan said.

Jack poured more for them both.

"Still not dating anyone?" Dugan said.

"No."

"How about fishing? I remember when you used to bore anyone

who'd listen about the pleasures of fly fishing."

It was true. He had started trout fishing when he was ten, quickly becoming familiar with all the small streams around New Canterbury, and during their first year of marriage when Zellie was pregnant with Julia, they'd spent a week in a cabin on the Beaver Kill River, where he'd taught her how to cast.

"Maybe this spring," Jack said.

"You should force yourself, take a break from this place."

"Yep," Jack said.

"I mean it," Dugan said, emphatically. "But enough preaching. I'll dive into my second point, which is that my new study has received final approval from the IRB. We begin enrolling patients this weekend."

"Remind me which study."

"The one I described to you in great detail last month sitting right here in this chair."

"Right. The witch doctor project."

"Kindly don't use that term. This is a case-controlled prospective trial designed to determine whether exposing patients to a shamanistic ritual might reduce length of stay in a post-ICU step-down unit through an enhanced placebo effect. My residents love it. They'll be doing the rituals in full costume . . . stop grinning."

"It paints an odd picture, Hal. Psychiatry residents dancing around a patient's bed waving rattles."

"The placebo effect is understudied. If we can use it to shave even one day off hospital length of stay, the national cost savings would be enormous."

"No argument. I wish you success."

Dugan plunked down the glass and averted his eyes. "Now, one last thing. Do you know Ms. Bansal, the administrator of the Patterson Psychiatric Institute?"

"No. Why?"

"She's going to be reaching out to you for a reference for me. You see, I uh . . . am being vetted for the medical directorship job at

Patterson. That was my third point."

Jack looked down at the lifeless bird and swallowed, his mouth going dry. "You're thinking of leaving? You should have brought this up at the beginning. Isn't Ralph Teitelbaum the medical director there?"

"He died in a car accident back at the end of the summer. A recruiter reached out to me last month. Listen, I've been administering this psych department and training residents for thirty years. I've paid my dues. It's time for a change. The workload will be light. It'll be almost a semi-retirement. And it's in the Adirondacks. Beautiful country. Not far away. There's plenty of trout streams there. You could come visit."

The desk lamp cast a pool of warm light on the polished surface that reflected up onto Dugan's face. Jack couldn't hold back a sigh. There'd been too many surprises today.

"I won't be but a couple hours away. We'll continue meeting every two weeks."

"How soon?"

"Assuming they'll take me, about three months. That'll allow me time to complete the shaman study."

Jack drained his scotch. "I've just never known this place without you."

"My young friend, please do not think of this as another loss. It's not."

"You think you'll be happy there?"

"I do. The only onerous aspect is that I'll oversee the unit there that houses the criminally insane. They've got some real monsters, like the one who strangled and dismembered those women in the Catskills. And also . . ." Dugan cleared his throat.

"Also what?" said Jack.

"Dr. Bryson Witner is there now."

Jack's neck muscles tensed, and a chill crept up his spine. *Bryson Witner.* The man's name still had the power to send a shock wave through him. He could picture Witner's cold eyes and thin smile. "I thought they were holding him in Attica."

"All of the state's criminally insane are now concentrated at Patterson. State-of-the-art confinement. Do you still have nightmares about him?"

"Yes."

"No surprise, given how close he came to killing you and your wife. But all of us here at New Canterbury still have Witner nightmares. I know I'm supposed to have sympathy for individuals who do bad things under the influence of psychosis, but he murdered too many people. If he'd been executed, I'd have said 'fair is fair.' But enough of that. How are things going with your niece from Ohio? Kaitlyn is her name, right?"

"Yes. She's been stable. Doing well in school."

"I recall you mentioning she had a resemblance to Zellie. Has that been problematic for you, grief-wise?"

Jack looked away for a moment before answering. "It's under control. She'll be going back to Ohio in two weeks."

Dugan stared at him, then released a breath. "There you go disappearing again. I worry about you."

CHAPTER SIX

Kaitlyn had finished geometry and was now working on *To Kill a Mockingbird*. After coming to the end of the same paragraph twice, she lay the book down. The sound of Conrad's head smacking the hard floor kept returning, how he'd gone limp, the coppery smell of the blood oozing from the big cut on his scalp. Just before he'd fallen, she had hated him from the bottom of her heart. But after that, the whole thing seemed stupid.

The tiny flowers in the wallpaper seemed to be slowly swirling. Even Conrad's friends said it was an accident. Mr. Brady told her about the meeting with Conrad's mother and Uncle Jack, and that Uncle Jack hadn't gotten angry. Probably because he didn't care. Early on she used to wonder what she'd done wrong. But Aunt Zoë told her it was *him*, not *her*, that he'd become a different person after Aunt Zellie had died. Zoë told her the story of their meeting, of how Uncle Jack had recognized her from a dust jacket photo on the book she'd written. But what did it matter? In two weeks, she'd be back to her old life, her old school, and a new and better relationship with her stepmother.

Kaitlyn heard the bedroom door creak open. There stood Julia draped in a dark blue blanket. "Trust me," Kaitlyn said. "You are not invisible."

"You promised to read me a book. Aren't you done yet?"

"No. And I'll never finish with you interrupting me. Now go. Vamoose."

"But you're just laying on your bed."

"Leave or I'm calling Aunt Zoë."

The door clicked shut. Being here had been okay. Better than she'd expected. She'd felt happy most of the time, which was . . . sort of strange. At first she'd missed the freedom she'd had with Stella—she could watch television or listen to music all night if she wanted because Stella was either out with Donald or zombified in her own room with the door locked. Thank God Stella would be back to normal.

The door cracked open again. "Out," Kaitlyn said. "Or I'll boycott playing with you completely." The door shut.

Stella getting sentenced to the rehab unit instead of prison had been the best thing that could have happened. She was getting help every day. They'd talked by phone a lot early on, Stella telling her how the death of Kaitlyn's father had pushed her into six years of bad decisions, one of which had been Donald. "Your father's love kept me in the right lane, honey. His love was like magic."

Now Donald would be out of their lives for good. Stella had begged for forgiveness, saying she'd again be someone Kaitlyn could trust and depend upon. Kaitlyn had promised to stop being critical, to think before she talked. "But Mom, it's scary finding used needles on the coffee table. That's got to stop."

"That's done, sweetie. I'm just asking for your help."

The last couple of weeks, though, Kaitlyn had begun feeling a little worried. Stella had seemed less interested in hearing how Kaitlyn was doing. She would ramble on about how she was getting tired of rehab. Those kumbaya moments during the first few weeks, when they'd cried together, were gone. Kaitlyn swallowed against an ache rising in her throat. *Please make this work.*

The door swung open widely. "It's after seven o'clock, Kaitlyn," Julia said, marching in without her invisibility cloak. "You said you'd be done." Kaitlyn watched Julia climb up on the desk chair and open her social studies book. "I'm almost five. I wish I had homework."

"I wish you did too," Kaitlyn said. "Please leave the book alone."

"Are you smart?"

"I'm a genius."

"My mommy was smart. She wrote a book."

"I know. I'm going to read it someday."

"Me too," Julia said. "Is it fun being a teenager?"

"It's about as much fun as having an interstellar dingbat run you through with a lightsaber."

"What's that like?"

"It burns and tickles at the same time."

"I want to be a genius too."

"Is that a fact? How much is two plus two?"

"Four," Julia said. "That's too easy."

"How much is two hundred plus two hundred?"

"How am I supposed to know that?"

Aunt Zoë appeared in the doorway, her eyeglasses dangling from a cord. "Julia, did Kaitlyn say it was okay to be here?"

"I'm done for now," Kaitlyn said. "She's okay."

"Kaitlyn's giving me questions, Aunt Zoë. She asked me how much two hundred plus two hundred is. That's too big."

"Don't they teach you anything in preschool?" Kaitlyn said. "How many apples are two apples plus two apples?"

"Four apples!"

"So, how many hundreds are two hundreds plus two hundreds?"

Julia squirmed and asked her to repeat the question. Kaitlyn did.

"Uh . . . four hundreds?" Julia said.

"Not bad," said Kaitlyn. "But here's the big test. Are you ready?"

Julia nodded, eyes gleaming.

"How much is two thousand plus two thousand?"

"Mmmm . . . four thousand?"

Zoë laughed.

"Wow, I'm impressed," Kaitlyn said. "How much is two million plus two million?"

"Four million!"

"Dang, girl," said Kaitlyn. "Aunt Zoë, are you listening to this?"

"I am."

"I want to be smart too," said the little girl.

"Did you want to read to her, Kate?" Zoë asked.

"Sure."

"When's Daddy coming home?" said Julia.

"He'll be here when he gets here. Stop pestering and go get a book for Kaitlyn to read. What would you like tonight?"

"*The Twits*!" Julia said, hopping off the chair. "I love *The Twits*."

"Takes one to know one," Kaitlyn said.

"You're a twit," said Julia. "I'm not a twit."

"True. You're a pest not a twit."

Julia laughed and ran to her room.

"What a scalawag," Zoë said. "You've got a lot of patience with her."

"Not always."

"She really adores you. She's going to be heartbroken when you leave."

"Are you saying that to make me feel better?"

"I don't know what I'm saying," Zoë said, folding her arms over her chest. "Have you talked to your stepmother tonight?"

"Not yet."

"Are you going to tell her about what happened in school today?"

"I guess I should, right? I still feel so bad about Conrad."

Zoë sighed. "Things happen. It wasn't your fault. Talking might help."

"Maybe," Kaitlyn said. Aunt Zoë had been great these past couple of months. She really seemed to get it. "Aunt Zoë, do you ever wish you had kids?"

"Sometimes. But God didn't put that on my agenda. Anyways, my whole career was taking care of animals, so that substituted to some extent, I suppose."

As the sister of Aunt Zellie's mother, Zoë was Kaitlyn's great-aunt. Before taking an early retirement to come stay with Uncle Jack and Julia, she'd been a veterinarian's assistant in California. She was divorced and had shared a secret with Kaitlyn one time. Her ex-husband had come out of the closet after they'd been married for fifteen years. He was gay, but they were still friends.

"You'd have made a great mother," Kaitlyn said.

Zoë put her glasses on. "I'd probably have been a tyrant."

Julia returned with the book. "Can I sit with you on your bed?" she said.

"If you promise not to fart."

"Ewww! I knew you were going to say that!"

With Julia finally tucked in bed, Kaitlyn called Stella's unit at the rehab center. The ward clerk answered.

"Could you get me Stella Andersen, please?" she said. "It's her stepdaughter."

"I recognize your voice, honey. You don't always have to tell me who you are. Let me go find her."

The phone went quiet. It was a refurbished iPhone that Aunt Zoë had gotten her when she'd first arrived in the summer. Stella had broken her old phone during an argument on the Fourth of July, the same day Stella wrecked the car, which was what finally led to rehab. Minutes passed. The hallway carpet was cool against her feet. Uncle Jack's bedroom door was open and light was seeping out. He still hadn't gotten home yet. She'd never seen inside his room. She looked at the phone. Why was it taking so long? Zoë was in the living room, reading. She stepped inside. The light was coming from Uncle Jack's closet.

The room didn't smell like the rest of the house. It was leathery. Almost musty. The curtains were closed and the bed was made. The only thing on the dresser was a wedding photo of him and Aunt Zellie. He always made his own bed, Zoë said, because he didn't want her to feel like a housekeeper. Zoë thought this was pigheaded because she didn't mind doing housework herself, but Uncle Jack was strange about some things. A wounded bird ever since Zellie died. "If he acts cold," she'd said, "it's not you. He's like that with a lot of people."

He was the dean of the medical school, but she didn't really know what kind of things he did. The very first time she'd met him was the day he and Zellie had gotten married, when her father was still alive. She'd been ten. She, Stella, and her father had driven to New Canterbury for the wedding. It was later that summer that her father was killed in the fire. Uncle Jack had seemed such a happy person. Everyone was happy that day, even Stella.

The light was coming from his closet. The door was wide open. She looked inside. On the right were men's shirts and pants and jackets. The opposite side, to her surprise, was hung with dresses, blouses, skirts, and sweaters. Zellie had been gone for three years and Uncle Jack still hadn't cleared away her things. She stepped in. It smelled of wood. Touching a black dress, she rubbed the fabric between her fingers. Flower-petal soft. She touched it to her cheek. It smelled faintly of flowers too. *Oh my God*, she thought, letting it go. How can he stand it? It was hard enough for her to look at her father's old baseball glove, which she kept hidden under her mattress after Stella had mentioned selling it.

The sudden sound of a voice startled her. The phone. She'd forgotten about it. She backed out of the closet.

"Sorry to keep you waiting," said the clerk.

Kaitlyn padded back into the hallway. "That's okay. Is anything wrong?"

"Listen, honey. We can't seem to locate Stella right now. I'd be happy to give her a message."

Somewhere toward the front of the house an outside door slammed shut. Uncle Jack was home. "You can't find her? What do you mean? What's going on?"

"Not to worry. She had a day pass today and it looks like she may not be back yet. It's about that time though."

"I didn't know she got passes."

"I was surprised too. But her doctor okayed it. Let me look. Yep. Today was her second. I'll have her call you when she gets in."

Zoë was sitting in her favorite chair, a recliner, a shawl over her legs.

"Is Uncle Jack home?" Kaitlyn asked. "I heard the door."

"No, that was Tony. He said to tell you to come over if you want to play some darts with him and Chad. Did you talk with her yet?"

"I tried but she wasn't available. I think I'll go play darts."

"Not available?" Zoë asked.

"She was out on some kind of pass."

Zoë's eyebrows arched. She set the Kindle on her lap. "Talk to me for a minute," she said.

"Later, okay?" Kaitlyn grabbed her heavy blue fleece jacket and slipped on her old running shoes. She went out. It was a bright, crisp night with a lot of stars and a three-quarter moon above the mountain behind the barn. Her breath vapor hung in the air. As she rounded the house heading for the barn, she could see way down into the valley in front of the house to where the lights of New Canterbury twinkled. Must be pretty here when it snows. But she'd be gone by then.

Tony was Uncle Jack's younger brother. He was about forty and lived in the barn. When she had first described him to Aishia, Kaitlyn had strung her along, saying that Uncle Jack made Tony, who had a type of autism, live in the barn. Aishia was shocked until Kaitlyn added that Jack had turned the barn's second floor into an apartment, and it was great.

She found Tony and his friend Chad, who had a less severe type of autism, on the far end of the barn's ground floor past the green tractor. The area was lit by two rows of hanging LED shop lights and was bright. Tony and Chad were wearing matching green sweatshirts with the name of their computer business on the front: *NetNuts*.

Kaitlyn had introduced them to darts, and now Tony and Chad

played all the time. Tony, maybe because of his special archery talent, was improving fast. The dartboard hanging there was the only thing she'd brought from Dayton other than her clothes. Her father had taught her to play when she was Julia's age.

"Hey guys."

She'd gotten used to Tony's condition. He just couldn't show much in the way of feelings and tended to hyperfixate on things. He didn't drive, and he didn't like to make eye contact. Old photos showed him with a bushy beard, holding a bow at a statewide archery competition. He had many archery trophies in his apartment and still practiced in the backyard. His dark brown beard was well trimmed now.

Chad was younger than Tony and had short blond hair. Chad waved her over. "Hey, Katie," he said. "You better watch out. We're warmed up. Hold out your hand and I'll get you started."

She held it out, palm up. Concentrating, Chad placed three darts side by side, lining them up with the vanes in the same orientation. She hid a smile. Chad's quirks were less noticeable than Tony's, but he had the same tendency to obsess over small details. Chad had a car, though he still lived with his mother. Both men were super smart, especially when it came to computers. Their joint business venture involved fixing them, salvaging components, setting up networks, and even building fast systems for gamers.

"You want to play 301 or 501?" asked Chad.

"301," she said. Chad turned and coughed into his elbow, to which she responded, "You've got a cold."

"Not much." He coughed again. It was coarse and didn't sound good.

She raised the dart, squinted, and threw a triple twenty. Chad and Tony cheered. She prepared to throw again, but her phone began chirping. Kaitlyn answered it.

"Hey, sweetie," Stella said. "Didn't know you were going to call, or I'd have left a message with Ida. But I'm supposed to be getting my own phone back in a few days, hallelujah. Ring the bells." Stella had a fit of giggling.

Kaitlyn felt a shiver of alarm. The phone tight against her ear, she strode to the other side of the barn, heart pounding. "Where *were* you?"

"Out on a little pass, Kaitlyn. No problem. Got one last night too."

"How did you get a pass?"

"By following the rules. Hey, don't pee on my parade. I can't tell you how good it felt to be out. I'm way ready to get my life back. Just two more weeks. Not even."

"You sound stoned. Are you stoned?"

"I wouldn't call it stoned. Half-baked, maybe."

"Are you crazy?"

"Listen to me, young lady. I don't appreciate that tone."

"I can't believe this, Stella."

"Whoa. Stop right there. Let's get something straight, young lady. You will call me *Mom* or *Mama*, like always, and you will show me the respect I deserve. That's that. How am I going to build up my own self-respect? That's a lesson I've learned. How many times have we talked about this?"

"The point is, *Mom*, where did you go?" She paused as a tremor passed through her like a mini earthquake. "Where did you *go*?"

"Don't be such a brat, Kaitlyn. I've been in this place for almost three months, all right? I've learned a lot about myself. I'm creating a toolbelt of good habits, which you will soon see. But a little weed now and then isn't going to hurt anybody, and it's everywhere here. I'm not alone. It's like drinking a beer."

"That's not what you said this summer."

"You sound so self-righteous. When I get out and we're a family again, everything is going to be just like we talked about. You'll be proud of me. You're not going to lose me like you lost your father."

"What do you mean?"

"I'm not saying anything about it being your fault, Kaitlyn, so simmer down. Please."

"All right, but where did you go?"

Stella sighed. "You don't know what it's like."

"And I never want to."

"You're a strong person, Kaitlyn. I love you and I miss you so much. And I need you just like I needed your father."

Kaitlyn drew a deep shuddering breath and let it out slowly. "I know," she said. "It's been hard for me too. Just tell me where you went."

"I had some pizza and wings and then I took a walk by the river. Hey, I saw a couple of shooting stars! Two of them. Maybe your mom is in for some good luck finally."

"Were you alone?"

"I thought you called because you wanted to talk."

"Just answer."

"Here we go," Stella said. "Albert Einstein. You know everything about everything."

"Was it Donald?"

"Listen, while you've been living in that big house with your doctor uncle, I've been alone. Certain people understand me, and Donald Citrian, for all his faults, is one of them. Yes, Donald took me to dinner. Yes, back in the summer I said that we were over. But I have a perfect right to change my mind."

"What does your therapist think?"

"That I need to make my own life decisions. I need your understanding."

"Is he coming back to live with us?"

Stella blew her nose. Kaitlyn reflexively moved the phone away.

"You know that he would never do anything to harm you. He always treated you like a daughter."

"It's not Donald or I that I'm worried about—it's you."

"I've got so many new life tools hanging from my belt now. I'm going to start working again. You should have seen those shooting stars, my God."

Kaitlyn looked over at Tony and Chad. Chad threw a dart and made a little jump as it hit the cork.

"Are you still there?" Stella said.

"Yes."

"What are you doing tonight?"

"I'm playing darts with Uncle Tony and Chad."

"I personally would not feel comfortable around a nutjob like Tony with a dart in his hand. Who's Chad? Did you find a boyfriend?"

"I've told you about him. He's Uncle Tony's friend and business partner. Chad Chadwick."

"His parents ought to be whipped for giving him a name like that. Jesus."

"He's very nice."

"I bet you miss your friends back here a ton. Won't be long now."

"I didn't have that many."

"What about Jody? You guys used to be joined at the hip."

"You forget that her parents pulled her out last year after that kid John Schultz overdosed in the bathroom."

"Oh, yeah. I remember that. Where was it her parents sent her?"

"St. Theresa's Academy."

"You still friends?"

"Sort of. I called her last week but all she talked about was some boy whose parents have a condo in Orlando."

"That's what you need. A boyfriend with a condo in Florida. I'll chaperone."

"It's not funny. Listen, something happened at school today. I got into a fight."

"Sweetie, I'm afraid it's going to have to wait till the next time we talk. I need to go and do a routine pee test. Fortunately, I've got a supply on hand."

"Please don't tell me that."

"Do you miss me?"

Kaitlyn's chest muscles were quivering. "I can't believe you're going to let Donald back in the house. I can't believe it. Shouldn't I have a say?"

"I have to go. Let me hear you say it."

"Say what?"

"How about *I love you, Mom*? And *I know how much you love and need me*?"

"I love you," Kaitlyn said, flatly.

Stella didn't respond for a few beats, then she said, "Take care of yourself, Kaitlyn," her voice going crisp and hard. "I'll see you in two weeks. And stay away from hamsters."

The line went dead.

Kaitlyn began to tremble. *Hamsters*. A powerful ache swelled in her throat. She was reminding Kaitlyn of how her father had died. She thought back to that terrible night, how the fire alarm had woken her, her father leading her outside, how Kaitlyn had remembered her hamster back in its cage, how her father had dashed back in, thinking he still had time.

CHAPTER SEVEN

Jack waded into a field just east of the barn that hadn't been cultivated in years, weaving through saplings and brittle weed stalks that scratched against his briefcase. A couple of months had passed since he'd last been out here. This is where three years ago he'd had them tow his wrecked Ford Escape. It had been rusting in the weeds ever since, its tires flat, the front end caved in and ugly.

The roof bore a scrim of frost. He opened the driver's door. It squealed like an injured animal. Brushing away a spiderweb, he slid in behind the wheel. The seat was cold and cramped, still in the position where she'd left it. He could feel her here, just as he could when he opened the closet door sometimes, half expecting to see her turn to ask his opinion.

"All is not well," he said aloud. "But I will keep trying."

Standing in front of the mirror, Kaitlyn tucked her blouse into her jeans, then turned to the left and right. Her face looked tired and slack. She tried smiling. While she held the smile, her face looked alive. But when she let it go, awful. She did not want people thinking she hadn't slept. What passed through her mind was nobody's business.

She noticed movement out the window and looked. It was Uncle Jack walking in the field toward Aunt Zellie's wrecked car. The early morning sky was dark gray. Kaitlyn had gone out there to see for herself once when Uncle Jack wasn't home. She watched him open the door and slip inside. What was he doing? Was he just going to just sit there? It was like the clothes in the closet. She grabbed her backpack. She was so far from figuring him out.

In the kitchen, Aunt Zoë was at the table, a cup cradled in her hand. The string from a tea bag hung down the side of the cup. Julia wasn't up yet. Her preschool started later, and she wasn't an early riser.

"I can tell it's Wednesday," Kaitlyn said.

"Good morning," said Zoë. "Why's that?"

"Because you're drinking tea. You only drink tea on Wednesday mornings. Please don't tell me I look tired."

Zoë smiled. "You look as bright as a robin in spring hunting for worms."

"I feel more like the worm."

"How about a pancake? Or maybe an egg and toast. You've got plenty of time."

"No, I'm fine. Don't go to any trouble."

"I didn't ask *if* you wanted breakfast. I asked *what* you wanted. Now choose."

"Pancake would be fine. I saw Uncle Jack go out to that wrecked car out back and get inside."

Zoë sighed, then pressed her lips together. "If I were him, I wouldn't want any reminders like that lying around. Not that he listens to me."

"Does he plan to fix it up or something?"

"I don't think it's fixable. The only thing he told me was he didn't want them shredding it."

"Shredding it?"

"That's what they do nowadays, drop them in a machine that chews them into little chunks they recycle. There's a scrapyard a few miles away. You can hear the shredder working some nights."

"Like a grinding, banging sound?"

"That's it," Zoë said.

"I've wondered. I thought it was a train."

Zoë poured batter into the skillet. "Were you able to get through to your stepmother last night?"

"She finally called back."

"How'd it go?"

Kaitlyn inspected her fingernails. She really needed to stop biting them.

"Kaitlyn?" said Zoë.

Without warning, Kaitlyn felt her eyes overflow. Zoë came and put her hands on Kaitlyn's shoulders. She kissed the top of her head. "Sweetheart."

"I'm sorry," Kaitlyn said.

"Nothing to be sorry for. You can talk to me. You are my BFF, dude. Tell me whatever."

"BFF, dude?" Kaitlyn said, half laughing, half sobbing. "Where did you hear that?" She dabbed at her eyes with a napkin. "I love you, Aunt Zoë."

Zoë kissed her head again.

Kaitlyn sighed. "Stella's been smoking dope and getting back with her boyfriend, Donald."

Zoë's hands tightened on Kaitlyn's shoulders. "Kaitlyn, I do *not* want you going back there."

"I can deal with it. She obviously needs me. And it's what I deserve."

"What do you mean, what you deserve?"

"Nothing. She brought up the hamster again last night."

"What hamster?" Zoë asked.

"Never mind. It's too complicated. I really don't want to get into it. I need to go."

"But breakfast," Zoë protested.

"I'm fine. I'm getting fat here anyway."

CHAPTER EIGHT

The day after his trip to New Canterbury, Dr. Lawrence Haines strode out to the Bell Jet Ranger helicopter based in the backyard of his estate on the outskirts of Raleigh. His mechanic, Alfredo, was waiting by the bird under a clear, balmy early morning sky.

"Morning, Dr. Haines," he said, wiping his hands on a rag and patting the tail boom. "She's topped up and ready."

Haines strapped in, donned his headset, and started the turbine. After entering the coordinates for Mikhail Potemkin's ship into his GPS, he lifted off, heading southeast toward the ocean, aided by a quartering tailwind. He wouldn't be filing a flight plan, and he'd be avoiding populated areas. Maintaining an altitude of five hundred feet, he soared over the scrub pine flats and sandy fields of eastern North Carolina. Half an hour later, a barrier island with its stilted houses and lapping breakers slid beneath him, and he was over the Atlantic. There would be nothing but waves below him now for the next twenty-five miles, until he reached Potemkin's ship anchored out in international waters, just outside of his home state.

The ship came into view fifteen minutes later. At 515 feet long with a displacement of 475 tons, it resembled something between a luxury yacht and a battleship. But it was more than either. Potemkin's nautical fiefdom was registered with the UN as an independent nation called Wiegatesland. Similar to a few other of the world's handful of sovereign microstates like Tuvalu, Nauru, San Marino, or Kiribati, Wiegatesland lacked extradition treaties with other nations.

On board his boat, Potemkin was immune from being hauled away to face justice.

Haines made radio contact.

"Ranger zero-five-one alpha," the controller replied in a British accent. "Roger that. You're cleared to land. Winds out of one-eight-seven degrees at fourteen knots. Standby to clear customs after landing."

Haines circled the massive ship, set up his approach, and brought the Jet Ranger down between two other helicopters, an Alouette and a Robinson, both painted in tan and green camouflage. A squad of five Wiegatesland marines in white shorts and shirts with blue caps marched up and saluted, AK-47s slung from their shoulders. Above the bridge, a huge purple and gold flag snapped in the breeze. One of the marines produced a trumpet and began playing the Wiegatesland national anthem, clearly a mash-up of "Mack the Knife" and "Hello, Dolly!" Potemkin had an odd sense of humor. As it died away, an officer with a razor thin gray mustache appeared at Haines's window.

"Hello, Colonel Spavin," Haines said.

"Greetings, Dr. Haines. The prime minister is waiting. Anything to declare today?"

"Do you really have to do this, Colonel?"

"No firearms, alcohol, tobacco, or produce?"

"Negative."

Spavin led him to the stern and then into a covered atrium-like area at the rearmost section of the superstructure, where the shaded air smelled of vegetation. The reason for the vegetation smell was the giant terrarium they now passed, which contained soil from Potemkin's birthplace near Murmansk. Within the glass walls, a small copse of birch and fir trees grew in mossy ground among scattered rocks and ferns, all bathed in the glow of pink and blue grow lamps, drops of condensation beading the interior surface of the glass. A placard said: *Welcome to Wiegatesland, Home to Those Who Roam*, with translations in a dozen languages. Spavin halted at a metal detector guarding the entrance, which led deeper into the superstructure.

"When did you install this?" Haines asked, nodding at the metal detector.

"Last month, Doctor," Spavin said, handing him a plastic basket. "Can't be too careful these days. Please empty your pockets and remove your belt. Sorry, that's the protocol. You can leave your shoes on." Spavin handed him back the basket and they proceeded down a mahogany paneled hallway, the left side of which was lined by doors bearing gilded labels: *Ministry of National Security and Intelligence*; *Ministry of Engineering and Foreign Affairs*; *Ministry of Commerce and the High Seas*; *Ministry of the Interior, Taxation, and Recruitment*; *Ministry of Social Welfare, Culture, Health, and Entertainment*.

There was only one door, however, on the corridor's right wall, labeled *Cyber Affairs*. As they approached it, the door swung open and a young man in a black T-shirt emerged along with the sound of many voices. The man smiled and saluted Spavin. As they passed, Haines saw rows and rows of computer terminals swarming with people. This was Potemkin's operational nerve center. At the end of the hallway was a double door labeled *Prime Minister*. Spavin flung it open and stood aside. Ahead rose a wide staircase of teak treads and brass railings.

Haines ascended into a vast, high-ceiled room that spanned the width of the superstructure and was sparsely furnished with pieces done in chrome, glass, and white leather. Tinted floor-to-ceiling windows gave expansive views of the open sea on either side. The floor was covered in deep pile, cream-colored carpeting. At the far end of the room lay a raised platform upon which sat a desk laden with two huge monitors. In the mirrored wall behind the desk, he could see the back of Potemkin's head, with its small bald spot at the crown. He was bent over, typing. Potemkin's Russian-accented voice boomed out: "Be right with you, Lawrence! Make yourself comfortable."

"Take your time, Mikhail."

A moment later Potemkin emerged from behind the monitors. Trim and in his early fifties, Potemkin had a large head and prominent cheekbones, and he would have been handsome were it not for a tarantula-shaped mole on his right cheek. When Haines had first met him back in Boston twenty years ago, he'd offered to refer him to a plastic surgeon, but Potemkin laughed away the suggestion. On the contrary—it was a badge of honor. His ancestor, a general in the army that helped defeat Napoleon, had possessed one similar.

Today he was wearing a white Icelandic fisherman's sweater, orange Bermuda shorts, and a pair of flip-flops. His long, graying black hair was in disarray, as usual. "Lawrence, please forgive that I was not outside to greet you when you alighted."

"I know you're busy."

"Always too much," the oligarch said, flashing a smile that revealed large white teeth. "But I watched you land through my security feed. As always, my friend, you fly as gentle as a dove. Before business, I've got something you must see!" He dashed back to his desk and returned to hand Haines a small glass box, inside of which lay a coin on a velvet cushion. "Now, tell me what this is."

This was a common routine between the two of them, showing off coins they'd acquired. They'd first met at the Boston Numismatics Society, one of the oldest coin collecting clubs in the nation, back when Haines was an internal medicine resident and Potemkin was studying computer science at MIT. Haines held it up to the light. It was obviously Greek, and its pale-yellow glow suggested electrum, an amalgam of gold and silver. Looking closer, he recognized the head of Arethusa, a nymph. On the obverse was a chariot pulled by four horses. The details were remarkably intact, the chariot reins still visible.

Haines shook his head in wonder and more than a little envy. "This looks like a decadrachm stamped from a die engraved by either Kimon of Syracuse or Euanitos, circa 400 BC. It's in sublime condition, Mikhail. Where'd you find it? A shipwreck?"

Potemkin squinted at him with a somber expression first, then brayed with laughter. "Ah, Lawrence. Ha, ha! This is fake! The real one, I have locked down in the Treasury Department. Good, no?

We have passed a number already on eBay. Want to know what I'm getting for them?"

Haines grimaced. "Not really, no."

"You keep it. A souvenir of Wiegatesland. Now, come and tell me about your visit to the hospital yesterday. You said there was a complication. I'm curious." He followed Potemkin over to a semicircle of white leather chairs around a glass coffee table. The Russian opened a cigar humidor. "Join me? They're the ones Fidel liked best, made in a factory where naked women read Tolstoy to entertain the rollers. And they give other things too, I hear." Haines declined. Potemkin sniffed the cigar but did not light up. "My wife asked me to say hello to you, by the way. She is in Capri for a few weeks."

"Sorry to have missed her," Haines responded. "Please give her my regards."

Potemkin ran the cigar beneath his nose again. "So, tell me about this *complication*. I handed you that hospital on a silver platter. It couldn't have been easier. A big green light. Why is it not done?"

Haines filled his chest. "It turns out the current dean has a potential plan to raise enough capital—enough capital that they might not need my help."

"You're saying they might not sell to you?"

"I seriously doubt he can pull it off, but that's not what I came here to discuss."

"Hmmm," said Potemkin, tapping his temple with the unlit cigar. "The dean you're referring to—would that be a doctor named Jack Forester, the same individual that our friend Bryson Witner had his trouble with?"

"Yes."

Potemkin laughed. "This is too good, Lawrence. Do you not find this funny?"

"Ironic, but not particularly humorous."

The Russian arched with laughter again. "Very ironic, yes," he said, putting a handkerchief to his eyes. "You do not overstate. The same man that Bryson Witner hates for getting him locked up, the same human spur who pricked Bryson into starting this whole thing in the first place, and who now may ruin everything, this Forester. We won't let him succeed, of course, but what is this little plan of his to stop the takeover?"

"I have no idea, Mikhail. I was merely told that Forester proposed something, and they decided to give him two weeks to see if it will work. I don't see how he could succeed, but there's a finite chance, I suppose."

"However, my tall friend, if there is any shred of possibility he might prevail, we need to prevent it."

"Which brings up why I wanted to see you. We need to talk."

The laughter bled from Potemkin's eyes. "Oh? About what?"

Haines filled his chest again and leaned back in the plush chair. "I'm going to put my foot down, Mikhail. I want no further interference."

"Is that what you call my work? Interference?"

"Our original plan was for you to monitor the finances there from the inside. Monitor and help me decide when to move. But given the scale of their losses and the fact that you were able to tell me exactly when to be prepared, I believe you moved beyond monitoring to manipulating. And I know you can do it." Haines nodded in the direction of the cyber affairs room.

Potemkin released a long sigh and smiled. "Lawrence, you receive what you asked for, and yet you express surprise."

Haines felt his temper rising. "Our agreement was that you would simply observe and keep me informed."

"Our agreement was that I would help you. Which I did. Why are you surprised? You know what I do for a living."

Haines glanced at the mirrored wall behind the desk, where the oligarch's snowy mountain screen savers reflected from his monitors. "How did you do it, Mikhail? I want the truth."

"Well, it was a big challenge, but I love a challenge. I experimented.

Once we got past the firewall with Bryson's help, we did a little of this and a little of that, and soon we had integrated ourselves into *every* aspect of their cyber infrastructure. I know all their business—their books, their communications, when the toilets flush, when the cash registers open and close, their cameras, their medical monitoring equipment, everything. Ha, ha!"

"Where did the money go, Mikhail?"

Potemkin licked the tip of his cigar and shrugged. "Here and there. Some of it they spent thinking they had more than they really did. Some of it they failed to collect. Some of it went to feed my own operating expenses, naturally." He pointed the cigar around. "All this is not for peanuts. Countries are costly." He sniffed the cigar again. "But don't let this disturb you. They will never find out. Trust me, they will never find out."

"How can you be certain?"

"Because I'm good at keeping my worms under the ground. Remember, I'm a man who helped design the Stuxnet virus. And because when you take over that crippled place, you will promptly install a new network with brand new state-of-the-art hardware and software, and we will have all the old things destroyed. Goodbye to any evidence, not that it's likely they'd be able to find it anyway. And no one will ever know of my investments in your business because of my shell companies. They will never find out because there will be nothing left of those computers. Unless, of course, Dr. Forester beats you out."

Haines was breathing heavily, his shoulders feeling rigid. Someone was climbing up the steps into the stateroom. It was an attractive young woman with dark blond hair, which she brushed as she walked. Seeing him, she stopped. She was wearing a terry cloth robe over a light blue bathing suit.

"Very sorry, Mikhail," she said. "I didn't know you had a guest."

Potemkin grunted. "No problem. Come let me introduce. Lawrence, allow me to present Gina Larsen—she was married to my nephew before he passed. Gina, this is Dr. Lawrence Haines, my old friend from Boston days I've told you so much about. He is building the greatest hospital system in the world, with our help."

"Hello, Dr. Haines," she said, setting the hairbrush on the coffee table and shaking his hand. "A pleasure to finally meet you."

"Lawrence, let me tell you about Gina. She is one of my intelligence operatives, you see. A person of many talents. She was a registered nurse in her previous life, as well as a trained actress. She's worked for me ever since my nephew, her husband, died. Now, Gina, please wait outside and you can escort him back to his chariot of the sky when we conclude."

When the doors shut behind her, Potemkin smiled. "Gina's very competent," he continued, picking up her hairbrush and waving it. "Even if she leaves things lying around sometimes, like many women do. It's a shame my nephew was killed before he could really enjoy life with her. They had one child, a little girl, you see, that I take care of in the UK while she works for me. You owe her many thanks. She has been helping me with the New Canterbury operation. Gina is the conduit of information between me and our insane comrade, Bryson."

"I would just as soon not know anything about this."

"Why not? She visits him once a quarter posing as his long-lost cousin. But, forget about her for now. Back to where we were with this crisis of conscience of yours. I understand that along with making money, you want to help mankind with your hospitals. I get that. And you know that I want my investments in you to return money and grow. We are in this together. My friend, if you are in for a penny, you are in for a pound. Do you follow me? I don't interfere with your work; you shouldn't interfere with mine. You need to trust me."

Haines sighed and allowed the anger building inside to seep away. Expressing it would get him nowhere. He rubbed his chin, realizing he hadn't shaved very closely this morning. "Mikhail, what's done is done. But for the greater good of HWA, I want no more manipulation. If the project fails now, it wasn't meant to succeed. No more."

His eyes narrowing, Potemkin lifted his niece's hairbrush and tapped it on his knee. "So, if this Jack Forester cuts you out, we should just let him win the prize? Is that what you mean?"

"Things have gone way beyond my comfort zone. I want the process to play out naturally from here on out. Do I make myself clear?"

Potemkin shrugged and smiled. "Well, my old friend, if you feel that strongly . . ."

"I do."

"Then so be it." Potemkin gave Haines his hand. "You and I must not argue, my big friend. I honor your Christlike feelings. They are more important than my investments. Everything will henceforth be above the board. I wash my hands. If my reward comes, I will take it. If not, I will at least have tried."

Haines nodded. "Thank you. I will hold you to your word."

Potemkin lit the cigar, the flame pulsating as he drew. "Adieu for now, Lawrence. Gina will walk you to your bird."

CHAPTER NINE

Kaitlyn and Mr. Brady walked down a brightly lit corridor in the medical center basement. He had driven her from school to help her get enrolled in her volunteer activity. They came to a door labeled *Volunteer Coordination Services* and entered an office suite.

The receptionist sprang up and greeted him like an old friend, giving him a hug. "So you've brought us a new recruit."

"Yes, indeed, Martha. This is Kaitlyn Andersen. Cassandra is expecting us."

"She'll be back from a meeting any minute. Why don't you go wait in her office?"

They had barely taken seats when a pretty middle-aged lady strode in and likewise greeted Mr. Brady warmly. Cassandra Simpson wore a string of pearls around her neck and a lot of lipstick. "And you must be Kaitlyn, Dr. Forester's niece." She shook Kaitlyn's hand. "Welcome. We always need the help."

"Kaitlyn had a study hall this period, then lunch," Mr. Brady said. "I thought we'd get the ball rolling."

"Excellent. I took the liberty of calling Dr. Forester's office so we can get a permission signed. How's everything with you, Jim? I hear you're thinking of retiring next year." As they continued talking, Kaitlyn studied Cassandra's office. There was a Boston fern like Aunt Zoë had, but not as healthy looking. Watering plants was one of the chores Zoë had given her. She never needed to worry about forgetting because Julia would bring her the watering can and ask to pour the water herself, which half the time she ended up spilling. Julia was easily distracted. She'd get excited if a fly landed on a leaf. *Oh look!* She was going to miss Julia. Having a kid-sister type around made you feel older.

"Kaitlyn, when would you like to start?" Cassandra said, interrupting her thoughts.

"I don't know. Maybe the day after tomorrow?"

"That would work on our end," Mr. Brady said. "That's Friday and they have a teachers' workday."

"What will I actually be doing?" Kaitlyn asked.

Cassandra described things like helping at the reception desk, transporting patients, delivering supplies, assisting the nurses, carrying flowers up to rooms, making coffee for families, helping in the medical library, and so on.

"Will I go into the operating room?"

"Would you like that?"

"Sure."

"We might be able to arrange that. Are you interested in medicine, Kaitlyn?"

"Sort of."

"Any particular specialty?"

She'd never thought of this before and said the first things that came to mind. "Pediatrics and psychiatry."

"Well, maybe you'll go to medical school here someday like your uncle."

"She's definitely got the brains for it," said Mr. Brady.

Kaitlyn felt a surge of irritation. She wished Mr. Brady would stop being so positive. She'd be lucky if she got into a community college somewhere. Suddenly, a knock came from Cassandra's door.

"What is it?" Cassandra called.

The door opened and there stood a tall, skinny young man wearing a dark suit. His head was shaved except for the back part, which was pulled into a bun. It looked like he had a wing tattoo on his neck. That was bold.

"A little busy here, Tré," said Cassandra. "Can I help you?"

"Hi, Ms. Simpson. Sorry to interrupt. Martha called the office and said the dean's niece was here, so I thought I'd stop by and say hello. You must be Kaitlyn. And—my lord—Mr. Brady! I didn't know you were here too. Remember me?"

"Well, if it isn't Tré Tannino. Look what the cat dragged in. I didn't know you were working here."

"Yes, sir. Five years this June. I'm Dr. Forester's administrative assistant and working on my MBA. I bet you thought I'd be in jail by now."

Mr. Brady laughed and denied that was the case.

Tré shook Kaitlyn's hand. "Nice to meet you," he said. "Welcome. I'll look forward to seeing you around. Maybe we can do lunch sometime." Then he shook Mr. Brady's hand again, repeated an apology to Cassandra, and was gone.

"Wow," said Brady. "That made my day."

CHAPTER TEN

Squinting in the sunlight, Gina Larsen watched Haines's helicopter soar off toward the mainland. In no hurry to return to Potemkin's big but chilly and mildew-smelling office, she ambled down the starboard deck. She did not enjoy Potemkin's company. He was so unlike his nephew Dmitry, her deceased husband. Potemkin needed to be in complete control, to keep others off-balance. Though if Dmitry had been more calculating like his uncle, he might still be alive, and she wouldn't be here doing Potemkin's bidding, waiting for him to reunite her with her daughter. Lydia was now almost two, and she hadn't seen her in over a year, a constant ache. If Potemkin kept his promise, however, they would soon be reunited and she'd be free.

A member of the maintenance crew, one-armed Yevgeny gave her a gap-toothed smile and tipped his hat as she passed. He was one of the few lower-deck people who never made passes at her, never treated her as if she were one of the ship's rotating cast of brothel girls. She had few friends. Most of the other females on board were either non-English speaking domestics or haughty software engineers who had their own neighborhoods, each populated with a personal bar, restaurant, and fitness center.

Back in the office, Potemkin was working at his computer. She settled into a chair by his desk. He finally looked at her and yanked the cigar from his mouth. "You forgot your hairbrush."

"I know. Why did Dr. Haines fly in today? Is there a problem?"

"Yes. But I have a plan. Let's ask Bodashka to join us." He turned to the two-way mirror behind the desk and waved. A hidden door opened and out stepped Bodashka Liski, the minister of national security and intelligence. Middle-aged and short, Liski wore his usual dark blue pinstripe suit with a turquoise shirt and red tie.

"Air getting unhealthy in there, boss," he said in English, his accent a little thicker than Potemkin's. "You need better circulation." When he and Potemkin were alone, they usually spoke in Russian.

"Then get it fixed and don't bother me. You were probably sleeping anyway. I should make you walk the plank. Come sit."

"I never sleep on the job," Liski said, laughing and pulling up a chair next to Gina. "Hello, Gina. I didn't mean to ignore you, my lovely."

She sighed and gazed out the window. A wall of clouds was approaching from the east. Potemkin tossed Liski a cigar. Along with being an inch or so shorter than Gina, who herself was only five-foot-four, Bodashka Liski had tiny feet and a bald, pear-shaped head. The only non-compact thing about him was a protuberant belly. She watched him slip the cigar into his mouth and apply the hissing flame of a lighter to its tip. He also had a strange mustache. The middle third was shaved clean, leaving two widely separated side sections that drooped beyond the corners of his mouth almost to the middle of his chin. His cheeks sunk in grotesquely as he sucked on the cigar. Gina waved the acrid cloud away from her face.

"So, Bodashka," said Potemkin. "What did you think of what you heard from the lips of Lawrence Haines today? Talk English so Gina can understand."

"I think his feet grow cold. How will you approach this, boss? What is up your shirt? I am excited to hear."

"Then be quiet and listen. I'm going to need help from both of you." Potemkin swiveled his chair around and stared at Gina. "I have two more important missions for you, niece." He held up his palm toward her. "Before you get riled up, let me tell you that this work will be your final duty. I promise you."

She saw Liski look down at his fingernails. *I knew it*, she thought, her face heating. *This is never going to end. Not until I'm dead.* "That's what you said the last time, Mikhail."

"You are mistaken. I did not say that. It's what you believed I said. So don't get angry, *zechka*."

"Don't call me that."

"But it's true. You *are* my captive. Not, however, for much longer. When this is done, you will make a great reunion with your beautiful little girl, my grandniece Lydia. End of story."

"He will keep his word," said Liski. "You know that."

"Yes," said Potemkin. "You will have a trust fund to live from, a nice little house in Aix-en-Provence—if that's still where you want—and you can raise the girl in peace and security. That is how my nephew would have wanted it."

Her eyes burning, she inhaled deeply and rubbed her temples.

"I never betray family," Potemkin continued. "You were Dmitry's bride when the gangsters murdered him, and your little girl is my blood. You were in bad shape when we took her from you. Don't forget that. It was to help."

"Blood is thicker than water," said Liski. "Have trust."

Trust? She looked at the diminutive, ass-kissing Liski and shivered. Light shimmering on the mirrored wall reflected off the top of his shaven head, making his skull appear like an open beaker of liquid. As he nodded at her, she imagined his brains sloshing over the edge. She turned back to Potemkin and clenched her jaws. "What is it you need me to do?"

"That's my girl. Okay, here's the plan. First, Gina, you will pay Bryson Witner one more visit at the Patterson hospital. You will tell him that things are going along as planned and that we will keep up our end of the bargain and help him get out."

"Is that true? Or will I be lying to him?"

"Of course it's not true."

"No way he gets out," said Liski. "He is a madman. It will be good for the cosmos with him gone."

"And he knows too much," said Potemkin. "His fate, though, is not a worry for either of you. I will arrange to take care of him at the right time."

"Like you recently did for the snoopy medical director Teitelbaum at Patterson, boss, where Witner is locked up, right?"

Potemkin glared at him. "Bodashka, you talk too much."

Gina looked at the two of them. "Is there something here I should know about?"

"It wasn't necessary for you to know, Gina," Potemkin said. "But I suppose there is no harm. You reported last month that Witner believed the medical director there at Patterson was becoming suspicious. That could not be allowed to continue."

Gina felt a twisting sensation in her upper abdomen. Dr. Teitelbaum had seemed to be a nice man. She'd met him a time or two. "So, what happened with his car wasn't an accident," she stated.

"No," Potemkin said. "In any case, Gina, you simply need to see Witner tomorrow and reassure that I will help him get out soon. That is all."

"Tomorrow?"

"Tomorrow."

She looked out the window again. The sky was darkening. "What's the second thing you want me to do?"

"Something even more interesting than when you befriended the Turkish ambassador last year and got so much good information for me. This second thing will require all your skills and talents."

With a sense of revulsion, she remembered the chubby, oily-skinned ambassador who reeked of cigarette smoke. "What is it?" she asked, clenching her jaws.

"A different type of seduction, Gina. Not to bed, but into the head. Witner's old enemy, Jack Forester, is now the hospital dean at New Canterbury. Lawrence tells me Forester has a mysterious plan that might prevent Lawrence from buying the hospital. They gave him two weeks to try."

"Do you think he can do it, boss?" Liski said.

"This is what Gina needs to discover. If Forester figures out a way to block me, she will make sure it doesn't happen."

"But, boss, why can't you just find out through their computer system? You roam it freely, I thought."

"Good question," Gina said. "Why go through all this if you can hack their communications?"

Potemkin blew out a cloud of smoke. "I will be doing that also, of course. But too much is riding on this. We need better information of the deepest kind, right from the horse's trough. That's what Gina will do."

She shifted in the chair. "But how, Mikhail? I can't just walk in there."

"Oh, yes you can." Potemkin strode to his desk. "Come and see. Both of you."

When they were standing behind him, he pointed to a photograph filling the screen. "You see this woman? Her name is Marianna Vlada Marina Kovalenko. This was taken last year in Kyiv, where the bitch lives."

The woman was slender, maybe in her late thirties, early forties. She had long chestnut hair, a smallish chin, and a no-nonsense expression on her somewhat pretty face. The photo was grainy, as if taken from a distance. She was standing on a city street corner in a summer dress, satchel slung on her shoulder, her hair lifted off her neck by a breeze.

"She has bowlegs," Liski said. "But nice too."

"This is the woman Gina will impersonate," Potemkin said. "Kovalenko is thirty-nine years of age, a little older than you, but close enough. Unmarried and has no children. For a living, she writes a lot of liberal rubbish for the *Ukrainian Week* magazine. Do you remember who she is now, Bodashka?"

Liski nodded and smiled. "I do, yes. She wrote the big article accusing you of eliminating that person who was going to rat you out in Kyiv, the one they put in a Ukrainian witness protection program. Some witness protection!"

"Right," said Potemkin. "She's one of those people who thinks their life's purpose is to write negative things about successful businesspeople from Russia, whom she believes make Ukraine more corrupt. As if they need our help."

Liski turned to Gina. "Her article about Mikhail made him seem like the devil."

Imagine that, she thought.

Potemkin sniffed. "In her stupid article she didn't once mention my orphanage in Crimea."

"Actually, she did," said Liski. "She said it was linked to sex trafficking."

"Which couldn't be further from the truth anymore," said Potemkin. "Fake news."

"I'm surprised you didn't punish her," said Liski.

"Who needs to swat at every fly? I am glad now I didn't bother. Marianna Kovalenko is going to be very useful. You see, she also writes things about health care and public policy garbage. She was once a nurse, like Gina."

"You actually read what she writes, boss?"

Gina stepped away from the computer impatiently. "Mikhail, what does she have to do with New Canterbury?"

"Patience," he responded, then turned his attention back to Liski. "Since she disrespected me in print, Bodashka, I read all her things. She writes well. She even won a little Ukrainian award for a story she wrote last year about . . ." Potemkin hesitated, giving them a teasing smile.

"About what, boss?"

Potemkin chuckled. "About some good hospitals in America that are situated in small cities, about how they survive. And New Canterbury was one of those she mentioned. I remember because of our project. You see why I read a lot?"

"Kindly get to the point," said Gina.

Potemkin let out an exasperated sigh and took another drag on the cigar. "Be patient. The point is that Kovalenko would have reason to visit New Canterbury and interview Dr. Forester to write some more for *Ukrainian Week*. That would be you, Gina."

"I can't speak Ukrainian."

"Don't be a fool. All you need is an accent. You can do that in your sleep. You will charm Forester and find out what he's up to. Simple."

Gina leaned forward. "But what if Forester knows what she looks like?"

"I just spoke with her editor at *Ukrainian Week*. She never met Forester. And I will have our web people remove every photograph of her that exists on the entire internet."

"But if you know Kovalenko's editor, boss, why did he publish her false news about you?"

"I didn't know him then. But he knows all about me now. And he doesn't want to know me any better, I promise. The day after tomorrow, after you visit Witner, you will go to New Canterbury as Marianna Kovalenko. You will pick Dr. Forester's brains and help stop whatever he is planning, if needed."

"How can I get in to see him on short notice like this?"

"How? I know that the hospital CEO was just fired a few days ago. So, you will call Forester and say you had made a deal to interview the CEO. I will provide you with a letter from his office. And my people will hack into his computer and put you on schedule. Now he's gone, and you've flown all the way from Kyiv. You're a poor little woman. Mew, mew, mew. While you're there, Bodashka will detain the real Kovalenko."

"You're not going to hurt her, are you?" asked Gina.

Liski glanced toward Potemkin. "Am I, boss?"

He waved the cigar dismissively. "We don't put blood on our hands when we do not need to. You will simply take her out of sight as long as needed. A week or so. She may come in handy again."

"Where do I take her?"

"The little dacha south of Kyiv. Her associates at the magazine will be told she's gone to the US to research the story. The editor will help me in this. No problem. Her only relative is a sister with two daughters and a husband. You will let Ms. Kovalenko understand that their safety depends upon her keeping a shut mouth after you turn her loose. She will agree, I am sure."

"One more question," said Liski. "How did you come up with this plan so fast?"

Potemkin swiveled his chair around to face them. He puffed the cigar, exhaling toward the ceiling. Then he tapped his finger against his forehead. "I didn't become one of the world's richest persons by being slow. Prepare to leave now. Gina goes to New York, first to visit Witner then to New Canterbury. Bodashka, you fly to Ukraine."

Gina squared her shoulders and met his eyes. "Mikhail, I need your absolute word that when this is over, I can have my daughter back."

"Absolutely," said Potemkin, crossing himself.

"I'd like to FaceTime with her before I go."

"No. Only when you come back. And then you can see her in person."

"That's cruel," she said, her eyes burning.

"I am not cruel," he said. "The sad fact is that my nephew Dmitry should have come to work for me instead of hanging around with those low-class Russian thugs in Brooklyn. Had he listened to me, he would be alive today, warming your bed and raising your daughter. You should have tried harder to talk him to sense. I warned you."

Gina's eyes suddenly overflowed.

Potemkin set down his cigar in a large green glass ashtray on the desk. He closed the photo and looked back at Gina. "No need to cry. You will have a contact close to New Canterbury in case you need help. Here—take this." He reached into his drawer and handed her a blue cell phone. "This is a burner phone with his number."

"Who is it?" she replied.

"His name is Freddy Sokolov. He manages a local scrapyard I own there."

Liski grunted. "I know Freddy. A good man."

Gina took the phone and stared at Potemkin in surprise. "You own a scrapyard in New Canterbury?"

"Why not? I have a few scrapyards here and there. I've got a little bit of everything everywhere. I happened to hear about this one when Lawrence first started looking at the hospital. It was close, and I got a good deal."

Gina shook her head. "Why a scrapyard?"

Potemkin smiled. "Do either of you know the two biggest raw materials needed in Russia today?"

"I have no idea," Gina said.

"Cobalt?" guessed Liski.

"Not so fancy. One is scrap iron for making steel. Scrap is much cheaper than ore dug out of the ground. The American countryside is full of old rusting cars, trucks, and tractors. They just leave these things lying around. So, I buy a scrapyard, and I put it in a big shredder machine. Then my men go hunting for junkers. Americans will sometimes even pay you to haul them away. I run my shredders day and night, turning old cars into chunks of iron that I load on railroad cars and then ship across the sea and *voilà*. The profit is not bad."

"Smart business," said Liski. "America wastes a lot."

"I also have scrapyards in California, Mississippi, and Oregon. From the west side of America, I sell to China. The second raw material Russia needs is recycled microprocessors for cell phones, missile guidance systems, new cars, you name it. Americans throw out thousands of computers every single glorious day!"

Liski chortled. "God bless America."

"I buy them for pennies and hire people to harvest the chips. I do it right at my scrapyards. Economy of scale."

Gina shook her head. "If this is lucrative, why not just drop all the illegal things and the hacking? It would be safer, for God's sake."

"If I cared about safety, I would have become a doctor like Lawrence. No, I am too creative. Before you go, Gina, I will also provide you with an ID badge that will give you free run of the hospital there. My staff is making it now. May come in handy."

Lightning pulsed within the greenish gray clouds now surrounding the ship, and water rose in huge greasy swells. Gina saw that Potemkin was watching the approaching tempest and smiling, his fingers raised like a conductor's baton, moving in little arcs.

CHAPTER ELEVEN

Jack hung up, leaned back in his chair, raised his arms, and laughed aloud. Then laughed again. A few seconds later someone knocked on the door. "It's open."

"All okay?" said Tré, peering inside.

"Most definitely. I just talked with Damien Falconi. He's flying in the day after tomorrow. Saturday morning. We've got lots of work to do. I'm going to text you the number of his assistant who'll help you with the arrangements. I'd like to set up a meeting as soon as he arrives with just him, Jan Cummings, Martin Bentley, and me. Then, we'll have a session with all the department chairs. Reserve the boardroom, please. Then we'll do a tour. And book us a dinner reservation at La Petite Maison. One of the private rooms."

"Shall do. Super exciting. By the way, chief, I met your niece Kaitlyn in the volunteer office. I guess we'll be seeing her around."

"I'm not sure if it's worth her effort," Jack said. "She'll be heading back home at the end of next week. But it's her choice."

The phone rang back out at Tré's desk, and he excused himself. He returned a moment later. "Chief, there's a call you may or may not want to take."

"Who is it?"

"Her name is . . ." Tré looked down at a Post-it Note. "Marianna Kovalenko, a journalist from some magazine in Ukraine. She wants to speak with you about an article."

"When's my next meeting?"

"Twenty minutes."

"All right, put her through."

He picked up his desk phone.

"Hello, Dr. Forester," said a woman with a pronounced accent. "I am Marianna Kovalenko. Thank you so much for talking with me. You are the new hospital CEO, yes?"

"Just the interim CEO," he said. "How can I help you?"

"I feel a little desperate. I'm not sure what to do. Back in summer, I talk to the CEO of your hospital, Mr. Everts, and he agrees for me to come visit a few days to start tomorrow to write article about the hospital. But I get to New York City and call his office this morning and they tell me he is gone and it is you in charge."

"I'm afraid that's true."

She sighed wearily. "That is not good luck for me. I have come a very long way. Dr. Forester, may it still be possible to come and have interviews? It would mean so much to me. I write about health issues because I was once a nurse."

"Under ordinary circumstances, I'd be happy to see what we could arrange, Ms. Kovalenko. But the timing isn't good right now."

"I understand. The notice is too short for you. If I had known, I would have tried to find other hospitals to visit. But I thought this was all arranged with Mr. Everts."

"You say you have a letter from him?"

"Yes. I have it in my hand right now. Maybe he did not tell other people. You could check his schedule, maybe? Many experts of health care in my country know of your hospital because you have good medical school and good research and are not in the big city. I had written an article about you in the past. I mentioned that you did not sell to the big company Health Wealth Associates when they wanted to buy you some time ago, that you want to stay free."

"So, you came all the way only to write about New Canterbury?"

"Yes. Call me Marianna, please. Is there any chance you might help me, please?"

"Could I put you on hold a moment?"

"Of course, Dr. Forester."

Jack picked up his cell phone and dialed Jason Everts's mobile number. It rang and rang, then went to voicemail. The mailbox was full. He buzzed Tré.

"Yes, sir?"

"Do you know if Mr. Everts's assistant is still in the office downstairs?"

"I believe she's taking some vacation time now that Mr. Everts is gone."

"Can you access his calendar?"

"Sure thing." The sound of keystrokes came over the phone. "Yep, here it is."

"Do you see any mention of an interview with this woman?"

"Yes. There's two hours blocked out tomorrow."

"Thanks."

He picked up the desk phone again and reconnected. "Ms. Kovalenko? Listen, I can't promise much, but if you come to my office, we'll do the best we can for you."

At a quarter past noon local time, 4,700 miles away in Kyiv, Ukraine, the real Marianna Kovalenko stepped out of the *Ukrainian Week* offices on Mashynobudivnykiv Street. The wind was gusty and cold, but it felt good to be away from her desk. It had been an intense morning of research and writing. The piece she was working on about the lingering health effects in villages close to Chernobyl was coming together.

Traffic was light. She could hear children playing soccer next to the secondary school. As she walked westward toward the Kvartal Shopping Mall to look for winter things at the new consignment shop, she heard a sudden scuffing of shoe leather on the sidewalk behind her. Her spine tingled as powerful hands vised her arms and a hand clapped over her mouth. Two men propelled her toward a gleaming white Mercedes and threw her into the back seat, climbing in on either side. The car sped away, the whole thing over a dozen heartbeats. She still had her canvas purse slung over her shoulder. The men pulled off their balaclavas.

"What is this about?" she asked, keeping her voice steady.

No response. They were big men and barely left her enough room to breathe. She glanced from side to side. One of them was beyond middle-aged and had shaggy gray hair and a flattened, misshapen nose that had obviously been broken many times—and never set. The other appeared in his twenties and looked athletic. His scalp was clean shaven. The tattoo of a snake curled around his neck and up the side of his head behind his ear. The smell of expensive seat leather mingled with body odor, onions, fish, vodka, and cigarette smoke.

"Please tell me what this is about?"

"You'll know soon enough," said the older one. His accent was eastern Ukrainian. Donbas.

"Are you sure you have the right person?" She stated her full name.

Silence.

A weird thought struck her. "Are you police?"

The younger man laughed. "No. We're much nicer than them."

The driver's eyes met hers in the rearview mirror. He had a broad Asiatic face, maybe Mongolian. What did all this mean? Which right-wing politician or oligarch had she insulted in print most recently? Aronofsky? Lemnitzer? Potemkin? The list was long. But she hadn't received any death threats in almost a year. If they were going to assassinate a journalist, it was usually a bullet to the back of the head in broad daylight. But other methods were used, like nerve poisoning or bombs or hacking into a car's computer system to cause accidents.

But if this wasn't a typical execution, what else could it be? The most obvious answer was that they wanted to torture her first. That was not unheard of with journalists. Yes, this was likely it. She groaned and felt nauseated. If she was going to suffer and die, she at least wanted to know who the bastard was.

For some reason they hadn't blindfolded her. Not a good sign. They didn't care what she saw. They were heading south through the residential and commercial streets of Holosiivskyi District not far from her apartment, the tree branches along the street almost bare of autumn foliage. Winter was coming quickly. Soon they were passing factories on the outskirts of the city. Then for half an hour they drove southward on the western side of the river, deeper and deeper into the countryside.

The car slowed and they turned left onto a gravel secondary road. If they continued, they would soon come to a bridge over the river. She shut her eyes and took a deep breath to steady herself. Her worst fear was of drowning. Did they know? The driver braked and turned onto an even less developed road cutting into the forest. Stones ricocheted against the wheel wells. This went on for some minutes as the brush on either side grew taller and denser.

Then they emerged into a clearing. It was small and scattered with little hillocks that could have been old burial mounds. On the far side sat a little stucco dacha with a green tin roof. A black Land Rover was already parked there. The driver pulled next to it. She closed her eyes and took three slow deep breaths, her heart pounding in her neck. She had imagined such a thing as this happening one day. Whatever her fate, she would soon know.

The driver leaned against the car and lit a cigarette as the other two men maneuvered her inside. The interior looked modern: one large room with a kitchen that had wood cabinets and a stove set in a small island. The walls were white. Dark beams crossed the ceiling. There was a bookshelf and a flat-screen television. A bald little man in a dark pinstripe suit and red tie sat on a couch watching a soccer game with the sound off. He leaped to his feet. He was short and slender except for a large belly, and he had an odd-looking mustache open in the middle.

"Ms. Kovalenko," he said. His Ukrainian had a Russian accent. "Welcome. Release her, boys." He motioned toward the table. "Sit, please. Let us have a drink and talk."

"I prefer to stand. Which oligarch are you doing this for?"

"Assist the lady to sit."

The two goons had remained standing on either side of her. They took her arms and walked her over to the table, forcing her into a chair.

"Thank you, boys," said the little man. "You can watch the game if you like. She's not going anywhere."

They marched to the couch and one of them turned up the volume. The sounds of cheering filtered through the room.

The little man sat opposite her. "Tea?" he offered. "Not to worry—no poison."

"No."

"Or maybe vodka or wine?"

"No."

"Seltzer with lime?"

"No."

"A Diet Coke?"

"We are out of Diet Coke," the older goon called over.

"Nothing," she said. "What do you want of me?"

"Just some help. We are going to borrow your identity for a week or so. That's all."

"What do you mean, borrow my identity?"

The main door opened, and the Asian-looking driver lugged in two suitcases that she recognized as her own. They'd invaded her apartment after she'd left for work that morning.

"Thank you, Boris," said the little man, switching into English. "Put them in her bedroom."

"Which bedroom?"

"The big one, of course. She's our guest." He turned back to Marianna. "Boris is new. He is from Mongolia and is a very distant relation to me, thanks to a philandering cousin of mine. He can't speak Russian or Ukrainian yet, but he did learn English, so use that to communicate with him. Your English is good, I assume?"

"Passable," she said.

Boris opened the bedroom door with his boot and dropped her suitcases on the floor, where Marianna heard them clatter and fall over.

"Now, Ms. Kovalenko, I will tell you what you need to know," said the little man. "An actress is going to visit the New Canterbury Medical Center in New York State to interview Dr. Forester, the dean, using your credentials as a journalist. She will tell them she is there to write a follow-up article to something you wrote in the past."

"You want to use my identity to spy on someone. Why?"

Reaching across the table, he patted her hand. She pulled it away. He continued. "After her work there is done, you will go free, and you will use her notes to write the article. Your magazine is being told you had a sudden opportunity. That's why you're gone. All is being explained to everyone. Your editor is our friend. Very clean. No mess."

"What gives you the right?" she demanded. "Who do you work for?"

"Ms. Kovalenko, just to confirm, you have never had contact with this Dr. Forester, correct?"

"I have only seen his photo when I did research."

"Good. We will be very fair to you, my dear. When you submit this article to your magazine, we will pay you an additional five thousand American dollars, whether they decide to publish it or not. Not a bad deal, right?"

"And if I don't go along with this, you will kill me."

"Not quite. First, we will kill your sister, her husband, and their two daughters. We know where they live. And then you will die. The same applies should you ever divulge any of the details I have just shared with you."

She closed her eyes, her head growing tight.

The little man continued. "Though you write nasty stories and fake news, you will not be harmed for that. This is just business. Boris, along with Ivan One and Ivan Two will not molest you. I also call them Ivan Nose and Ivan Snake, but I don't suggest you do the same. Boris even brought your jogging clothes from your apartment, didn't you, Boris?"

"Yes," said Boris from the doorway to her bedroom, standing there and filling it, his arms folded across his chest.

"Of course, you will only be able to do your jogging on the little road right here where we have CCTV, and you must be out for no more than twenty minutes. Enough to work up a good sweat upon your athletic body. If you do not return, then we will go to your sister's house."

A terrible thought seared across her mind. "What if something happens to the actress over there?" she asked.

"What do you mean?"

"If she dies or is caught, will harm still come to my sister and her family?"

The little man raised his bushy brows with an impression of surprise that almost looked genuine. "If it is not you who causes the problem, your loved ones will face no danger. Solemn promise. We do not hurt our fellow man for the fun of it." He made the sign of the cross.

"It's Potemkin, isn't it?" she said, unable to hold back a sob.

"I hope you will never know," he said.

She dabbed at her eyes with her jacket sleeve.

"Boys, tell Ms. Kovalenko that my word is good."

"His word is better even than good," said the younger of the Ivans. "It is like fine Japanese whiskey."

The little man rose to his feet, placing a straw fedora on his head. "Till later, Ms. K," he said. "I'll drop in to join you for dinner from time to time. In the meanwhile, ciao!"

CHAPTER TWELVE

The Patterson Institute rose like a precarious castle near the mountaintop across a deep valley. Although it was Gina Larsen's eleventh visit here—posing as Bryson Witner's cousin, the only family who ever visited—to communicate with Witner for Potemkin, this view never failed to make her palms go moist on the steering wheel. Perched on a cliff edge, the structure looked as if it might come loose in a storm and crumble into the abyss.

Many minutes of winding roads later, she pulled into the parking lot and stepped out of the car. Adjusting the hidden shoulder straps that helped support the fat suit she was wearing, she trudged up the steps to the entrance doors and pushed inside. They showed her to a waiting area where a guard brought in Witner, hands cuffed behind his back as usual, then led them into an open inner courtyard. During her initial visits she'd been surprised that they'd permitted her to walk with Witner alone in the exercise area. But there were multiple layers of security. His hands were cuffed, his medication regimen was powerful, several armed guards kept them in view from cubicles on the roof, and the guard who'd led them there kept vigil by the door, constantly in sight. No other patients were allowed out at the same time. It turned out to be ideal for sharing information privately.

Her last visit had been on a warm summer day. Now the outdoor exercise equipment had been cleared for the coming winter. The Astroturf was clear of everything except dead leaves that rustled underfoot as they strolled. A few snowflakes filtered down, vanishing on contact with the ground.

"Bryson, you seem happy today," she said.

Witner, wearing an unzipped green parka, gave her a crooked smile as a gust ruffled his graying hair. "Well, it can't be my physical liveliness," he said. "The medications have seen to that. Look, see how I shake—" He lifted his hands behind his back.

His long bony fingers had a coarse, involuntary, clenching sort of tremor that made his hands resemble spiders trying to crawl away from his wrists. Potemkin once told her that when he first befriended Witner at the coin club in Boston, back when Witner worked at Harvard, Witner kept venomous spiders in a terrarium in his flat. He had a black widow and a banana spider, one of the deadliest in the world. Potemkin, who was a fan of the BBC show *Doctor Who*, had given him the nickname "Doctor Witch," a wordplay on "Doctor Which." *Who, which, where, why.* Stupid, but that was the way Potemkin's mind worked.

She shivered. "Looks uncomfortable, Bryson."

"Oh it is. If I seem lively today it's because my soul is entertaining the idea that my body may soon be free of this place, meaning I won't have to wander around here talking to myself. Do you know that I spend most of my days conversing with various parts of my mind?"

"You've told me."

"Fortunately, I find myself good company. So, any news from Mikhail about him springing me?"

She'd been waiting for this. She must avoid him sniffing the slightest whiff of betrayal. "Things are moving along well. Dr. Haines will soon own the hospital and then Mikhail will arrange your escape."

"I'm curious as to how soon, my dear."

"Certainly it will be soon. Unfortunately, there's been a little complication with the takeover."

His expression faltered. "Of what sort?"

"Apparently Dr. Forester is trying to undercut the deal. The hospital has given him two weeks."

Witner broke into laughter, his breath vapor curling up. "Forester! In the way again. Amazing. Always tilting at windmills. What's his plan?"

"We don't know. I'm going there tomorrow to find out. I'll be interviewing him as a Ukrainian journalist."

"Why a Ukrainian journalist?"

She explained the scenario.

He nodded approvingly. "Good plan. I wish you luck. There was a time when I might have asked you to hurt Forester for me. Lord knows I tried myself. But I've scratched that itch. Speaking of vengeance, I suppose you've heard that our director here recently died in an accident."

She looked away, her mouth feeling dry. "Dr. Teitelbaum. Yes, I did."

"Mikhail's work, I assume?" Witner asked. "After you told him of my suspicions?"

She nodded grimly.

"What if I told you, my friend, that perhaps I was wrong about Teitelbaum being onto something about this arrangement?"

She stopped. The vacant look in his eyes made her shiver. *Doctor Witch.* Not for the first time, she wondered what would happen if he turned violent with her. She knew that the numerous people he had murdered included one of his patients, his protégé at the hospital, and his own lover. "Wait," she said. " What are you saying?"

"I'm saying that I may have dreamed it." He glanced away and shrugged. "Or maybe some part of me just wanted to see what Potemkin would do. Strangely enough, Teitelbaum's replacement may be one of my old colleagues from New Canterbury. Hal Dugan, a hopeless moron." He barked a laugh that echoed across the courtyard. Then he slowly turned and fixed her with his eyes again. "I sense a conflict inside you today, my dear. Are you hiding something?"

She met his gaze. "Of course not. This fat suit's killing me."

CHAPTER THIRTEEN

Jack walked into the kitchen, dressed to leave for the hospital. He'd been examining the day's schedule on his phone, searching for things that could be canceled or skipped. With so much to get organized before Falconi's visit tomorrow, he should never have said yes to the Ukrainian journalist. Julia, Zoë, Kaitlyn, and Tony were at the table.

"We need to be heading out in a few minutes," he said. "Are you about ready, Kaitlyn?"

"Yes, sir," she said.

"Sir?" said Julia. "You just called Daddy *sir*."

She hasn't finished breakfast," Zoë said. "Come get something to eat. They're not going to fire you if you take ten minutes to get some nourishment. You're setting a bad example."

"That's right," said Julia.

He dropped the phone in his pocket and pulled up a chair between Tony and his daughter. In the middle of the table lay a tray heaped with bacon, scrambled eggs, French toast, strawberries, and a pitcher of orange juice. The feast was likely for Kaitlyn's benefit, it being her first day of volunteering.

"Breakfast is the most important meal of the day, Daddy." Julia pushed a plate closer to him.

Jack took some strawberries and bacon. Julia dropped a piece of French toast on his plate. Getting in on the act, Tony did the same with a slice of bacon. There came a knock on the door. "It must be

Chad," said Tony. "He's picking me up."

"Julia," said Zoë. "Please let Chad in and ask him if he wants some breakfast."

Julia, still in pajamas, hopped down and ran to the door. She returned with Chad Chadwick in tow.

"He says he's hungry," Julia announced.

"I did?" asked Chad.

"You could use some nourishment," Julia said, parroting Zoë and climbing back up on her chair. Chad stopped well away from the table and coughed into his hand.

"You look pale, Chad," said Zoë. "Don't you feel well?"

"Just can't get rid of this cold," he responded. "But I'm okay."

Jack motioned for Chad to sit. "Sit here," said Jack. "We're about to leave."

"I better stay away from the table. I don't want to give you this bug."

"I hope you're feeling a little better, at least," chimed in Kaitlyn.

Chad glanced her way. "Hi, Kate," he said. "You're all dressed up. I thought it was a teacher's workday."

"She's going to the hospital with her uncle," said Zoë. "It's her first day as a volunteer."

"Very cool," replied Chad. "You excited?"

Kaitlyn shrugged. "I guess. What are you guys doing today?"

"Just another day of tearing down old computers at Aldiss Scrap."

"The way you look, I think you should go home and go back to bed," said Zoë.

"I feel better than I look. It's not hard work anyways. We'll be sitting all day."

Jack looked at his watch and glanced at Kaitlyn's plate. It was empty. He pushed back from the table. "Kaitlyn, time to go," he said.

"Daddy, can I go with you and Kaitlyn today?" asked Julia.

"No, sweetie," said Zoë. "When you're older maybe, but not today."

"Daddy, I'd like to get a tattoo like Kaitlyn has. But just one. For Mommy." She pointed to her left wrist.

Jack looked at his daughter and buttoned up his coat. "No, Julia. There are other ways to remember her."

A strikingly attractive woman with red hair drawn into a loose ponytail was standing by Tré's desk in the reception area. She wore a light gray business suit and black high heels. She beamed as Jack entered and held out her hand. "Marianna Kovalenko," she said, shaking his hand warmly. "Thank you for your time, Dr. Forester. So wonderful to meet you. Mr. Tré said I could have an entire hour with you now. Very kind. I have given him the letter I have from Mr. Everts."

"Here it is," said Tré, handing over the sheet.

Jack glanced it over and handed it back to him. "Welcome to New Canterbury, Ms. Kovalenko," he said, giving Tré an annoyed glance. "I'm afraid I can only spare half an hour now, but Mr. Tré will make sure you have other knowledgeable people to interview. Will that be possible, Mr. Tré?"

"Certainly, sir. I'll get on it. By the way, where's your niece? I thought she was coming with you today."

"She's downstairs getting an orientation with Cassandra."

"Your niece is here, Dr. Forester?" said the journalist. "A physician too, is she?"

"No. She's a volunteer."

He ushered her into the office. Taking a chair, the journalist set a notepad on her lap and licked the tip of her pen, a gesture Jack hadn't seen anyone do since medical school.

"Dr. Forester, in honor of your limited time, may I leap right into the chase with important question my editor want me to explore?"

"Please do."

"As I told you on the phone, I did not like the thought of your wonderful hospital being taken over by big chain business and am so glad that didn't happen a few years ago. In Ukraine, you see, there is always the threat of Russia eating us up, so we must work to remain free."

Jack looked at her carefully. Given the current situation, that statement cut a bit close to the bone. She was referring, of course, to HWA's previous attempt. There was no way she could know they were making a far more aggressive move right now.

"What exactly is your question, Ms. Kovalenko?"

"Forgive me, Dr. Forester. I mean to ask, how does a hospital like yours keep itself independent of the big health care business?"

"In general, you mean?"

"Yes, of course," she said, flashing a smile. "In general. What are the strategies for best success and stability?" She sat there poised and attentive with eyes that radiated good humor and intelligence. "This is, I know, a big question. But important to us."

"It is a big question," Jack said, glancing at his watch. "It's a matter of finding the right balance between financial stability and providing quality services. In our case, those services include patient care, education, and health care research." He rattled off some additional general information, which even to himself sounded like boring boilerplate. He was giving her nothing of substance and again regretted agreeing for her to come. "In addition, sometimes it is necessary to innovate, to expand your services and find new sources of revenue."

"This is wonderful information, Doctor," she said, looking up from her notepad, her pen stopping. "Thank you so much. What kinds of innovations do you mean? For any ideas you can share with us, we would be so grateful."

The intercom on his desk buzzed. "Dr. Forester, I'm very sorry to interrupt."

"Excuse me," he said to her. "What is it, Tré?"

"We're confirmed. Mr. Falconi is flying in tomorrow morning with one of his vice presidents. Sounds like they're really excited to talk about the project. I've got all the rooms reserved and the invites are going out now. How much time should we plan for the hospital tour?"

Jack thought this over for a second, then responded, "Four hours."

"Roger that, chief." The intercom went silent.

"I can see you are very busy, Dr. Forester," she said. "You have a new project to work on. When do you find time to sleep?"

"There are always challenges."

"Might I ask what the new project is?"

How much should he share with her? The plans for a possible genomics research center weren't something that needed to be kept secret, though it was far too early to talk in any detail about it. All the department heads would be hearing about it at the presentation tomorrow morning anyway. It wouldn't hurt to divulge a bit—though she didn't need to know how much depended upon its success. He would keep that part under wraps.

He took a deep breath and looked at her. "Ms. Kovalenko, this must be kept off the record for now."

"Of course." She folded her notebook, dropped it into her briefcase, and crossed her legs. "Doctor, you have my word I will not share until you say I should." Smiling, she made a zipping motion with her thumb and forefinger across her lips.

He looked at his watch. There was no time left. "I'll tell you what," he said. "I need to leave for a meeting now. How about I drop you off at your hotel at the end of the day. We'll have a chance to wrap this up in the car." He rose and extended his hand.

"Perfect," she said, still smiling.

CHAPTER FOURTEEN

Waiting outside the office for Cassandra, Kaitlyn wondered what was going on in all the rooms upstairs. Nurses and doctors seeing patients, women having babies, kids getting their appendixes removed, people being treated for gangrene and cancer and diabetes and who knew what else. There were IVs running and people getting anesthetized, and probably even insane people getting strapped into straightjackets.

She had experienced nothing like this before. What would she see and do today? She imagined telling Aishia about it tonight. What if she told Stella too? That was dicey. If she were in the wrong mood, she might mock her for showing interest in something. It was a depressing thought.

Cassandra came out and handed Kaitlyn her own lavender-colored volunteer jacket. Then she took her to another office where a technician made an ID photo key card with a lanyard to hang around her neck. Everyone was so welcoming. Back in the main office, Cassandra issued her a little walkie-talkie to use during her shift. After that, she watched an orientation video that gave a visual tour of the hospital and talked about patient confidentiality. Then Cassandra gave her a CPR booklet to study. Next week Kaitlyn would take a CPR class along with nursing and medical students. Time flew. It was almost noon.

"Looks like you're enjoying yourself," Cassandra said. "Tré just called. He wonders if you'd want to have lunch with him."

Kaitlyn walked with Tré to a cafeteria-like restaurant on the ground floor with windows overlooking a courtyard, which was surrounded by buildings on all sides. He offered to pay for her lunch, but she thanked him and declined. Aunt Zoë had been giving her a weekly allowance for babysitting and helping around the house, and she'd been saving it. She was aiming to have enough for a used laptop when she got back to Ohio. She ordered a slice of cheese pizza and a lemonade, and Tré got a salad in a plastic bowl. They went to a table by the windows. Outside, the sky was a mixture of clouds and patches of blue.

"So, how did it go this morning? Do you like it?"

"I do," she said.

"What's this I hear about you leaving town so soon?"

She felt her face warming. "Who told you that?"

"Your uncle mentioned it."

Kaitlyn looked down at the pizza, which was good. She took another bite and glanced at him. He was shoveling down the salad like he was starving. "You've got a big chunk of radish on your chin," she said.

His face colored and he raised his napkin. "Did I get it?"

She smiled. "Yep."

"Hate that. By the way, I noticed your tats. Nice. How long have you had them?"

She looked down at her wrists. On the inner surface of each was a small eye with falling teardrops. "About a year. How about your neck wings?"

"Six years. I was nineteen." He tugged down his shirt collar to expose more of it. "I was just coming out. Life was insane. Do you mind me mentioning the coming out thing? If you do, I'll shut up. I don't have a great filter."

"Why should I mind?" she said. "Do you regret it?"

"Coming out or the tattoo?"

"The tattoo."

"I might need to get it removed someday depending on job opportunities. We'll see."

He took the last forkful of salad and closed the lid of the plastic bowl with a snap. "That was a treat running into Mr. Brady yesterday," he said. "My high school days were weird. I was on the wrong end of some bullies. Including my father. But I could always talk to Mr. Brady."

"He's nice, but I'm not sure I like the way he tries to get inside my head."

"He means well. What brought you here from Ohio, if you don't mind me asking?"

She felt a familiar ache in her throat and looked away. An older couple at the next table was staring off into space. She suddenly felt angry. *You want to know about me? My real mother died from a blood clot just after I was born, and my father was killed in a fire when I was ten. And I've got an uncle who doesn't like me.*

She took a deep breath. "Why am I here? Because things were chaos at home. My stepmother's an addict. She's in rehab again, thanks to a judge, and I'm going to send him a Christmas card."

"I'm glad to hear she's getting help."

"I was too. But I just found out she wants to get back with her creepy boyfriend." She looked away, wadding up her napkin and feeling her face start to burn. "Why am I telling you this? It's gross and embarrassing. Forget I said anything."

He caught her eyes and nodded. Kindly. "It's okay." After a pause, he added, "You know what I think?"

She dropped the napkin on her plate. "What?"

"That you keep it together very well."

She looked at the old couple again. They were looking at each other now and smiling. "I know what you're going to say next. Why am I going back there if things are so messed up?"

He raised his eyebrows. "Okay . . . Why are you going back if things are so messed up?"

Out the window a few weeds rose above the grass. She sighed. "It isn't like I have a choice, you know. And I really don't want to just desert her. She needs support, right?"

He drummed the tabletop. "When I started college, I majored in psychology because I thought I wanted to be a counselor. I did my big thesis paper on codependency. Do you know what that is?"

She shrugged. "Sort of. Why did you do it on that?"

"Because I was in a codependent relationship, and it wasn't good. I finally figured it out."

She turned this over in her mind, her throat tightening. "So, wait . . . are you saying I'm codependent with my stepmother or something?"

"Hey, I don't mean it personally. It's just a thought."

"I really don't want to talk about it," she said.

"Understood. I've got a bad habit of talking before thinking. So forget the psychology. I just want to be your friend."

She closed her eyes and sighed. He was just trying to be nice. And he was smart and sensitive—a lot of people talked before they thought. A friend. Like Aishia. She looked at him. "That would be okay."

"Good."

"But tell me something," she added. "What's my uncle like at work? When I'm around him, I feel like I've got to walk on eggshells. I don't think he's smiled at me once since I've been here."

Tré pursed his lips and nodded. "They tell me that after his wife was killed in the car accident, he went from warm to cold. It's probably not about you. He's still twisted up inside."

"That's what my Aunt Zoë says."

"On a different topic, do you know what Cassandra has you doing this afternoon?"

"I'm not sure. Why?"

"There's a special visitor coming to the medical center from California tomorrow. It's a really big deal and I have tons of things to do. To top it off, a foreign journalist arrived today and I've got to arrange interviews for her. I could use the help of a smart volunteer. Would you mind if I asked Cassandra to sublet you for the rest of the day?"

CHAPTER FIFTEEN

There wasn't a sunset that evening, just clouds and rain when they left the hospital. Jack had to stop for gas immediately if he was going to make it to Ms. Kovalenko's hotel then get back home. With the rush hour traffic sizzling by on Bangalore Boulevard, he pumped gas into his SUV and could see through the car window that Marianna had turned to talk with Kaitlyn, who was in the back seat. He heard faint laughter and could see they were smiling. Kaitlyn was a bright kid. Tré clearly enjoyed her company—he'd kept her busy all afternoon. The resemblance between his niece and his wife was uncanny sometimes, but he noticed it less this evening, for some reason. Maybe the thought of Falconi's visit was lifting his spirits.

Back in the vehicle, he set the GPS for Marianna's hotel and got back into traffic, which was heavy.

"Dr. Forester," said Marianna. "You were going to tell me something about your new project. I would very much love to hear."

Ah, yes. How much should he share? Giving her some generic details shouldn't be a problem. Genomic medicine research. Powered by AI. The possibility of building a new center here at New Canterbury. But it was all only a remote dream at this point.

"My God," Marianna said, listening intently. "That is wonderful. What a super idea. I hope that you may you have great—"

She was interrupted by the ringing of his phone over the vehicle's speakers. It was his brother Tony. He tapped the answer icon and Tony's voice erupted before he'd even said hello.

"Slow down," Jack said. "You're saying Chad is sick? Repeat what you just said." He glanced over at Ms. Kovalenko and whispered, "It's my brother."

The details emerged. Tony was still at Aldiss Scrap. Chad was too sick to drive them home. Lots of coughing, and he'd fainted and thrown up. Now he's having trouble breathing. His skin is hot. He's on the floor shaking.

"Okay, Tony. Hang on. I'm going to head over right now. We're not that far away. I'll call an ambulance to meet us there."

He hung up and looked over at Marianna. She'd already grasped the situation.

"Please, not to worry about me," she said. "Go now. I can be at hotel later. This is more important."

On the outskirts of town already, he kept the vehicle moving as quickly as the potholes would allow.

"What do you think's going on, Uncle Jack?" asked Kaitlyn, sounding worried. "Does Chad have pneumonia or something?"

Jack glanced back at her and nodded. "That's a good thought, Kaitlyn. We'll know soon."

Gina braced herself as Forester sped through the dark and rain. They were soon passing through countryside that looked almost uninhabited. He took a particularly sharp corner, and she looked back to see the girl Kaitlyn swaying from side to side with the same focused looked in her eyes that Forester had.

"The night is dark," Gina said.

"Stygian," said Kaitlyn.

"Good word, yes," she said. "From where did you learn that word?"

"It's a band I like."

"We're close," said Forester. "It's right after this hill."

They crested the rise and she could see the sprawl of a few large buildings and many lights down in a small valley.

"That's it," he said.

Gina relaxed at the presence of light. The pieces were falling into place. Forester had been stingy with details, not surprisingly, but he'd now let enough slip. The answer lay with Damien Falconi. She had Googled him that afternoon while waiting to interview a professor of internal medicine, which had been a total waste of time. Falconi was a very wealthy tech entrepreneur, and he was coming to New Canterbury tomorrow. Forester wanted him to bail the hospital out and finance the creation of a genomic research center. That had to be it. She would call Potemkin with the news as soon as possible.

Then would come the hardest part of her job. How to disrupt those plans? She could not let herself fail.

Windshield wipers slapping, they passed a sign that read *Aldiss Scrap and Recycling, LLC*. Well . . . It was a small world after all. She had to smile. This must be Potemkin's local scrapyard, the one run for him by the man she could reach out to for help via the burner phone. This was a good omen. She crossed herself.

Forester noticed. "Does my driving scare you that much?"

"No, Dr. Forester. Of course not. It is just my habit when reaching destination."

The scrapyard's main building was a warehouse-like structure. Off to the right lay a field strewn with junked vehicles. The complex appeared to be bisected by a rail line they now thumped across. Forester turned the car into a gravel lot and parked in a row of cars and pickups.

"We beat EMS," he said, leaping out. She climbed out into the drizzle and watched as he opened the hatchback and grabbed a black plastic suitcase, then dashed for the door, his niece close behind. Hindered by her heels on the gravel, Gina strove to keep up. A tall man at the counter was waiting for them. He had a brush cut and biceps bulging inside a long-sleeved black T-shirt. "You must be Dr. Forester," the man said, and Gina registered his Russian accent. "Your brother said you were coming. Follow me."

He introduced himself as Freddy Sokolov. That was him. Her contact. Fabulous. He looked capable. Sokolov led them behind the counter into a high open space divided by shelves rising to the ceiling, stacks of old computers, and monitors everywhere. A thunderous noise was vibrating through the building, a horrific banging sound. She clamped her hands over her ears. Forester slowed and his niece glanced around with a frightened expression.

"It's just the shredder," Sokolov shouted, laughing. "I'll ask them to stop for a while." A group of people were hovering around a man lying on the concrete. "Doctor's here," Sokolov shouted, and they moved aside. The awful din suddenly ceased. Gina had been bracing herself against it, and when it vanished, she felt slightly off-balance.

"Hi, Chad," Forester said, as he knelt beside him and opened the black case. The young man's eyes were half closed. He was pale and sweaty, and his respiratory rate was extremely fast.

"Dr. Forester," Gina said. "Remember that I am a nurse. I once work for a while in the ICU. May I be of help?"

"Absolutely. You start the oxygen and check his vitals, and I'll get an IV in."

He took out a small green canister and she retrieved the oxygen tubing, fitting the cannula into the man's nose, introducing herself as she worked. He smiled at her.

Forester got out the IV supplies and ran scissors up the man's shirtsleeve to expose the arm. She clipped a pulse oximeter onto his fingertip and wrapped a blood pressure cuff around his other arm. Even on oxygen, his saturation was only 89 percent. His blood pressure was 85 systolic and his heart rate was over 120.

"Please get us a bag of saline," Forester said, as he slipped in the IV needle.

She reached for the saline in his emergency kit, impressed by the contents. It was a mini crash cart. It contained intubation gear with various laryngoscope blades and endotracheal tubes of different sizes, along with a labeled plastic rack of medication vials. Though it had been a few years since her ICU days, she recognized most of the drugs—epinephrine, atropine, norepinephrine, adenosine, metoprolol, lorazepam, rocuronium, etomidate, and ketamine.

Ketamine. *Interesting.* A dissociative anesthetic agent, it was extremely useful in the ICU and ER for procedural sedation, including for intubations. It also had abuse potential as a hallucinogen.

She hooked up tubing to the IV bag and Forester opened it wide. "Let's give him the whole liter ASAP." Surprised at how much she remembered, she stood, holding the bag high while Forester started a second IV in the other arm. They needed to get in as much fluid as possible, two or three bags.

Gina motioned Kaitlyn to come closer. "Please hold this bag up while I get another one ready."

Forester was doing a more thorough physical exam now, listening for heart and lung sounds, and palpating. "Look at this," he said to her, pointing to a long scar running diagonally on the upper left abdomen.

She bent and peered more closely. "A scar of surgery?"

Forester nodded. "Chad, do you still have your spleen?"

The man looked more alert now. "No, Dr. Forester. I fell out of a tree when I was eleven and they had to take it out. Is that important?"

"It can make you more susceptible to some infections," Forester said. "Marianna, is the other bag of saline ready?"

Retrieving it from the kit, she glanced again at the ketamine vial. Special K was its street name. Dmitry had tried it once and talked about the hallucinations, had asked her to steal him some from the hospital, which she refused to do. Its place was for patients, she'd told him. In the right dose it turned people into zombies for about half an hour, during which time they felt no pain and were oblivious to what was going on around them, sitting there with eyes wide open, breathing. You could kill them and they'd never know it.

The EMS unit arrived shortly thereafter. The medics greeted Forester like an old friend. They soon had the septic young man, this friend of Forester's brother, loaded on a gurney. As they began rolling him outside toward the ambulance waiting in the rain, an idea came to Gina. She was walking next to Dr. Forester.

"I would like to ride in the ambulance to help," she said. "They could use assistance of a nurse, I think. I have no license here, of course, but I have an extra pair of hands to be used."

"That would be against our standard policy," said one of the EMTs. "Unless you want to make an exception, Dr. Forester."

Forester looked over and smiled at her. "If you could, please. She's a nurse and she'll only do what you order."

"Fair enough," said the EMT. "I'll put it in my report. But if you trust her, it's good enough for me."

Forester reached out and shook her hand. "I am going to drop Kaitlyn off at home, then I'll head right for the hospital with Tony to see how he's doing. I'll take you to your hotel."

"Thank you so much," she said, preparing to enter the ambulance. "By the way, Dr. Forester, I overheard early today that you are having a tour of the hospital tomorrow for the visitor. Might I be able to join in this?"

He looked at her for a moment, seeming to consider something, then smiled and agreed. "That's the least we could do," he said. "Thanks for your help."

CHAPTER SIXTEEN

The next morning Kaitlyn had been helping Tré "break trail," as he called it, for the VIPs' four-hour tour of the hospital, making sure that nurses and other staff were prepared and helping stragglers avoid wrong turns. One of her duties was to hold open doors as the group marched by like a centipede, with Uncle Jack as its head and President Jan Cummings striding on either side of Damien Falconi.

The VIPs were now in one of the ICUs, milling around and talking.

"Okay, Kaitlyn," said Tré, checking his wristwatch. "You and I will head for the next stop, which is the new step-down unit. After that, we break for lunch. You getting hungry?"

"A little. What's a step-down unit?"

"It gives a level of care between an ICU and a regular floor."

She considered this. "I wonder if that's where they'll put Chad."

"Wouldn't be surprised. How's he doing?"

"Pretty well. His pneumonia is improving. Uncle Jack and I visited him in the ICU this morning before Uncle Jack's presentation. They said he'd be moved out soon." Kaitlyn's cell phone chimed. It was Aishia. "Do I have time to take this?"

"Sure," said Tré. "Talk while we walk to step-down."

She answered.

"Hey, girlfriend," said Aishia. "How's it going?"

Kaitlyn stepped over to a window and stopped. "It's been fun. They're all nice."

"What's Damien Falconi like?"

Outside the sky was a deep blue. "He talks very fast and he's got a geeky sense of humor. Very tan. Guess who he brought with him from California?"

"Somebody famous?"

Kaitlyn laughed. "Nope. His mother. Her name is Leigh Falconi, and she's got a PhD in molecular genetics and is on the board of his company. Very friendly." Kaitlyn smoothed her hair and noticed her reflection in the glass. She was smiling. "She asked me what I wanted to do with my life. I said maybe a doctor."

"Really? That's cool. You never told me that."

Kaitlyn glanced down the hallway. She was falling way behind. "I hadn't really thought about it. It just popped out. Listen, I've got to go. I'll call you later."

"Wait. I almost forgot. Will you come to my house tomorrow? My brother Hassan and I can drive over and pick you up. My mom makes a feast for Sunday dinner. They all want to meet you."

Kaitlyn started jogging. "Sure. Awesome."

"I'm so sad, Kaitlette. This will be the last and only time you come to our house."

"Stop—don't remind me."

"I wish you didn't have to leave."

"Cease and desist. I'll see you tomorrow."

Jack let Jan Cummings shoulder the conversation with Falconi as they walked toward the new step-down unit. She was telling him about a run-in she'd had with a California politician they both knew.

"But I can tell you this much, Damien," she said. "New Canterbury University will be fully committed to this project, and that won't change."

Jack was finding it difficult to read Falconi. He was a fountain of questions, some of which were tangential to the matter at hand, like what was the annual snowfall here (Jack looked it up on his phone—84 inches), and did the university have a good hockey team (yes).

Immediately behind them strode Martin Bentley, looking unenthusiastic. The provost was walking between Damien's mother and Marianna Kovalenko. Interesting that the only time Bentley displayed any animation was when he was chatting with Marianna, with whom he seemed to be charmed. Trailing after them came a group of department chairs and senior administrators from the medical center and the main campus.

Just before the entrance to the step-down unit, Falconi stopped. The procession halted. He turned back to Bentley. "About your financial crisis: do you think you've really gotten to the bottom of it?"

The provost cleared his throat and flashed a strained smile. "Well, yes, sir, I think it is fair to say that we are very close."

"Would you mind reminding me?" asked Falconi.

"Of?"

"Of what you understand to be the root causes."

"Might be best if Ms. Cummings does that," Bentley said, nodding toward her.

Jan stepped forward. "I'd be very happy to, Damien. Aside from the report . . ."

Jack felt a tap on the shoulder. It was Tré, with Kaitlyn at his side.

"A quick word, chief," Tré said.

The three of them stepped away from the group.

"What's up?" Jack said.

"Dr. Dugan's shaman study is about to get started in there," Tré said, indicating the step-down unit, where the tour was headed. "The nurses are in a tizzy about it."

"Find Dr. Dugan and tell him to hold off until we're out of there."

"Will do."

"Hurry."

"FYI, Uncle Jack," interjected Kaitlyn. "I just found out that Chad was already moved in there. He's sedated. Out like a light."

"Okay, thanks."

"FYI?" said Tré, turning and grinning at her. "Listen to you, girl."

"Get a move on, Tré," said Jack, stepping back to Falconi's side where he caught the tail of Jan Cummings's explanation.

". . . an aggregated accumulation of incremental accounting discrepancies over several years that surprisingly didn't trigger any alarms. Unfortunately, given the—"

Falconi raised his hand, interrupting her. "That reminds me of something, Jan. Want to hear a funny story?"

"Damien," said his mother, "let's not hold things up."

"This will just take a minute," he said. "One of my partners asked me if I set this up myself—screwed up your books, that is—so you'd reach out to me. He was joking, of course."

"Ah," said Jan, smiling and looking around.

"But my point is," continued Falconi, "have you ruled out the possibility of a cyberattack?"

Jack saw Kaitlyn by the doors to the step-down unit, waiting for them. Tré would be inside talking to Dugan. She'd been working hard to make sure the day went smoothly—he needed to thank her after all this was over.

"Good question," Jan was saying. "We don't believe that's likely. The IT people say our firewall is as good as it gets."

Jack checked his watch and raised his arm. "Friends, shall we continue? Next stop is our state-of-the-art post-ICU step-down unit. Then, lunch back in the boardroom, followed by a tour of the med school and the research labs."

The step-down unit consisted of twenty rooms arrayed around the large plexiglass windows of a central nursing station full of computer terminals and equipment. As the group gathered in the nursing station, Jack spotted Tré coming in the rear access with Kaitlyn close behind him.

"I haven't found Dr. Dugan yet, chief."

"Keep looking. Help him with this, Kaitlyn."

The group coalesced around the charge nurse who stood in front of a large flat-screen monitor hanging from the ceiling. The monitor displayed a checkerboard of video and vital sign feeds, along with EKG strips, for each room.

"Are we ready, Dr. Forester?" the nurse asked.

Jack nodded.

"Welcome, everyone," she said. "This is our newest step-down care unit." She pointed to the big monitor behind her. "Thanks to this, it's a *step up* from what we had before. It allows us to keep track— "

"Excuse me," interrupted Damien Falconi, pointing at the screen. "What's going on in that room there? Second to the left."

The nurse craned her neck to look at the monitor. A look of dismay crossed her face. "Good lord," she said. Reaching up, she tapped the image and it expanded to fill the screen. She tapped again to activate the audio. Someone wearing a feathered headdress, bead necklaces, a leopard skin cape, and a baggy loincloth was prancing around the patient's bed shaking a rattle and chanting, his face painted in white and red stripes. Two black horns protruded from his forehead.

"Dr. Forester, what the devil's happening in there?" said Bentley.

"This is a study," Jack said, his throat tightening.

Several people laughed.

"Of what?" asked Jan.

"I can explain!" boomed Hal Dugan, bursting into the nursing station, a clipboard in hand. "I didn't expect an audience, or I'd have forewarned you. I'm Dr. Halverson Dugan from psychiatry. What you're viewing up there is an exciting new clinical trial."

"I trust you're joking," said Jan.

"Not at all, my friends." Dugan smiled and gestured at the screen. "This is a prospective trial designed to quantify the placebo effect of shamanistic rituals on hospital length of stay. This is the first subject you see up there. The individual performing the ritual is my chief resident. It's never been done before—you're witnessing history."

"This is not an opportune time, Hal," Jack muttered under his breath, anger rising.

"Don't you mean prehistory?" Bentley said.

"Nurse, would you please turn that noise down?" asked Leigh Falconi.

"Shouldn't we stop this?" said the charge nurse. She reached up and the cacophony died away.

"Yes, we should," Jack said.

Falconi spoke up again. "Interesting, Dr. Dugan. But I think I've just noticed a flaw with your study design."

Jack felt a tap on his shoulder. It was Kaitlyn.

Dugan looked defensive. "What do you mean, *flaw*?"

Kaitlyn whispered something in his ear he couldn't make out.

Falconi strode to the screen and pointed. "Your study can't gauge a placebo effect if the patient is unaware of what's going on. He looks asleep."

Kaitlyn raised her voice. "Uncle Jack, that's Chad in there."

Jack started. It was indeed Chad, lying there with his eyes closed while the resident pranced, rattling and chanting.

"He can't be asleep," said Dugan, slipping on the glasses strung around his neck.

"That patient is the young man just transferred from the ICU," said the nurse. "He's mildly autistic and was a little anxious, so his attending ordered sedation."

"You need to stop this immediately, Hal," Jack said.

"Autistic? That's impossible," said Dugan. "Psychiatric conditions are an exclusion criterion for enrollment. That's room fifteen, correct?"

"Yes," said the nurse.

"What's the patient's name?"

"Chad Chadwick," said Jack. "Call this off *now*."

"Why wasn't I told?" asked Dugan, his face reddening. "It's supposed to be John Colony. That's who we consented yesterday. In that room."

"John Colony was moved to a regular floor half an hour ago," said the nurse. "He's on 4D now."

"If you don't stop this, I will," said Jack.

Face flushing, Dugan turned to the charge nurse. "Can he hear me in there through this contraption?"

She tapped a different area of the screen. "He can now."

"Alvin!" said Dugan. "Terminate the protocol." The resident kept dancing and chanting. "Turn the volume up." The nurse tapped the screen several more times. "Alvin!" called Dugan again. The volume in the room was now loud enough that they could hear the echo inside the nursing station through the plexiglass.

Startled, the resident froze. At the same moment, Chad opened his eyes—and let out a terrified yell. By then, Jack, the nurse, and Dugan were racing toward the room. Jack got there first, where he found the resident-turned-shaman backing away from the bed, ankle bells jingling.

"Chad, it's okay," Jack said, bursting into the room.

But Chad was trying to crawl backward up the head of the bed. "Go away!"

"No one's going to hurt you, honey," the nurse said. "Settle down. You're safe." She gave Dugan a sharp look.

"This wasn't supposed to happen, son," said Dugan. "That person is just a doctor."

"That's no doctor," Chad said, his voice quaking.

Jack touched his shoulder, but Chad pulled away. Then Jack turned to the nurse. "Please call his attending. He's going to need something more."

Kaitlyn sidestepped Jack and approached the bed. "Chad, it's Kaitlyn."

"Let's not overload him," Jack said to her. "Maybe you should wait outside."

"No," Kaitlyn replied. "I'm his friend."

He started to reply but something in her tone made him pause.

"Kaitlyn," said Chad, starting to calm. "This place is crazy."

"It's going to be okay," she said. "They're doing an experiment and got the wrong room. He honestly is a doctor."

"She should stay with him," said the nurse, motioning toward Kaitlyn.

Jack hesitated a moment. "All right, then." He turned and went out into the hallway. The lights were bright. For an odd instant he felt as if he were in another building at another time. He shook his head. Falconi and his mother were nowhere in sight.

"Chief?" It was Tré, walking toward him and looking despondent. "I tried to find him, sir. I really did. I hope this doesn't hurt our chances."

Jack rubbed his eyes. "I know you did your best, Tré. Please shepherd the rest of the group over to lunch while I find a rock to hide under."

Tré gave him a sympathetic look. For an awkward moment Jack thought Tré was going to pat him on the back, but instead the young man strode away. He was a good kid.

"Jack."

Jack turned. Hal Dugan was striding up to him, eyes glaring. "I can't believe they didn't tell us about the bed change. Those nurses . . . So, you know this patient?"

Jack felt his jaw clenching. He took a deep breath. "That's neither here nor there, Hal." He pointed at the psychiatrist. "It was your responsibility to check, not the nurses. The study is suspended until you revise the protocol so this can't happen again."

Dugan straightened, his eyes blinking rapidly. "Listen here, this was a freak accident—"

Jack shook his head. "End of discussion." He spun away and strode into the nursing station. Jan Cummings and Marianna Kovalenko were the only members of the tour group still there.

The university president turned to him and blew out a breath of air. Her face was flushed. "Good holy Mother of God, what a mess," she said. "Is the young fellow going to be okay?"

"Yes, and the study is on hold."

"What a terrible thing to take place," Marianna said. "He looked scared out of his head."

"Scared shitless is the common expression, I believe," Jan said, motioning toward the screen. "Ms. Kovalenko tells me that the young lady in there is your niece. You should have told us. I chatted with her during the tour. Looks like she's doing a good job. She told me she was interested in medicine."

Jack looked up at the monitor. Kaitlyn was holding Chad's hand. "She did?" said Jack.

"You should be proud. You're setting a good example."

Jack looked at her, not sure what to say. He paused. "Well, shall we head to lunch?"

Jan sniffed. "You can. I've lost my appetite. We need to talk with Falconi. Let's hope his sense of humor stays intact. You want to come with us, Ms. Kovalenko?"

"Thank you, but you both please go on ahead of me," said Marianna. "I will catch you up. I must find the women's room. I meet you there."

After Forester and Cummings had left, Gina approached the charge nurse, who was just returning from room fifteen. "May I ask you a question?" she asked, careful to stay in the accent.

"Of course."

"This is a grand monitor system. Very modern."

The nurse looked tired. She had on too much mascara. "Thanks," she said. "Glad you think so. It sure came in handy a few minutes ago. What a fiasco."

Gina shot her a sympathetic smile. "For my curiosity, please, could you tell me does it keep a record of everything for permanent?"

The nurse's brow wrinkled. "I'm not sure what you mean?"

"I mean, does it store what it records, the system you have?"

"Ah, I see what you're saying. The answer is yes and no. The telemetry records are permanently stored in the patient's electronic medical record, but the video recording module was an expensive add-on that we didn't get."

"So, the camera doesn't keep a record?"

The nurse nodded. "Correct. No video is saved. And, honestly, I'm glad we didn't have a record of this dumpster fire."

Gina gave her another smile of sympathy. "I understand. Thank you. And thank you for the tour. I wish we had more places like this in my country."

CHAPTER SEVENTEEN

Gina slipped out of the luncheon in the boardroom and found an alcove that contained a couch and a potted tree. She took out the secure phone for Potemkin. A headache was coming on. It rang once before he answered.

"Gina," he said. "How is it going?"

"Well."

"What does that mean? Is Damien Falconi there like you told me last night? He's not as rich as me, but he's got a lot."

"He's here. I overheard them discussing details this morning. Forester is going to ask Falconi to invest something like several hundred million dollars and loan them even more to start this genomic research center."

"It's a smart thing, I hate to say. He will make and sell patents, start new companies. Very wise. So, is the Falconi man interested?"

"It looks like it to me. But Forester only has nine days to seal a deal."

"Then you must stop this. Do you have a plan?"

She hesitated. "I think I see a way to drown this place in negative publicity. But I'll have to do something I don't want to do."

"You have to kill someone?" Potemkin asked.

She squeezed her eyes shut. "Yes."

"Then we'll get Freddy to do it. He's no virgin like you."

Gina considered this. "That won't work. I'm the best one to do it."

"Fine, you do it."

"I want your absolute promise, Mikhail—even if it fails—you will return my daughter."

He laughed. "I was expecting you to ask for more money. But you do it for your daughter. Dmitry's spirit is proud." He quit laughing, and his voice turned sincere. "You have my word. Swear on my parents' grave. I will be generous to you, regardless of success. Cross my heart."

"I'm going to need some logistical help," she said. "I'll be making my way into the hospital tonight. Can you still access their entire computer system?"

"Of course. You still have that ID badge I gave you?"

"Yes. Can you change the telemetry monitoring in a specific room?"

"You mean those heart machines that go *beep-beep*? Yes, of course. I could make their clocks run backward if I wanted."

"Then I will need you to set one monitor on a blind loop so that it looks normal and doesn't change."

"Which room?"

"Room fifteen in the new step-down unit on the eighth floor of the north tower. And at the same time, I will need you to set off an alarm in a different room."

"I will get my people working on this now."

"And you must erase any segment of me that might be caught on their CCTVs, and any record of when I swipe in using my press badge. Thankfully, they don't record video in the rooms. And I need an interior map of the building."

"Yes, of course. I believe this is all feasible. You know, if Forester wins, I will become a ground floor investor in their new research center. One way or another, in ten years I will be the richest man in the world. Other countries will be petitioning to ally themselves with Wiegatesland . . ."

She moved the phone away from her ear. "Mikhail," she said. He continued. "*Mikhail*! Enough, please. This is all very . . . inspiring. Just remember your promise."

Rain pelted the hotel awning under which Gina waited that evening, wind swirling around her legs. Light from the Italian restaurant next door glimmered on the sidewalk. She watched a young couple dash across the street, laughing. The girl ducked inside while the man collapsed his umbrella. Their palpable carefree happiness deepened the dread she felt. Forester's SUV glided up to the curb, windshield wipers thudding like a heartbeat. She climbed in. He was smiling. It was the most relaxed looking she'd seen him. She asked how things were going with Damien Falconi.

"The signs are good," he said.

"Even with that problem today?"

"It didn't seem to faze him."

"And your brother's friend," she said, "is he good?"

"I saw him a little while ago. He's fine now. Thanks for asking."

She set her purse on the floor in front of her, which is where she would leave it. They arrived at the restaurant. A young lady led them to a private dining room already full of people. Martin Bentley came up to her. "Ah, Ms. Kovalenko. Glad you could make it."

A willowy woman walked over and laced her arm around his elbow. Bentley cleared his throat. "Marianna, let me introduce you to my wife. Sydney, this is Marianna Kovalenko from Ukraine, the journalist I mentioned."

"Ah, yes," she said. "Charmed." She gave Gina's hand a limp shake. One of her eyes wandered away.

"Marianna, allow me to get you a drink," said Bentley.

"Please, not necessary."

"As long as you're offering, darling, I'll take a cosmo," his wife said. "Do you know what Martin's middle initial stands for?" Without waiting for Gina to answer, she continued with a giggle. "Ford. His father was a car enthusiast. Get it—Martin *Ford* Bentley. Martin, as in Aston Martin."

Bentley frowned. "Are you sure you'd like another drink, Syd?"

She fixed a look at him and arched one of her eyebrows. "Marty . . ." she said. "You're not being a good boy."

He sighed and turned to leave.

"Get one for yourself and loosen up," she remarked to his departing back. Then she turned to Gina. "What on earth would you find to write about in this town? It's a nest of nincompoops. What's the word for 'nincompoop' in Ukrainian? I have a friend who can say dickhead in Mandarin. It's hilarious."

"I am not sure of the translation."

"How about bastard? Surely you can translate bastard."

Gina saw with gratitude that Forester was approaching.

"Sorry to interrupt," he said to her. "We've saved a seat for you. Shall we?"

"I'll catch up with you later, my dear," said Bentley's wife. "Think dirty!"

Gina's place was between Forester and Leigh Falconi. A beaming Damien Falconi sat on Forester's left next to Jan Cummings. The conversation rippled with laughter. Suddenly something vibrated between her breasts. Before leaving the hotel, she'd placed the Potemkin phone in her cleavage. After buzzing three times against her sternum, it stopped. "I must excuse myself," she said, rising.

She reassured Forester that all was well and stepped out. A restroom wouldn't be private enough, so she went outside under the portico. The rain had stopped. Potemkin answered immediately. "We are in business, Gina. I can do all that you ask. Call when you are ready."

She returned. During the meal, Leigh Falconi wanted to chat. Gina deflected her way through several questions about Ukraine, and Falconi's mother soon turned to her other seatmate.

When the main course was cleared, Gina turned to Forester. "Oh no," she sighed. "I left my phone in my purse in your car and I need to make a call. So stupid. May I borrow your keys?" He offered to go for her. "No, you stay. I know where you park. I insist. I will be soon back."

Hands trembling, she opened the rear hatch, lifted the lid on Forester's emergency kit, and found the vial of ketamine and a syringe. Half an hour later, while Jan Cummings was making some remarks, she leaned toward Forester. "I am getting a headache. I think I will return to hotel now. I will take Uber. No—it's not too bad. Like usual. I just need sleep. You have been too kind already. I will be working on my article tomorrow in hotel, then leave the morning after. I will say goodbye before I leave."

At least the part about the headache was true.

CHAPTER EIGHTEEN

Gina parked on a quiet street two blocks from the hospital. Wearing a short blond wig streaked with gray, she exited her rental car and slung the backpack over her shoulder. The night was dark, the sidewalk deserted. She heard the sizzle of car tires behind her and a chill climbed her spine. She didn't change pace. Once the car passed, she took out her Potemkin phone. "I'm almost there."

"Good," he said. "We are ready."

Hearing a murmur of voices in the background, she envisioned the cyber room with its engineers and servers and monitors. Grand Hack Station, he liked to call it. "I'm using the southeast staff entrance, ground floor. Can you tell if there is a security camera there?"

"Yes. We are watching you right now."

"Make sure they erase footage of me entering."

"Don't tell me my business. Images and badge swipes will disappear."

It wasn't worry about Potemkin's expertise that was gnawing at her. At the door she waved the plastic press badge that Forester's assistant had given her over the sensor. Nothing happened. She flipped the badge over and moved it more slowly. She heard a *click*.

The hallway was brightly lit, and the few people she passed paid her no attention. In the locker room, she found a set of clean blue scrubs. She folded her street clothes into the pack and found a white lab jacket, which she also donned, clipping her press badge to it so that it was partly obscured by the lapel and would pass for a nurse's if no one looked closely. And if someone should discover the deception, she would admit to being a journalist hoping to get a better look at the hospital at night from the perspective of a staff member. She would become weepy. Call Dr. Forester. He'd vouch for her.

She rode an elevator to the eighth floor and made her way to the back entrance of the step-down unit. She took out the Potemkin phone. "Now," she said. An instant later, she heard the clang of an alarm. Through the glass doors she could see nurses and staff members racing toward room one, far to the left. She strode over to room fifteen, her heart pounding. She opened the door. He was sleeping. The room was dim. The cardiac monitor displayed steady, normal heart rhythm. If Potemkin was successful, it would stay that way no matter what happened, on a replaying loop.

Chad had been having a dream. In his dream a man with face painted red and white and horns coming out his skull hovered over him, murmuring and waving his arms as if conducting an orchestra, something rattling like a nest of rattlesnakes.

Now, he felt a stirring of air and opened his eyes. In place of the witch was a beautiful angel, her face sad. Vaguely remembering her, he smiled. "I must still be dreaming."

After finding his clothes in a blue plastic bag in the room's tiny closet, she removed the belt from the pants and went to the bed. The belt would be easier than fashioning something out of a sheet or the cord of a hospital gown. She injected the ketamine into his IV and within seconds he was staring straight ahead, his eyeballs twitching side to side. He was in another place. Insensate. He would never know a thing. Around his neck, she fastened the belt, then attached it to the stretcher rail. It took effort, but she managed to slide him off the bed. As he settled, the belt tightened and his face turned a darker and darker blue. And darker still. His mouth worked, but his eyes remained fixed in that zombie-like stare, widening.

When he stopped breathing, she picked up the backpack, waves of nausea cresting. Up on the cardiac monitor, all looked normal. She took the Potemkin phone and texted: *set off alarms in room twenty*. An instant later, bells rang out from far down the hall in the opposite direction. In a moment, her way out was clear.

CHAPTER NINETEEN

The rising sun blinded Jack as he eased up his driveway back at home. It was Saturday morning. He had been at the hospital all night, the nursing supervisor having called him at midnight with the horrifying news that a patient on the step-down unit had just committed suicide. Rushing into town, he'd arrived at the same time as Chad's mother and sister.

Rolling to a stop near the garage, he killed the engine and leaned back against the headrest, his eyes feeling gritty. It didn't look like anyone was stirring in the house. Over the past several years, he'd gotten to know Chad well and admired how he'd struggled through a disability, glad his brother had found such a friend. Now that was all gone, and what happened didn't make any sense.

There was something he must do before he could rest. Walking out to the barn, he picked up a handful of gravel and threw it into the woods, the pebbles spattering against leaves and branches. As he climbed the stairs to Tony's apartment, he remembered for some reason the way Zellie used to smile as she lay with eyes closed after making love. His heart twisted through multiple layers of grief.

An hour or so later—he was starting to lose track of time—Jack trudged from the barn to the house and entered by the side door. The kitchen was empty, but the smell of coffee told him Zoë was up and about. He poured a cup. Zoë came down the hallway wearing her blue housecoat, eyes puffy, a wad of tissue in her hand. Before leaving for the hospital last night, he'd told her.

"I still can't believe it," she said, slumping into a chair at the table. "You talked with Tony? Is he all right?"

Jack gave her shoulder a squeeze. "It was like when our parents died. He just withdraws into himself. Back then he didn't talk or show emotion for about two weeks. Then he got weepy, and that lasted a month."

"Poor man. They were like brothers."

"The suicide angle was tough. Tony couldn't believe it."

She shook her head and sighed. "Did you have to break the news to Chad's family too?"

"Yes." He saw motion in the hallway. It was Kaitlyn, still in pajamas.

"What did you say about suicide?" she asked timidly.

"Come here, honey," said Zoë.

"What's the matter?" she said, pulling out a chair. Its legs screeched against the floor. "What happened?"

Zoë took Kaitlyn's hand and told her.

"No," Kaitlyn said, her lip quivering. "I just saw him yesterday. He was getting better. Why would he do that?" Tears came. "Why didn't he say something to me?"

As Zoë hugged her, Jack looked over at the key hook on the wall by the kitchen door and he relived it—Zellie calling to him, asking him if she could take his car, him distracted and not remembering why she shouldn't.

"Does Uncle Tony know yet?" Kaitlyn asked.

"Yes," Jack replied.

"This will be terrible for him. I feel so bad."

Jack was startled by the chiming of his cell phone. It was Tré. "I've got to take this." He strode away from the table and answered.

"Chief, I assume you know what happened at the hospital last night. The suicide."

"I've been there most of the night."

"Have you seen the news yet?"

"No."

"It's not good." His words tumbling out, Tré described that all the national news outlets were running it as a headline story. Hospital approved a shaman ritual study that drives a patient to commit suicide. "I don't know how it got out already, sir, but it's moving like a California wildfire. I don't know what we can do."

Jack felt the blood draining from his face. He saw Julia come padding through the kitchen and over to the table. "Let me gather my thoughts," he told Tré. After hanging up, he returned to the table. Julia was sitting on Kaitlyn's lap, crying. He sagged into the chair.

"Jack, what's wrong?" said Zoë.

"Daddy, why couldn't you save Chad?"

"Shush," Zoë said. "Daddy's tired. He didn't have a chance to help Chad. If he could have, he would have saved him."

"I should go over and see how Uncle Tony's doing," said Kaitlyn. Moving Julia off her lap, she started to rise.

Jack cleared his throat loudly. "No," he said. "He just needs to be alone now."

She froze, staring at him. "But he must be really hurting."

"I think I know what my brother needs."

The room went silent. Kaitlyn's face reddened. Julia stood next to her, staring.

"You're wrong, Jack," Zoë said. "I think Tony might appreciate her company."

Kaitlyn rose. "That's all right. Don't worry about it."

"Come back," Zoë said. "Where are you going?"

"To my room. I've got to get ready anyway. Like I told you last night, I'm going over to Aishia's house. They'll be here to pick me up." She strode down the hallway and disappeared.

"That was uncalled for, Jack," Zoë said, glaring at him. "Why did you say that?"

Jack didn't have time to respond. His phone chimed again. Feeling the throb of a headache coming on, he looked at the phone. *Jan Cummings.* The headache blossomed. "Excuse me again." He went into his home office and shut the door before answering. "I was just about to call you, Jan."

"I should damn well hope so. This completely blindsided me. Why didn't you call me last night?"

"I should have."

"I don't mean to sound like a heartless bitch, but I'm the president of a university whose medical center is about to be dragged through a huge steaming pile of shit. You should have called me immediately. We've had no time to get ahead of it."

Jack felt as if someone had reached down his throat and yanked out his heart.

"Are you still there?" she continued.

"Yes."

"I'm calling a meeting for ten a.m. with all the necessary people, including Damien Falconi. I've already talked to him. He's rattled. We can only hope this doesn't scare him off."

"I'll be there."

"And one more thing—not that it makes any difference—but I'd like to know who the son of a bitch was that alerted the media." The connection went dead.

In the kitchen, Julia was sitting on Zoë's lap. "Daddy, why were you mean to Kaitlyn?"

Trying to keep his voice gentle, he said, "I'm not trying to be mean, sweetie. I just think Uncle Tony wants to be alone."

"I'm really going to miss Kaitlyn when she goes."

Jack looked at Zoë. "This is what I was worried about. Attachments developing. The pain of separation."

Zoë frowned at him. "For God's sake, what do you expect? Kaitlyn's a fine person. There *should* be attachments."

"This is not about Kaitlyn."

"Well it should be. I really don't understand you."

He felt his jaw tightening. "This shouldn't be a mystery. Kaitlyn is just a guest here."

"No. She is family."

"And for that matter, you're a guest here too," he said.

"Are you asking me to leave?"

He sighed. "I didn't mean that. I'm sorry."

She looked away, her eyes glistening.

"Aunt Zoë, you're not going to leave, are you?" Julia said, a sob in her voice.

Zoë blew her nose. "No, sweetheart. I'm not. Your father is just tired."

"Daddy, you need a nap."

CHAPTER TWENTY

Jan Cummings slowly rapped her knuckles on the conference table, and it reminded Jack of a funeral dirge. He watched her glance up again at the clock.

"I hope to heaven he hasn't had an accident," she said.

Bentley cleared his throat. "Are we certain he knew the meeting was at ten?"

She snapped a glance at him. "Do you think I'd forget to convey that detail?"

"Should I try calling his assistant?" inquired Tré, sitting beside Jack.

"No," Jack said. "Not yet. He's probably stuck in traffic."

"Sunday morning traffic jams in New Canterbury?" murmured Bentley. "There's a novel concept."

Jan sighed. "Martin, why don't you read us what you've come up with for a press release."

"Certainly." The provost took up a sheet of paper. "This is just a draft. Here we go. Last night at eleven thirty-five p.m.—"

He was interrupted by Jan's cell phone buzzing on the tabletop. "It's him," she said, pressing it to her ear. Jack watched her face. He did not like what he saw.

"You're on the plane already?" Her lips tightened and she glanced upward. "Yes, of course. That's true, but are you sure we can't talk about this?" She paused. "I hope that you *do* realize what this means for us." She caught Jack's eyes and shook her head. "Right. Goodbye then." Setting down the phone, she heaved a much longer sigh and looked away. Jack felt numb. He stared into the glare of the window.

"You obviously heard," she said.

"It would have been nice of him to call before flying off," Bentley started. "But I always feared this opportunity wouldn't materialize."

"Stop that," said Jan. "It would have worked. If it weren't for, as the Joan Baez song goes, a simple twist of fate."

"Bob Dylan," said Tré.

"Pardon?" asked Jan.

"Dylan actually wrote the song," said Tré.

Jan gave the assistant a sharp, prolonged look. "Any other balloons you want to pop, young man?"

Tré's cheeks colored deeply.

"Speaking of busted balloons," said Bentley. "At least we have a parachute. Shall I go ahead and call Dr. Haines and get the HWA deal moving forward?"

Jan flared her nostrils. "I'll do it. Meeting adjourned. Leave that press release with me."

Jack opened his mouth. She held up her hand. "All of you, go."

Late in the afternoon, Jack was sitting at the desk staring at a half-finished sentence on the computer screen. There was a knock, and the door swung open. It was Tré.

"I thought you'd gone home," Jack said.

"Not yet," Tré replied. "Anything I can help with?"

"No. I'm working on a letter to the medical center staff about the transition to Health Wealth Associates. I'd like them to hear it from me first. I'm going to stay till I finish."

"Will you be taking tomorrow off, chief?"

"Tomorrow's Monday. No."

"It sounds like you haven't slept much since Friday night. I'm sure people would understand."

Jack leaned back in his chair. "I used to be an emergency doctor. I'm used to sleep deprivation. Go home. And *you* take tomorrow off. I'm serious. You've been here all weekend too."

"Thanks for the offer but . . ." He stopped. Someone was entering the outer office. Jack heard a woman's voice. "Ms. Kovalenko is here, chief."

Jack inwardly groaned. "Okay. Show her in."

Tré stepped aside and she entered. "Dr. Forester, I'm so glad I can catch you. I tried your number, but it goes right to word mail. The switchboard says you might be here."

Jack tapped his phone. Nothing. The battery must have died. "My fault," he said.

"Not your fault," she said. "Listen, I leave very early tomorrow and I wanted to thank you again and to say goodbye. You are so kind, and I hope your plan with Mr. Falconi is still a great success."

Jack sighed and shook his head.

"What is wrong?" she asked, looking from Jack to Tré and back.

"I'm afraid that won't be happening."

"Not happening?"

"You must not have heard the news this morning."

"What news?"

"It's a long story. I'll just say that we've had complications. I can't say any more now. And I shouldn't keep you. Thanks for stopping by, and I wish you safe travels. I suggest you wait a couple of days and read the news before you write your story." He rose and held out his hand. "It was nice to meet you."

She paused, her brow furrowing. "I'm so very sad to hear this, Doctor." She shook his hand. "I hope your complication can be overcome. But there is one more favor I must ask. I am certain that I dropped an earring in your car last evening."

"I'll find it and send it to you. Leave your address with Tré."

"That is so kind, Dr. Forester, but it was one my mother gave to me, may she rest in peace. I couldn't leave without it. I know you are busy, so may I borrow your keys to go look? I will, of course, bring them back."

"You can if you'd like," he said, reaching in his pocket. "It's on the ground floor in section D. Third one on the right. You know what it looks like."

"I can show you the way, Ms. Kovalenko," said Tré.

"No, no, please, Mr. Tré. You both have helped me so much already. Absolutely no. But thank you. I can find." She took the key fob from Jack.

"No need to bring it back," Jack said. "Just leave it with the parking attendant."

She stood there for a moment looking at him. There was a glint of moisture in her eyes. She gave him a sudden hug and went to Tré and did the same. Then she was gone.

Jack heard the phone on Tré's desk ring. Tré went out. "It's your aunt," he called to Jack.

"Send it back. Then go home. That's an order." He picked up the receiver.

"Jack, your phone is going straight to voicemail."

"Sorry. The battery died."

"You should be more careful. But listen, something's happened."

Jack drew in a breath. "Is Tony all right?"

"Yes. It's Julia. Don't be alarmed. She's had a little accident."

CHAPTER TWENTY-ONE

Dinner at Aishia's house had been all that Aishia had described and more. Kaitlyn was stuffed. So many great new flavors and foods she'd never heard of before. She'd made mental notes of some of the dishes: *biryani*, *dolma*, *kuba*, and the *kanafeh*. Her parents were nice too. Her mother had a great sense of humor. And it had been so good to talk to Aishia about everything. The day had flown by, and now it was time to go home. If you could call it home.

Kaitlyn had just climbed into the back seat of Hassan's old gray Civic with Aishia when her phone chimed. It was Aunt Zoë.

"I'm glad I caught you," Zoë said. "Listen, your cousin took a spill. She's okay—but I'm taking her to the hospital. We're in the car now."

"What do you mean, a spill?"

"You know that old apple tree on the far side of the garage?"

"The one she's not supposed to climb alone? Let me guess."

"This time she might have broken her arm."

In the background Kaitlyn heard Julia say, "Tell her it wasn't my fault."

"Kaitlyn, why don't you meet us in the emergency room?" Zoë suggested. "Ask them to drop you off there."

"Sure. It's pretty much on the way. Tell Julia to be brave. How's Uncle Tony doing?"

"He came to the house for lunch. Other than not saying anything, he seemed calm."

"He's not talking?"

"Quiet as a mouse. I'm almost at the hospital. See you shortly, sweetheart."

Hassan hadn't come out to the car yet. He'd been watching a soccer game with his father and brothers. Aishia had overheard the conversation. "So Julia fell out of a tree and broke her arm?" she asked. "How did she do that?"

"Julia does what Julia wants," Kaitlyn said. "This is completely in character."

"Has to learn the hard way." Aishia looked out the window. "Here comes Hassan. Looks like he combed his hair for you."

A tall young man of twenty, Hassan opened the door and climbed behind the wheel. He was in his second year of community college studying engineering and still living at home. He was a nice enough person, for certain, but he hadn't given Kaitlyn any inkling he was interested in her.

"Finally," said Aishia. "Why do you always keep me waiting?"

"Because I enjoy hearing you complain, turtlehead," he said, starting the engine.

"I'll tell Dad you called me that."

"Don't forget I'm doing you a favor."

"You're doing it for Kaitlette because you're secretly in love with her."

Kaitlyn sighed. You would think that if someone wanted to give her a nickname, they'd call her Kate or Katie.

"It's true," Hassan said, as he backed the car out of the driveway. "She and I have decided to get married, and we're not going to invite you because you're a turtlehead."

"Hassan," said Kaitlyn. "There's been a change in plans. My aunt is taking Julia to the hospital, so could you drop me off there instead of home?"

"No problem," he said. "Is she all right?"

"Just a broken arm," said Aishia.

He nodded, sympathetic. "I hope she's okay."

"I'll tell you who's not okay," Aishia said. "Kaitlette."

"Don't go there, Aishia," Kaitlyn said.

"Your Uncle Jack doesn't treat you the way you deserve."

"I'm sorry I told you," Kaitlyn said. Feeling her face burn, she stared out the window. It was dusk, and the house windows were glowing yellow.

"I wish I could make you my sister and keep you here," Aishia said.

"Let's drop it, all right?" Kaitlyn insisted.

"I can't believe you go back to Ohio in just a week."

Kaitlyn stared out the window.

"There's got to be a way," Aishia pushed.

Kaitlyn swung to face Aishia, her breath coming faster. "Please, shut up."

"But you won't help yourself—"

The car braked and Hassan steered it toward the curb, stopping in front of a convenience store. He turned to face them. "Aishia, I know you mean well, but you really need to leave it alone. You're making her sad."

"But she's my best friend," Aishia said.

Hassan turned to Kaitlyn. "Are you okay?"

Kaitlyn was staring out the window. *No, she was not going to cry.* A skinny teenage kid was riding a skateboard in the 7-Eleven parking lot, wearing a T-shirt despite the cold. She could hear the thin rumble of the skateboard's wheels on pavement, could feel it inside her mind. "I'm okay," she said. "Would you take me to the hospital, please?"

Kaitlyn watched until Hassan's car turned out of sight. There were tall buildings all around and lots of people passing on the sidewalk. She walked toward the door. The last time she'd been in an emergency room was when she was twelve and had a fever, unable to keep anything down. Not feeling well herself that day, Stella had sent Kaitlyn there by taxi and stayed home. Ambulances were too expensive. Memories came rushing back—the sense of chaos, the dingy corridors and little rooms, the wheelchairs speeding by, the smells, the old woman in the next room yowling. But the staff had been kind, especially when they learned she was alone. An elderly man, a volunteer, came to stay with her, talking and telling stories about his days as a fireman, the time he'd rescued a cat and almost fell off the ladder. They gave her medicine and took some blood. When she was able to drink ginger ale and eat saltine crackers, they sent her home in another taxi. The driver had dreadlocks and told her a joke that she couldn't understand because of his accent.

The waiting area was quiet. The young receptionist led her past curtained room after curtained room until she saw Aunt Zoë sitting in a chair next to a stretcher, where Julia lay with her right arm wrapped in some kind of splint.

"There you are," said Zoë. "Julia's been anxiously awaiting your presence."

"Look at my arm," Julia said.

"I see." Kaitlyn went to the bedside and rumpled Julia's hair. "I heard you tried to fly." That got a little smile.

"No. Do I look like a bird?"

"Well, you *do* remind me of a woodpecker sometimes." Kaitlyn moved a lock of Julia's hair off her forehead.

"And you remind me of an ostrich."

"Thank you," Kaitlyn said. "Does it hurt much?"

"Just a little. Do they give tattoos here?"

Zoë gave a surprised laugh. "Of course not. Why would you ask such a thing?"

"Because I want a tattoo on my wrist, like Kaitlyn."

Zoë sighed.

Kaitlyn turned to Zoë. "Is her arm broken?"

"They haven't taken her for an x-ray yet, but the doctor thinks so. But not a bad one."

"Where's Uncle Jack?"

"I don't want you to leave, Kaitlyn," said Julia. "Not ever."

"Jack should be here shortly," Zoë said.

Kaitlyn pulled a chair over and Zoë put an arm around her shoulders, drawing her close. Feeling a wave of affection for Zoë, she sighed and her breath came out in a shudder. Zoë pulled her still closer.

"Your Uncle Jack's had a bad day too," Zoë said. "You shouldn't pay attention to what he said this morning. His plan to start the research center has fallen through. He just told me."

"That's too bad."

"I left my elephant in the car, Aunt Zoë," Julia said.

"You left Ellie in the car?" asked Kaitlyn.

Julia nodded.

"I'll get her for you," Kaitlyn said.

"Oh, I think she'll survive without Ellie for a little while," Zoë said.

"I don't mind." Kaitlyn rose.

Zoë got to her feet too and spoke softly. "I'm sorry your uncle hurt your feelings this morning. I don't think he understands anything sometimes. Himself included."

Kaitlyn nodded and stepped back. "No more flying until I get back," she said to Julia, then went into the hallway. She felt lost, all these machines and lights and people. Then she saw Uncle Jack approaching. Yes, that was the way out. She walked by him, keeping her eyes fixed straight ahead. He called her name. She clutched Zoë's car keys and didn't stop.

CHAPTER TWENTY-TWO

Her hands trembling on the wheel, Gina drove through the outskirts of town in deepening darkness. If ever she needed his help, now was it. She took out the Potemkin phone and called again. It kept ringing and ringing. This was not like him. Stopping at a red light, she turned to get a good view of the girl on the back seat.

Kaitlyn the niece was lying on her side, deeply sedated, wrists bound behind her. Her eyes were blank and unblinking, twitching slowly with nystagmus. A line of saliva oozed from the corner of her mouth. Her breathing was regular but sounded coarse. Gina chose to put her in the back seat because it would have been impossible to lift her in the trunk. But this was dangerous. There wasn't even a blanket to cover her with.

The light changed and she drove on, trying Potemkin's number again. Finally, she got through to him. "Why in the hell haven't you answered me?"

"I'm here now, so no problem," he said in a genial tone. "I was on the upper deck celebrating. Have you been watching the news about our favorite hospital? It gets better and better. Why are you calling?"

"Mikhail, there's been a problem."

"What kind of problem? Tell me now."

Gina sighed. "Someone saw me putting the medication vial back in Forester's car."

"What are you talking about?"

"The medication I used last night came from Forester's car. It couldn't be seen missing, so I had to put it back. I replaced what I used with water."

"You should have been more careful. Who was it that saw you?"

"Forester's niece."

Potemkin grunted loudly. "This niece, she knew you?"

"Yes. She spotted me and came over to say goodbye. I didn't see or hear her until she was right there. I had the vial in my hand."

"How old is this niece?"

"Sixteen. She's sedated in the back seat right now. I gave her the same medication I gave the boy."

"Enough to kill her?"

Heart sinking, she opened her mouth but stopped, glancing back again and swallowing.

"Well?" he pressed. "That would be the simplest thing, no?"

She knew there was no point in arguing. "I don't know how much it takes," she said. "I'm not a pharmacist."

"So, what do you plan to do when she wakes up, Gina—take her to Ben & Jerry's and buy her some good American ice cream?"

"Don't say stupid things." A police car was approaching from the opposite direction. She checked her speed. It slipped by. "I need help."

"No one saw you take this girl?"

"No."

"Are you sure? Did you check to see if there were any cameras around?"

"Of course." Her hands were cramping on the wheel.

"Then you need the help of Freddy Sokolov at my scrapyard. I'm texting you the address now for your GPS. Once there, you can shoot her. Freddy will dispose."

A painful lump forming in her throat, Gina started to say something that came out as a sob. She glanced back and saw the girl's eyes glow in the passing light of a streetlamp.

"Ah..." said Potemkin. "Once was too much for you. No problem.

Freddy can do it. You have his secure phone. Call him. He's reliable."

"Okay," she said. "Okay."

Potemkin went quiet. She knew he hadn't hung up because she could hear him breathing.

"I tell you what, Gina. We will make it more simple. I will call Freddy myself. You just drive straight to the scrapyard."

"He'll be there on a Sunday?"

"Yes. Freddy loves to shred those junk cars, and he likes the money. I give him bonuses by the ton. We had a big shipment of junkers yesterday. He's probably been shredding all day and most likely alone. It only takes one person. You put the car on the conveyor, then the big machine chews them up. After this, you dump the bits into a train car. If he's not working now, he will come. He lives close. Just go to the front gate and flash your lights three times. Simple."

At the scrapyard, Gina pulled up to a tall chain-link gate topped by barbed wire. Even with the windows closed she could hear the shredder's racket. She blinked her headlamps. The girl in the back seat still wasn't moving. She saw a man silhouetted by high intensity floodlights walking toward the gate inside, flashlight in his hand. His height and build resembled the Freddy Sokolov she'd seen the other night. As she rolled down the passenger window, the shredder's din increased. He opened the gate and came to her, beaming the flashlight in her eyes.

"You are Gina?"

She held up her hand to block the glare. "Yes. Do you have to shine that in my eyes?"

The beam moved away from her face as he directed it into the seat of the car through the window. "Is that the kid?"

"Yes."

"How long will she be out?"

"I don't know. A long time."

"Okay," he said. "Pull inside and stay in the car. Wait for me."

He opened the gate wider. She eased in, stopping. Returning to her window, he again directed the light in her eyes.

"Stop," she said. "You're blinding me." But as he moved the light away, she saw the unmistakable black hole of a pistol barrel. Then everything ended in a smear of fire.

CHAPTER TWENTY-THREE

It was a very strange feeling. Kaitlyn was soaring over a city just above the buildings, and it was cold. When she brought the frigid air into her lungs, it filled her with a happiness she had never felt before. Then the city faded and she was circling the moon. She had never been this close to the moon. It was made up of many hues, shifting and mingling. She drifted downward, the happiness fading. Now she was in a room with chandeliers, which drizzled flecks of ice. Someone had hidden oranges, and it was her job to find them. But she smelled fire. This was frightening. Where was she, and what was happening?

Now when she tried, she discovered she was able to move her toes and her eyelids. She was lying on her side. Her arms were behind her. It was hard to breathe. Her shoulder ached. She touched her tongue to her lip. It was dry. Her face was numb and tingling.

She felt a swaying movement. Then another. She was in a car. A rush of nausea came and went. She thought she saw a woman looking at her, but she couldn't tell. Now she could move her eyes and look up. She saw the back of the headrest in front of her. It was doing something strange, morphing into the shape of a face she remembered. Marianna Kovalenko.

Memories returned. Slowly, she recalled being in the parking garage, seeing Marianna, going to her, the look of surprise on her face. And the gun. And the way Marianna had injected her in the thigh, the needle piercing through her jeans, the burning pain.

She could move her hands now. And now her wrists. There was something binding them together, a strap of some kind. She had seen Marianna reaching into Uncle Jack's emergency kit. Her chest tightened with fear. Marianna had pointed a gun at her. Marianna had drugged her. She was lying on her side in the back seat of a car that Marianna was driving. Why?

The car suddenly slowed and turned. She heard the tires grinding over gravel. Then it stopped. She heard Marianna roll down the window. There was a deep banging, clanking noise outside. It was familiar, but she couldn't remember why. Her mind was still foggy. She heard a man's voice. Then she saw the glare of a flashlight. She lay still. It played on her face, then went away. She tried moving her legs and wiggling her wrists. They worked, but everything felt weak.

The car began rolling again, slowly, then after a moment it stopped. She heard Marianna say something, and then there came the flare of a different light, followed by a powerful bang that made her flinch and blink as wet drops sprinkled her face. Marianna slumped toward the passenger side and took a rattling, gurgling breath, then went quiet. The smell of blood hit Kaitlyn, making her throat clench. She had a quick vision of Conrad's head hitting the floor.

Was it her turn next? *She had to get out and hide.*

She twisted her wrists and felt the rope loosen. Where was the man now? She heard the motor of a big truck or tractor roar and rumble closer and closer. Something heavy banged onto the car's roof, making it creak and jiggle. Then everything was pulled upward. The car was being lifted. It swayed, rising. The strap gave way and her hands were free. She rubbed her wrists. Her joints were stiff and her muscles still weak and sluggish. She forced herself up until she was sitting.

The car was swaying like a pendulum, moving forward. She looked out the windows. The smell of blood made her gag. She could see that the car was being lifted by some kind of crane, and they were inching forward. In the floodlights she could see objects scattered around—old cars, tractors, trucks, refrigerators. And there was a building.

She looked down. It was hard to tell, but it looked like it wasn't too high to jump. She grabbed the door handle. *It was locked.* She tried again. It still wouldn't budge. She tried rolling down the window. Nothing. She was trapped. Everything must be locked from the front.

Where were they going?

And then she saw it up ahead, what looked like a huge metal box. The source of the rumbling and banging noise. She recognized the sound. It must be the shredder machine. And that's where the crane was taking them. *This had to be the scrapyard where they'd gone to help Chad.*

As she stared, her chin trembling, an old car moved up a long conveyor to the mouth of the machine. It reached the top and slid down into the opening. It bounced and revolved—the roaring, banging sounds coming to a crescendo, the car being ripped to pieces by huge whirling teeth.

The swaying stopped. She felt the car lurch and descend. The crane was lowering it onto the conveyor. She slammed her feet against the rear door, then hit the window. A few seconds later the car came to rest on the conveyor, landing hard enough to pitch her forward. She could feel the car inch upward toward the mouth of the shredder.

Launching herself forward between the seats, she scrambled until she was kneeling on Marianna's body. She moved toward the door lock, starting as her left knee pressed into Marianna's stomach and a gurgle came from her still mouth. She clenched her teeth and kept moving. She was in the driver's seat now, sitting on Marianna's hips. She could see through the windshield that the car was near the top of the conveyor.

She tried the door handle. The door cracked open with a rush of cold air. Her scalp tingled with terror. Would he see her? *Don't be stupid. It was either him, or it was the shredder,* which was now shuddering so close she could feel the vibrations in her spine. She opened the door further. There was a railing of metal meant to keep the cars on the conveyor. It was close enough to leap over, but she couldn't tell how far the drop was. There were shadows everywhere—but in seconds now she'd be at the top, and it wouldn't matter.

She took a deep breath, swinging her legs under her. Now, with the edge of the door in her right hand and the frame in her left, she stood, shivering, her knees quaking.

It had begun to rain again.

CHAPTER TWENTY-FOUR

Blinking against the rain, Kaitlyn braced in the doorway of the doomed car—now close to the top of the conveyor—and jumped. As she'd planned, her right foot landed on the railing of the ramp, helping her vault over and clear the edge, launching herself into the shadows.

She landed hard on the wet gravel with her feet under her, pitching forward and catching herself with her hands, then falling onto her knees, a sharp pain blossoming in her left ankle. The shredder's roar intensified with more slamming and crashing. The car was being eaten alive. She smelled oil and dirt. She rose to her feet, testing her ankle. The pain was bearable.

Above the racket she heard a man shout. "Hey!"

She began limping away, trying to stay in the shadows. She could feel the grinding and clanging—the monstrous anger—of the shredder in her bones. The rain ran down her hair into her eyes. She wiped them with her sleeve, shivering.

"Hey you! Stop!" He was closer. She flattened against the outer wall of the shredder. "I won't hurt you."

She bolted toward a little shed and made it to cover, her chest heaving. She had to find a place to hide—and a way out of this place.

"I promise I won't hurt you." She shivered. He was even closer now. "Just come on out. Nothing to be afraid of." Closer still. She froze and held her breath, her back pressed against the shed. Raindrops pattered on the metal roof. She crouched and felt something hard and sharp edged against her ankle. Her hand trembling, she touched it.

"You'll get soaked and freeze out here." He was just on the other side of the shed. His voice was deep, with an accent like Marianna's. Her heart was beating so hard she was sure he would hear it. "She was a bad woman," he said. "She was trying to hurt you. I didn't know you were in there."

What was it she has just touched? She felt again. It was a jagged chunk of metal about the size of an apple. Her fingers closed around it. It was heavy, but not overly so. She thought of how the shredder tore things apart, compressing and twisting and hammering cars into things like this.

"I want to help you." He was coming around the shed now.

She hefted the chunk and rose. It was slightly larger than a baseball. She thought of Mr. Brady. He was close enough now that she could hear his boots scuffing gravel.

"Just let me know where you are so I can help you." She saw the splash of yellow made by his flashlight as he swept it around, the raindrops slanting through the beam of light like needles of silver. Light glinted off a puddle. In a moment he'd be around the corner. The arm holding the flashlight came into view. "Let's make this easy." Then she saw the gun in his other hand. "I'm your friend."

Her breath was coming fast, her heart crashing inside her chest. Then his entire body came into view, and she could see him silhouetted. In a moment he would turn and shine the light in her direction. She cocked her trembling arm back, braced, and threw. She heard the crack and saw his neck jerk.

The chunk had hit the side of his head. The flashlight and gun clattered on the gravel. The flashlight twirled once around. He said nothing. He stood there for a few seconds before his silhouette fell forward, hitting the ground like a chopped tree. The flashlight was still burning. She limped over and picked it up, her hand shaking so badly she had to steady it with both hands. She shone the light on him. He was very still. Blood was pouring out of a gash on his temple, trickling in rivulets that dripped off his nose and the stubble on his chin, mingling with the rain. Had she killed him? *The gun.* What if he came to and started chasing her again? He might still shoot her. She thought of taking the weapon with her, but she had no idea how to use it. Instead, she kicked the pistol into a puddle, where it disappeared.

And then she began running as fast as her ankle would allow, back past the shredder and the crane. She saw a chain-link gate, locked with a cable and a padlock. She tucked the flashlight in her back pocket, wiped the rain from her eyes with her sleeve, and began climbing. There were two strands of barbed wire on top. They were fitted on an extension of the fence that tilted away from her. This would hurt. She grabbed hold of the top strand and swung her leg up. The wire bit into her arms and hands and caught on her clothes, but gradually she worked her way over. Knowing that jumping would make her ankle worse, she managed to climb down the other side.

The road was dark. There were trees on either side, and there were no stars or moon. She used the flashlight only when she needed to. The rain was easing, but she had never been so cold in her life.

After a long time walking and shivering, she saw a light in a window.

CHAPTER TWENTY-FIVE

Jack stared at the kitchen clock. Ten minutes past midnight.

Zoë was sitting across from him at the table, her eyes red and swollen. Julia was on her lap, head resting against Zoë's chest, hugging the stuffed elephant. Half-empty cups of coffee on the table had long since gone cold.

"At some point we'll need to let Stella know," Jack said.

Zoë shook her head. "I'd rather we wait until morning. She won't handle news like this very well. Why make her worry all night? Fingers crossed, we'll have Kaitlyn back by then."

"Nonetheless, Zoë, I feel an obligation to notify her that her daughter's missing. And what if Kaitlyn's called her already? Maybe she knows more than we do."

"That's guilt talking, Jack. This is not your fault."

"She was angry. She walked right by me."

"I know," Zoë said, hugging Julia closer. "She only wanted to comfort Tony. But she wouldn't just up and leave because of that."

The thought of some predator luring Kaitlyn into Jack's car outside the ED kept sending waves of dismay through him. The best-case scenario was that someone she knew picked her up to help her run away.

Zoë sniffed. "And if Kaitlyn were in trouble, the last person she'd call would be Stella."

"Their relationship is that bad?"

"Worse. Kaitlyn talks to me a lot."

"Nonetheless, I feel a responsibility to call."

"I'm not going to argue with you, Jack. Do what you think best. They've given Stella her phone back. The number is on a card on the refrigerator."

Jack rose to get it.

"Was Kaitlyn still mad at Daddy?" Julia asked.

"Hush," Zoë said.

"Was she mad at me?" she continued, her eyes sad.

"Heavens, of course not."

Jack came back with the number. "Julia, it's time for you to go to bed."

"Not until Kaitlyn's home," she said, yawning.

Stella answered after several rings. But her greeting was not cordial. "*Fuck you*," she said. "My car doesn't need an extended warranty. I don't even have a car. And if you're calling for a donation, I don't give a damn about politics or charities. So cut me from your list and leave me alone."

Before the line went dead, Jack heard male laughter in the background. He lowered the phone. In his mind's eye he saw Kaitlyn back in the ED, marching by him, no expression, no reaction.

"So how did that work for you?" said Zoë.

"You heard?" he replied.

"Enough. She didn't recognize your number." Zoë nodded toward a sleeping Julia in her lap. "Julia's asleep. Do you want to carry her to bed?" Before he could answer, her phone on the table began chiming. She swept it up. "It's Aishia calling back," she said. "Please God, let her have some good news." She answered. They talked for a moment, then Zoë thanked her, set the phone down, and looked at Jack. "She and her brother have been looking for her. Nothing."

Her phone suddenly chimed again. Zoë snatched it quickly and stared at the display. She frowned.

"Who is it?" Jack asked.

"I don't know the number, but it's local."

Jack followed the GPS deeper into the countryside south of New Canterbury. The rain had stopped and the only light in the sky was the pale-yellow glow of city lights against the clouds behind him. He descended into a valley of apple orchards. A two-story farmhouse came into view on the right, window lights illuminating two trees in front. This was it. Before he was halfway up the driveway, he saw headlights in his rearview mirror. Another car was approaching. The lights of yet another car swung in behind it.

He stopped by the house and got out. The first car behind him was a police cruiser, and two uniformed officers stepped out. The second car pulled up next to it, and a woman in a blue down jacket emerged. The three strode toward Jack, switching on their flashlights. The woman stopped in front of him and held out a badge, shining her light on it. "I'm Chief Investigator Frances Dirkens, New Canterbury Police. Who are you and what brings you here?" The two in uniforms hovered behind her. He couldn't see her clearly, but she appeared to be in her late fifties.

"I'm Jack Forester. I'm here to pick up my niece, Kaitlyn Andersen." He described her disappearance, and her call a little while ago.

"That's why we're here too," she said. "Where are the girl's parents?"

"I have temporary guardianship. Kaitlyn's been staying with us for a few months." He explained the situation.

"I see." The investigator passed the light over his face. "I thought I recognized you. You're Dr. Forester from the university. I met you half a dozen years ago when we arrested your colleague, Bryson Witner, after his murder spree. My husband works at the university too." She shone the light at her own face. "Ring a bell?"

"Not really."

"I hope that doesn't mean I've gotten uglier."

The front door of the house opened and a man yelled out, "Come on in. We've been waiting for you."

"Thank you, sir," she called over. "We'll be there in a moment." The door banged shut. "Lionel and Joe," she said, "go ahead and start collecting information. Give me another moment with the good doctor."

"Will do, Frankie."

"Do you know who lives here, Doctor?" she asked.

"No idea," Jack replied.

"It's an older couple by the name of Ted and Bea VanDyke. They told our dispatcher that your niece had been taken against her will to the Aldiss Scrapyard. But she escaped and made her way here. Were you aware of any of this?"

"The scrapyard?" Jack said, shivering as the cold seeped through his light jacket. "No, I wasn't. Kaitlyn didn't give us any details when she called."

Dirkens pointed with her thumb. "It's about three-quarters of a mile south of here."

"I know. I was there a couple evenings ago. Friday."

"You were just there?"

"Yes."

"Why?"

He described how his brother had been doing some electronics salvage work there and that his business partner had gotten sick. "I went to help. As a matter of fact, Kaitlyn was with me. She'd been volunteering at the hospital."

"Do you go to the scrapyard often?"

"First time ever."

"Doctor, as you probably know, most missing kids turn out to be runaways. Sometimes they say they've been kidnapped. That still may be the case here. We'll see. But she told the VanDykes that the woman who kidnapped her was murdered at Aldiss Scrap. I've got officers heading there . . ." She paused and stepped toward him. "Is something wrong? You look a little shaky."

Jack steadied himself against the fender. The world had begun to spin, but it was already passing. "No, I'm fine," he said, straightening.

"It's been a long, strange weekend. Haven't had much sleep since Friday."

"I heard about the suicide at your hospital and that shaman business. Sounds like a big hot mess."

"If you don't mind, I'd like to see how my niece is doing."

"Just a couple more questions. Any chance your niece is involved in drugs like the stepmother you mentioned?"

"I'd say no."

"Does she have any history of running away?"

"Not that I'm aware of. But I've been out of touch with her past, I'm afraid."

A man in his seventies wearing a Buffalo Bills sweatshirt ushered Jack and Dirkens into a living room where the smell of dinner roast lingered in the air. Kaitlyn sat on the sofa next to Bea VanDyke, who had a halo of thin white hair and an arm draped around Kaitlyn's shoulder protectively. Jack introduced himself. Kaitlyn was wrapped in a blue and white quilt. Her hair was moist and she had gauze wrappings on her hands and arms. The two officers were seated on chairs flanking the sofa.

Kaitlyn's eyes met Jack's, then shied away. "Sorry you had to come out in the middle of the night, Uncle Jack."

"I'm just glad you're safe. We were so worried."

"Aunt Zoë knows you got here," she said. "I texted her."

"Good." He felt at a loss for words. "Are you okay?"

"She's got some scratches," said Bea VanDyke. "From barbed wire. Didn't look to me like they needed stitches. But you're the doctor. I cleaned them with peroxide and put on some ointment. And she was wet and very cold when she got here. There's an electric heating pad under that quilt. She rolled her left ankle too."

"Let me have a look," said Jack.

"It's okay, really," Kaitlyn said, pulling her legs up under the quilt.

"Later then," Jack said. "We're going to stop by the ER on the way home anyway."

"Why?" asked Kaitlyn. "I don't need that."

"Your uncle's right, Kaitlyn," said the investigator, who pulled over a chair. "We need to have you checked." She introduced herself and showed Kaitlyn her badge. "Is there anything you'd like to talk to me about in private?"

"She didn't get sexually assaulted, if you're worried about that," said Bea VanDyke.

"Is that true, Kaitlyn?" asked Dirkens.

"Yes."

"Good. For the record, your full name is?"

"Kaitlyn Zelinda Andersen. With a K and a Z."

Jack was surprised. He didn't know her middle name was the same as Zellie's first—Zelinda. All the Andersens' given names started with Z: Zoë, Zack, Zelda, Zeke, Zara, Zeb.

At Dirkens's request, Kaitlyn detailed what had happened that day—being at her friend's house, getting dropped off at the hospital, where it happened.

"And what exactly happened at the hospital?" inquired the investigator.

"I was going out to the car to get my cousin Julia's stuffed animal. I saw Ms. Kovalenko pull into the parking garage. I followed her inside." Kaitlyn's voice trembled slightly. "She had a gun, and she kidnapped me."

Jack interrupted, startled. "You're saying Marianna kidnapped you?"

"You know this person, Doctor?" said Dirkens.

"Yes, and I find it hard to believe."

"Just be quiet and listen," added Mrs. VanDyke. "You should be very proud of this young lady after what she's been through."

Jack cleared his throat. "Kaitlyn, this is a serious accusation."

"I need to do the questioning," said Dirkens. "Kaitlyn, tell me in your own words who this person is."

"Well, she was a journalist from Ukraine who was supposed to be writing an article about the hospital for her magazine. I met her on the hospital tour. That's how I knew her."

"That much is correct," Jack said.

"Keep going, Kaitlyn," said Dirkens. "So, you saw her pull in and..."

"I knew she was going home tomorrow and I wanted to say goodbye. She'd seemed very nice before." Kaitlyn inhaled deeply. "I saw that she'd driven down to the lower level, so I took the stairs down and saw her car at the end where the doctors park. She had stopped right behind my uncle's car. She was opening the back hatch and getting something."

"Stop there for a moment," said Dirkens. She turned to Jack. "Do you leave your vehicle unlocked?"

"No," Jack said, sagging into a chair. "Marianna had stopped by my office. She was catching a flight the next morning. She told me that she'd lost an earring and asked to borrow the keys so she could retrieve it."

Dirkens raised an eyebrow. "How did she lose an earring in your car?"

"I assume she dropped it. I'd picked her up at her hotel Saturday night—last night—to take her to a dinner for a special guest at the medical center."

"So, you had a close relationship with her?"

"No. Not at all. Purely professional."

"That's true," said Kaitlyn.

"Did she return your keys?"

"She left them with the parking attendant, as I'd asked."

"What would you have been doing while this happened, Doctor?"

"Like Kaitlyn said, my daughter was in the ER with a broken arm. I went there."

Dirkens turned back to Kaitlyn. "Okay, honey, tell us what happened next."

"I went up to her, and that's when I saw what she was doing. And . . ." She suddenly shivered.

Bea VanDyke rubbed her shoulder. "It's okay. They need to know."

"She had this little glass bottle of medicine in her hand. It looked like she was putting it into the emergency kit."

An electric tingle crawled up Jack's back. "Kaitlyn, it's extremely important that you tell the truth."

Kaitlyn glared back. "Thanks, but I don't need to be told that telling the truth is important."

"Doctor," said Bea VanDyke, "I know an honest person when I meet one—and this girl is that and more." She looked at Dirkens. "You'd better catch the people behind this."

"Bea," said her husband. "Let them do their job."

"Dr. Forester, what's in your kit?" asked Dirkens.

"The same things we have in an ER crash cart—intubation and IV equipment, cardiac meds, airway meds."

Dirkens turned back to Kaitlyn. "Did you see what medication she had?"

"No."

"Dr. Forester, is the kit outside in your vehicle now?" Dirkens continued.

"Yes."

"We're going to need to take it as evidence."

"I understand," Jack said. "Please do. The vehicle isn't locked." He turned to Kaitlyn. "Listen, I'm sorry for sounding like I didn't believe you. This is just all so strange."

She sniffed. "You're telling me."

"Lionel," Dirkens said, turning to one of the officers. "Please secure the doctor's emergency kit and treat it as a source of prints."

"Will do, Frankie," he said, rising.

Dirkens redirected her attention to Kaitlyn. "So, you saw her putting what looked like a medicine vial back into the emergency kit?"

"That's what it looked like."

"What happened next?"

"Well, she saw me, stood up, and hit the back of her head on the door of the hatch. I apologized for frightening her. But then she took out a pistol, and she got a strap or something from the back of the car to tie my hands. Then she went and finished whatever she was doing in his emergency kit, and a minute later she pushed me in her car and gave me a shot in my leg. Here in my left thigh." Kaitlyn stopped and rubbed her forehead as if trying to remember something. "Could I have a drink of water, please?"

Ted VanDyke hustled into the kitchen.

Dirkens turned back to her. "Then what?"

"I started feeling weird and then I couldn't move. I lost track of time. It was like being inside a dream. I was seeing strange things. I don't remember us driving away from the hospital."

Dirkens turned to Jack. "What could cause this, Doctor?"

"Sounds like ketamine. There was a vial in the emergency kit."

"Why would you have ketamine in your car?"

"Lots of uses—procedural sedation, severe agitation. In lower doses, it's a good analgesic. Decent safety profile. No respiratory dep—"

Dirkens raised her hand. "Enough detail, thanks. How might this woman have known how to use it?"

"She said was once a nurse."

Mr. VanDyke handed Kaitlyn a glass. She took a long drink.

Dirkens continued "Then what happened, Kaitlyn?"

Jack listened. As the details gathered, his doubts evaporated. She was describing how Marianna had spoken to a man with a flashlight at the entrance. And then her voice broke.

"It's okay," said Bea VanDyke. "Just tell them like you told us."

"He shot her in the head. I saw a flash of light and heard the bang."

Jack felt his throat tighten. He'd seen many gunshot wounds to the head in his career. They were always awful.

"When Kaitlyn got here, she had blood all over her," said Bea VanDyke. "At first, I thought it was hers. But it wasn't, except for where she hurt her arms. I cleaned her up the best I could. These are my clothes that she's wearing. I put hers in that plastic bag your officer has."

The policeman raised a bag that was sitting by his chair.

"Investigator," Bea continued, "I've always hated that scrapyard. Ted and I have been trying to sell the orchard here for three years so we can move south where the kids have gone. But thanks to all that noise and the big trucks hauling in junk cars, nobody wants to—"

"Bea, let them continue," her husband interrupted.

"All I'm saying is that I hopé you close it down."

Dirkens's phone rang. "I need to take this. Be right back." She strode off into the front hallway.

Jack used the lull to get out his own phone and call Zoë. As he gave her a brief update, he studied Kaitlyn. Bea VanDyke was whispering something to her. Yes, there was a part of her that reminded him of Zellie. But there was another part that was simply her. She was a strong person.

Dirkens returned. "That was one of the officers at the scrapyard. They've found a middle-aged male lying unconscious with what looks like a skull fracture."

"That's him," said Kaitlyn. "The one who shot her. I can explain."

CHAPTER TWENTY-SIX

Jack waited for Kaitlyn on the VanDykes' porch. It was two o'clock in the morning. Gusts of wind rustled leaves on the yard. The investigator had gone to her car for a minute. She returned. "Your niece still inside?"

"She's using the bathroom."

"I just talked to our people again. We're not going to get any answers from the man at the scrapyard. He died en route to the hospital. Heck of a lucky throw on her part."

"It may be more than luck," Jack said. "According to the school, she's got a great pitching arm."

"Interesting."

"Her dad was a semipro ball player."

"The apple doesn't fall far from the tree. In any case, the man's green card says he was a Russian national named Frederick Sokolov. Hasn't shown up on any of our criminal databases yet."

Jack straightened. "Sokolov? I met him Friday evening at the scrapyard. He was the manager."

"Good to know. They found the handgun just where Kaitlyn said she'd kicked it—in a pothole full of water." Dirkens blew air through her pursed lips. "They also spotted human remains and blood in the dump truck that the shredder was emptying into. What color was this reporter's hair?"

"Dark reddish."

"That jibes with the remains. We'll see what DNA tells us. They may or may not be able to get usable prints."

Jack looked down, shook his head, then glanced up at Dirkens. "Marianna was with us at the scrapyard Friday evening."

She stared back. "You're saying she was with you. Why?"

He described how he'd been taking her to her hotel when he'd gotten the call from his brother, and that when they arrived Marianna had helped him take care of Chad Chadwick, who was extremely sick. She'd acted like she really had been a nurse. She knew what to do.

"Which means she'd met this Sokolov and had seen your medical kit, right?" Dirkens asked, to which Jack nodded. "Wait . . . wasn't Chad Chadwick the name of the man who'd committed suicide at your hospital?"

"Correct."

The investigator exhaled, her breath vapor trailing off in the dark. Jack's gloveless fingers were going numb. He stuffed them in his pockets and glanced at the front door. "You mentioned your husband works at the university," he said. "Is he a physician?"

She smiled. "Not hardly. He teaches classics. He investigates old texts, and I'm out here." She scuffed her shoe against the porch boards. "I'd trade places with him tonight. I don't know what the hell to make of all this. Your niece is kidnapped and sedated by a person tampering with your emergency kit. She was a Ukrainian journalist who'd come to write a story about your hospital. She gives your niece ketamine, takes her to a scrapyard, and allegedly gets murdered by the manager, a Russian she'd recently met while helping you take care of a young man there. The young man then commits suicide the next day. Wouldn't you say this is a bizarre chain of events? Bad things happen to four people who were at the scrapyard Friday night. A kidnapping and three deaths, counting Freddy Sokolov."

"I can't see any connections," Jack said. "I don't envy your job."

"Nor I yours. In any case, with the kidnapping and the deaths of two foreign nationals, we'll be involving the FBI. And I'll need forensic blood samples from your niece to confirm that sedative."

"I'm taking her to the ER now."

"One of our officers will meet you. The tests need to be run at our lab."

The front door opened. "She's ready," said Bea VanDyke.

Kaitlyn was limping, the quilt draped over her shoulders. Jack reached to take her arm. "I'm fine," Kaitlyn said. "I can walk. Thank you again."

"You keep the quilt, honey," Bea said to Kaitlyn. "I want you to have it."

Dirkens held out a card. "Kaitlyn, I'll have to talk with you more, but if you want to speak about anything in the meantime, call me. Twenty-four seven. You've done a great job."

A moment later, Jack and Kaitlyn were in the SUV driving northward between the orchards. Hearing Kaitlyn's teeth chatter, he turned on the heat full blast. She made a long sighing sound. He looked over. She was holding the quilt to her face and quietly crying.

"It's going to be okay," he said, and handed her some tissues from the door panel compartment.

"Do we really have to go to the hospital? Couldn't it wait till morning?"

"I'm afraid it can't. But it won't take long."

She paused, then added softly, "Thanks again for coming to get me."

"Of course."

Kaitlyn looked over. "I still can't help but feel bad for Marianna. I just don't know why she did this. I never did anything to hurt her. Why did *any* of this happen?"

"We don't know yet. But the most important thing is that you're safe."

"Investigator Dirkens seems nice," she said. "Did she tell you how the man's doing?" Jack glanced at her and hesitated. "If you know something, please tell me," she continued. "I'm not a child."

"The investigator told me that the man died before he got to the hospital. He was the manager we met there the other night." He looked at her. She was staring ahead. "You did what you had to do. You had no choice."

"I know that." She drew in a breath. "I didn't think. I just threw." She was quiet for a moment, then turned to him. "Can I ask you a personal question?"

"Of course."

"Why did you want to be a doctor?"

The last person who'd asked him that question had been Zellie, on their first date.

"If you don't feel like answering, it's okay," she added. "I know it's late."

"No, that's all right. Well, for most doctors, I think it's just a gut feeling that this kind of life is where they belong. For me, I'd always liked science and I had a good memory, but when I look back, I think the seed was planted when I saw a friend of mine die and I couldn't help him. I was fifteen." He told her the story of how his father had moved them to Bolivia that year for his construction engineering work and how he and his friends had been mugged in La Paz one day. Enrique had fought back, getting stabbed in the chest.

Kaitlyn was looking intently at him. "Could you have saved him with what you know now?"

"A good chance, yes. The knife had nicked his heart. If you act quickly, you can rescue people with an injury of that nature."

"How quickly?"

"Very. It's usually just a matter of minutes."

"Have you ever saved anybody like that?"

"A couple of times, but the opportunity doesn't come along often. It's usually too late."

"I can see why you wanted to learn it."

They were quiet for a moment. Then Jack looked over at her. "When I think back, there was something else that motivated me too—Tony's mental disability. I saw the way it affected his life, and I couldn't stop wondering why disorders strike certain people—what causes them in the first place, and how they can be treated."

"I can understand that," she said. "Thinking about my stepmother's problem makes me curious too. Why is she like that? Why is it so hard for her to be normal?" She paused. "Were you in high school when you realized you'd like to be a doctor?"

"No, it was in college." He glanced over at her again and swallowed. "Actually, I lost my way for a while back in high school."

"What do you mean, lost your way?" she asked.

Jack felt his face warming. "Well, it's a boring story. More embarrassing than boring, maybe. You see, I did something stupid and got arrested when I was seventeen."

Out of the corner of his eye he could see her staring at him. "For what were you arrested?"

He clenched and unclenched his hands on the steering wheel, noticing that his palms were moist. There was goodness in honesty. No matter when. "I hung around with the wrong people for a while. Not that I'm blaming them." He looked over at her. "One night we broke into a house and stole some alcohol. Very stupid. Someone recognized me running away, one of the neighbors walking his dog, and he called the police."

"What did the police do?"

"They came and hauled me out of school the next day. Pretty embarrassing. I was terrified."

"I would be too," she said.

"They offered to be lenient if I'd tell them who was with me, but I refused, so they charged me with a felony."

"You had to stand trial?"

"I did. I spent a week in jail and had to do six months of community service."

"I bet your friends felt bad."

"Actually, we never talked about it. I didn't see them much after that."

"And you did community service like what I'm doing?"

"Very much so," he said. "At the same hospital, in fact."

"Was it good for you?"

"I met some good people there who helped me get into med school later on."

She sighed. "Wow."

"I was lucky in that way."

"That was after your parents died in the plane crash?"

He paused and looked at her again, her features indistinct in the minimal light from the dashboard. "Did Zoë tell you about that? I guess she must have. But, yes. It was after they were gone."

"She said it happened when you were in Bolivia. A plane crash."

He swallowed and nodded. "In Bolivia, yes."

They were quiet for a minute or two. Then Kaitlyn shifted in the seat and cleared her throat. "I guess that means we have something else in common. Losing parents."

Again he glanced at her, tightening his grip on the wheel, impressed by the maturity he heard in her voice. "That's true. I hadn't thought of that before. Except you were younger when you lost yours. That must have been very rough."

"I never knew my mom. I was just a baby. Like Julia was. How long till we get to the hospital?"

"A few minutes." No wonder Kaitlyn and Julia seemed so close.

"So, that's why you want to start that new research center, right, to find better cures? Like for Uncle Tony and Chad?"

"And many other things," he said.

"Aunt Zoë told me you had some problems with the plan."

"Yep," he said. "Big problems. I'm afraid it isn't going to happen."

She sighed. "Maybe sometime in the future it can," she said.

"I don't know about that. We'll see." He felt a sudden urge to change the subject. "Tell me something, Kaitlyn."

"What?"

"Are you thinking about going into medicine? Ms. Cummings mentioned that."

"A little bit maybe. I don't know. We'll see. But thank you for talking with me."

They were in the city now, nearing the hospital. "And thank you, too," he said.

"For what?"

"For listening..."

He wanted to say more, but he was tired and felt suddenly tongue-tied. They were pulling into the emergency department parking lot now, and he let a flood of concerns about what would happen to the medical center overwhelm him.

CHAPTER TWENTY-SEVEN

Late Monday morning, Mikhail Potemkin took the elevator to his private observation bridge. His mood was foul. Bolting the hatch behind him, he hopped onto the leather upholstered chair, buckled in, and jabbed a button. With a silky whine, the chair rose on a gleaming hydraulic pillar, easing to a stop fifteen feet higher than the ship's tallest antennae. The chair began swaying side to side, reflecting the ship's gentle movement on the waves far below. He gazed about and sniffed. The balmy southwest breeze was perfumed with a hint of vegetation from the coastal marshes many miles beyond the horizon. He spat, lit a cigar, then pulled out his phone and called Bodashka Liski.

"It's me," Potemkin said. He could hear laughter and talk in the background. "I have some bad news for you."

"What bad news, boss?"

"What the hell is going on there? Some kind of orgy?"

"Not yet." Liski chuckled. "I've just arrived at the restaurant to have dinner with a most delightful lady."

"Well ditch her and stroll outside. I need to talk with you in private."

"Sure." The phone went silent. Liski returned a moment later. "I'm outside now, alone. What's the news you mentioned?"

Potemkin blew twin jets of smoke out his nostrils. "Gina met her maker last night."

A moment of silence. "Gina's dead?"

"You heard me."

Liski blew air into the phone. "How did it happen?"

"Bad luck and carelessness. She let herself be seen in a compromising situation by a teenage girl who happened to be Forester's niece. His niece saw my niece. Too damn many nieces."

"What was the compromising situation?"

"The kid sees Gina with the medicine she used to terminate someone. Gina grabs kid, takes kid to my scrapyard where I told Freddy to deal with them both. But Freddy only got to Gina. The kid bashes in his head and escapes. Freddy's dead too."

"A teenage girl whacked Freddy Sokolov and escaped? Maybe you should hire her."

"Is that supposed to be funny?"

Liski cleared his throat. "Funny, no. I'm in despair, boss."

"Get over it quick, because there are some things I need you to do."

"You want the Forester niece dead?"

"No. She doesn't know enough to hurt me. It would only make things messier."

"Yes, Mikhail. Too many corpses spoil the plot."

Potemkin tightened his grip on the phone. "Have you been drinking?"

There was a pause. "Very little. I'm just a little off-balance by this news. Gina could be a pain in my ass, but she was okay. She came so close to getting her daughter back."

"True, and bad luck for her. But thanks to the work she did there, Forester is out of luck and Lawrence Haines is back in business."

"Then may she rest in peace. As for Freddy getting whacked by a teenage girl, it's just as well. He would have died of embarrassment if she hadn't killed him."

Potemkin sniffed. "That is a very stupid comment."

"Sorry, boss."

"I didn't tell you everything, Bodashka. After Gina was shot, her car went through Freddy's car shredder. With her inside."

"Argh. At least she was dead first. I wish you hadn't told me."

"I'm telling you because it will serve a purpose for us."

"How can going through a car shredder serve our purpose?"

"Gina's remains were shredded. So, how will she be identified?"

"By DNA," Liski said.

"Of course. DNA. And it so happens that Gina left a hairbrush full of hair here in Wiegatesland."

"So?"

"I already had the brush taken to my special friends at the Ukraine consulate in New York. They will give it to the local police in New Canterbury and attest that it came by direct courier from Kovalenko's apartment in Kyiv. By tonight, Gina will be DNA identified as Kovalenko. The consulate will request that her remains be cremated and returned to the real Kovalenko's sister in Ukraine. No one will know the difference. End of story."

"You are a genius, Mikhail. A pure genius."

"Now, Bodashka, you must make the real Marianna Kovalenko go away for good."

"Do you mind if I do it in the morning? I have a special evening planned."

"Kovalenko won't be going anywhere, so go have your fun tonight. She has no access to the news at the dacha, right?"

"Of course not. What about Freddy? Can he be connected to us?"

"He was under many layers of cover. No traceable links to Wiegatesland or me. The poor fool didn't even have a criminal record. The police will be scratching skin from their scalps for years trying to figure this whole thing out."

"Ha. It will become the mother of all cold cases. It would make a good plot for a Netflix mystery, wouldn't it? Whoever writes it could make a killing."

"Enough foolishness. There is more to finish with. It's time to take care of Bryson Witner."

"How will you do it?"

"I'll explain later. For now, go enjoy whatever you have planned, if you still can after what I've told you. Then, first thing in the morning, dispose of Ms. Kovalenko."

CHAPTER TWENTY-EIGHT

Kaitlyn awoke late the next morning. She and Uncle Jack had gotten home at four in the morning. As she lay there, daylight seeping through the curtains, memories resurfaced—the gunshot, how Marianna's body had slumped, the sickening give of it as she'd climbed into the front seat, jumping from the car, the sound of the shredder, standing by the shed and waiting for that man, the way his head jerked when the chunk of metal hit him, being in the emergency room, blood flowing from the vein in her elbow into the test tubes. And fear. Not fear itself, but the memory of what the fear had felt like.

She changed into jeans and a sweatshirt. The blue and white quilt Mrs. VanDyke had given her hung over the back of her desk chair. When she opened the door, she saw a large, dark blue object lying in the hall.

"Boo!" Kaitlyn's heart skipped a beat. Then Julia threw off the blanket. "Aunt Zoë told me not to wake you, so I stayed out here. Are you okay? Look at what I got." Julia held up her arm to show a pink cast encasing it from the hand to the elbow.

"Very cool."

"The doctor said it can come off by Christmas."

"How long have you been here?"

"Forever."

"I'm sorry I didn't bring you back your elephant at the hospital," Kaitlyn said, leaning back against the wall.

"It's okay. How come you've got all those bandages?"

"Just some cuts. No big deal."

"And what's that on your ankle?"

"It's an ace bandage. I've got a sprain."

"Can I see?"

Kaitlyn lowered herself onto the carpet and unrolled the bandage. Her ankle was a little swollen and black and blue on the outside. "It doesn't hurt much. Probably less than your arm."

"I missed breakfast too, like you, because I stayed up late waiting." Julia crawled close to her. "Aunt Zoë said someone tried to kidnap you, but you got away. Is that for real?"

Kaitlyn nodded. She didn't want to talk about it, but how did you tell that to a four-year-old? She felt warm air from the register waft across her feet.

"But why?" Julia pressed.

"Bad people do bad things. It's over now."

"It's almost time for lunch," Julia said. "Are you hungry?"

To her surprise, she was.

Zoë was sitting at the kitchen table reading. She hugged Kaitlyn long and tightly. "I was going to make a pizza for lunch but got lazy," she said. "How about toasted cheese sandwiches instead?"

"Where's Uncle Jack?" asked Kaitlyn.

"Back to the hospital—where else? Before I forget, he tried to call your stepmother last night but had trouble getting information across. You might want to give her a ring, before she reads about it in the paper."

"I don't think she reads the paper much."

"Still, a good idea."

"My phone's gone," Kaitlyn said. "I think the lady took it last night. It was probably in the car when it went through the shredder."

"Shredder?" asked Julia.

"Use mine," Zoë said. "You make the call, and I'll round up some grub."

"Don't say *grub*," said Julia. "It sounds like *bug*."

"By the way, Kaitlyn, Investigator Dirkens called. She wants to come over and talk with you."

"I've already told her everything."

Zoë handed her the phone, and Kaitlyn went to her bedroom. For a moment the spinning sensation she'd felt when she had woken up in the car returned. Lying down, she draped the quilt over her and pulled it up to her chin. The quilt still had the warm, wholesome smell of the VanDykes' house. The spinning went away but an ache rose behind her eyes as more memories resurfaced. She muffled a sob and heard the door creak open. Julia's head appeared. Kaitlyn sat up and blew her nose.

"Where'd you get the new blanket?" asked Julia.

"A nice lady." She let Julia climb up, awkwardly because of the cast. Kaitlyn put one arm around her, and with her free hand she called Stella's number. It rang several times before her stepmother answered.

"Hey," Kaitlyn said.

"Why are you calling from Zoë's number? What happened to your phone?"

Kaitlyn sighed. Julia was listening. "I don't have it anymore. Something bad happened last night."

"What was that?"

Kaitlyn hesitated. "I got kidnapped."

Stella was silent for a moment then made something like a laugh. "Oh, really? And what was his name?"

"How can you say that?" Anger swelling, Kaitlyn sat up straighter. "Do you want to hear what happened or not?"

"Did he take you to a motel?"

"That's awful," Kaitlyn said, trembling. "You have no idea."

"I was *kidnapped* when I was your age too. His name was Vince. So why don't you level with me?"

Kaitlyn moved Julia aside and stood, trying to hold back tears, feeling her throat tighten.

"Kaitlyn?" peeped Julia.

"I tell you one thing," said Stella. "You're getting a pregnancy test as soon as you get home. But that can wait till next week. Donald and I are going to celebrate my graduation. He's booked us an Airbnb at Reno Beach near Toledo for the weekend."

"He's what?" Kaitlyn closed her eyes and felt her chest tighten. Stella and that jerk were going to spend a weekend celebrating. The familiar ache bulged in her throat. Julia hugged her leg.

"It's not that far away, Kaitlyn," Stella said. "You'll be fine at home till we get back."

Her breath was coming faster. "I was almost killed, and you don't even want to listen to me! I'm coming home Friday and you're going away Saturday?"

"Actually, we're leaving Friday, sweetie. He's booked us starting Friday night. So we'll be home Sunday. You know where the spare key is. No friends over. No *kidnappings*. No booze, no drugs, no hamsters."

Kaitlyn wanted to scream. She wanted to throw something. She wanted to stab herself. Julia looked frightened, still sitting on the bed.

"Are you there?" Stella continued.

"I have to go now," Kaitlyn said sharply. "Aunt Zoë's made lunch. Julia's hungry."

"Did you hear what I told you?"

"Loud and clear."

"So, what time will you be getting here on Friday?"

Kaitlyn's breath was coming faster yet. Sharp pains jabbed at her breastbone. "Not sure. I've got to go. Bye." She threw the phone on the bed and moaned.

"Kaitlyn?" Julia said, her lower lip quivering. "Why doesn't she like you?"

Kaitlyn couldn't stop the tears. "I don't know. Because she's crazy. Because she thinks I killed my father."

"She thinks you killed your father?"

Kaitlyn looked at Julia. That was a stupid thing to say. "Forget I said that, okay? Just forget it, please."

Julia's cheeks were wet now too. "Why do you have to go back? Stay here."

Kaitlyn grabbed tissues. "I hate this. I hate this."

CHAPTER TWENTY-NINE

Time passed slowly for the real Marianna Kovalenko in the dacha south of Kyiv. The two goons watched television and ignored her, except to bang on the bathroom door if she spent more than a few minutes inside. They were stupid. The little man with the strange mustache had come by once and brought Chinese food. From overhearing the goons, she learned that his name was Bodashka Liski, and she filed that in her memory.

When they'd confiscated her tablet computer and cell phone on the first day, they'd also asked if she had a radio or any other electronics. "Just this MP3 player," she'd told them. She'd been gifted it for Christmas a couple years ago by a man she'd been dating, her last serious relationship. He'd gotten it with wireless earbuds.

"We don't care about that," the taller one had said, apparently thinking she'd meant it was just a music player and nothing else. "Listen to songs if you want."

What she didn't mention, however, was that the device was also an FM radio. It would be nice to follow the news. They also let her keep a notepad, pencils, and the books in her satchel. Thanks to that, she had completed an article and made good progress on translating a book of stories by the American writer Christine Sneed for a publisher in Kyiv. And she had revised some poems. But concentrating was difficult. They let her jog, so long as she stayed within range of the cameras that covered the dacha and several hundred yards up and down the road. She would run short loops for an hour each morning.

Which was what she was doing this Monday, the dawn air dark and misty. She was listening to music through her earbuds and imagined she was in Mariinskyi Park, her favorite place in Kyiv. It was time for the seven o'clock local news, so she switched the player to radio mode. The program's theme music began. Then came a commercial for Kompaniya Z's free retirement consultations, and after a fanfare of trumpets, the anchor spoke. Marianna knew her. Inna Limonov was a nice person, a new mother.

"Good evening, Kyiv and environs. Again, this morning we bring you the news and the truth behind the stories." But something was amiss. Inna's tone was dark. After a pause, she continued. "Some stories contain personal grief. I am sad to report that a Ukrainian citizen was killed over the weekend in New York State in America. The police are investigating her death as a homicide. The victim's body had suffered significant damage, we are told, making identification difficult. But a DNA match using a hairbrush has confirmed that the deceased was the award-winning *Ukrainian Week* writer, Marianna Kovalenko."

Marianna's heart began thudding violently. She stopped running and promptly vomited into the dirt. Inna Limonov's words became unhinged from any meaning. Swallowing back another wave of nausea, she fumbled to turn off the device and glanced at the dacha. There were lights in the windows. If she didn't move, they would think something was wrong. She began jogging again, her legs feeling waterlogged.

DNA identification using a hairbrush. What hairbrush? She only owned two. One was in her car and the other was here. It could not have been hers. How they managed it, she had no idea, but they were capable of such tricks and would do anything to cover their tracks. As clearly as if a photo had materialized, she saw what this meant. The woman had run afoul of something, then been killed. To protect themselves, she would also need to die. Her own identity had been murdered with the actress across the sea.

She jogged slowly, breathing hard through her nose, her skin prickling. *She would soon be dead.* Through the mist, she could see one of the cameras up on a pole. They hadn't come out when they saw her stop, meaning they weren't watching the monitor closely. Not surprising. They were not only stupid, but lazy. She must do something.

She saw a white car approaching through the trees. As it drew nearer, she heard the tires slithering on the dirt. It was Liski's vehicle. A tentacle of fear tightened around her neck. He was coming to kill her. If she tried to run off and succeeded, they would go after her sister for revenge. A plan took form. She would run away, get to a phone, and warn her sister to take the family and disappear. And if she could not reach her sister, she would return to the dacha and accept her own fate. What other choice did she have?

His car drew closer. She didn't think he had seen her yet. She ran to a corner where she believed the camera had a small dead zone and plunged into the forest.

CHAPTER THIRTY

At the knock on his office door, Jack took the phone away from his ear. He'd been listening to the same generic new age piano loop for the past ten minutes, waiting for someone who was supposed to be locating Damien Falconi.

"It's open," he called out.

Tré appeared. "They're here, chief."

A frosty-eyed Jan Cummings marched through the doorway, followed by Bentley. Jan's assistant had called to set up this meeting fifteen minutes ago. They hadn't wasted time getting here. Neither met his eyes.

"Finish your call," she said. "We can wait outside, if you'd like."

"No need." He set the phone down. "I was on hold."

As they gathered at Jack's conference table, Bentley said, "If by any chance you were calling Mr. Falconi, be advised that we've signed a letter of intent with HWA this morning. The ink is dry."

Jack inhaled sharply. He'd been expecting this, but it still packed a gut punch.

Bentley continued. "I didn't see you at Judy Marsh's memorial service yesterday evening."

"Couldn't make it. We had a crisis at home."

"I would say you did," said Jan. "It's the talk of the town. Please reassure me that your niece is all right. She seemed like such a fine kid."

"It was a major ordeal, but she's safe and sound."

"What exactly happened?" Jan inquired. "The news story was light on details."

Jack spent several minutes describing last night's events. Though he spoke quickly and evenly, looking down at the top of his desk and revolving a pen in his hand, inside he was reliving it all again. When he finished, he looked up at them, both Jan and Bentley were staring at him in silence.

After a moment, Jan shook her head and spoke. "Good God. So this Marianna woman was trying to get drugs out of your car and Kaitlyn was in the wrong place at the wrong time."

"That's what it looks like. All we have are questions right now."

Bentley cleared his throat. "The major issue to my mind is why a foreign journalist was invited into the inner circle of this university without having been properly vetted. PR says they weren't given so much as a courtesy call, which is standard procedure. You are not aware of that?"

Jack felt heat rush into his face. "I'm not going to make excuses. I made the wrong decision. She had a letter from Jason Everts and she was on his schedule, but I didn't check it out thoroughly."

"True," said the provost. "Had Jason vetted her?"

"I don't know."

"You definitely should have gone through channels, Jack," Jan said. "But I must admit, I did *not* sense anything strange about her." She sighed. "So much for my powers of intuition. And, as a matter of fact, Martin, you didn't look too suspicious when you were with her, either."

"This is why we have protocols," Bentley retorted. "At any rate, isn't it reckless to keep medications in your car, Forester? Is it even legal?"

"I'm still an emergency physician, remember?"

"But how much do you practice?"

Jan held up her hand. "Enough, Martin. We didn't come here to put Jack on trial. What's done is done." She heaved another sigh. "But that said, Jack, I won't beat around the bush." Her eyes shifted to the window. "After the signing with HWA this morning, we had an emergency board meeting."

Jack felt his throat tightening.

Jan went on. "Owing to your approval of a flawed study protocol in the step-down unit that may have resulted in the suicide of a patient—and your failure to vet that journalist—the board questions your ability to continue leading this medical center. I've been asked to request your resignation." She leaned back, folding her arms.

He stared at the tabletop. Its surface glowed with reflected light, making it look as if you could throw a stone and watch ripples radiate.

"This was a difficult decision," she said.

"You've had a good run up to now," Bentley said. "But there's too much water over the dam. Or under the bridge. The optics of you remaining are too negative. Thankfully, things are going to start running more smoothly. Immediately."

Jack glared up. "How do you mean?"

Bentley shot a look at Jan Cummings. "How much can I divulge about the IT situation?"

"I see no harm in sharing it."

"Sharing what?" Jack demanded.

"The analysis of the possible causes of our financial meltdown is complete," the provost said. "Our firewall wasn't breached, but the experts couldn't rule out the potential of some tampering with the software. HWA is going to be proactive and install a brand new, state-of-the-art, intrusion-hardened electronic information system, and all the hardware will be upgraded. For both the med center and the main campus. New accounting software too. It's a ninety-million-dollar investment that Mr. Haines is triggering today. I'd say this bodes well for the acquisition."

"Our whole IT department is in need of reorganization," Jan said. "They discovered that scores of individuals no longer with the university—some who have been gone for as long as ten years—still had full network access."

Bentley sniffed. "One of them, Forester, you'll be interested to know, was your old acquaintance, the psychopath Dr. Bryson Witner. He was still logging in occasionally over the past six years from wherever they've got him locked up now. I imagine that sends a chill up your spine the way it does mine."

It did. Could the news get any more dismal? He gazed out the window where the edge of the eastern clinical tower looked like a razor slicing the gray sky.

"Martin tells me that you were responsible for bringing that murderer to justice," said Jan.

"My wife and I just followed up on some suspicions."

"And I understand he almost killed you both."

"He came close, yes."

"It's a shame you didn't have suspicions about the Ukrainian journalist," chirped Bentley.

It was a gratuitous jab. Jack looked at Jan, half expecting her to rein in the arrogant bastard. But she didn't. It was as if he'd never seen her before, had never noticed how angular her face was, how deep the shadows beneath her cheekbones were.

"What now?" asked Jack. "Do I get escorted out to the parking lot?"

"Of course not," she said. "You can thank me for that. For the sake of the institution, I'm asking—and hoping—that you stay for the rest of the week."

"But if you want to leave sooner than Friday, we'd understand," said Bentley. "We could live with it either way."

I bet you could. He glanced at the table again and considered the situation. Looking up, he said, "I'll stay till Friday."

Jan nodded. "Good. I'm sure that's not easy. Thank you."

"Nothing to thank me for," Jack replied, stiffly. "I'd like to be the one to tell the staff about the acquisition by Health Wealth Associates."

Bentley straightened and looked at Jan. "I'm not sure that's wise."

Jack felt a flare of fury. "Only a real son of a bitch would suggest I might poison the well," he said, trying to control his tone. "These are my colleagues and friends, and I love this place. My only goal would be to reassure them."

Face darkening, Bentley visibly swallowed.

"This is my call, Martin," Jan said. "I think his request is reasonable. Let me think about it, Jack. I'll let you know later today. Fair enough?"

"Thank you," he said.

"And I am sincerely glad your niece is okay," she added, rising to her feet. "Pass on good wishes from me. I'm sorry things played out this way."

CHAPTER THIRTY-ONE

After the interview with Investigator Dirkens was over, Kaitlyn went into the bathroom and cried. In the mirror her face grew red and blotchy. Was she going to feel like this the rest of her life? She splashed her face with cold water and went out. Back in the kitchen, the investigator was putting on her coat, still talking with Aunt Zoë. Their voices lowered when Kaitlyn entered.

"That's an excellent idea, Ms. Andersen," Frances Dirkens said, glancing with a smile at Kaitlyn. "I highly recommend it."

Kaitlyn stopped. They were talking about her. "What's an excellent idea?"

Zoë folded her arms and looked at her. "I told the investigator that you're going to be seeing a counselor."

Kaitlyn sighed. It wasn't the idea of seeing a counselor, but the fact that Zoë didn't talk with her first. "Do I really need that?"

"You'll be glad you did," said the investigator.

She sighed again and looked away. Zoë came over and put her arm around her. Kaitlyn relaxed.

"Got to be going," said Dirkens.

Zoë and Kaitlyn walked her to the door. The air was cold outside. As Dirkens got into her car, Kaitlyn saw another vehicle coming up the driveway.

"Who now?" Zoë sighed. "This is turning into Grand Central Station."

"It's Aishia and Hassan," Kaitlyn said. "She wanted to come over after school and I told her it was okay. Do you mind? I forgot to tell you."

When Aishia had called Kaitlyn to ask why she wasn't in school, Kaitlyn had told her everything about the previous night.

"Of course I don't mind," Zoë said, going out with Kaitlyn to meet them.

Hassan eased his car up near the garage, making room so that Dirkens could turn around and depart. Aishia was out of the car before it completely stopped. She jogged over and hugged Kaitlyn. "My God, I'm so glad you're okay. I couldn't think of anything else all day."

Hassan had stayed in the car. They could hear music playing through the closed windows.

"Is he coming in?" asked Zoë.

"He's shy," said Kaitlyn.

"No, he's just antisocial," offered Aishia.

Zoë looked at the boy through the windshield. "Well, he's not going to sit out there," she concluded. "Tell him to come on in."

Down in the basement, Hassan pulled up a chair by the TV and switched it to ESPN. Kaitlyn and Aishia sat together on the couch. Julia knelt on the rug and wrapped her arm around Kaitlyn's leg.

"How are you, Miss Julia?" Aishia said, scratching the top of her head. "I love your cast. I want one too."

"Do you guys want to go outside and play hide-and-seek?" Julia asked.

"No," said Kaitlyn. "*We* guys are going to talk now."

"But Aunt Zoë won't let me go out by myself."

"It'll be dark soon anyway," Aishia said. "And it's cold."

"I've been thinking a lot about something, Aishia," Kaitlyn said.

"I'm surprised you can still think at all. The whole thing sounds like such a nightmare."

"I hate nightmares," added Julia.

"Hey, Jules," said Kaitlyn. "Would you do me a favor?"

"If you take me outside and play hide-and-seek," Julia said.

"Not today. But I promise I will soon. Would you go up to my room and find my blue scrunchie?"

Julia bounded up the stairs.

"Do you really have a blue scrunchie?" asked Aishia.

"Yes, but I haven't seen it in weeks." Kaitlyn lowered her voice and leaned closer toward her friend, smelling the bright floral scent of fabric softener. "I'm not going to go back with Stella."

Aishia grabbed Kaitlyn's arm. "Yes, Kaitlyn! Yes! When did you decide?"

"Just this morning. I haven't even told Aunt Zoë."

"Do you think your Uncle Jack will let you?"

"I'm not sure. We actually had a really good talk when he drove me home last night, but he's under a lot of stress. I don't know how to go about this. Maybe it isn't even legal. Could Stella try and have the police take me back?"

"I can't believe they'd do that."

"If I need to run away, that's what I'll do. I am never going back."

"Guys," said Hassan.

They both looked at him. He had muted the TV. Kaitlyn felt her face flush. "You shouldn't eavesdrop, Hassan," said Aishia.

"You shouldn't talk so loud. If you want my advice, Kaitlyn, you should talk to a lawyer or somebody like that. You need a solid strategy."

"I don't know any lawyers."

"How about Mr. Brady?" offered Aishia.

Hassan raised his eyebrows. "Is he a lawyer?"

"No, silly. He's our guidance counselor. But I bet he would know the best way to do this."

Kaitlyn nodded. "Good idea. I'll talk to him tomorrow."

"Found it! Found it!" shouted Julia, hopping down the stairs waving a scrunchie.

Julia was already in bed and Kaitlyn was in her room when she heard a car in the driveway. It was a quarter past nine. The garage door hummed as it opened. She'd been rehearsing what she would say. *Uncle Jack, I really like it here, so what would you think* . . . No, she couldn't just jump into it like that. Or should she? She hadn't told Zoë yet. Maybe she should start there. But she wanted him to respect her, not to think she was hiding behind Zoë. She would discuss it with them both together. *Yes.*

She set down her book. Steeling her nerves, she walked up the hallway. He was standing in front of the microwave. "Hi, Uncle Jack."

"Hi, Kaitlyn." He sounded tired, but he looked at her kindly and asked how she was doing. "By the way," he said. "Ms. Cummings from the university sends good wishes to you. You made a fine impression."

The microwave dinged and he took out a plate of leftovers just as Zoë came in from the living room. "Jack, I would have gotten that for you."

"No problem." He set the plate on the table, then got a bottle of wine out of the fridge and poured a glass. His eyes looked half closed.

Zoë sat across from him. "You're home later than you said. I was about to give you a call." Kaitlyn sat too. Zoë looked at her, raising her brows. "You still hungry, dear?"

"No, I'm fine," she said. "Just wanted to take a break."

Zoë turned to Jack. "Investigator Dirkens came and talked to Kaitlyn. She seemed very kind."

He looked at Kaitlyn. "How did it go?"

"Not bad. Lots and lots of questions."

"I'd say," said Zoë. "She still doesn't have any idea what that woman was up to."

"We're all in the dark," Uncle Jack said. Then he sighed and set down his fork, pushing the plate away. "Something else happened today. I might as well tell you now."

"Yes?" Zoë asked. "What is it?"

He folded his hands. "There's no reason to sugarcoat this. Long story short—the university asked me to resign."

"You can't be serious," said Zoë.

Kaitlyn could feel the muscles along her back tighten. She watched him take a long sip of the wine. Color seemed to leave his face.

"I'm afraid so. It's all the recent things. The board lost confidence."

"But you've been there for so long and have done so much good. They're making you a scapegoat."

"I don't disagree," he said, looking over at her.

"They can't sacrifice you like this. You should get a lawyer and sue those idiots."

"Zoë, I know you mean well, but enough, please. The hospital is being sold to HWA and that's that. We'll get through it."

Kaitlyn could see his eyes glisten in the light.

"I've got a right to be angry on your behalf," Zoë added.

"Me too, Uncle Jack," Kaitlyn said, her heart sinking further as she realized this was not going to be the night to talk about her staying.

"I'm going to be okay," he said, his voice firmer. "We're all going to be okay. I'll be staying for the rest of the week. I haven't had time to think about what comes next."

"Could they change their minds?" urged Kaitlyn.

He looked her in the eyes, his expression tired but warm. Her heart melted.

"They don't usually walk back decisions like this. No more talking about it tonight, though, okay?"

Uncle Jack finished his glass of wine and poured another. Zoë took the bottle and poured herself a glass. Kaitlyn thought of Mr. Brady. She needed to talk to him, get his advice on everything.

"By the way, Jack, before I forget," Zoë said. "I called the psychologist you mentioned this morning. Kaitlyn has an appointment Thursday afternoon. I talked to her when she returned my call. She said that if Kaitlyn was having trouble sleeping, she could take a single Benadryl tablet. Is that okay?"

He nodded.

"I don't have PTSD," Kaitlyn said.

"You don't know that," Zoë replied firmly. "And I think you should stay home again tomorrow and get some more rest."

"No," Kaitlyn said. "I'm okay talking to a counselor, but I'd really like to go back to school tomorrow and finish up."

Uncle Jack looked at Zoë. "I think it would be good for her."

Zoë seemed to resign. "Fine, then."

"How was Tony doing today?" he added.

"Pretty much the same," Zoë said. "He was napping on and off most of the day. But he did talk to Kaitlyn a little over supper, which was good."

Kaitlyn looked at him to see his response.

"Good," he said.

CHAPTER THIRTY-TWO

Anticipating an avalanche of questions, Kaitlyn didn't ride the bus to school on Tuesday morning. After Aunt Zoë dropped her off, she went straight to Mr. Brady's secretary and signed up for his first open slot. Eleven o'clock.

Strangely enough, it was as if no one seemed to have heard about what happened to her on Sunday. Or if they had heard, they were shy about approaching her. No one paid her any unusual attention as she walked toward the lockers. Maybe a few extra looks.

Aishia dashed up to her by their lockers. "Did you see Mr. Brady yet?"

"Not yet. Eleven o'clock."

Aishia hugged her then pushed away, cleared her throat, and spoke in a whisper. "You'll never guess who's coming this way."

"Who?"

Kaitlyn turned and stared. Conrad Greer was walking hesitantly in her direction. She looked away, then looked back. When he got a couple of steps away, he stopped and did something with his lips that resembled a wobbly smile. She met his eyes, noticing that he didn't smell like a gym sock today.

"Got to get going," said Aishia. "See you later." She scurried away.

"Hi," Conrad said.

"Hi."

"Listen, that was pretty strange the other day," he said. "You know—what happened with everything." His cheeks were turning pink.

"Yeah," she said. "It was. So, how are you feeling?"

"I'm okay. Pretty good." He touched the back of his head. "I'm getting the stitches out in two days. They itch." He turned so she could see the back of his head. An area on his scalp the size of a lemon had been shaved to the skin, which was white. A row of black stitches ran diagonally across the open area like a set of railroad tracks.

The thought occurred to her that someday she might sew up a cut like that. "Looks better than it did," she said. "It really bled a lot."

"I don't remember much about it. But what I wanted to say was, like, this whole thing wasn't your fault. What I was saying was dumb. I'm sorry about that."

"Okay," she said. "But it takes two to tango."

"What?" His blush deepened.

"Never mind."

"So, I'm working on some things inside myself," he said. He looked so awkward she almost smiled.

"That sounds good," she said.

"Sweet," he said. "Well, hey, listen, take care." He turned to go but glanced back again. "By the way, do you like to be called Kaitlyn or Kate?"

"Kaitlyn."

"Okay, cool. Kaitlyn. See you around."

At eleven o'clock she went to Mr. Brady's office.

"Kaitlyn Andersen," he said, rising. "A sight for sore eyes. I wasn't sure we'd see you back this week."

"I wasn't either," she said.

"Sit down, please. If a tenth of what I read is true, you went through a lot. Are you doing all right?"

"I'm okay."

"A little okay or a lot okay?"

"In between." She looked down and wondered if this was such a good idea. But it was too late. "Aunt Zoë made me an appointment to see a counselor, but I'm not sure I really need it."

"I think it can't hurt, right?" he said. "Listen, we're really going to miss you. Are things going okay in Dayton with your stepmom?"

"That's what I wanted to talk about."

"Okay. I'm all ears."

"I don't want to go back there." She cleared her throat. "No, what I really mean is that I'm not going to go back. Period. She hasn't changed. I can't handle it anymore." She described the call with Stella the previous day, the boyfriend coming back, the trip to Reno Beach, Stella not being there on Saturday. "I know what'll happen if I go back there. I'm going to be angry and sad and frustrated. I'll want to hurt her and I'll want to hurt myself for being so stupid to ever care about . . . her. Or about anything."

He'd been listening intently. Nodding, he said, "Have you talked to your uncle about this?"

"Not yet. He's under a lot of stress. But he's been . . . I don't know exactly why, but he's been friendlier to me. I almost think he likes me."

"Why would he not like you?"

"Zoë thinks he's still mourning for Aunt Zellie. But I don't know why that should make him hate me."

"Well, sometimes grief can mess people up. I wondered about that. But this is good, Kaitlyn, this decision. You're thinking for yourself."

"Mr. Brady, I know that my stepmother is going to explode when she finds out. I'm not sure what to do." She hesitated. "Do I need a lawyer?"

"Yes. You will. But this isn't the first time I've helped someone in this situation. I know an attorney who works with Child Protective Services. She'd help you and your uncle file a petition with a judge showing why it would be in your best interest to stay here. I would be more than happy to testify in favor of that."

"How long does it take?"

"Probably just a few weeks."

"Would I have to go back with Stella in the meantime?"

"The lawyer can file for an emergency order of protective custody so you could stay here."

"That would be amazing. But I need to talk to Uncle Jack."

"Yes. As soon as possible."

"He won't have to pay for me," she said. "I'll get a job and give him room and board. And I'll babysit Julia for free."

Brady smiled. "Well, I'm sure you'll work it out. But please tell Dr. Forester that I'm one hundred percent on board and will help however I can. I'll reach out to the attorney now."

"Mr. Brady, thank you."

"No, thank *you*, Kaitlyn," he said, extending his hand. "You've made my day."

CHAPTER THIRTY-THREE

Jack arrived at his office and stopped at Tré's desk. "Hey, come on back with me," he said. "Let's talk." Inside the inner office, Jack motioned toward the upholstered chairs in front of the little gas fireplace, and they sat across from each other.

"Let's go out for lunch on Friday, just you and me," Jack said. "Someplace nice."

"I'd enjoy that, sir."

"And Tré, on a personal note, you've done a terrific job in this position. The incoming dean will need your experience. I hope you'll consider staying."

Tré looked down and grimaced. "They've already reached out to me. I got a call from their corporate office first thing this morning."

Jack nodded and clenched his jaws. This would be his life over the next few days as his power drained away. He wasn't running a ship anymore. The ship had sunk and the current was flowing around him. He might as well steel himself. It was only going to get worse.

"And you accepted, I hope?" he asked.

"Not yet. If you need a good administrative assistant in your next job, sir, please think of me. I'd much rather work for you."

"That's kind, but I have no idea what I'll be doing. In the meantime, we've got work to do. I know it's short notice, but I'd like you to set me up a meeting this afternoon with all department chairs, program directors, the VP of Nursing, the Chief Medical Officer, and any senior resident that can make it. Reserve the Gavin Lecture

Hall. It should be open then. We'll need about an hour. Call it an 'announcement of coming changes,' or something like that. I want to give them my take on what to expect with the HWA transition and tell them about my departure."

"Sounds good, sir. Are you sure you only want an hour?"

"Better make it ninety minutes."

"Will do. By the way, an Investigator Dirkens called and wants to stop by and see you. I told her I'd call her and let her know a good time."

"Thanks. Tell her I'll be free after this meeting with the staff. About four thirty. And as for HWA giving you an offer to stay, I recommend you take it. See how things go for a few months. There are a lot of changes coming, and you've got a steady hand."

He spent the rest of the morning and early afternoon tying up loose ends and jotting down ideas about what he would say. Ten minutes before the meeting, he headed to the Gavin Lecture Hall, reviewing those ideas in his mind. Preoccupied, he collided with someone barreling out of a side corridor. It was Dr. Annabel Singh, the chief pathologist, a tall lady with graying hair in a ponytail.

"Jack, I'm so sorry," she said. "Did I hurt you?"

"No. My fault. How about you?"

"I'm too tough for you to injure. But this is fortuitous. I was hoping to catch you before going to the meeting."

"Let's walk and talk. What's on your mind?"

"It's about Chad Chadwick's postmortem results. I understand you knew him."

Jack told her about Chad's friendship with his brother. They came to the elevators. He pressed the down button and checked his watch, wondering if this meeting was a good idea after all. Did he have what it took to balance honesty with reassurance? He was going to get hammered with questions.

"What do you know of this boy's usage of street drugs?" she was saying. "Was he a drug user?"

"Chad Chadwick? I highly doubt it. Maybe a little cannabis occasionally, but he was a solid individual. To the best of my knowledge. Why do you ask?"

"Something may be showing up on the tox screen. Not sure yet. I'll get back to you when I know more."

"Sounds good."

They entered the elevator, and it began a slow descent into the lion's den.

The Gavin auditorium was already packed and loud with conversation when Jack strode onto the elevated speaker's platform, feeling the old floorboards creak. He went to the lectern. This was the same sturdy prop upon which his professors in med school two decades ago had placed their notes. Made of cherrywood, it bore an intricately carved wooden vine around the top edge that was worn smooth by generations of professorial hands.

He gazed out over the rows of seats sloping up to the back entrance a floor above, his throat tightening. There must be over a hundred fifty people here already, with more trickling in. The senior faculty were well outnumbered by the junior faculty and chief residents, many of whom wore scrubs in colors keyed to their department—blue for ED, green for OB, black for anesthesia, maroon for surgery.

Though he still got butterflies before giving a lecture, he felt a different kind of anticipation now, one mingled with anger and frustration. He inhaled deeply several times to settle his nerves and remembered the first time he'd sat in this room. It was twenty years ago, his first day of med school, when Dr. Gavin, one of the school's longest-serving deans who would later become a friend and mentor, gave the class a "welcome to this honored profession" talk.

The clock on the back wall said three minutes after three. He tapped the microphone and spoke. "Can you hear me in back?" This would be his last time standing here. He would go out with dignity. Quiet settled over the auditorium. "Thank you for taking time out of your busy schedules. You all received an email today from President Cummings regarding the fact that the university has decided to move forward with a plan for the medical center to be acquired by Health Wealth Associates. You may have also heard rumors that I'll be leaving. My intention today is to share with you everything about the situation that I've been made privy to. After that, we'll open the floor to questions."

He paused. The calm before the storm. Scanning the rows, he noticed a woman in the very back with hair the same color and length as Zellie's. His chest contracted, and for an instant he was all but certain it was her. But that was insane. He heard people stirring in their seats, throats clearing.

For the next half an hour, he described the financial crisis, the lack of options, and so forth, then devoted the final minutes to his imminent departure. He ended by expressing his gratitude for having had the opportunity to occupy a role he'd never dreamed possible when he was a boy growing up in New Canterbury.

Then the questions. All the frustration in the lecture hall burst forth. It felt like he was standing at the base of a dam that had sprung multiple leaks. *Would HWA be cutting staff? Why weren't other options explored? Would the academic mission change? How will this affect grant funding or promotions? Might the medical school close? Why weren't they involved in the decision?* Many, many variations of this last question. On and on.

As he attempted to give considered responses, his eyes were drawn from time to time to the woman who resembled his dead wife, but with each glance, she resembled Zellie less and less. Underneath his blazer, the back of his shirt was soaked in sweat. Droplets trickled down the sides of his chest. It was not until five fifteen that he brought the session to a close and the attendees departed, leaving only one person sitting in the back row. It was Investigator Frances Dirkens. He had completely forgotten about their four thirty meeting. She rose and descended as Jack climbed off the platform.

"No need to apologize," she said. "Your assistant brought me down." She wore a blue sweater and was carrying a tan overcoat on her arm. "Sounds like you've got a mess on your hands. Did I hear rightly that you're leaving?"

"That's correct"

"Sorry to hear it, and your colleagues here sure didn't sound happy either. So, the finances are bad enough you need to sell the hospital to a chain. I'm surprised. I thought the place was healthy."

"So did most of us."

"But is merging with a larger organization necessarily a bad thing?"

"HWA is coming here to exploit, not to develop. That's just my opinion, for what it's worth."

"I'm inclined to believe you," she said. "And I'm very sorry. Shall we talk here? I won't keep you long."

"Here's fine." They settled into front-row chairs.

"I interviewed Kaitlyn again today," she said. "A very articulate young lady. Among other things, she told us that while you pumped gas, Marianna told her she had a three-year-old daughter. Which is interesting, because the profile we got from Kyiv indicates she was unmarried and childless. But maybe she'd given it up for adoption. Who knows? I was tempted to give my son away a few times. Did Marianna mention having a child to you?"

"We never discussed anything personal."

"But you found her credible? No cracks in her story?"

"Nothing. But there were no deep dives."

"In any case, we've got DNA confirmation. We received hair samples and prints from a hairbrush of Kovalenko's, and they all match up with what was found at the crime scene. She was Marianna Kovalenko from Kyiv. And those same prints match the ones on the ketamine vial from your kit. Oh, and your niece indeed had ketamine in her blood."

"That's what it sounded like."

"According to Interpol, one of her coworkers at *Ukrainian Week* said it was strange she didn't tell anyone before she left. But her editor didn't think it was unusual."

"It all makes no sense," Jack said.

"We can assume she kidnapped your niece because Kaitlyn saw her getting it. My big question is why she wanted ketamine in the first place. Dr. Forester, did you see any indication that she might have been addicted to it?"

"Ketamine addiction is possible but very uncommon."

"Maybe ketamine abuse is more prevalent in Ukraine. I'll check that angle. But even if she were a ketamine junkie, why take Kaitlyn to the scrapyard? Why did the manager allegedly shoot her? Not your typical response to a trespasser."

"The whole thing makes my head spin," Jack said.

"Yep. Some puzzle pieces are hiding in the weeds. It must be like you trying to name a disease when all you have are a few mysterious symptoms." She rose. "Thanks for your time. Call me if any ideas pop up. And good luck with all of this."

CHAPTER THIRTY-FOUR

It was after nine o'clock at night when Kaitlyn borrowed Zoë's phone and donned a jacket. Out on the front deck, she slid a chair over where she could see the lights of New Canterbury sparkling like a nest of fireflies. Draping Mrs. VanDyke's quilt over her legs, she leaned back and found herself yawning.

She hadn't slept well last night, visions of the scrapyard's shadows and silhouettes in the glare of harsh lights intruding as she would start to drop off. Before she'd gone to bed, Aunt Zoë had offered her a Benadryl, but she'd left it on her nightstand. What if she ended up like Stella and all her pills? But she'd searched Benadryl, and everything said it wasn't addicting. Maybe she'd take one tonight, depending.

It was so quiet out here. Only the occasional sigh of a distant car. After days of clouds, the sky was clear. No moon, just stars that were so much brighter than back in Dayton where streetlamps burned from dusk to dawn and trucks roared by on the highway at all hours. This sky was magical. Staring up, she wondered what the stars were all about. Why were there stars instead of just nothing? Why was there anything at all? It was not a frightening thought. Just mysterious. She hadn't been to church since before her father died. As a sense of wonder blossomed, she resolved never to forget this moment. She keyed in Aishia's number on the cold glass of the screen.

"Who is this?" answered Aishia.

"Hi, it's me. This is Zoë's phone. I wish you were here. I'm out on the deck and the stars are amazing."

"Isn't it cold?"

"I'm under a quilt."

"I like to be outside when it's snowing and I'm dressed for it," Aishia said. "But I don't like the wind so much. Especially when you're wearing a dress. In college, I'm only going to wear dresses when I go on dates with handsome millionaires."

"Why don't you just become a banker or something?"

"Too boring. So, tell me! What did your uncle say? You don't sound sad, so it must be good news. I'm so excited."

"I didn't ask him yet."

"Kaitlyn! You have to. Don't put it off."

"He got home late again tonight. He looked so tired—I felt sorry for him. He went right to bed after supper."

"Are you sure they really fired him? I've never heard of a doctor getting fired."

"I know. But as soon as he comes home tomorrow, I'm going to get him and Zoë together and talk."

"Have you told her yet?"

"Not yet."

"You're procrastinating!"

"By tomorrow I'll have more information about the lawyer that Mr. Brady is going to talk with. Whatever it costs Uncle Jack to keep me here, I'll pay him back. I'll even sign a legal IOU."

"You're so funny. Hey, listen, tomorrow's a half day at school. Why don't you ride the bus home with me at noon? Hassan can drive you home after supper. Then you can talk to them."

"I promised Zoë I'd babysit. She's got a doctor's visit tomorrow afternoon and then a hairdresser's appointment. Seriously, I wish you were here to see this crazy beautiful sky. I'll Instagram you." Kaitlyn couldn't stifle a huge yawn that morphed into a long sigh.

"Are you okay?"

"Just super tired."

Marianna Kovalenko was also having difficulty sleeping. For the past nine hours, she had been mulling over the past week's events as she sat cramped between a large Polish woman and a tall Polish man in the middle aisle of an Airbus A330. It was only when the flight attendant announced they would be on the ground at Kennedy Airport in fifteen minutes that her concentration, like the legs of a marathon runner just past the finish line, gave in to gravity and relaxed. The attendant's voice became a lullaby as she described the sunny weather and the temperature as a mild fifty-eight degrees. The aircraft bumped through some turbulence, swaying, and she let her eyes drift shut. The past folded back over the present and the Polish man's snoring became the rustling of her footfalls and her own breathing as she fled through the forest. She had struck out eastward toward the river, but fearing they would intercept her, she'd angled south then west, using the sun to keep her bearing, halting every few minutes to listen. She could no longer hear Liski shouting at the goons. The beech trees gave way to oak and poplar. Half an hour later she came to a road and waited for a break in traffic, then darted across and climbed an embankment into dense trees again. Then came a smaller road where she saw a Renault pull up to the single pump of an ancient gas station. A woman in a black dress emerged. A man came out and pumped. After he went back inside, Marianna approached the woman. Yes, she was going to Kyiv. Yes, she would take her.

The woman kept glancing over at her and finally said that if she was running away from someone, she should go to the police. Marianna shook her head. Even after the reforms of 2014, many police still could not be trusted. The woman turned to talking about God, Christ, and Satan. She was a Jehovah's Witness—and she'd lectured Marianna on how to save her life and seek justice.

It was early afternoon when the woman had dropped her off, giving her a handful of pamphlets. Her own apartment wouldn't be safe, so she had gone to her old friend Anatoly, using the back stairs. Once there, she called her sister Olesia and described what had happened. *You must take your husband and daughters and flee immediately. Just go.* Then with Anatoly's help, she withdrew money, secured travel, and called another friend for a new passport. She got a burner phone and hair dye. It would not be safe to depart from the Kyiv airport, so shortly after midnight, she had lifted off from the little private strip in Bucha in a single engine plane flown by the friend of a friend who navigated them to Chopin Airport in Warsaw, three hours of flying through darkness. At five in the morning she boarded LOT Flight 2587 in Warsaw and flew westward, the sunrise always behind them but slowly gaining as they passed through six time zones

The impact of the wheels slamming onto the runway jolted her awake. For a panicked moment she feared she was packed in a cell with the others. Then the lights came on and window shades slid up. The flight attendant welcomed them to New York. Remembering her burner phone, she grabbed it and switched off the airplane mode. The man beside her was shuffling things in his briefcase. A skyline appeared outside. She'd always wanted to visit New York, but not like this.

The phone suddenly vibrated, startling her. Two text messages, initially sent sometime during those hours above the ocean, had hit her inbox. The first was from Olesia, who had promised to give her regular progress reports as she and her family made their way to Rennes in northwestern France, where Olesia's husband had a close friend. The message had been posted six hours ago while Olesia was passing through Frankfurt. They were safe and making good time.

She opened the second message. It was from Aleksander, her graphic designer friend who had created her new passport. A tingle of horror crept up her spine. Anatoly, whom she had gone to first, was in the hospital, badly beaten, still unconscious. They had tortured him for information. *Marianna, be on high alert. He may have told your plans.*

A bell chimed, and the sound of seatbelts clicking open was like the scuttling of crabs. She could not repress a sob. The Polish lady asked if she was all right. Waves of guilt and anger washed over her. Inhuman monsters. They had left Anatoly for dead. All he had done was try to help her. He had known where she was going. It was possible that American henchmen of the oligarch were already waiting, scanning flights. Their reach was very long. Her only disguise was her hair, now short and black instead of long and chestnut. The passengers were rising. She stood, pulled her hat low—it was a Boston Red Sox baseball cap Anatoly had lent her—and retrieved her bag, a small canvas valise, from the overhead. It was all she had. Please God, let Anatoly survive.

She followed the others past the flight attendant. Cold air carried the smell of a city and jet fuel. She strode up the ramp, head down, gazing at the legs of the kind Polish lady who was wearing red flats, her ankles puffy. She needed to find someplace private to make the call. In the wide hallway of the terminal, sunlight poured through huge windows and the sky was a pale hazy blue. She kept pace with the others. The English language flowed around her like a muddy river.

She came to a concourse lined by restaurants and stores and felt a stab of hunger. The last thing she'd eaten was a package of smoked salmon in Warsaw, the taste of which still clung to her teeth. To her left she saw a men's clothing store. It was large and empty. She strode in between a rack of dress shirts and a display of ties and belts. She came to the rear by a row of blazers. Taking out the burner phone, she looked around. A young Black man with dreadlocks was coming toward her. He was dressed in a black suit with a thin orange tie.

"Could I help you find something?" he said. His smile displayed silver braces.

"May I make a call here?" she asked. "I will try not to bother anyone."

He smiled with cheer. "Not much danger of that. I thought you were going to be my first customer. Sure, help yourself."

While waiting in the Warsaw airport, she'd found the number on the internet, committing it to memory. It rang twice before a man answered. "FBI," he said. "Callahan, here. How can I assist you?"

She took a deep breath. "Sorry, my English is now a little rusty."

"Take your time, ma'am."

She thought of the earnest, gray-haired Jehovah's Witness woman in the Renault who had driven her to Kyiv, proselytizing her faith. "It is urgently necessary that I be placed under witness protection."

"I'm afraid the Witness Protection Program falls under the US Marshals Service."

"They are not you?"

"It's a separate branch of the Justice Department, ma'am. You've reached the New York Field Office of the Federal Bureau of Investigation."

"You cannot help me with witness protection?"

"Why don't you tell me what's going on?"

"I was kidnapped in Ukraine and my identity was stolen. I escaped. They will be searching for me to kill me. I have information of great value to you about Russian criminals."

"Where are you right now?"

"I am at the JFK airport. I just flew from Poland. I was taken off the street in Kyiv by the men of a Russian oligarch. But I was able to get away."

"And when did this all happen?"

"My escape was yesterday. I made my way to Kyiv where friends helped me. But one of them was tortured for information, so they know I am here."

"Why didn't you go to the police there?"

"These have too many connections. Too much corruption in Ukraine."

"But you said you just flew in from Poland."

"Yes. I was flown in small plane to Warsaw. I leave under a new passport with a different name."

"You're using a false passport?"

"So that I could escape, yes. But I believe they now know I am here, and they will kill me if they find me. When I am in witness protection, I can give you much important information. I know witness protection is very safe in this country. I wrote about it one time. That is my work. I am a journalist. I believe these men work for the oligarch Mikhail Potemkin. Do you know who he is?"

"No, ma'am, I'm afraid that Russian oligarchs are not my area of expertise. Why would they kidnap you?"

"It was to steal my identity as journalist so that someone could impersonate me and come to New Canterbury Medical Center to spy on Dr. Forester. I do not know why. I can only ask you to please help me. Do you know of Dr. Forester?"

The man made a sigh then he chuckled. "Doesn't ring a bell."

She was breathing faster, her palms moist. "Can you help me find the right person to talk with? My life is at risk. The woman impersonating me was killed, and they proved with some fake DNA that she was me. To keep their lies hidden, they must kill me. Can you follow what I am saying?"

"Sounds like the plot of a spy novel."

"This is not a story, and I cannot help you if I am dead."

"I agree with you there," he said. "And you say the person they proved was you with DNA is dead?"

"Yes. And my sister will need protection too. They will seek revenge. And her family. They are fleeing to France now."

"Listen, ma'am, do you know how many prank calls we receive any given week?"

Her jaws tightened. "What are you saying?"

"Are you a Ukrainian citizen?"

"I am, yes."

"And you entered the US on a false passport, correct?"

"Thanks to my friends in Kyiv, yes." A band of frustration tightened around her chest. "Please, I don't think you under—"

"Here's what I think, ma'am. You should go to the Ukrainian consulate. It's on 49th Street in Manhattan. Let me check." A keyboard clicked in the background. "Yes. 240 East 49th Street."

"The consulate?"

"They should be able to help you."

"But I cannot trust anyone there. These people are smart."

"Are you talking about the consulate staff?"

"No! Those who kidnap me, who send the woman who died here."

"Ma'am, I'm going to have to hang up now. To get to the consulate, take the AirTrain from Kennedy to Jamaica—"

"Jamaica?"

"Jamaica, New York. It's not far from JFK. You can catch the subway from there into Manhattan. The subway maps will tell you how to get to 49th Street. The consulate can deal with your passport issue and help you apply for asylum. If your story checks out, they can put you in touch with the US Marshals Service for witness protection. If that's warranted."

Her arm holding the phone trembled. "You do not believe me."

"I don't believe or disbelieve. This is the best advice I can give you."

"But I need your help. I am not crazy!"

"Is there anything else I can help you with today?"

Tears streamed down her cheeks. She brushed them away. Sharp pains were stabbing her chest and her fingers tingled. The clerk was walking toward her, a concerned look on his face.

"But please, I need help," she said. "I can make you understand if you'll let me try. Can we meet?"

"I don't mean to be rude, ma'am, but I'm going to hang up now. Good luck to you."

The connection went dead. Her hand holding the phone dropped and the phone fell to the carpet. The clerk bent and picked it up. "Doesn't sound like that went well," he said.

She grabbed tissues from her purse. "I could not make him understand."

"Would you like to sit down? A water, maybe?"

She sighed, her chest shuddering. "I am not sure now what to do." She brought the tissues to her face and then looked sharply at him. "How much did you hear of what I said?"

"That he didn't want to meet. Looks like you've come a long way. You just arrived from overseas?"

"Yes. Warsaw." She stuffed the tissues into her coat pocket. "It is my fault. I thought it would be more simple. Stupid."

"You can hang out for a while here, if you need."

"I cannot stay. But thank you." She picked up her valise. "Do not concern yourself."

"Do you have any friends here? Have you ever been to New York before?"

"No." She straightened her shoulders. "The only one I know of here in America is the enemy of my enemy," she said.

"I'm not sure I follow."

"Maybe to him is where I should go. I will find out how to do this. Thank you for the kindness. I must leave."

"Hold on a minute," he said. "I might be able to help you."

"Why are you so kind? I have nothing to offer."

"Why? Listen, my mother was a refugee from Ghana. She came here with ten dollars. When we were growing up, we heard all these stories of people helping her. She would have wanted me to do the same."

"This might put you in danger."

"I can take care of myself. So, you're from Poland?"

"Ukraine."

"And you said you didn't have a friend, but you have the enemy of your enemy. Is this a good person?"

"Yes. He is in New Canterbury in the state of New York. Do you know?"

"I've heard of it. Let's go look on the computer. My name is Cornell."

Cornell found New Canterbury and showed her the map. It was reachable by bus and only three hours away. He bought her a

Greyhound ticket online and printed it. She tried to give him more than the amount, but he wouldn't take any extra. The bus was leaving from the Port Authority Bus Terminal in an hour and a half.

"Not much time," he said. "There are lots of ways to get lost for somebody new to the city. I'll take you to Port Authority myself."

He laughed away her protests. He would not get into trouble if he wasn't gone long. His boss owed him favors and was a friend of the family. He would get his car and meet her at the Uber pickup area out front in five minutes. He drove for Uber when he wasn't at the clothing store or studying.

She wended her way out of the terminal, staying within groups of people and looking for any sign of men following or lurking. Waiting close to a pillar outside, she saw him pull up. There appeared to be no one even looking at her. Sprinting out to the car, she climbed in and held her valise on her lap as he drove through the city of Queens and across the bridge onto the island of Manhattan, pointing out sights. He told her he was going to school at night to become an occupational therapist. He was learning the saxophone. If she had not been carrying the weight of Anatoly and Olesia and everything else, she would have enjoyed the conversation, the buildings, the people out walking, the broad river, and the wide streets.

He did not ask her too many questions, which was good—she hated to lie. When they came to the bus station, she thanked him from the bottom of her heart. "If all Americans are similar to you, Cornell, I know why this is a great country."

"Don't worry," Cornell said. "They're not."

CHAPTER THIRTY-FIVE

Tré hadn't laid eyes on Dr. Lawrence Haines before, but when an extremely tall man with a chiseled forehead and regal bearing strode into the reception area, he had a hunch and rose.

The man smiled and said, "Just passing by and thought I'd see if Dr. Forester could slip me in." Haines introduced himself, extending a hand as large as a baseball mitt.

"He's still at a lunch meeting, sir. He should be back very shortly. I can text and let him know you're here."

"Excellent," Haines said, glancing around. "Are you his receptionist?"

Tré introduced himself. "I'm his administrative assistant."

"The dean doesn't have a dedicated receptionist?"

"No. I'm the jack-of-all-trades."

"You must be stretched thin, Tré."

"Would you like to wait in the inner office, Dr. Haines?"

"That would be kind. So, Tré, have my people reached out to you about staying?"

"They did."

"And?"

"I believe I will, yes. Dr. Forester encouraged me."

"Excellent. We'll honor your experience, and we've got plenty of work to go around." The cell phone in Tré's belt holster chirped with a text. "Go ahead and check that if you need to," said Haines.

Tré read the message. "I'm being asked by one of the office

managers down the hall to help move a file cabinet. Could you excuse me for a minute?"

"You *are* a jack-of-all-trades. I don't see why we even have file cabinets anymore. May have to do something about that."

Soon enough Marianna had reason to appreciate Cornell's remark about all Americans not being like him. The taxi driver who ferried her from the New Canterbury bus station to the hospital gave her no hello, no smile, no warmth. "This is it, lady," he said, stopping near the front entrance.

"How much do I owe?"

"What it says there." He jabbed a finger at the meter. "Seventeen fifty."

Marianna handed him one of the twenty-dollar bills she'd gotten in Warsaw and waited for the change. He craned his neck and stared at her. "You really want something back?"

Realizing he was talking about a tip, she flushed and remembered reading that tipping was more expected and costly in America. But her resources were so limited. "Yes, please," she said. "The change."

He handed her two dollar bills and two twenty-five cent pieces. When she passed him back the two coins, he grimaced as if she had just dropped a turd on his palm.

"Thanks, lady," he said. Your bag's in the trunk. Get it yourself."

"And if you knew what I've been through," she said in Ukrainian, "maybe you wouldn't be such an asshole."

She got her valise and headed for the entrance, leaving the trunk lid open. She heard him get out and say something. No time to worry about it. The trees lining the walkway were decked in fall colors. The main doors whooshed open automatically. It was an elegant lobby. Tall windows of colored glass. The layout reminded her of the Feofaniya Hospital in Kyiv. She headed for the restroom. It was empty and warm and smelled very clean. Taking out her toilet kit, she washed her face, brushed her teeth, and applied deodorant, perfume, and a little makeup. Several women came in and out. "A long day for you too, honey?" one lady asked. "I've been here three days."

Her reflection in the mirror looked like a nightmare. The black hair made her resemble an anime character. Getting directions from a security guard, she rode an elevator to the fifth floor then strode down a long corridor that transitioned from modern to traditional, with dark tiles and wooden doors. Finally, she saw an arched entrance of dark polished wood with a placard that said *Dean's Suite*.

She was almost there when a man suddenly walked out. He was too young to be Dr. Forester, whose photo she had seen on the website. This man was skinny, and his hair was in a bun at the rear of his skull. He gazed at a cell phone and whistled as he sauntered past her. Standing at the entrance, she felt lightheaded and tired, her mouth dry. What if he wouldn't see her? What if he had gone away? What if he didn't care or wouldn't believe her? *What would she do next if this didn't work?*

She marched in past a glass case displaying antique medical instruments. There was a desk on one side and a waiting area on the other with a potted tree, a couch, and a coffee table laden with magazines. There was no one here. At the end was a closed door with a placard that read: *Jack Forester, MD, FACEP, Dean*. She went to the door, mouthed a silent prayer, and knocked.

A deep voice emerged from inside. "Come in."

She opened the door. A gray-suited man stood by the windows. He was silhouetted in the bright light and she could not distinguish his features. "Dr. Forester," she said, "please forgive my intrusion. But I am someone who has traveled far." She swallowed. "I need your help, and you may need mine."

"Miss, I'm afraid you're talking to the wrong person. I'm waiting for Dr. Forester myself." As he ambled toward her, she could see it was not Dr. Forester. "I'm Dr. Haines. Larry Haines."

"I am so sorry," she said, backing out the door. He was very tall. Very.

"No need to apologize."

She spun about, her face burning. At that moment the same skinny young man with the hair bun marched in under the archway. "Hello," he said, looking startled. "Can I help you?"

She glanced back toward Dr. Forester's office. The man was standing in the doorway watching. "I would like to talk please with Dr. Forester," she said to the young man.

"Do you have an appointment?"

She had thought of calling during the bus ride but decided against it. What would she have said? Better to beg forgiveness than ask for permission. "I tried to call but I could not get through," she lied.

"And your name is?"

She must only use the name on her new passport. "I am Vlada Marina." They were her two middle names. Easiest to remember.

"Vlada Marina," he repeated. "Does he know you?"

"Not at the present, but I have information he needs. A confidential thing that he will understand." She took a long breath. "He will want to see me. You can believe me."

The young man seemed skeptical. The big man still stood in the doorway to Dr. Forester's office. He suddenly cleared his throat. "Tré," he said. "I'll just be saying a quick hello to Dr. Forester and won't take much of his time. Let me give up the remainder to the young lady. This sounds important."

The young man looked at him, then back at her. "Okay, Ms. Marina. Have a seat please."

She gave the tall man a look of gratitude, which he returned with a nod and smile. Then she went to the couch and took up a magazine, her fingers trembling. *The enemy of my enemy is my friend. I can only pray.*

CHAPTER THIRTY-SIX

"I hope you don't mind me dropping by unannounced," said Haines. "I was just having a little unofficial walkabout and thought I'd see if you had a moment." Jack accepted the handshake warily. "I'm hooking up with my team shortly and we're meeting with Jan Cummings on the other side of the campus, so I can't linger long," Haines went on. "And you've got some kind of unexpected visitor waiting. I wanted mainly to say that your board's decision to show you the exit had no input from me. I think it's a stupid waste of talent. With your permission, I'll ask them to reverse course. I'd like you to stay."

There was something about Haines's enunciation of *stay* that brought visions of dog training to Jack's mind.

Haines continued. "I know you wanted to prevent this transition. That simply tells me you've got qualities my organization needs—independent thinking and creativity, not to mention experience." Haines laid a hand on his shoulder, gently. "I don't need an immediate answer. Take your time." Giving the shoulder an almost imperceptible squeeze, Haines smiled. "This isn't selling your soul to the devil, Jack. You and I are on the same side. Quality health care and service to our patients." Haines dropped his hand. "And—not that it should or would influence your decision, my friend—by national standards, you're underpaid. We will fix that. Let's make a time to talk more." His smile grew charmingly crooked. "We'll even get you a proper receptionist, so strangers like me and the lady waiting out there don't just walk in on you."

The ember of anger that had begun glowing in Jack's chest broke into an open flame. He looked out the window, his face burning. The workforce here was about to be decimated, and this man had just offered him a raise to help wield the scythe.

"I've already submitted my resignation. I'm not rescinding it."

Haines nodded indulgently. "I expected that to be your first reaction. You're still upset. That must have stung like hell. But your colleagues would certainly be relieved to know you're staying. Think of it from their angle."

"There's no chance I would stay," Jack said flatly.

"Sleep on it, at least," Haines said, extending his hand to shake. "For what it's worth, Jack . . . we did a deep dive on your background and found a little skeleton in your closet."

Jack cocked his head.

"Yes," Haines pushed on. "You've got a police file. You're lucky to have risen this far."

Jack drew in a breath sharply. "That was expunged a long time ago."

Haines smiled. "As I'm sure you're aware, that kind of blemish will make it hard for you to find an equivalent position elsewhere in the country. But for me and HWA, what you've done since is all that matters."

Jack met the tall man's stare, his throat tightening.

"If you don't mind me asking, Jack, what *would* you do otherwise?"

"Practice emergency medicine somewhere," he shot back.

Haines grinned broadly. "Reminds me of a story. The president of a coal mine, you see, got fed up with paperwork and meetings, so he decided to don a helmet and work up a sweat with his old friends down one of the shafts. But after an hour working the seam, he came back up into the light and never went underground again. With us, Jack, you could rise as high as you'd want. Maybe you'll have my job someday."

Jack kept his eyes locked on Haines and said nothing.

Haines was undeterred. "Well, if you change your mind, reach out. At the rate we're acquiring hospitals, you may have no choice but to work for us someday somewhere. Get in now while the getting's good." He turned and strode out the door, ducking to miss the lintel.

Tré stepped in a moment later and found Jack standing where Haines had left him. "Is everything okay, sir?"

Jack nodded, his heart still pounding.

"Do you want some more time, or should I send in that lady now?" Tré asked.

"Tell me again what it's about."

"Like I said, she wouldn't tell me. It was weird, but she reminded me of that journalist. Her accent. I don't want us to get burned again."

"That makes two of us. What was her name?"

"Vlada Marina."

"Let me see her." Jack strode out into the reception area. The woman was sitting on the couch, a magazine on her lap. He noticed the bleary expression of someone who'd been up all night with a sick family member. She had short black hair, was attractive in a sharp-edged way.

"Ms. Marina?" Jack called.

She sprang to her feet. Of medium height, she had an unusually long neck.

"I know who you are," she said, hesitantly. "I am very grateful for your time." Her small Adam's apple moved as she swallowed. Her lips looked dry.

"Have we met before?" he questioned.

"No, but I have seen you on the website. I have come a long way. I must talk with you, please. Something very important."

Jack saw her glance at Tré, who was puttering a few feet away at a cabinet, obviously eavesdropping.

"Is this about a patient?" he said.

"May we talk in privacy?" She lowered her voice to a barely

audible whisper. "I beg you, please. It's about the woman from Ukraine who came to see you."

A strong tingle crawled up his spine. He stared at her for a long moment. "What do you know about that?"

"Please, Doctor. Privacy."

He took a deep breath. "Tré," he said over his shoulder. "We'll be in my office for a moment."

Inside, she gazed around then strode to the middle of the room, turning to face the windows. Jack closed the door and watched her set down her valise, her back to him. Then she leaned her head forward and brought her hands to her face. Her shoulders shuddered.

"I am sorry, Dr. Forester." She straightened. I am not usually a person who shows emotion. It is such a relief to be here. A miracle."

"No need to apologize. Your coat?"

"My coat?"

"It's warm in here. May I take it for you?"

She opened her mouth as if to refuse, then handed it to him. "Thank you."

He hung the tan woolen coat by the door. It carried a faint odor of mothballs. "Please have a seat." He gestured toward the sofa. He sat in the armchair across the coffee table. She folded her hands on her knees.

"So," he said, "what do you know?"

"I know that last week a woman came to see you who said she was a journalist from *Ukrainian Week*."

"That's correct."

She hesitated. "She was an impostor. I know because I am Marianna Kovalenko. Not her."

He stared at her. An urge to laugh passed through him like a shooting star and left in its wake a sense of wonder. How much more insane could life possibly become? Would Haines return dressed as a gangster?

"Wait," she said. "I see you don't believe. But please listen to me. If you do nothing else, just listen. I am not lying."

"Marianna Kovalenko was identified by DNA from a hairbrush," he said.

"It was not true. They somehow arranged for that to happen, the ones behind this. It is not the truth."

"They?" Jack said. "Who do you mean by *they*?"

"The Russian oligarch Mikhail Potemkin, I believe, and his mob. Very big mob. Very powerful. Please, I beg you to listen. There is a way I can show you who I am."

"And how's that?"

"They said they would remove my few photographs from the internet. Potemkin is capable of this with the power of his internet skill. But after my escape when I got to Kyiv, my friend Anatoly who was almost beaten to death, he located one picture they didn't take down. I was in gymnastics club at university in Ukraine for 2005 and 2006. Anatoly was there too. Kyiv Polytechnic. He said our group photo is still on the internet. Please look. I'm not that much different."

She looked so earnest and beseeching. He went to his desk and opened a search engine, navigating to the website of Kyiv Polytechnic. The text was in Ukrainian. She strode up next to him. "I can do," she said. He gave her the chair.

A moment later, he was looking at a photo of twenty young men and women. She expanded it and pointed at a slender girl with a short ponytail, leaning against the vaulting horse, one knee drawn up, and looking seriously at the camera. She was identified in the caption as Marianna Kovalenko. Jack studied the image, then looked at her again, back and forth. His neck tingled. It was her. Beyond a doubt.

Her eyes were boring into him. He nodded. "Yes. I believe you are the person in that photo."

"I will never lie to you like she did."

He looked away. "Why haven't you gone to the police?"

"If you would listen to my story, you will understand."

He looked at his watch. "Listen, I have several appointments coming up. I need to leave here in ten minutes. Tell me your story."

She took him through a series of events that began one day the previous week when she'd left her office to shop and get a slice of pizza—her being grabbed, the dacha, the little man with the fedora, hearing the news about the actress's death on Monday morning, her running away through the forest, the idea for witness protection, Anatoly's help, calling her sister, the flight across the ocean, being brushed aside by the FBI, the clerk in the clothing store taking her to the bus station, and finally mistaking the tall man in Jack's office for Jack himself.

Though his trust in his own judgment had been shaken, he listened with a growing sense that she was telling the truth. He looked at his watch. She'd been talking for fifteen minutes. He had to leave, but he no longer wondered who she was.

He wondered why the other woman had come in the first place.

She was dry-eyed and calmer now. "So that is why I am here. I somehow must prove that the other woman was not me. Then I can get into the Witness Protection Program. Otherwise, the criminals will find me and get away with this. Whatever was the reason for this deception, I do not know."

"Ms. Kovalenko, an excellent local detective, is working on the case. We must get her involved."

She rose. "*No!*"

"But—"

"Please, no. I'm asking you not to tell anyone. Not police. They will not believe. They will just say I am dead."

"That's not rational. This is not Ukraine. I can help."

"And you do not know how powerful these people are. Please. Not until I can prove beyond doubt who I am. I need to have them take DNA from my apartment in Kyiv and do the comparison again. Not from the consulate. And why did they not check fingerprints?"

"They did. They matched prints from the hairbrush."

"This only proves it was that woman's hairbrush. How they got it to them, I do not know, but it is within their power, I am sure. We cannot trust fingerprint records from Ukrainian police. But I studied journalism in Leeds, England, for a year and had to have fingerprints taken at the school. They will be on record."

"Okay, I hear what you're saying. But I'm in danger of running late. I've got three appointments this afternoon. I'm making the rounds saying goodbye. I'll be back in a couple of hours. Wait for me here."

"Why are you saying goodbyes?"

"Because I'm leaving this job the day after tomorrow."

"Leaving?" she said, color draining from her face. "Why?"

He glanced at his watch and briefly summarized the unexpected financial crisis, his plan to avert the HWA takeover, the board losing confidence. "That's the abridged version of a long story," he said. "I'll explain more later."

"I am very sad to hear this," she said.

"The important thing is finding out what the devil is going on. I'll be back as soon as I can."

"Please, I ask you again," she said, following him to the door. "Tell no one."

"Tré is my assistant," he said. "You can trust him."

"No," she said, her face set. "No one, please."

CHAPTER THIRTY-SEVEN

It was a sunny afternoon, not exactly warm, but pleasant in the full sun.

"I'll be back by five," said Aunt Zoë, joining them outside. "Kaitlyn is in charge, Julia. Understand?"

"We're going to take a walk," Julia said, hopping up and down.

Kaitlyn yawned. "I said maybe."

Zoë came over. "How did you sleep last night?"

Kaitlyn held back another yawn. "I took some of the Benadryl," she said.

"Did it help?"

"I think so." She had taken one tablet at about ten the night before. But by two in the morning, she was groggy but still awake, so she'd taken another. The next thing she knew, her alarm was going off.

"You still look tired," Zoë said.

"I'll be okay." She'd felt sluggish all day, her mind numb. From what she'd read, this was a possible side effect of Benadryl. She'd never take it again. She'd rather feel ordinarily tired than have this fogginess.

"Well, if you don't feel like a walk, just say no. Lord, where are my car keys?" Zoë fumbled in her purse.

"Can we go trick or treating tonight, Kaitlyn?" pleaded Julia, tugging her arm.

"Halloween's Sunday. Today's only Wednesday."

"Why can't we go more than once?"

"It's illegal," Kaitlyn said.

Finding her keys, Zoë looked up, shading her eyes. "It's certainly a beautiful day for a walk, though. Indian summer. Wish I could join you. Just be careful. Someone we know likes to run off. I'll bring back some pumpkins and we can make jack-o'-lanterns tonight."

"Oh, Aunt Zoë," said Kaitlyn. "Mr. Brady should be calling for me today. I gave him your number."

"The guidance counselor?"

"Just tell him I'll call him back."

Zoë gave her a glance. "What's he want to talk about?"

"Nothing bad. I'll tell you tonight. I'd like to talk with you and Uncle Jack about something anyway. Maybe after supper?"

Zoë smiled. "Good," she said. "We can do that."

"When's Daddy coming home?" asked Julia.

"Not sure, honey," Zoë said, then she got in her car and left.

"Let's go, let's go!" said Julia.

"Please don't yank my arm. You'll dislocate my pitching shoulder. Put on your coat and hat."

"But the sun is warm."

"We'll be in the shade a lot."

Kaitlyn worked Julia's coat sleeve over the cast and worked a stocking cap onto her head. Then she donned her own fleece and put on the school baseball cap that Mr. Brady had given her the day he'd watched her pitch. They started up the trail behind the barn that went through the forest up the mountain. It really was beautiful, the sky deep blue and the sun glowing through the trees. She inhaled deeply. The air smelled of fallen leaves.

"Let's go all the way up where we can see the river and the valley," Julia said.

"Okay, but don't run ahead."

Julia laughed and proceeded to run. "Catch me!"

"If that's the way it is, we're going back."

Julia returned. She grabbed a handful of leaves and flung them in the air. They continued walking, then Julia darted off and picked up a stick. She returned to walk next to Kaitlyn and began tapping the path in front of them with the branch. "Look, I've got a cane. Do you want me to get you one?"

"The only thing I need is a leash."

"I'm going to be a witch for Halloween!" Julia exclaimed. "This can be my broom. What are you going to be?"

"A cannibal."

"Yuck. Why do you want to be a cannibal?"

"No, actually, I'm going to be Spider-Woman."

"Or you can be Hermione Granger and cast spells. You can make me disappear!" Julia's excitement faltered. "Are you going to be here for Halloween? I heard Aunt Zoë talk about having to drive you back on Sunday. I hope you don't go."

Kaitlyn smiled, tempted to mention she might be staying for good, wanting to see the look on Julia's face. But the time wasn't right.

The trail grew steeper. She could see the hills on the far side of the valley. She was feeling relaxed. All last night she had thought about what it would be like to call this place home, to have Zoë to talk with, to feel her warmth. Kaitlyn could imagine being like the daughter that Zoë had never had. The thought made her chest swell with the urge to cry. Why should happiness be painful?

"Almost there," said Julia.

And then there was Julia. It would be fun to watch her grow up. She could also imagine a time in the future when she and Uncle Jack could become like friends. If only he'd stop closing himself off. Zoë was probably right about how losing Zellie had damaged him. Could such a scar be permanent? How much damage did the loss of her own parents do? Stella would explode at the news of her staying. Kaitlyn knew she'd have to be strong and wait for the shock waves to settle. On the other side of that explosion was a new life.

They came to the top where there was a big open area without many trees. Kaitlyn felt a jolt of alarm as Julia took off running toward the big flat rock that ended in a steep drop. Zoë had a fear of heights, wouldn't even go near the cliff.

"Julia! Stop and wait for me."

The little girl jumped up and down, laughing. They stood there on the flat boulder together and looked over the valley.

"I wonder if it's like this on the moon," said Julia.

"I don't think there's quite as many trees."

"Are there a lot of bears down there?"

"Thousands."

"What kind?"

"Most of them are Teddies, I think," Kaitlyn said.

"Teddy bears? No they're not."

"Actually, at night, whole flocks of dingbats come out and fly around."

"Why do you lie all the time?"

"I'm not lying. I'm standing."

"Stop making fun of me."

Kaitlyn looked at her and sighed. "Hey, I'm sorry. I'm just in a good mood. I feel a little silly."

"I like it better when you're in a bad mood. Can we play hide-and-seek?"

"Sure. Do you want to hide first?"

"No, you."

"Okay. But let's get away from the edge. You go by that tree and close your eyes."

"And count to twenty?"

"Yes. Twenty."

"Out loud?"

"Yep." Kaitlyn went a little ways into the woods and stood behind a big pine tree.

"Ready or not, here I come!" Julia shouted.

Kaitlyn maneuvered to keep the tree between them.

"I see you!" said Julia. "My turn to hide now. This time you count to one hundred."

"Okay, but don't go too far and don't go that way." Kaitlyn pointed toward the cliff. She went and sat beside a large stone, leaning back against it. It was in the shade, but the stone had absorbed heat, and its contours matched the shape of her back. It felt warm and comfortable. She closed her eyes and began counting. A sensation of moving air swept across her forehead. She yawned and stretched drowsily. No more Benadryl, ever. She lay her head back. Her eyes were heavy. So comfortable. Julia was moving somewhere near the woods.

CHAPTER THIRTY-EIGHT

His meetings over, Jack returned to his office. The curtains were drawn and the room was dark except for the greenish glow of his desk lamp. He eased the door shut. She was sleeping on the couch, her head pillowed on the valise, her coat for a blanket. Her shoes were side by side near the coffee table, upon which lay an empty plate and an empty bottle of apple juice. Tré had followed through with his request to bring her food.

He went closer and studied her face. She had prominent cheekbones, a high forehead, a slender nose and delicate chin, a small mole on her neck. Her skin was pale and clear and her hair fine textured. He smelled perfume mingled with perspiration and the mothball scent of her coat. Her breathing sounded like distant waves receding. He pulled the coat up over her shoulder. A lock of hair falling across her right eye might scratch her cornea when she woke. He carefully moved it back in place. She stirred, then settled.

Questions churned through his mind. There was something behind all of this that made no sense. Why would a Russian oligarch go to the trouble of kidnapping her and sending an impostor? If the oligarch was an internet criminal, might that be related to the hospital's financial collapse? But they'd found no evidence of hacking. His overriding instinct remained to get Frances Dirkens involved, the sooner the better. But he wasn't going to break the woman's trust by talking to the police without her knowledge. Her ability to trust the authorities had obviously been shredded. She knew about corruption a thousand times better than he did. Maybe these people really did have eyes and ears everywhere. But why this subterfuge? It felt like he was crawling through a labyrinth of rabbit holes with no glimmer of light.

His phone chirped with an incoming text from Tré. *Dr. Singh the pathologist is here to see you.* Marianna shifted and sighed. He went out to the reception area, closing the door quietly behind him.

Annabel was talking to Tré. "There you are," she said. "I've got some follow-up about Chad Chadwick's toxicology findings."

"What did you find?" asked Jack.

"The test turned up positive for PCP, which didn't make sense after your comments about him being a straight shooter. So either you were wrong, or somebody slipped it to him. Or..."

Jack felt something cold stirring in his chest. "Or it was something different," he said slowly. "PCP cross-reacts with ketamine on the drug screen."

She broke into a smile. "A-plus, Dr. Forester! Exactly. I did a quantitative assay for ketamine. Very positive. His level was in the therapeutic range at the time of death. I checked his medical records from the ER and the step-down unit. He was given sedation—but not with ketamine. They used lorazepam. You were with him in the field. Did the medics give it to him?"

"No. I'm sure they didn't."

"Then the most likely explanation is that he was given it in the chaos of the ER when he arrived there, and they failed to document it. This is a serious breach of protocol. I'll notify the quality assurance office. They need to start a full root cause analysis." She hesitated at the look on his face. "What's the matter—don't you agree? You look like you've seen a ghost."

He studied her. After a pause, he said, "I'm not sure what's going on."

"Well, I'm sure you're busy. This is such a crazy time. I'll get the process started, not to worry." Her expression turned serious, and she held out her hand. "And, if I don't see you before you leave, Jack,

I enjoyed working with you these years. I wish you the best of luck."

Standing there by Tré's desk, lost in thinking the unthinkable, he watched her stride away. On the night of Chad's death, the woman posing as Marianna Kovalenko had gone out to his car because she'd forgotten her purse. Shortly afterward, she'd complained of a headache and left the dinner early. This meant she'd potentially had access to the ketamine in his vehicle not long before Chad died. Maybe when Kaitlyn surprised her, she wasn't taking it out—she was putting it back.

"Tré, listen to me," he said, pointing at his closed office door. "Thanks for bringing our guest some nourishment. And let me remind you again that we need to keep her visit here completely confidential."

"When are you going to tell me who she is?"

"Not yet. You'll understand why when the time's right."

Back in the office, he found Marianna awake.

"Thank you for the food, Dr. Forester. And for the nap. I'm feeling more like myself. Are you done with your meetings?"

"I am. But we hadn't discussed where you're going to stay tonight."

"I will find a place."

"There is plenty of room at my house."

"Oh no," she said, springing to her feet. "Do not even think this thing, please. It would bring possible danger to you and your family."

"Not if no one knows you're here."

"Because of what they did to Anatoly, they know I have come to America. They could be listening, maybe right now." She pointed to his computer. "You don't know what they can do. I don't want to risk any chance of them hurting you or your family. Maybe I already say too much."

"Ms. Kovalenko—"

"I ask you to stop repeating."

Her paranoia had some justification, he realized, but he must find a way around this. "Okay," he said, taking a piece of paper and a pen. "I understand. There could be bugs or informants here. So, here's an idea. You find a safe place to stay and contact me. We'll talk again tomorrow."

As he spoke, he wrote on the piece of paper. He handed the note to her. *Go to the basement level, section D-1. I'll be waiting outside the exit next to the physiology lab. 30 minutes. This will be safe. Trust me.*

As she read the note, he continued talking. "But honestly, Ms. Kovalenko. I still believe you'll be safer with me. We have a lot to talk about."

She finished reading and looked up at him, the hint of a smile on her lips. She nodded. "Please stop asking," she said. "Besides, I would be imposing on your wife. No."

Jack tensed. "My wife is deceased."

"I am sorry. I did not know."

"But she would have wanted the same thing."

"Again, this is so kind. I will find somewhere safe. I will make sure I'm not being followed."

"Okay, if that's your final say," he said. He gave her a thumbs up. As she returned the gesture, his cell phone rang. It was Investigator Dirkens. "I have to take this," he said. "It's the police." He saw her expression turn alarmed. "Don't worry," he added. "I will *not* tell them about you—until you agree."

She took the slip of paper he had written on and waved it, her eyes wide with consternation. He understood the need to mollify her and nodded, then he answered the call.

"Doctor, can you converse now?" asked the investigator.

"Could I call you right back?" he said.

"Sure."

He hung up. "Come with me," he said to her. "We'll go outside. Just in case."

A few minutes later he emerged with Marianna onto the roof of the building and closed the door behind them. There was a chill wind and the sound of traffic below.

"We'll be safe here."

"Good," she said, folding her arms against the wind. He had not thought to bring jackets.

He redialed Investigator Dirkens and put it on speakerphone so Marianna would be able to hear. The number rang. In the distance, the rotor blades of an approaching helicopter thudded.

"I can talk now," he said as the investigator answered. Marianna leaned closer.

"Is that wind noise?" said Dirkens. "Are you outside?"

"I needed to get some fresh air. Listen, Investigator, I wanted to talk with you anyway. I've got some news for you. Our pathologist just told me that Chad Chadwick had a therapeutic level of ketamine on board when he died, but there's no record of it being given in the hospital."

"Ketamine again?" Dirkens said. "Good Lord. Ketamine here, ketamine there, fricking ketamine everywhere. What are you thinking?"

"Here's what I know." He went on to describe how the woman who claimed to be Marianna Kovalenko's identity had access to the ketamine in his car the night that Chad died. She'd gone to get her purse, then had left the dinner early. With ketamine on board, someone could have strangled Chad without a struggle.

"Interesting," said Dirkens. "You're suggesting she murdered him and made it look like suicide?"

"Or maybe she gave the medication to whoever murdered him. I don't know. It makes more sense to me than Chad killing himself. Maybe when Kaitlyn saw her in the parking garage, she was just putting it back."

"But what's her motive?" questioned Dirkens.

"No clue."

"Remind me. You said Chad was a friend and partner of your brother. Could Kovalenko have had any other connection with him?"

"She helped me take care of him at the scrapyard and she rode in the ambulance with him to the hospital. That's their only contact, as far as I know."

"Okay. I've heard enough. We'll reclassify his death as a potential homicide and open a full investigation. I'll need to talk with your brother."

"That may not be easy now." He explained Tony's condition.

"Understood," she said. "But backing up a little, you said 'the woman who claimed to be Marianna Kovalenko.' We have DNA evidence confirming that's who she was. You know that."

"I do, but maybe we're wrong. Listen, I was doing a little searching on the internet, looking for photos of her and—"

"But there weren't any. We checked."

"I know there weren't any individual photos, but she'd told me that she'd graduated from Kyiv Polytechnic."

"You didn't mention that before. When did she tell you that?"

"Oh, I don't know. When she first came, I think. At any rate, I searched their website. It turns out she was in the gymnastics club. I found group photos from the years she attended. Even accounting for the age difference, the real Marianna Kovalenko didn't look anything like the one who was here. Maybe the DNA needs to be confirmed using other sources, say directly from her apartment. From what I've heard, you can't trust the Ukrainian consulate that gave you the hairbrush. Are there FBI agents in Ukraine?"

"Yes. There's a legate in Kyiv."

"That's where it needs to come from. And you should get a new set of fingerprints—not from Ukraine. I know she spent a semester at Leeds University in England. I'm sure they keep a set of foreign student fingerprints at English universities. That would be more reliable."

Dirkens was silent for a moment. Then she cleared her throat. "You seem to be doing a lot of extracurricular investigating."

"Can you blame me?"

"No. Not at all. Good finds."

After hanging up, he caught Marianna's eyes.

"Thank you," she said. "This is smart." It was the first time he'd seen anything like a smile on her lips.

CHAPTER THIRTY-NINE

In Kaitlyn's dream she was climbing a tree. As she struggled higher, the tree began to sway. There was nothing to do but continue until she reached an escalator. The escalator led to a shopping mall, where she found Stella getting her hair done. She went in and sat on the chair next to her. The chair was very hard against her back. Something had gone wrong. Stella's hair was falling out. Clumps of it lay on the green tile floor. Stella glared at her. "Look at this! It's your fault. From now on you'll have to share your hair with me."

Kaitlyn tried to rise but something bright and hot was pushing against her face. She opened her eyes. It was the sun. She squinted and sat up. Her neck hurt and it was hard to focus her eyes. She'd been sleeping. She saw the trees and the mountain, the blue sky. Then she remembered why she'd been leaning back against a rock. The sun had moved. She had been in the shade and now it was full upon her.

Where was Julia? Springing up, she felt a wave of lightheadedness. "Julia!" she yelled as her vision darkened and her stomach lurched. She was going to throw up. She leaned forward, hands on her knees. How could she have done this? The nausea passed. She straightened and looked around.

"Julia!" She waited, breathing rapidly. "Julia!" How long had she been asleep? Why didn't Julia wake her up? The little monster. "Julia! Come back here immediately!"

Oh God, oh God. Don't let anything happen to her.

She continued calling out as she dashed this way then that, darting into the forest, trying to scan through the trees. *What have I done?* Her legs quaking, she walked out on the big flat rock and approached the cliff. "Julia!" Dropping to her hands and knees, she crawled to the edge. If she saw her little body down there, she would get a running start and throw herself out too. How could she live with herself?

She inched forward until she saw the sheer drop to rocks and trees. "Julia!" Nothing but an echo, a return of her voice—absolute and terrifying. "Julia!" She stayed there listening and scanning for several more minutes, her heart throbbing against the inside of her chest. She could see no sign of the child down there. But that didn't mean she hadn't fallen. There were so many places for a tiny body to be hidden from view.

She rose to her feet and sobbed. Maybe she should just jump and get this horrible life over with. *It was just like with her father, rushing back into the burning house. She was worthless.* She could just close her eyes and let gravity pull her down. She would never have to face the mirror, or Stella, or Zoë, or Jack, or memories of her father. It wasn't the first time she'd thought of ending her life. Did she have the courage? It would be over in a moment.

Then a thought intruded. What if Julia had gotten lost in the woods and needed help? Or what if she was hiding nearby, laughing as Kaitlyn called her name? Or what if she had just grown bored and decided to go back home? She retreated from the edge, stood there swaying and wiping her face. The sun was still above the mountain but slipping behind a band of clouds. A cool wind stirred over her. She faced the forest.

"Julia! If you're hiding, please come out."

But Julia didn't have neither the patience nor the meanness it would take for such a cruel joke. She ran toward the forest but stopped at the edge. It was too big. She could end up getting lost too. No—the best thing now would be to see if Julia had gone home. And if she hadn't, she could ask Uncle Tony to help search the woods. *Would Zoë or anyone else ever forgive her?*

She took off running, hating herself as her legs churned and her chest heaved.

CHAPTER FORTY

Striding down the brick walkways that wound through the campus, knitting it together like a living nervous system, Lawrence Haines headed for the parking garage where he had left his rental vehicle, taking his time. He passed by the new building that housed the English department, looking up to admire the sleek limestone facade, vertically oriented windows, and crenulated eves. Equally interesting was the ornate Georgian building made of bricks imported from England and devoted now to the chemistry department, a historical marker identifying it as the oldest structure on campus, built in 1853.

He drew in a lungful of the crisp air that was perfumed with the oak, beech, and maple leaves crunching underfoot and felt exhilarated. It had been a splendidly productive afternoon of meetings with senior university leaders. He and his acquisition team were getting a good lay of the land and already establishing relationships with the key decision-makers. Now the sun was lowering over the hills past the river, and he was going home.

A phone rang in his overcoat pocket, breaking his chain of thoughts. It was the secure satellite device that connected him to Potemkin. His heart immediately sank. He'd known this call would be coming at some point. Potemkin would be wanting a progress report. He was tempted to ignore it. But the Russian would keep trying. It was unavoidable. Get it over with. Keeping up his pace, he answered.

"Hello, Lawrence," Potemkin said. "You sound winded."

"I'm walking."

"Congratulations again. You have won. Or I should say, we have won. How does it feel?"

"As expected."

"What? You don't sound as happy as I would expect."

Haines entered the ground floor of the parking garage and headed for the stairs. "I've got a lot on my mind. I've had a busy day."

"Good," said Potemkin. "I picture you there having many meetings with grateful people who hail you as the hero that will rescue them with his sturdy HWA lifeboat. And you let them know, I hope, that you will begin by blessing them with a brand-new computer system, highest quality, as we discussed?"

"Of course. The funds are being transferred to make it happen."

"Very well. Excellent. We will bury the past in some landfill."

Entering a stairwell, Haines climbed toward the level where he'd left the vehicle. The air inside was stale. A wave of anger swirled in his chest. He might as well address it now. "Mikhail, there have been some strange happenings here in the past few days since we talked. Suicides and kidnappings and people going through car shredders. Were you involved in any way? Don't lie to me."

Potemkin's answer was delayed a second or so. "Well, Lawrence, I have heard some rumors about those things, yes," said the Russian. "But my work there is now done, my friend. Done. As you requested. To change subject, tell me how is your Dr. Forester taking his loss? Did you see him today?"

"I did see him briefly. I made him an offer to stay—it would have lubricated the transition—but he's holding out."

"For money?"

"No. More out of spite. He's a proud man."

"I'm surprised you couldn't bring him around. I thought you were good at that."

"I *am* good at that. It'll be his loss."

"Would you like me to help convince him?"

Haines nearly stumbled on a step. "No! I said no more interference. How can I make that any clearer?"

"I only make a joke, my friend. Relax."

"It's just as well he goes. He's not an efficient administrator. I saw how he runs his office. He's got an administrative assistant who doubles as his receptionist and looks like a manicurist. Strangers barge into his office unannounced. While I was waiting for him, some wild-eyed foreign woman sauntered in and mistook me for him."

Potemkin didn't respond immediately.

"Mikhail?"

"A foreign woman, you say?"

"To judge by her accent, yes."

"Tell me more about this person."

"I was merely giving you an example of his chaotic management style."

"Tell me about her, please. The woman."

"What's the relevance?"

"Humor me, Lawrence. How old? What was her accent? Just tell me."

"I'd say she was in her mid-thirties, the accent resembled yours a bit. Maybe thicker. Slavic sounding. Why?" Reaching the third floor, he pushed open the heavy metal door. The hinges needed oiling.

"Did you happen to get her name?"

"I don't have time for this, Mikhail." He marched toward his car. "Why would I have asked her name?"

"This may be of importance. Did you get her name?"

The car was a white Mercedes. "She did give his assistant her name. I think it was Vlada Marina." He pressed the key fob and its lights flashed. "Yes, the name Vlada stuck in my mind because I assumed it was the feminine form of Vladimir. Like Putin. Not that I'm a fan of your friend over there."

"Most interesting . . ."

Haines rolled his eyes. "Why is that interesting?"

"I must go," asserted the Russian. The connection suddenly went dead.

Haines slid behind the wheel and stared at the phone. That was the shortest conversation he'd ever had with Potemkin. Hopefully, it would be the last.

CHAPTER FORTY-ONE

The soles of Kaitlyn's running shoes crackled over the dead leaves on the path. The barn came into view. "Julia!" She ran into the backyard, slowing, her heart sinking. There was no child on the swing set. She leaped up the steps to the back door and burst into the kitchen. "Julia!" She leaned over, gulping air as a sharp pain stabbed her side. The living room was empty. She dashed down the hallway to Julia's room. Likewise.

She opened the basement door. Flicking on the lights, she flew downstairs into the den. Empty. Back outside, she ran to the barn and flung open the side door. "Julia!" She sprinted up to Tony's apartment and banged the door. She could hear the TV going. "Uncle Tony!" The door swung open. Tony still wore a blank look.

"Kaitlyn?"

"Julia is lost," she said, gasping. "We were up by the flat rock. I fell asleep. She's not back here. I've checked everywhere."

Understanding dawned in his eyes. He turned and took his jacket off the hook and picked up a flashlight. "Let's go look."

"I'm scared, Uncle Tony. I looked down the cliff, but I couldn't see her."

Tony had short and slightly bowed legs but could move very quickly when he wanted to. He was already jogging away when Kaitlyn got outside. The sun was now close to the horizon, the light changing.

"Wait for me," she said. But a car was crunching up the driveway. It was Aunt Zoë. She froze, trembling.

Zoë's door flew open. "Kaitlyn, what on earth is going on? What's wrong?"

She tried to explain, seeing a look of alarm blossom on Zoë's face. "Slow down, child. Stop crying. I can't understand you."

"Julia is lost. Uncle Tony is looking for her now."

Zoë straightened. "What do you mean she's lost?"

"We were playing hide-and-seek, and it was my turn to seek and . . ."

"And what?"

"I fell asleep. I didn't mean to. I think the medicine . . . When I opened my eyes, she was gone. I can't find her, Aunt Zoë. I am so scared."

"Where was this, Kaitlyn? Down in the basement?"

"Up the hill. By the flat rock."

"You were playing by the cliff and you fell asleep? Oh God, Kaitlyn."

"I just closed my eyes for a minute and the next thing I knew she was gone."

"Oh, mother of mercy," Zoë said, a catch in her voice.

"I'm going to go back up and help Uncle Tony look," Kaitlyn said.

"You are *not*. Not in the state you're in."

"I've got to." Kaitlyn swung around but Zoë grabbed her arm. She tried to break free, but Zoë gripped harder.

"Go in the house, Kaitlyn. Listen to me! This isn't helping. Go in the house. *Now*."

It was the first time she'd heard Zoë raise her voice, and it jolted her like an electric shock. She saw Zoë yank out her phone. "I need to call the police. They can bring search dogs. We'll find her. *Now please, go in the house*. That's an order, Kaitlyn."

"You hate me now."

"Stop it."

Jack's car was halfway up the driveway when he noticed two figures in front of the barn. Dusk was approaching and he couldn't clearly see them until he coasted near. It was Zoë and Kaitlyn. Something was obviously wrong. Zoë had hold of Kaitlyn's arm and Kaitlyn was trying to pull away, almost dragging the older woman with her.

Hearing their voices through the closed windows, he glanced at Marianna in the seat beside him. He had spent the entire ride from the hospital filling her in on the details of what had transpired since he'd learned of the financial crisis last week. She was staring at the scene with a puzzled expression.

"From your description of your family, Dr. Forester, I imagine that would be Zoë and Kaitlyn," she said. "They look to be having a struggle."

"I need to see what's happening." He stepped outside. "Zoë?" he called, striding over. Zoë turned. Kaitlyn jerked free and dashed into the barn. "What the hell is going on?" Marianna came up behind him.

Zoë's face was pale and contorted. "I need to make this call," she said, her voice trembling. Her chest rose and fell.

"Who do you need to call?" he said. "Talk to me."

"I'm calling 911," she said, putting the phone to her ear. "Be quiet a minute."

He had never seen Zoë agitated before. She began talking rapid-fire into the phone. Through her words, he pieced together what had transpired. A dark sensation—as painful and potent as anything he'd ever felt—bored into his chest.

Zoë ended the call and turned to him, dropping the phone in her pocket and closing her eyes.

"How could this have happened?" he demanded.

"They were playing hide-and-seek up by the flat rock and Kaitlyn fell asleep. Tony's up there now and the police will be here shortly."

"She took my daughter up there and fell asleep?"

Zoë's eyes went hard and her face firm. "Don't blame her. It's my fault, Jack. I knew she was tired. I never should have asked her to babysit. She didn't mean for this to happen. We'll find her. That's the important thing."

Jack stared at the path leading into the woods and strode in that direction. The sun was setting below the western ridge, and the forest was deep in shadow. He stopped. Should he get a light and run out there or wait for the police, show them the way? When he turned back to Zoë, he saw that Marianna—*he'd forgotten about her*—had gone to Zoë with her hand outstretched.

"You must be Aunt Zoë," she was saying. "Dr. Forester has told me all about you. I'm Vlada Marina. Is there anything I can do to help?"

"I'm sorry—you're who?" Zoë asked, staring.

Jack went to them. He and Marianna had devised a cover story during the drive. "Vlada is the daughter of a visiting professor we had here a few years ago," he said. "She's from Estonia and came for a job interview. I've invited her to stay with us while she's—" He heard Tony's voice calling far off from the direction of the trail. "Excuse me." He turned and ran in that direction. He hadn't gone a hundred yards when he saw Tony emerge, carrying the child in his arms. He handed her to Jack.

"Daddy, I got lost."

Jack squeezed her tightly and kissed the top of her head. "Thank you, brother," he said, his eyes burning as he looked over at Tony. "Are you hurt, sweetie?"

"No."

"You gave us a scare." They started back down to the yard. "What happened?"

"Not much."

Though he felt immense relief, the dark sensation was still churning. "Not much? What sort of not much?"

"We were playing, and I found a really good place to hide inside a bush. Kaitlyn got tired and took a nap, so I went to find some flowers. Then everything looked the same. I heard her calling me, but she didn't hear me back. But Uncle Tony did."

The K-9 unit was there when they got back to the yard. There were two dogs on leashes, a black lab and a border collie, and three officers equipped with lights and a bullhorn. Marianna was kneeling between the dogs, petting them as they tried to lick her face. Jack set Julia down and Zoë picked her up. He thanked the officers.

"No problem at all," one of them said. "These are the kinds of S&R calls we like."

"Who's that?" Julia inquired, pointing at Marianna.

"This is Ms. Marina," Zoë said. "She seems to be a friend of your daddy's."

"Would you like to pet the dogs?" Marianna said to the little girl.

"Sure," she said, writhing out of Zoë's arms.

"Is Kaitlyn still in the barn?" Jack asked Zoë.

"Yes. I went in to talk with her, but she isn't saying anything. I'm worried. She didn't need this."

"No one needed this. What could she have been thinking?"

"She was dead tired, and I should never have left her to babysit. She took a Benadryl last night and I'm sure that made it worse. It's my fault." She faced him directly. "Do you hear me, Jack Forester? Don't be angry with her. I've seen nothing but responsibility from that girl."

"I just need to talk with her."

"Fine. But be gentle. You know how much she's been through."

"She'd have put herself through a lot more if something had happened to Julia."

"Obviously. And I think if the worst had happened, she wouldn't have been able to live with herself. So, thank God that wasn't the case. I'm warning you, if you're angry, do not go in there."

"I understand."

"She needs understanding. Something you really haven't given her much of."

"That's unfair, Zoë." He sighed. "I'm okay. I get what you're saying."

Zoë nodded toward Marianna, who was petting the dogs alongside Julia. "Your friend Vlada seems like a very nice person."

"I apologize for not giving you a head's up, Zoë. She'll be spending the night with us. Maybe longer. This was unexpected. I'll explain later."

The officers were loading the dogs back into the van. As he headed for the barn, Jack saw Marianna following him with her eyes. He found Kaitlyn sitting in the corner behind the old tractor, her knees drawn up. Her eyes were puffy, her cheeks chapped and raw. She was staring straight ahead, unfocused, her breathing shallow, mouth half open.

"Julia's back," he said. "Tony found her. She's fine."

She nodded, not looking at him. "You don't have to say it. I'm a loser and an idiot."

Jack heard movement and glanced in its direction. Julia came into the barn leading Marianna. She dropped Marianna's hand and ran to Kaitlyn, who continued staring ahead.

"Kaitlyn, I'm sorry I got lost. I went to find you some flowers."

Kaitlyn shrugged. "Don't be sorry. It was my fault."

"I didn't want to wake you up. Is Daddy mad at you again?"

"It doesn't matter," Kaitlyn said. "He doesn't like me and he never did."

"Yes, he does. Can I give you a hug?"

"No." Julia tried anyway, but Kaitlyn put up her hand. "Please, don't. I'm glad you're okay, but you need to stay away from me."

"Marianna," Jack said. "Would you take Julia back outside?"

"You mean Vlada," said Marianna.

"Sorry. Vlada."

"I don't want to leave," said Julia, sniffling. "Kaitlyn?"

"You must do as your papa says," said Marianna.

"My papa? We don't call him that."

"Well, you could," Marianna said, taking her hand and leading her back outside. "It's a good word."

"Kaitlyn . . ." Jack began.

"I don't want to talk. You've never wanted me here. I used to wonder what I could do to change it."

"I'm sorry I gave you that impress—"

"I used to think it was all my fault," she said, interrupting him. "But there's something wrong with you too. It's like, I don't know, something is dead inside of you."

He looked away and drew a deep breath.

She went on. "But who am I to talk? Julia could have died because of me." She took a deep shuddering breath and exhaled. He remembered how Zellie had cried after her father's death, the way her breath had shuddered like that. "I don't blame you anymore for thinking I'm worthless. And I'm stupid. I took two of those pills for sleep last night."

"The Benadryl?"

"I know you probably think that, like, I'm just pitying myself. But it's more than that. I don't want to be an evil person, but I can't help hurting people. I don't want to be like this."

He stared down at her and remembered the night they had talked in the car. His throat contracted and he heaved a sigh. "Kaitlyn, you're not a bad person. Not at all. Far from it. Come inside and let's get some supper. We'll talk more. It's going to get cold out here."

She shook her head and didn't glance up. "Just leave me alone."

CHAPTER FORTY-TWO

Ordinarily, Bryson Witner's thrice weekly exercise walks were a time to relish the fresh air and the rhythm of movement, a time to let his thoughts emerge and converse. But a sharp blade of foreboding had wedged in his mind ever since he'd read about the murder of a Ukrainian journalist in New Canterbury. Gina was dead. Something had gone awry with her spying mission. The subsequent news that the medical center would be acquired by HWA had lightened his mood a bit, but not entirely. With Haines in possession of the hospital, what relevance did he himself now possess to either of them, especially Potemkin? Trust was a dodgy business, and Potemkin was one of the dodgiest persons on earth.

A crow screeched overhead. He gazed up, jingling the handcuffs at his back. The bird soared away, leaving a sky full of cold clouds, as impenetrable as the questions he'd been asking himself. With Gina dead, his communication link to Potemkin had been severed. How and when would Potemkin reach out to him regarding the escape plans? During his final meeting with Gina last week, he'd had a fleeting sense she was hiding something. He should have dug deeper. Now he was in limbo, waiting, reliant on the goodwill of others. Because of that, he had begun collecting information that might be useful as leverage against them someday, keeping it in a safe location, to be revealed only if the need arose. It was, he liked to think, a healthy exercise of paranoia.

A frigid gust rinsed across his scalp as he strode over the

Astroturf back toward the doorway where Gordon the guard stood leaning against the cinder block wall, his eyes fixed on a cell phone as intently as if it contained the tablets of Moses.

Gordon looked up. "You done already, old guy? You've got a few more minutes."

"A fact of which I'm not unaware, but I want to go in," Witner said. "Thank you for the nugatory solicitude."

"The what?" Gordon puzzled. Then he shrugged. "Never mind. Your room inspection probably isn't done yet. But suit yourself. You want in, we'll go in." They shuffled down the dingy beige corridor toward Witner's quarters. "Looked like you were having quite the talk with yourself out there today, Witner," Gordon said. "I heard you've got multiple personalities. Is it for real?"

Guards didn't last too long at Patterson. The pay was poor. Not surprising that many of them liked to add a little spice to the job by probing into the lurid histories of their charges. Gordon had only been here a few months and was still soaking it in. But Witner wasn't in a mood to humor him.

"We all contain multitudes, Gordon," he said. "Somewhere inside of you, for example, there's a Buddhist monk seeking to become one with the universe."

Gordon laughed. "You sure come up with lots of crazy crap," he said. "But seriously, you look a little, I don't know . . . somewhere else today."

They came to his room. A notice was taped to the door. *Cleaning and inspection in progress. Do not interrupt.*

"See, like I told you, Witner. He's not done yet."

"How thorough of him. Behold your tax dollars at work."

These weekly room shakedowns had been instituted after a patient in a different state had fashioned a knife out of a toothbrush and took out the eye of a visitor a few years ago. One of the guards would rifle through his dresser, his toiletries, his books, look beneath his bed, under the rug.

The door swung open and a guard emerged, one that Witner had never seen before. He was a scrawny middle-aged man with a ropey neck and a robust five o'clock shadow.

"All is in order," he said, peeling the notice off the door. "Back in you go, amigo."

"Merci beaucoup," said Witner. "Amigo."

Gordon undid the cuffs and Witner stepped inside. The heavy door slammed shut. Ordinarily this would have been the end of his daily contact with other human beings, supper being served in a cardboard box slid through a slot. But his weekly counseling session with Geoffrey Nettles, MSW, scheduled every Wednesday at 1 p.m., had been pushed back to 4 p.m. today. It was 3:50 now.

As was his habit, he strode around the room and into the bathroom, checking to see if anything was missing or disturbed. A guard last year had made off with his deodorant. At least one could say he needed it. The last thing he checked was his desk drawer where he kept his favorite coin. He liked to look at this piece regularly, and the guards would never be brazen enough to steal it. Everyone knew it was there, and the room was under constant video surveillance.

There it was, safe and sound, tucked into a clear plastic case—a 1970 Washington quarter from the Denver mint, one of a small number of them that had been inadvertently stamped onto blanks intended for dimes and released into circulation before the mistake was caught. He'd bought it at an auction at the Boston Numismatic Society back in 1987 for thirty-five hundred dollars, outbidding Potemkin, who had ridiculed him for spending so much money. But the last laugh was his. Two days later he'd refused a four thousand dollar offer from another collector.

Looking at it pleased him inordinately. In its bungled creation and distribution, this disc exemplified the potential for human beings to foul things up. And being a rare mistake, it was of value. Humanity in a nutshell. He wondered again when and how Potemkin would make contact.

Closing the drawer, he settled into a chair. He'd come to enjoy these "stability assessment sessions" with Geoffrey, a well-read person who possessed a quick wit. Their relationship had grown relaxed over the years. Geoffrey had made the guards dispense with handcuffs, comfortable in the knowledge they were being video monitored. After the usual questions about hearing voices or having suicidal or homicidal thoughts, they'd chat, often about politics (the counselor was a rabid Democrat), and Geoffrey would go away and file his report.

At exactly 3:58, the lock clattered and the door creaked open. Geoffrey sauntered in wearing a brown fedora and a black trench coat. He was a pudgy man with a blond crew cut and a red-veined nose, the only clue that he'd once been a tippler, on the wagon—or so he claimed—since the birth of his first child.

"Forgive the change in schedule, Bryson," he said, shuffling off his coat. "My wife needed to see the OB."

"All is well?"

"Yes, thank you. The pregnancy is on track."

"Your third, right?" Witner asked.

"Fourth."

"You're quite the satyr."

"Nature calls; I respond. And how are you doing? The guard tells me you were talking up a storm with yourself in the yard this afternoon. Are you having any auditory hallucinations?"

"I'm not hearing voices, per se," said Witner. "I'm simply communicating with various aspects of my stunning personality. My internal committees and I meet frequently to discuss the general situation."

"Well, just so long as you and your inner colleagues talk about the real world. Anything else new?"

An image of Gina came to mind. "Not really. They didn't disturb the spiderwebs during the inspection today. That's something new."

"Ah, yes, your arachnid pals," Geoffrey remarked, smiling.

"I believe there are three of them living in my room now. Two yellow sacs and one daddy longlegs. Seriously, don't you think it strange that spiders conjure such revulsion in us humans? Imagine if we were similarly repelled by the sight of a robin hopping in a puddle."

"I'd rather not." Geoffrey set his hat on the table and picked up Witner's Kindle. "Mind if I see what you've been reading?"

"When have I ever denied you that pleasure?"

Geoffrey took the reading device, settled into a chair opposite Witner, and began swiping away. "You must really like P. G. Wodehouse," he said.

"I enjoy his tragic dimensions."

"Right," said Geoffrey. "Find me a tragic passage in Wodehouse and I'll . . ."

"You'll what? Eat your fedora?"

"It's awfully hot in here," Geoffrey said, looking up. "Or is it me?"

"Must be you," Witner said. "You're flushed. Don't you feel well?"

"No," Geoffrey said. "I don't. I'm getting nauseated."

"Maybe that intermittent fasting is catching up with you. I warned you."

A sheen of sweat had blossomed on the counselor's forehead and his mouth was sagging open. Witner leaned forward, feeling a surge of clinical interest.

"Geoffrey?"

Geoffrey shook his head as if to clear it. Then he began blinking rapidly and swallowing. "Bryson, could you pass me a waste can? I'm going to vomit. Something is not right."

Something was definitely amiss. When Witner returned from the bathroom with a trash can, Geoffrey was staring blankly, straight ahead, a string of saliva oozing onto the e-reader. As Witner slid the trash can between the counselor's legs, the Kindle slipped from Geoffrey's hands and clattered into it. Geoffrey made a moaning sound.

"We'd better get you lying down," Witner said.

"Oh God," said Geoffrey, hunching forward. A stream of vomit gushed from his mouth, most of it flying over the can. Then another and another, leaving him gasping and choking. He swayed and pitched forward onto the floor, upsetting the trash can and hitting his head. Witner looked up at the monitor camera above the door. Where were the bloody guards? They usually appeared at the drop of a piece of toast. Geoffrey began convulsing, his limbs jerking rhythmically, neck drawing back, face turning purple, eyes fixed and bulging.

Glaring up at the camera, Witner waved his arms. "Yoo-hoo! Damn you! We could use some help here." The control room was only a hundred feet down the hallway. They should have been here immediately. He waved again. "Get the paramedics, you imbeciles!"

No response. Very bizarre. He was on his own. As a physician, he'd witnessed many people seizing. You protect them from banging their heads and keep your own fingers out of their mouth. They will not swallow their tongues, but they will bite off your finger. Mainly, though, you medicate them to stop the seizure activity.

He grabbed a blanket off the cot, eased Geoffrey onto his side so he wouldn't aspirate, folded the blanket, and put it under Geoffrey's thrashing head to protect it from the concrete floor. The most common reason people seize is an inadequately medicated underlying convulsive disorder, but Geoffrey had always said he was in good health and took no medication.

There was nothing more to do but wait for help. Where the devil were those blockheads? Seizures could go on for a long time, but eventually they would stop. Only very rarely did people die from a convulsion. Geoffrey's seizure activity was weakening and growing more sporadic, with longer and longer pauses of no movement.

Witner stared again at the camera. Obviously there'd been a malfunction. Two guards monitored the bank of screens. The chance of both taking naps simultaneously was about that of a meteorite landing on one's doghouse. This was odd. Nefariously odd. Something malign was afoot.

Typically, when a seizure finally ends, the patient goes into a coma-like postictal state that might last half an hour or more, and they would sleep it off. Geoffrey's seizing had finally stopped.

But so had his breathing.

His face was growing bluer and bluer, his eyes wide open and bloodshot, his lips flecked with froth and blood. Witner ground his knuckles into Geoffrey's sternum, checking for any response. None.

Then came a slow, gurgling expiration of air, followed by silence. Witner felt for a carotid pulse. Nothing. This was not a postictal state. Geoffrey was *dead*. His left arm was extended as if he were reaching for the vomit-streaked Kindle that had slid out of the overturned trash can.

He thought of starting CPR but found himself staring instead at the Kindle. He took a deep breath as a realization blossomed. "Yes," he said. He looked up at the camera, noticing how it resembled a one-eyed snake. Rising to his feet and gazing around, he imagined himself encircled by a team of residents and medical students, his clinical committee.

"So, ladies and gentlemen, we have a moderately overweight Caucasian male in his forties—recovering alcoholic, occasional cigar smoker, in otherwise good health—who became suddenly flushed and diaphoretic. Shortly afterward, he vomited forcefully, collapsed, and experienced generalized seizure activity, followed shortly thereafter by death. All this transpired within the space of ten minutes after he'd picked up and handled my e-reader. Would anyone hazard a diagnosis?"

"Hypoglycemia, Professor?" he answered himself in a reedy voice.

"Not at all likely," he replied in his normal tone. "Anyone else?"

"Anaphylaxis, Professor?"

"Not convincing. How about you, young Bryson?"

"Thank you for calling on me, Dr. Witner," he said. "This looks like an acute toxic exposure. There are very few poisonous substances that act this quickly. Cyanide is one. Another is the highly potent cholinergic nerve agent called Novichok, developed by the Soviets and often used by modern Russians to murder their enemies. It is rapidly absorbed across intact skin and requires only a minuscule dosage to be lethal. It is often smeared onto a surface that the victim will touch. The symptoms resemble this."

"Ha! Brilliant, Bryson," he said. "And what do you think might have been the vector for this agent?"

"Obviously, the Kindle, sir. It was lying on the table after the inspection today. You were the intended target, but your counselor got to it first."

"Yes, poor Geoffrey. I will miss him, as will his wife and children. But continue with your analysis. We so love to hear your mind at work."

"Thank you, sir. It's likely that at least one member of the Patterson security force is a clandestine agent for whoever is behind this. The one who inspected the room today is a prime candidate. But he obviously wasn't aware of the change in Geoffrey's schedule. You have been betrayed, sir."

"And I think we know by whom."

"Yes."

"And the camera? Why didn't they see and respond?"

"It's playing a pre-recorded loop. At some point, the agent who did this will switch it back to the live feed and sound the alarm. He'll use a solvent to swab the Kindle and remove traces of the poison. Unaware of the foul play, the authorities will call his death a cardiac arrest. An autopsy will be performed, but Novichok doesn't show up on the standard tests."

"Indeed," Witner said. "Interestingly, the pre-recorded loop on the CCTV is currently rendering us invisible to the other guards. Does that not present us with a window of opportunity to turn the table?"

"I believe it does, sir. For how long, I do not know. But yes, a window has opened."

"By heavens, Bryson. What would we do without you?"

"You'll never know, sir."

FORTY-THREE

It was ten o'clock at night and Jack was sitting alone in the living room, the ice in his scotch long since melted. Everyone else had gone to bed. Among other things, he'd been thinking of Hal Dugan's comments about him not taking losses well and reliving the feeling that had grabbed him when he'd learned that Julia was lost, a nightmarish sense of sinking and paralysis.

He took a long sip. It was natural, of course, to feel overwhelmed at the potential loss of one's own child. But even though Julia was now safe, the feeling continued to surge like the surface of a wind-tossed ocean, something irrational in its power.

He could see down the hallway toward Kaitlyn's room. She had not joined them for supper, had locked her door. Julia had stood in front of it crying until Jack picked her up. He had given his daughter a bath and put her to bed while Zoë got Marianna set up in the spare bedroom. Then Zoë had gone to bed herself, and Marianna hadn't reappeared, was probably sleeping. Understandable, given what she'd been through.

There was light at the bottom of Kaitlyn's bedroom door. This was not how he'd wanted her stay to end. He thought of their conversation in the car the night she'd been kidnapped. Before she went home, he at least wanted to let her know that he respected her and wasn't angry, that he wished her the best.

Other issues crowded into his mind. He would soon be unemployed. How long could they coast on his savings? A month or six weeks at most. He would need to start looking for a position quickly. And he should go to bed himself. He was still sleep deprived. He should take an Ambien. Two Ambien maybe. He recalled Kaitlyn's anguished look when she told him in the barn about taking the Benadryl for sleep. He remembered her bravery at the scrapyard and how deftly she had been able to comfort Chad the day of Falconi's tour. His heart twisted.

A door opened in the hallway. He looked up, hoping it would be Kaitlyn. But it wasn't. Marianna walked down the hall and into the living room, wearing Zoë's old white bathrobe. "Am I disturbing? I was hoping for a drink of water."

He stood. "Of course. I thought you'd fallen asleep. Would you like a drink of something stronger?"

"Yes, that would be nice, thank you. My mind is restless."

"Scotch okay? Or wine?"

"Scotch is good."

When he handed her a glass, she was sitting on the couch with her legs drawn up under the robe. "How are you feeling?" he asked.

"The shower was good. I finally feel clean. But not calm inside. It is good to be here, and I thank you again, Dr. Forester. Your daughter, Julia, is very sweet. Very intelligent. Zoë says that your niece, Kaitlyn, is most intelligent too. But I did not have any chance to talk with her. Zoë tells also that Kaitlyn's situation at home is difficult and that she must go back soon. I overheard what Kaitlyn said—that you do not like her? That is difficult to believe."

He sighed. The sliding glass doors that gave onto the deck reflected the table light by Marianna. It resembled a bright star in the sky. "I don't dislike her," he said. "Not at all. But looking back, I could have been warmer toward her."

"Why are you not warmer to her?"

He sipped his drink and sought the right words. "The first time I saw her this summer, it was like looking at my wife. You'd think that it would make me feel more positively toward her, but it didn't. That bothers me because I know she's a great kid. And she's had it rough."

"She stirs up grief in you?"

"I think so."

"You told me you buried your wife three years in the past."

Jack looked at the reflection in the glass, that false star, and nodded. "That's correct."

"Three years is much long to hold grief," she said. "In Ukraine we know grief. So many died from the Nazis in the war, and then the way the Soviets treated us after the war was terrible."

"I can only imagine," he said.

"You and your wife must have been special together for it to still be hard after this much time. Zoë tells me she was a writer. Wrote novels, not articles like me. I don't have such a big imagination. I can't make up things."

"She wrote articles too, and she was a teacher." Jack shifted in his chair. "Maybe you could tell me more about yourself."

"You don't like to talk about her?"

"I'm interested to hear more about you."

"I'm a very ordinary person. I was raised without major personal trauma, mostly in Odessa. Do you know Odessa? It's a beautiful city."

"I'm not that good at geography, but it's a seaport, right? Or am I thinking of Sevastopol?"

"Very good. They are both port cities on the Black Sea. But Sevastopol is in Crimea, which Putin stole from us four years ago. Odessa is more north and west. All my grandparents, though, were from Eastern Ukraine, near Donetsk. They went through World War II there, which was difficult. After the war it was hard for them too. My father's father was a professor of history, but he was arrested by the Russians in 1959, and they never saw him again. My father was only eleven then."

Jack shook his head. "Sad to hear that. Why was he arrested?"

"He wrote things they didn't like, so they took him away to reeducate. My father's mother was a nurse. I knew her for a little while when I was young. Lovely person. Also died too young, from cancer. My mother and father are both gone too. She was a teacher and a bossy person, my mother. My father was hurt by the loss of his father and had troubles all his life, no good jobs for long, too much alcohol. So now there is just myself and my sister, Olesia."

"The one you told me fled with her family to France?"

"Yes. And that I hope I can get her and her family into the Witness Protection Program here in America with me."

"And you were a nurse yourself for a while?"

"Like my grandmother, yes. I worked in a pediatric hospital for almost two years. But I had always wanted to be writing, so I changed my career. I began working for *Ukrainian Week* after returning from study in England. I write about medical things, and about the ways that the influence of Russia and Putin are working to destroy my country."

"You're following in your grandfather's footsteps."

She nodded and sipped her drink. "Yes. I like that expression. Follow in footsteps. Like dry path in a swamp. They say I even look like him. I often hope that he would have been proud of what I do. Is that right—*would have been*? The conditional?"

"Yes, and I'm sure he would have. The way you escaped and made your way here is astonishing. You're a very resourceful person."

She shrugged and smiled. "And a very dead person on paper."

"That will soon change."

She lifted her glass. "Here is hoping that we can help each other find the truth."

"*Salut.*" He watched her take a long sip then look over at him, questioningly. "Yes?" he questioned.

"If I may ask, Dr. Forester, how did your wife die?"

"Zoë didn't tell you?"

"No. You do not have to talk of this, if you do not want."

He looked down at his shoes. He was suddenly aware they were scuffed and dirty. He hadn't cleaned or shined them in weeks. "It was a car accident." He looked up at her.

"Very sorry to hear, Dr. Forester."

He nodded, feeling his throat constrict as memories returned. He cleared it and took a sip of the scotch.

"I had a favorite uncle who lost his life that way," she said. "Of course, that is not like a spouse. The other person was very intoxicated. Was that what happened?"

"There wasn't another vehicle involved," he said. "She'd borrowed my car because hers wouldn't start." He hadn't intended to share that. But it came out.

"I see," she said.

He breathed in deeply and released the breath slowly. "She had an old Jeep that I couldn't get her to part with. It wouldn't start one day." He stopped, his eyes stinging. "If only I'd have . . ." He felt suddenly cold. Why was he burdening her like this? He looked at his shoes again. They were filthy.

"If only what, Dr. Forester?"

"Never mind," he said. "I was just rambling."

He heard soft footfalls. Julia shuffled into the living room, her stuffed elephant, the one Kaitlyn had gone out to get for her that awful night, dangling from her hand.

"Daddy, I can't go to sleep."

CHAPTER FORTY-FOUR

Mikhail Potemkin ascended to his private observation bridge where the night air was humid and still and the only sound an occasional surge of muffled laughter coming from the crew's bar near the bow. The water was a black shroud. No stars tonight. Setting his jaw, he called Liski.

"Bodashka, we must talk. Rapid action is in order."

"At your service," Liski said, his tone deferential, as it had been since the escape of Marianna Kovalenko. "What's going on, Mikhail?"

"First, my plan to eliminate Bryson Witner went completely to hell."

"But how? You are the most thorough planner I've ever known."

"No cat can catch every mouse that chews at the wires. In this case, Witner's counselor was exposed to the Novichok instead of him. Good plan, bad timing. The counselor is dead instead, and Witner turned this misfire to his advantage. He escaped."

"Escaped?" Liski made a hissing sound. "My God. The devil must be on his side."

"Maybe so, but Dr. Witch has played his last trick. Get over here immediately. Use the Lear. You need to find him and finish the job."

"What if the police get to him first?"

"Don't let that stop you. Find a way to destroy him however you can. You will be given a full briefing by Colonel Spavin after we talk. All resources will be at your disposal."

"It will be done," said Liski. "We will not fail."

"I want action, not words," Potemkin said. "Now, let us talk about

Marianna Kovalenko. I remain unhappy about her escape, Bodashka. Very unhappy. This is a personal humiliation. No one can do this to me. This must not stand."

"I understand, Mikhail. I take full responsibility. It was my fault, not yours. At least we extracted from Kovalenko's friend in Kyiv that she was heading for America."

"America is a big country, in case you forgot. You used to live there. Like a big shot."

"But I have people keeping an eye out for her. She will have to surface, and we'll be waiting."

"You don't have to wait."

"What do you mean?"

"I have found her. *Me*—I found her. With no help from you."

After a pause, Liski broke into excited speech. "How? This is good. Where is she?"

Potemkin described what Haines had told him about the woman in Forester's office. "And I had my people review footage from the hospital. They found her coming through the lobby. She's changed her hair color, but it's her. I'm sure of it.

"Unbelievable," said Liski. "How did she do it?"

"How is irrelevant. She obviously had access to the news in Ukraine and knew what was going to happen to her. She has a nimble mind and she wants to live. The question is what to do now. But I know one thing that gives me an advantage."

"What do you know?"

"Her going to Forester proves she did not go to the American police. They think Marianna Kovalenko is dead because of the DNA. She knows they wouldn't believe her. So she goes to Forester instead, hoping to enlist his help. She will try to convince him that he was tricked, then she will get him to help her. She is very clever."

"I wish she were on our side."

"But she is done making a fool out of me. You must find and eliminate her—and show her no mercy. Make her know terror.

Forester will probably try to hide her. Start by surveilling his house. The colonel will help you with all the resources you need for both jobs. Stay in contact."

"Yes. I will divide my crew into two teams—one for Witner and one for Kovalenko. They will begin even before I arrive. I'm on it like a hawk, like a ferret. I will not sleep till this is done."

"Leave no witnesses with Marianna. Have her dig her own grave. If she is with Forester, have him dig one for them both." Liski laughed at this. "I didn't say that to be funny. I mean it."

"You really want them to dig their own graves?" asked Liski.

"Why would I say it if I didn't mean it?"

"But what if I find a safer way to dispose of them?"

"There is no better way to create terror. Have them dig their own graves. In the ground. End of discussion."

"Not to contradict you, but that could be risky. Cadaver dogs could find them. With all respect, maybe you are taking this too personally."

"*Excuse* me? What are you suggesting? That maybe I'm insane?"

"No, no. Of course not. Just saying there could be more efficient ways—"

"Shut up and follow my orders. No more talk. She brought this on herself."

CHAPTER FORTY-FIVE

Marianna watched Dr. Forester lift his daughter onto his lap and smooth the little girl's hair. She thought of her own childhood, of how her mother and father's nearness would erase the ugliness of the world. The gift of parents is to hide the real world until one is old enough to cope. He is clearly a good father to Julia, but from what she'd seen and what the talkative Zoë had told her, the bond between him and his niece was broken. That was not good for either of them. It saddened her to think of a fatherless girl like Kaitlyn having a stepmother with many problems. Her roots had been torn away. It would be hard for her to grow strong. She may not.

A song her mother used to sing at bedtime came to mind. *Oi Khodyt Son Kolo Vikon.* She still knew it by heart. Why not share now? She began singing. Dr. Forester and the little girl looked over at her with surprise. She smiled at them and kept singing.

"What do the words mean, Daddy?" Julia wondered aloud. He put a finger to his lips.

For some reason the melody always reminded Marianna of a river twisting by bare trees under a moon. As she sang, she thought of Anatoly, praying he would survive, forgiving him if he betrayed her. And she thought of Olesia, how they had sung this one night in harmony to their mother before she died. Three times Marianna sang the verses for Julia, each one a little softer. By the last, the girl slept.

Jack smiled over at her, which was nice to see for a man with much weight on his back, a man of many layers. He was a person made to help others; she could see that. A person who would sacrifice. Maybe too much. She had known some doctors like that. Their need to give became almost a sickness, a death wish.

He carried the little girl to bed, then returned and asked if he could freshen her drink. She accepted.

"Thank you," he said, returning from the kitchen and handing her the glass. "That was lovely. You have a very nice voice."

"Not as good as my mother or sister."

"What was the song?"

"In English the name would be 'The Dream Passes by the Window.'"

"The melody was very soothing," he said. "It almost made me forget all the puzzles we're dealing with."

"Yes. We have more questions than answers. Most true."

"One of my big questions is this," he said. "If the impostor they sent over here was involved in Chad's death—why did she do it?"

"I was thinking this too. I believe it was nothing personal against the young man. We have an old saying that when the wolf is hunting for sheep, he attacks the nearest lamb to make them all run. That way he can see which ones are too slow."

"I'm feeling dense," he said. "I'm not sure how that applies to this situation."

"Maybe she wanted to see what would happen because he died. He was just the lamb. But I don't know."

He gazed ahead and took a deep breath. "Interesting. A murder of opportunity. His death certainly ruined our best chance to avoid being taken over by HWA."

"I met the leader of this company—Dr. Haines is his name?"

"You did?" he said, surprised.

"By accident. He was in your office when I first arrive today. Very tall man. When you were talking with him, your assistant Tré told me who he was. You mention while we drove home that for HWA to get your hospital would be like Russia devouring Ukraine."

"Yes. That's a comparison the impostor gave me."

She sipped and felt the liquid warm her chest. "She came to spy on you, this I know because they told me. Could it be that the oligarch had her kill him to help the HWA people?"

He looked up at the ceiling and seemed to turn this idea over in his mind as he swirled his drink. Then he shook his head. "That seems far-fetched. Too complicated. Why would a Russian oligarch be in cahoots with a thriving American health care company? Nope, I think HWA was just a lucky bystander."

"I do not know the word *cahoots*."

"It means to be in association with. To be partners with."

"I see. *Cahoots*. Nice word. I will remember it."

"Marianna, who exactly is this oligarch, Potemkin? Tell me more about him."

"I believe the one involved is Mikhail Potemkin, the most open criminal of them all. That is saying much. I wrote a story about him when he had a witness against him murdered in Kyiv, and again when he created his own country. I know he was unhappy about me because I make it harder for him to do business in Ukraine."

"He created his own country?"

"Not of land. He turned his very big yacht into a floating nation with him as leader. A mobile state. Gives him much impunity from laws. The process was blessed by Vladimir Putin, his old friend. They are all old friends, the oligarchs. That's how people become rich there, and this Potemkin is beyond dreams wealthy."

"Where does his money come from?"

"Many businesses. Some of them not criminal. But his main work is with—what's the phrase—cyber . . . ?"

"Cybercrime?" Jack offered.

She nodded. "Yes. He is a computer genius with advanced degree in computer science from what Americans call 'MIT.' He helped create some famous spyware programs there, like Pegasus. He worked on the Stuxnet worm, the one that attacked Iran. His ship is full of computers, a floating factory for these crimes. Lots of money."

"You're a brave person to take on someone like that."

"Brave maybe, but more than anything, I am an angry person. These people follow no humanity. Life is all a jungle to them. Kill and prosper. Kill to get what you want. Potemkin has killed many people. One of his favorite ways to assassinate inconvenient people is to hack the computer of cars and cause accidents. He uses poison too. And old-fashioned bullets."

"I didn't know cars could be hacked."

"Anything that connects with internet can be hacked, Dr. Forester. Don't you know this? Cars, phones, refrigerators, all these things. They tell me that cars are not that difficult. They plant a worm in the car that lets them follow with GPS and take over brakes and steering when the car is at the right place. Then *bang*. Very cruel."

She watched him frown thoughtfully.

"The university comptroller died in an accident last week," he said. "After the medical center's financial crisis was discovered. It made it look as if she felt responsible."

"This is something Potemkin could do. Maybe he wanted people to think that she felt guilty. We don't know anything right now. And anything is possible."

His cell phone began chiming. Taking it out, he looked at her. "It's Investigator Dirkens. Maybe she has news about the DNA."

Out of the speaker came the same female she'd heard over the phone in his office. After apologizing for the lateness of the call, she hesitated a moment, then said she had some unwelcome news.

"What's that?" he asked.

"You'd better sit down. I need to let you know that Bryson Witner escaped from the Patterson Institute this evening."

"I don't believe it," he said, sagging back in the chair.

"Neither did I at first," she said. "But it's true, and given that you were once a target of his, we're sending out a car to keep an eye on your place twenty-four seven until he's caught."

He shook his head and sighed. "How did he do it?"

"It looks like he killed a counselor and used the man's clothes and ID to waltz out. Then he stole the counselor's car. The state police suspect he had inside help. The CCTV in his room failed at just the right time. A patrol car should be arriving at your place right about now. Please confirm."

He strode to the deck doors and looked out. "There's a car. It's blinking its lights."

"That's them. Doctor, you and your family need to remain in place until this is over. I don't need to tell you how smart and dangerous he is."

"No, you don't. By the way, do you have anything on new DNA samples from Kyiv or the fingerprints from England?"

"Not yet. We should have results tomorrow or the next day. I'll contact you. Listen, if you step out of the house for any reason, let the officers know. I'll text you their cell number."

The call over, he sat staring at the wall.

"Dr. Forester," Marianna said, "who is this person who escaped?"

"A ghost from the past," he said. "Do you like Stephen King novels?"

"I am not the best fan of those books, but I have read a couple, yes. He makes the pages turn with fear. He is skilled at frightening."

"I'm not sure that even he could have invented a villain like Bryson Witner."

She leaned forward and listened as he talked. Bryson Witner was a brilliant physician who, after leaving a position at Harvard, had joined the endocrinology department faculty at the New Canterbury Medical Center. That was about seven years ago. He was very charismatic and charmed many people at the medical school. When the previous dean was killed in a scuba diving accident shortly after Witner arrived, he became the acting dean and tried to bring about ambitious innovations, obviously aiming to take the place over. But there were some, including Dr. Forester and his wife, who felt that things were not right with Witner. They became suspicious that

Witner was behind the death of the previous dean, which turned out to be true. Turns out Witner was a high-functioning paranoid schizophrenic and a serial killer. He'd also murdered one of his colleagues at New Canterbury and killed his own lover.

"Nobody thought him insane before he came?" she asked.

"He'd had a nervous breakdown while working at Harvard and was hospitalized for a good while. But, in hindsight, it was more than just a generic episode from overwork. It was a full-blown case of psychosis, and he may have been responsible for the death of a patient, though it was never proven. In any case, Harvard was happy to see him leave and didn't go into great detail on their reference letter."

"The investigator said you were his prime target. Why is this, Dr. Forester?"

"Witner never liked me from the beginning, and the feeling was mutual. At first I just thought he was overly ambitious and arrogant. But my wife was a journalist then, and when she interviewed him for an article she picked up the fact that he was a master manipulator. She thought he was hiding something. We weren't married yet, had just started seeing each other. Meanwhile, it turned out he tried to kill one of my mentors, who was also putting two and two together.

"She must have been a very good journalist." He looked away and appeared to lose himself in thought. "I'm sorry," she said. "It is still hard for you to talk about her."

"It is," he said, clearing his throat. "But in any case, I went to Boston and managed to get a look at the records from his hospitalization. What I saw was very scary. He'd had this whole bizarre delusional worldview where most people were infected by some sort of virus, and it was his duty to take them out. While I was gone, Zellie put herself at great personal risk by visiting his home before I had a chance to tell her what I'd learned. To make a long story short, we finally flushed him out into the open. But just before he was finally arrested, he tried to kill us both. With a shotgun. Almost succeeded."

"My God. He really is like a villain from Stephen King. Or the

Inferno of Dante. The investigator was smart to send protection for you. I hope they catch him soon."

"I'm sure they will." He caught her eyes. "I hate to drag you into this."

"No—it is me who drags *you* into trouble," she said. Then, unable to hold back a yawn, she set down her drink and yielded to it. Exhaustion swept over her.

"You should get some sleep."

She stifled another yawn and stood. "Yes. I will sleep. Thank you for everything."

FORTY-SIX

After Marianna retired, Jack went to the window again. The police cruiser was stationed halfway up the driveway, its headlights like a pair of benign yellow eyes in the darkness. He pulled up the number that Dirkens had texted him and notified the officers in the car that he was going out to make sure Tony had locked the barn door.

Outside, the air was still and frigid. The door was secure. He thought about waking Tony to warn him, then decided against it. Tony would never get back to sleep. What was the point? Back inside, he checked the doors and windows, and also decided against waking Zoë for the same reason. It might keep her up all night for no benefit. He eased into Julia's bedroom. She was sleeping soundly. A line of light still filtered beneath Kaitlyn's door. He thought of knocking. But it was late. He'd talk to her first thing tomorrow.

In his own bedroom, he lay down fully dressed and picked up the book on his nightstand. It was *The Nutmeg of Consolation*, the fourteenth book in the Aubrey–Maturin series by Patrick O'Brian. He opened it but his concentration drifted away after a few words. Slipping in the bookmark, a birthday card made by Julia in preschool, he closed his eyes and reviewed the strange events of the day. Marianna's idea to enter the Witness Protection Program here was a stroke of genius. She was a remarkable person—her resilience, her courage, her integrity, even her singing. The melody of the lullaby she'd sung for Julia replayed in his mind.

Then something she'd said that evening resurfaced. Potemkin used car hacking as a tool of assassination, planting malware in a vehicle's computer to take control. What would it feel like for your vehicle to develop a mind of its own and try to kill you?

His eyes shot open and a cold chill ran up his back.

Sitting up, he switched on the nightstand light as memories from several years ago came flooding back. A week or so before Zellie's accident, something strange had happened to the Ford Escape's steering. The mechanism had frozen momentarily as he was rounding a corner. Then it had suddenly overcorrected. If he hadn't slammed on the brakes, he would have been off the road and down an embankment. He drove slowly the rest of the way home, and everything had seemed back to normal.

But the experience had rattled him and he called the garage. His mechanic gave him an appointment for the following week and suggested he not drive the Escape until the hydraulics had a good checking out. He'd parked it in the garage and used his old F-150.

His heart began pounding and his scalp prickled. He hadn't told Zellie about the Escape's steering issue. She had her own vehicle, her Jeep. It hadn't seemed necessary. But why hadn't he at least mentioned it to her in passing? And even worse, several days later, a Saturday, with him sitting there concentrating on tying a goddamned trout fly, thinking about the hospital, Zellie had decided to run some errands. Julia, just a baby then, was taking a nap. She came back in the house, said her Jeep wouldn't turn over, could she use his Escape? "Sure," he'd called to her. *Sure.* Why hadn't he set aside what he was doing and stopped to think? It was the most horrific mistake he'd ever made in his life. She knew that the keys to the F-150 were hanging in the kitchen—right there next to the keys to the Escape. He just assumed she would take the truck. But why had he assumed that? He should have checked, should have used his goddamn brains. But no. He hadn't thought. He hadn't *thought*. It wasn't until half an hour later when the police called to notify him of the crash that he'd looked to see which keys she'd taken, and when he saw the F-150 keys still hanging there, he knew she'd taken the Escape—and that it was his fault. But by then she was dead. He might as well have killed her himself.

He was sitting rigidly upright in the bed now, sweat dripping into his eyes, his fists gripping the sheet. She deserved so much better. She had loved him and trusted him. She should have had a more caring and intelligent life partner. If he'd been less careless and not so self-involved, Julia would still have a mother. He would still have the love of his life. The police said there had been no skid marks, no indication of why she'd veered off the road. The hydraulic system was too damaged in the crash to assess for flaws. The only demonstrable flaw was his negligence—and he still could not bear to share his shame with another soul because he was a coward. It should have been him who died.

But maybe it was supposed to have been him who died. And who would have wanted that?

He jerked his legs off the bed and shot to his feet. The world went gray. He reached for the nightstand and steadied himself as nausea and lightheadedness receded. He trudged into his home office, sank into the chair, opened a browser, and on the same line he typed the names *Bryson Witner* and, guessing at the spelling, *Mikhail Potemkin*.

It didn't take long. Less than a few seconds. The first link led to photos of the annual gala of the Boston Numismatics Society, 1987. There were about thirty individuals, all standing in three rows. He easily picked out the young Witner in the first row, dapper in a tuxedo. Using the legend in the caption, he found Mikhail Potemkin a row behind and to the left of Witner. Potemkin had longish hair and an unusually large head with prominent cheekbones.

The way dye spreads in hot water, a bitter sensation billowed throughout his core. He called the officers in the driveway and let them know he was going out to his brother's apartment. The sky was clear, the air frigid. He clumped up the stairs. It was one thirty in the morning. He knocked, waited, and knocked again. The door swung open. Tony was in plaid pajamas. "What's the matter, Jack? You don't look good."

"We haven't had much of a chance to talk in a couple of days," Jack said, his throat raspy. "Are you feeling better?"

"Starting to," Tony said. "I'll never have a friend like Chad again, but I have other things to be thankful for."

The news that Chad may have been murdered was not something Jack was going to share yet. Tony offered him something to drink. He declined. Jack informed him of Witner's escape and the police protection. "Whenever you need to go outside, give me a call and I'll let the officers know. Best if you stay with us in the main house starting in the morning." Jack stopped as a shiver passed through him. "But the main reason I came over is to ask you a computer question."

"Why now?"

"Just listen to me. If a car computer gets infected with a virus so that it can be controlled remotely, would you be able to find it?"

"Should be able to, yes."

"The Escape has been sitting outside for three years. Could you analyze it for a virus?"

"I think so. The hardware's sealed and the ports are all standard. You sure you don't want something to drink? Orange juice?"

"Please check the computer out there first thing in the morning. I need to find out if it was infected."

"What makes you worried about it?"

Jack opened and closed his mouth. Nothing came out.

Tony tilted his head and drew in a deep breath, a look of understanding flashing in his eyes. "You think that's what happened to Zellie?" Jack exhaled. "How about a cup of tea?" Tony urged.

"No. It's late. You get some rest."

"That's what Zellie used to make when I was concerned about something. Tea. Are you sure?"

Jack closed his eyes. They were burning, had started flowing. "Okay."

CHAPTER FORTY-SEVEN

It was nearly three o'clock when Jack returned from Tony's apartment. Slumping onto a chair at the kitchen table, he fell asleep, forehead resting on the place mat. He dreamed that Marianna was standing in the field by the garage. The sun was gleaming on her hair. He walked over and she turned. But it was the impostor, whoever she was, not Marianna, and her eye sockets were hollow. He went into the house looking for Marianna, but in the kitchen he found Kaitlyn and Zellie making pasta. While Kaitlyn kneaded dough, Zellie cranked the machine and strands of spaghetti cascaded like a waterfall over the edge of the table. They ignored him. Back outside it was spring, the apple tree in blossom. Marianna had returned to Ukraine.

"Jack."

He opened his eyes. Zoë stood there, tightening the belt of her housecoat. "Don't tell me you've been here all night."

Early morning light filtered through a yellow curtain above the sink. The left side of his face was numb. She rested a hand on his shoulder and the recollection of why he had gone out to talk with Tony flooded through him like ice water. He thought of Witner.

"Zoë, I have to fill you in on something."

"Talk while I'm making coffee," she said. He followed her into the kitchen, his legs and neck stiff. He needed a shave and a shower. "The girls are still asleep. I haven't seen Vlada yet. I hope she rested well. That bed's a little hard but it's better than a hotel."

"I'm sure it was," Jack responded.

"Lord, Jack, I hope Kaitlyn is settled. That was awful. I feel so bad for her."

"Zoë, I don't suppose you've noticed the police car in the driveway yet."

She stopped pouring water into the coffee maker and looked at him. "Why is there a police car in the driveway?"

Her face went slack as he described Witner's escape. "It's unlikely he'd come here, but they're not taking chances."

"I'm grateful for that, at any rate," she said. Coffee began dripping into the carafe. "I wonder what's going to happen next. Maybe an earthquake. That would be interesting. Or a volcano erupting out back. By the way, Vlada is very nice, but I'm not sure I believe her story. The hotels in New Canterbury are never full unless there's a big football game. Maybe you just wanted her to stay here. Are you not telling me something?"

"She can be trusted, I'm sure."

"That wasn't my question. So, if the police want us to stay in the house until your friend Witner is caught, Kaitlyn won't be going to school. With what happened yesterday, I'm not sure she'd even want to. Julia's preschool doesn't start back until next week, so we're fine there. Assuming that monster isn't still running amok."

"They'll get him."

"Vlada will be stuck with us here too. She didn't pack very much. I can give her some of Zellie's clothes from the closet. They're close in size."

Jack hesitated. She caught his expression. "Does that bother you?" she asked.

"No, it's fine."

She handed him a cup. "Good. It's time you cleaned it out anyway."

He heard footsteps in the hallway. Marianna entered, still in Zoë's old robe. "Good morning," she said.

"And a good morning to you," said Zoë. "How did you sleep?"

"Most well, thank you. Dr. Forester gave me some whiskey before sleeping and it helped."

"Did he? Wasn't that nice of him."

"Bed is comfortable. House is warm. Dr. Forester, you look rumpled. Did you not sleep?"

"He never made it to bed," said Zoë. "Ready for some coffee, Vlada?"

"That would be good, thank you. But I don't want to cause you work. Let me help."

"You'll have your turn. Go sit."

Marianna took a chair next to Jack. "Why did you not go to bed?" she inquired.

He looked at her and lowered his voice. "I discovered something," he said.

"Tell me." She lifted the cup and inhaled. "Smells good. Zoë, will you come sit too?"

"In a bit," Zoë said. "I need to let Kaitlyn know she can sleep in. Jack, you'd better tell Vlada about the police car."

"I already know of this," Marianna said. Zoë looked at them, then padded down the hallway. "What did you discover, Dr. Forester?"

"Something hit me last night," he began. "A thought. An intuition maybe . . ."

"A thought of what?"

"I wondered if Bryson Witner and Potemkin might have any connection."

"Why would you think that?"

He looked into her eyes and through a trick of light saw his own reflection. "So, I put their names together and searched . . ."

Her brow furrowed. "What did you find?"

"Let me show you."

They went down the hallway to Jack's office. "In case you ever want to use this computer, the password is juliA!1415. I'll write it down for you." He pulled up a screenshot of the photo he'd found last night taken all those years ago at the coin club in Boston. "That's Bryon Witner. And you know who the other man is."

Her eyes widened and she said something in what he assumed was Ukrainian. Then she leaned back and folded her arms over her chest. "Too strange for coincidence."

"Yes," he said.

Zoë called out. "Jack!" An instant later she swept into the office, her face flushed. "Kaitlyn's gone."

The smaller of Kaitlyn's two suitcases was missing, along with some of her clothes, her toiletries, and her jacket. Jack phoned the officers in the driveway and detailed the story. "Has anyone seen anything unusual out there?"

"Per the log, sir, there's just your trips to the barn. Are you sure she's not hiding in the house somewhere?"

"Let me repeat, officer—we found an open window and a missing suitcase and clothes. She was upset yesterday evening."

"Do you know when she went missing?"

"I could see a light under her door around one in the morning. But the light was off when we just discovered she was gone. It had to be sometime between then and now." He heard the officer talking to his partner in the car. Zoë was at the kitchen table with Marianna, their heads close.

"Sir, we've only been on station half an hour and we've seen nothing. I'll check with the previous shift."

He saw Zoë reach for a tissue and sob. Marianna was talking too low for him to hear. Julia came shuffling down the hallway in her pajamas, holding the elephant.

"That would be good, Officer," Jack said. "And let's get a search going. There's a lunatic on the loose out there, as you know. He could be taking advantage of this."

"We're aware, sir."

"I'm going out to the barn now," Jack said.

"Why?"

"My brother lives out there."

"Your brother lives in the barn?"

"Didn't they tell you?"

"The location wasn't specified. I'll meet you out there."

He didn't bother grabbing his jacket. Tony was just rising. Jack filled him in as Tony dressed. When they got outside, one of the patrolmen was standing there, a cell phone to his ear. A steady cold wind was blowing. The officer had silver hair and red cheeks. "Good morning, Dr. Forester. I'm Officer Daniels. I've gotten hold of one of the people on duty last night. Here, you'd better talk to her." He switched to speaker mode and turned the phone toward Jack.

"Good morning," she said. "I'm Officer Volta. They caught me just as I was about to head home. I saw something last night that might be relevant. Only three cars went by all night. The last one stopped and picked someone up about a tenth of a mile or so west of your driveway, near the curve. We only noticed because it was just getting light, about five forty-five."

"By the red farmhouse?"

"Yes. I'd assumed someone was getting a ride to work."

"That house is vacant," Jack said.

"They moved three years ago, the Millers," added Tony, coming up next to him.

"That could have been her," Jack continued. "She might have seen your car and snuck behind the barn. From there she could have gotten to a field where the hedgerow would have hidden her from you." He looked over in that direction. A row of tall arborvitae swayed in the wind.

"That's possible," replied Officer Volta.

"Could you tell if that person you saw getting picked up had a suitcase?" Jack asked.

"No. It was too far and too dark."

"If you came out here to surveil, I'm surprised you didn't have the equipment to track the plate numbers going by."

Her brows rose. "This was a short-notice assignment, sir."

"I'm not complaining. The important question is who picked her up."

"You need to file a missing person report," the officer said.

"I realize that. We just filed one for her not many days ago. Kaitlyn Andersen."

"I remember. She's the teenager who was kidnapped. And now she's run away? Sounds like she needs help. I'm giving you to my sergeant."

The sergeant came on. "Dr. Forester, I just pulled up the basic information on your niece from the previous file. We'll get on it. Contact us if she comes back in the meantime."

Jack shivered as the cold wind cut through his shirt. Tony tapped his shoulder. "Jack, I'm going to go pull the computer from the old car now and bring it to my workshop."

"How long will it take?"

"I don't know."

CHAPTER FORTY-EIGHT

When Jack went inside, Julia was at the kitchen table sitting between Zoë and Marianna, her eyes moist and puffy.

"Did you find Kaitlyn, Daddy?"

"Not yet, honey. We will."

She wiped her nose. "The last time it was because she went to get Ellie. And now it's because I got lost. I said I was sorry."

"I told you it's not your fault, pumpkin," said Zoë. "She loves you. She will come back, and she will be okay."

"That's right," said Marianna. "We must think good thoughts for her."

"Are you going to the hospital now, Daddy?"

"No, Julia. We're all going to stay here today."

"Jack," said Zoë. "I called Aishia. She says she knows nothing."

"Can Vlada sing for us again?" asked Julia.

Zoë raised her eyebrows. "Vlada sang for you? When was that?"

"Last night," Julia said. "She's good. She sings like one of those 'got talent' people on the show you like."

"But that's the only song I can sing," said Marianna. "Everything else sounds like I'm a goat or a sick cat."

Julia giggled. "Really? Can I hear?"

"Zoë, we need to call Stella," Jack said.

She gave him a look and blinked. "We? Remember the last time you tried?"

"But it's possible Kaitlyn made contact with her."

Zoë blew air out her nose. "She would never reach out to Stella if she were in distress."

"Julia," said Marianna. "Let's you and I climb down to your playroom in the basement."

"We don't say *climb* down the stairs, Vlada," Julia said. "We say *go* down the stairs."

They left the table, and Marianna closed the basement door after them.

Once they were out of earshot, Jack turned to Zoë. "Let's get this over with," he said. "We can use your phone. She'll recognize the number."

"If you insist. I'll put it on speaker so we can both enjoy her sparkling personality. You start."

Stella's line rang half a dozen times before she picked up. "Zoë?"

"It's Jack, Stella. But I'm sitting here with Zoë. You're on speaker."

"Well, well . . . both of you at once. Are we still on track for bringing her back Sunday? If that's a problem, you can push it back a few days."

"Stella . . ."

"What has she done?"

Jack breathed deeply. "I'm afraid she ran away last night."

Stella said nothing for a few seconds, then her voice came over crisp and loud. "What's wrong with you people?"

"I hear your anger," Jack said.

"No, you hear diddly-squat. Or should I say jack shit. All you had to do was keep track of her for a few more effing days. Let me know when you find her. It better be soon, or you'll be hearing from my lawyers. And don't think I don't have them."

The connection went dead.

Zoë shook her head. "I wouldn't let that woman babysit my dead cat. Why Zachary ever decided to marry her, God only knows. Love can be both blind and stupid. I count myself a survivor. I escaped my marriage after five years and it was the best thing I ever did."

Jack remembered Zach and Stella's wedding, how lovely Stella had looked. She'd seemed a little jumpy, her conversation a bit unfiltered, but she'd been nice.

Zoë went on. "I'm going to call Aishia again. I think she was holding something back. Do you want to listen in?"

"I don't need to," he said. "But there's something I need to mention." He described the sighting of someone being picked up near daybreak by the old Miller farm. "It had to be her."

"Thank goodness," Zoë said. "This is a relief."

"Relief, Zoë? My worst nightmare is that it could have been Witner."

"Absolutely not. You're being paranoid. Kaitlyn would never have gotten into a car with a stranger. Never in a million years. She'd have taken off running. This means she's with someone she knows."

Zoë entered Aishia's number. Aishia had no sooner answered than Jack's own phone chimed. It was Dirkens. The investigator informed him there was no word yet on either Witner or Kaitlyn. "In the meantime, Doctor, I'd like to come over and interview your brother around noon today."

"Noon's fine," Jack said, and asked about the fingerprints and DNA.

"Nothing yet," she said.

"Investigator, there's something else. Have you ever heard of a Russian oligarch named Mikhail Potemkin?"

"It's vaguely familiar. Why?"

"You mentioned that Witner might have had some help escaping. Potemkin and Witner belonged to the same coin collecting club in Boston in the late eighties. I discovered a photo of them together on the internet."

"Why is this important?"

"Potemkin runs an international cybercrime operation, among other things. And he apparently knew Marianna Kovalenko."

Dirkens was silent for a moment, then she chuckled. "So, you're still nosing around on the internet. Keep it up. I'll get some people to dig a little further into this Potemkin. Interesting."

Jack poured himself another cup of coffee. Zoë was saying goodbye to Aishia. She looked at him. "Who were you talking to?"

"Investigator Dirkens. No news yet, but she's coming over this afternoon to interview Tony."

"Well, I was right," she said. "Aishia was hiding something. Kaitlyn has been talking to her guidance counselor about staying here." Jack felt his face warming. Zoë sighed. "I wish she'd have told me."

"The counselor's name is Jim Brady," Jack added. "I talked with him after Kaitlyn had that dustup."

"Aisha thinks he was helping her get some legal advice. He called here for her yesterday on my phone, but I was at the doctor's and missed the call. He didn't leave a message."

"I need to talk to him."

Zoë handed her phone to Jack. "Good idea. I've already pulled up his number from yesterday."

While Brady's number rang, Jack slipped on a jacket. It was time to see if Tony was making progress. The call went to voicemail. He identified himself and requested a call back.

After informing the police outside he was going to the barn, he stepped outside, carrying Zoë's phone. He was striding over to the barn when it rang.

"Mr. Brady, thanks for returning the call."

"I was going to be reaching out anyway, Doctor. I'd expected to see Kaitlyn in school today. Is everything all right?"

"No. It's not. She ran away early this morning."

Brady made a sigh that came across the line as a rasping sound. "I'm so sorry to hear that. You folks must be worried sick. Do you know where she might be?"

Jack reached the side door of the barn. "Honestly, Mr. Brady, I was hoping you might have some information. We know that she talked to you about staying in New Canterbury." The wind was ugly and biting. He stepped inside the barn. A faint smell of motor oil hung in the air.

"Yes, she did talk about that," Brady said, seeming a little hesitant. "Two days ago. She told me that she'd made up her mind not to go back with her stepmother. Has she not talked with you yet?"

"No. What all did she tell you?"

"She was wondering about the legalities of it. Because I know an attorney who deals with this kind of thing, I told her I'd get some advice. As you and I discussed in my office recently, I think it would be good for her to stay."

"Why didn't you reach out to me? Kaitlyn is a minor. You should have contacted me."

"She told me she wanted to ask you herself, Doctor, which seemed highly reasonable and appropriate. She said she would talk to you that evening. Today is Thursday. That was Tuesday. If, for whatever reason, she didn't, I'm deeply surprised and sorry. But it was not my intent to keep anything from you."

"She said nothing." Jack released a breath and glanced at the stairs leading to Tony's apartment and workshop. He thought back to Tuesday evening. He had come home late, was exhausted, had soon gone to bed. He remembered her sitting at the table, her expressions of sympathy.

"Dr. Forester, are you still there?"

Then yesterday, Wednesday, when he got home with Marianna, there was the Julia situation. He felt a wave of sadness. And guilt.

"Dr. Forester?"

"I'm here."

"If she didn't speak with you, she must have had a good reason. I truly believe she's a trustworthy individual."

"Nonetheless," Jack said, his voice tired. "I wish someone had spoken to me."

"I'm going to speak frankly, Dr. Forester. Not that she doesn't respect you—I'm sure she does—but I believe she feels intimidated around you. Regarding her decision to stay, I was happy to hear it. For her own good. Short and long-term."

The light was playing tricks with his vision. The steps seemed suddenly far away. He shook his head and climbed, stopping on each tread, could hear Kaitlyn's words from yesterday as if they were still echoing off the old beams.

"Have we lost connection, Doctor?"

"You said you'd reached out to a lawyer on her behalf. What did you find out?"

"The attorney believes that an emergency protective custody order is the best way to go, assuming you give your blessing. After that, there'd be a formal hearing. The attorney was optimistic that Kaitlyn could prevail. It's all about her well-being. And speaking of that, I'm very distraught about this running away business. If there's any way I could help, please . . ."

"Thank you, Mr. Brady. I mean that. The police are on it. We will let you know. And I look forward to talking with you about the other matter. She should stay here."

He reached the landing and knocked on Tony's door.

CHAPTER FORTY-NINE

Tony didn't answer repeated knocks. Jack wondered if he was still outside extracting the computer. Through the east-facing window on the landing, he could see past an outbuilding to where the wrecked Escape lay among the weeds and saplings. No sign of Tony. He tried the door. It swung open as slick as a pair of Crocs on wet tile. Tony had a habit of oiling hinges every week whether they needed it or not. Warm air tinged with the aroma of coffee wafted out.

There was no one in the kitchen or living room. He felt an unprecedented urge for a drink. Tony had once kept a bottle of Jack Daniels in a cupboard above the fridge. It was still there, still full. He poured out half a tumbler, drank deeply, poured more, and strode toward Tony's workshop at the rear of the apartment, carrying the glass, his chest burning with the liquor. As he passed the open bedroom door, he saw that the bed was neatly made, as always, covered with the old comforter that had once lain on their parents' bed. He continued to the workshop and found Tony perched on a bench in front of three monitors, wearing a set of noise-canceling headphones. On the wall hung several gleaming compound bows that Tony had used in past archery competitions.

In front of his brother lay a rectangular device the size of a cigar box, its outer casing lifted to reveal a green circuit board studded with microprocessors. Cables ran from it to a large CPU below the bench. Tony's attention was focused on the middle monitor where rows of numbers and symbols scrolled by as he tapped at a keyboard, near which lay his cell phone.

Not wanting to startle him, Jack took out his phone and texted. *I'm in the room with you.* Tony's phone by the keyboard lit up. Tony looked at it, then swiveled toward Jack, removing the headset.

Jack pointed. "Is that it?"

His brother nodded, tapping the device with his fingertip. "Yes. The connections were corroded, but it works."

Jack took a long drink and set the glass down, his throat burning. "What did you find?" Tony glanced away, evasively. It wasn't something Jack often saw in him. It sent an icy wedge into his chest. "Tell me," he said. "I need to know."

Tony picked up a pencil and pointed at a line of letters and symbols on the middle monitor. "It starts there, Jack. The virus. It looks Russian. It's very big." The back of Jack's neck tightened as Tony ran the pencil down the screen. "Looks like the code is integrated into the operating system in such a way that they can access everything."

The coldness in Jack's chest swirled and turned hot. He felt the whiskey going to his head. "Goddamnit," he said, his fists clenching. He poured some more in the kitchen, drank it, and marched down the stairs into the barn, a storm now raging inside. Tony yelled after him. Jack grabbed a sledgehammer. He waded into the field grass and dead weeds, brambles grabbing at his pant legs. The rusted whiteness of the ruined Escape rose in front of him, ugly and malignant. He stopped, breathing deeply.

"Jack!" Tony had followed him. "What are you doing?"

"Go back inside," Jack said over his shoulder, and raised the sledgehammer. He slammed it down on the middle of the hood, just behind where it had been creased when the car caromed off the tree and killed the love of his life, who had done nothing wrong.

"Dr. Forester." The officer had jogged up next to Tony. "What's going on here?"

Jack slammed the hammer through the already starred and cracked windshield. Swinging again, he bashed in what remained of the headlamps, blinking as glass shards peppered his face. Then he drove the sledge into the remnants of the radiator grill. *Everything we love is eventually destroyed. But we persist in believing we can make a difference.*

"He's never been like this," Tony said.

The sledge banged into the passenger door. *I want to see Witner. I want him to come here. I want to kill him with my bare hands.*

"Dr. Forester, you're not thinking straight."

He brought the sledge down with full force on the trunk lid, caving it in.

"Talk to me, sir."

He dealt a blow to the trunk again, then straightened, his chest heaving. He looked at the officer. "I'm not hurting you, so kindly, leave me the hell alone."

Bashing the trunk again, he saw Zellie lying in the casket. The undertaker had worked to hide the wound on her forehead where the skull had been broken and the skin was torn. But it still showed. He had run his finger across the wounded place, feeling the slickness of the makeup, the coldness, and kissed her forehead, her cheek, her lips, all hard and cold.

He drew back the sledgehammer and aimed a blow at the left taillight, but it grazed off the bumper and ricocheted into his shin. A wave of pain shot through his leg. He stopped, feeling blood drip into his shoe. He aimed one more blow, bashing in the rear window, then threw the sledgehammer into the weeds and limped away. Tony and the officer were talking to him, but he was encased in a shell of dark, suffocating air.

As he hobbled down the driveway, the other officer climbed out of the cruiser. "Whoa, let's take it easy here," she said.

He continued toward the road.

Hearing bangs and shouting, Marianna, Zoë, and Julia had gone to the back window.

"What on earth?" questioned Zoë.

"Why's Daddy hitting the old car?"

Marianna stared out with growing concern. Something had gone wrong inside of Dr. Forester.

Zoë made a deep sigh. "I always feared this might happen."

"What does this mean?" Marianna asked.

Zoë looked at her, her face grave, and explained what the car was. Marianna blinked with surprise and then comprehension. He was trying to kill the thing that had killed his wife. But what had triggered this anger?

"I don't want Daddy to go crazy," said the little girl, on the edge of tears.

"He won't, honey," said Zoë, sighing again.

Now he was limping away from the wrecked car. His brother and two policemen were following. As he came closer, she saw the blood on his leg. Then he walked around the house out of sight. She expected to hear him come in the door, but he didn't. While Zoë was reassuring Julia, Marianna threw on her coat and went outside. The wind was bitter. He was now almost to the end of the driveway. Tony and the police officers were following but keeping at a distance, as if not wanting to provoke him. She ran toward Jack. He had stopped at the end of the driveway.

The police and Tony stared as Marianna rushed by. "I will talk with him," she said. She drew near, and he turned. She stopped. His eyes were red, his nostrils flaring, his mouth set.

"You've hurt your leg," she said.

He took deep breaths. "It's not bad."

"You are very angry." She came up to him. "You should hold some back for when you need it."

"I apologize for this." He looked down, his expression faltering.

"You do not have to apologize," she said, smelling alcohol. She glanced over at Tony and the officers. They were hovering just out of earshot. "Are you ready to come inside?"

"I've let a lot of people down," he replied. "I'm not who people think I am."

"Why do you say that?"

"I've let Kaitlyn down too. She was going to ask to stay here. I don't know why."

"You don't know why she wants to stay, or why you let her down?"

"Both. You're shivering, Marianna." He paused, looking at her warmly. "You're a good person. I mean that. I'll try to help you the best I can."

"I know that." She steered the conversation back toward him. "What makes you so angry now?"

"It's everything," he said. "Everything."

"I think you are like me—similar to a lake where you can see down to the bottom, except when wind wrinkles the surface. There is much wind now. Let's go in and take care of your leg. Julia saw you through the window. You need to tell her you are good now and that she will be all right."

"Okay," he said.

She continued. "Zoë told me about that car. Why do you keep something like that at your home?"

He didn't answer. They started up the driveway. He was limping more, but she wasn't sure he would appreciate her hand. They walked past Tony and the officers. "We are going inside," she said. "He will be all right."

"You asked why I was angry, Marianna," Jack said, stopping by the steps leading up to the kitchen door. "There are some things I need to catch you up on since last night. And there's something I've never told anyone before about why my wife took that vehicle."

Zoë watched Vlada and Jack trudge back up the driveway toward the house. Jack seemed to be talking nonstop, Vlada focusing on him. Julia was standing beside her, propped against her leg. They didn't come right inside but stopped just outside the door. Jack was doing most of the talking, but she could not make out what was being said.

"It looks like Daddy's crying," said Julia in that objective, clinical sort of way that sometimes made her seem much older.

A few minutes later, they came in. As the door opened, Zoë heard Vlada say, "If a patient told you a story like this, you would tell them to forgive themselves. I know that. Come, we will clean your wound."

CHAPTER FIFTY

Several hours later, Jack was in the living room reading *Charlotte's Web* to Julia when someone knocked on the side door.

"Who's that?" asked Julia.

"That would be Investigator Dirkens," Jack said, looking at Marianna. "He's done talking to Uncle Tony."

Marianna rose quickly from the couch. "I will go to your office for a little while," she said. "I was just texting with my sister. They are safe in France now."

"Doesn't Vlada want to meet the investigator?" Julia prodded. "She's cool. They call her Frankie."

"Why don't you come with me, Julia?" Marianna offered. "We can keep reading while your papa talks to her."

Marianna held out her hand and Julia took it. The knocking came again. Jack limped through the kitchen and opened the door. Zoë had gone to lie down again, her stomach pain having returned. He ushered the investigator inside and offered to get some coffee.

"No time, I'm afraid. I wanted to let you know that we're talking to Kaitlyn's classmates and teachers. No leads yet, I'm sorry to say, but it remains a priority. Bryson Witner, unfortunately, is still at large, but the state police and the Feds are going all out."

"How did it go with my brother?"

"No new information," she said, glancing at her watch. "We talked a little about archery, which my son is into. He showed me some of his trophies. Impressive. But let's quickly address the elephant in the room, shall we? What the hell was going on with the sledgehammer and the old car? Is this some new kind of Pilates? My officers filled me in."

His face warmed. "Bottled up anger mixed with Jack Daniels. I'm fine now. It's a long story."

"I'm afraid it'll have to wait. I've got to run, but I'll call you later. The officers told me that a woman came out and calmed you down. Who was that?"

"Just a house guest. A family friend. I know you've got to go, but do you have any news on the fingerprints or DNA yet?"

"We received a bag of items this morning from the apartment in Kyiv. It's in the FBI lab now. Knock on wood, we'll have results by tomorrow morning, maybe sooner. And the prints will be here this afternoon. Where's Zoë, by the way?"

"Not feeling well. Stress, I think. She's worried about Kaitlyn."

"We'll find her."

As Dirkens reached for the door handle, her phone began chirping. She glanced at the screen. "Hmmm. It's the chief's office. I need to take this."

Soon after answering, a smile bloomed on her face. After hanging up, she gave Jack the news. They'd found the car that Witner took from Patterson in front of a Dave and Buster's in Raleigh, North Carolina. It was loaded with his fingerprints, and CCTV showed that it had been there since eight forty-five that morning.

"They don't have him in custody yet, but at least we know he's a long way away. The chief is going to pull your surveillance officers. Some good news, at any rate."

He went to the office. It was dark, curtains pulled. Marianna was at the computer, her face bathed in the monitor's glow. Raising a finger to her lips, she pointed to where Julia lay on a folded blanket in front of the bookcase, covered by the sweater Marianna had been wearing.

She beckoned him and said in an intense whisper, "Dr. Forester, you must see something."

He came behind her. The screenshot that he'd taken last night of the Boston Numismatic Society filled the screen. "Look. You will not believe." She pointed to one of the individuals in the third row, behind Potemkin. It was the image of a very tall and slender young man standing head and shoulders above the others. The face looked familiar, but he didn't immediately recognize him. He hadn't noticed this last night.

She pointed to the caption. "Dr. Lawrence Haines," she read. "This is the man who was in your office. The leader of Health Wealth."

Jack straightened, his back muscles tensing. His voice came out in a hoarse whisper. "Good God, Marianna."

She pulled up another photo. "Here too," she said. It was of a dining room, men in tuxedos and women in gowns. "This was from the coin club dinner the next year, 1988. See there." Four men and two women sat around a table laden with glasses. Haines was flanked on either side by Witner and Potemkin, the latter smoking a cigar.

"It cannot be coincidence, Dr. Forester," she said, keeping her voice just above a whisper. "When that woman murders someone in the hospital, it causes your plan to fail and the plan of Haines to succeed. I found another web page. Look."

She opened a different window and pulled up an archived newspaper article. "This is a story about Lawrence Haines buying two hospitals and starting his company. Newspaper from Atlanta, 1990. Not too long after the coin club pictures. See, it says he has 'received additional funding from foreign investors, including the Russian software entrepreneur, Mikhail Potemkin.'"

Marianna's face was flushed, her nostrils flaring, eyes gleaming. "It is all here," she said. "If they work together, it explains very much. This is not all for revenge."

Jack nodded slowly. "Revenge for Witner, power for Haines, profit for Potemkin."

"Yes. I think this is the story."

"Marianna, I think we have them. I can't believe you found this all so quickly. Brilliant work."

"This is what I do for a living. Research. You don't tell me yet if the police have gotten my fingerprints or the DNA?"

"Investigator Dirkens is expecting results tomorrow morning or sooner."

"Good. We will have much to share with them, Dr. Forester."

"Please call me Jack. I've been calling you by your first name."

"I would be shy to do that," she said, smiling. "But I will try."

He glanced back at the monitor. "Marianna, when you met Haines yesterday, did you give him your name?"

"I give the same name I give to everyone except you. *Vlada Marina*. They are my two middle names. From my two grandmothers." The computer screen suddenly went blank. "What happened?" she asked.

"Our cable gets glitchy sometimes. Try rebooting."

Zoë's called out from the living room. "Jack? We've lost the internet again."

Not wanting to wake Julia, he stepped into the hallway. "Try resetting the modem, Zoë."

"Were you expecting anyone?" Zoë asked. She was standing by the window. "An SUV is coming up the driveway. The police car's gone."

CHAPTER FIFTY-ONE

Jack went back to the office window and opened the curtains. Marianna joined him. A large white Suburban had pulled up close to the garage and men were climbing out. One of the men opened the rear door, and a small man emerged. He was wearing a dark suit and a straw fedora.

Jack heard Marianna take a sharp breath, and her fingers gripped his arm painfully tight.

"Oh my God . . . it's him. Liski—the man who kidnapped me. And the others. Boris and the two Ivans."

Her tone of certainty and terror chilled his heart. Letting the curtain fall, he grabbed his phone and punched in 911. Nothing happened. There were no bars of service. Marianna pushed away from the window, her face draining of color. "You must hide, Dr. Forester. All of you. I will go out to them."

"No, you will not," he said. "Go into the closet in my bedroom. There's a trapdoor in the ceiling. Grab the rope and a ladder will come down. Climb up there and pull up the ladder behind you. *Now.*"

"But it's only me they want."

"Please don't argue. Just go."

"Daddy, what's the matter?" whispered Julia, rousing.

Exhorting Marianna to hide, he scooped up his daughter and dashed into the kitchen.

Zoë was looking out the side window. "There are four of them. Who are they, Jack? The phone's not working either. What's happening?"

He took her arm. "Come with me. I don't have time to discuss."

"Where are we going?"

"The basement. I'll explain everything later. This is serious. No delay." Holding Julia tightly, he steered Zoë down the stairs. "You and Aunt Zoë are going to hide for a while," he said.

"Is this a game?"

"No. Just do as Aunt Zoë says and stay very quiet."

In his workshop area, he set Julia down, grabbed a flashlight, and ducked under the workbench. He slid aside a plywood panel. "This is a crawl space, Zoë. Take this flashlight and do not come out until I tell you."

She reared her head back. "That's a dirt floor. I'm not going in there."

"Yes, you are. Now."

She groaned, knelt, and began crawling forward. Julia followed. He replaced the panel and sprinted back upstairs. He reached the kitchen as the doorbell began chiming. He was startled to see Marianna standing there, as if frozen.

"Go and get up in the attic, please," he said.

"No, Dr. Forester. They must take me. It is the only way. You hide, please."

All options vanished when the door burst open with a crash. In strode a tall, burly man with Asian features, followed by the man with the fedora. He had a thin mustache, open in the middle. He was brandishing a large black pistol.

"We meet again, Ms. Kovalenko. Both of you stay where you are."

"Take me and leave him alone, Liski," she said, stepping forward.

"I said to stay where you are." The little man turned to Jack. "Hello, Dr. Forester."

Jack stared back. "Whoever you are, I suggest you leave before the police get here. I called them."

The little man laughed. "You're going to play the brave man, I see. But the police have no idea we exist. Your phones have been jammed and your cable is disrupted. Who else is here?"

Jack's mouth was going dry. "No one."

Liski turned to his huge helper. "Boris, tell the men to search this house and the other buildings. But first, please pat down these two and secure their hands. I will keep you covered." The helper forward. "Wait, Boris," continued Liski. "Give me your pistol. I've told you never to take a weapon close to an enemy unless you are pointing it at them. For all we know, Dr. Forester may be an expert in martial arts. Not likely though."

"Sorry, boss." Boris gave Liski his handgun and began patting down Marianna, breathing heavily. Jack saw Marianna close her eyes and shudder, and the big man's hands lingered over her breasts.

"Stay still, Dr. Forester," said Liski.

Boris bound Marianna's wrists behind her back with a plastic zip tie. Then he moved to Jack, frisked him, and zip-tied his wrists tightly. Jack smelled onions.

"Allow me to formally introduce myself. I am Bodashka Liski. There are four of us, all well-armed. Please don't mistake Boris's missteps for stupidity. He is a distant relation of mine and still in training. Let us go into the living room and be comfortable while we wait."

"Please," said Marianna. "Just take me and leave Dr. Forester alone. He knows nothing and he will not hurt you."

"I am a patient man, but not a stupid one. You got lucky once. That's enough. Into the living room, now."

"No," she said. "Take me and go."

"You want me to help her?" Boris asked.

Liski nodded. Boris grabbed the front of her blouse, shoving her. Scrambling backward, she fell.

"Stop," Jack demanded.

Boris swung and backhanded Jack in the jaw. Unable to break his fall, Jack landed on his shoulder. Boris picked up Marianna and propelled her onto the couch. He returned, grabbed Jack by the back of his shirt, lifted him to his feet, and shoved him into a chair.

"Thank you," said Liski. "Here's your pistol, Boris. Go search, and make sure the cell signal jamming device remains on."

Marianna was lying on her side on the couch, her cheeks glistening with tears. "I am sorry, Dr. Forester."

"Jack," he said.

The two other men stomped into the kitchen. Liski ordered them to search the house. As one man disappeared down the hallway, Jack heard the footsteps of another thud down the basement steps. His heart twisted. Liski ambled into the living room. He tossed his hat on the coffee table and settled into Zoë's recliner. Raising the footrest, he made a sigh of comfort. "Do you mind if I smoke in your house, Doctor?" he asked, pulling a cigar out of his breast pocket.

"I do."

"Then I apologize." He charred the end of the cigar with a butane lighter and lit it, his cheeks billowing inward as he drew. He sent a stream of smoke toward the ceiling. "There," he said, leveling his gaze at Jack. "You are an educated person. I myself lack only twelve credit hours from my bachelor's degree. I once wanted to become a comedian. It's true. But the competition was brutal, so I became otherwise employed."

"And you became a monster," spat Marianna.

Smoke trickled out his nostrils. "Ms. Kovalenko, I must compliment you on getting away from me in Ukraine. My boss was very unhappy, and it did not help my reputation. She's very smart, don't you think, Doctor? And not unattractive."

Jack kept staring at the little man. What might his weakness be?

Liski turned to Marianna and smiled. "I think you have an admirer in the doctor, Ms. Kovalenko. Or have you already experienced this?"

"You are disgusting," she said. "What do you intend to do?"

"We are going to wait until twilight, then we are going to take a walk."

Jack heard footsteps approach. Boris and another man marched into the living room. Between them stood Tony, his wrists bound.

"Look what we found in the barn," Boris said. "He's the doctor's brother."

"Good work," said Liski.

Tony looked at Jack and Marianna, his expression neutral. "This is strange," he said. "Are we being arrested?"

"It's okay, Tony," Jack said. "Just do as they say."

Marianna struggled to sit. "Let them go. Can't you be decent?"

"He doesn't talk much, Bodashka," said Boris, shoving Tony onto a chair next to Jack. "Should I give him encouragement?"

"Stop," said Jack, his voice going tight. "He has autism. That's the way he is."

The two other men stomped into the living room. "Boss, we don't find anyone else," the older one said. "There's a little kid's bedroom with dolls and toys. And also the room, I think, of a teenager."

"Thank you, Ivan One." Liski turned toward Jack. "I discovered you are a widower with two children living here, and that your aunt stays to help you. Where are they?"

Jack looked him square in the eyes. "They all left this morning to visit my sister in Baltimore. They won't be back for five days."

Liski eyed his cigar. "Really? You checked the basement, Ivan Two?"

"Yes, Bodashka. Empty. And messy. He hoards."

"All right. Boris, you stay with me. Ivan and Ivan—go out back and find a place in the woods where the ground isn't too hard that's nice and private. Mark your trail well because we'll be taking these people out there in the dark. And look for shovels. We need two."

As they left, Jack heard what sounded like footsteps on the basement stairs. A chill swept up his back. Liski raised his eyebrows and looked at him. "Yes, I heard it too, Doctor," he said, with a shake of his head. He took out his pistol and stood. "You were not being honest with me."

☙ ☙ ☙

Investigator Dirkens called Jack Forester's number. It went straight to voicemail. "Doctor, it's Frankie Dirkens with some news. We've received the fingerprints from Leeds University *and* the new DNA data from our lab here. You were spot-on. The person who came to see you was not Marianna Kovalenko. Repeat: NOT her. Call me when you get this, and thanks for the suggestions. You might consider changing professions."

CHAPTER FIFTY-TWO

Haines flew the Jet Ranger low and fast, wanting to get the flight over as quickly as possible. They were now over the Atlantic where waves glittered with tones of orange and ocher in the late afternoon sun descending behind them. They were heading eastward toward Potemkin's ship. Haines glanced at Bryson Witner, who was sitting to his right in the copilot's seat. Eyes fixed straight ahead, Witner's lips were curled into a tight smile, but tiny beads of sweat had broken out on his forehead, looking like coarse grains of salt. From under the band of his headset, his gray hair spilled in unkempt greasy strands.

Haines swallowed, his mouth bone-dry. He was all for helping old friends to whom he owed a favor, but this was way beyond the pale. He was secreting a psychopathic serial killer out of the country so that he might live out his days in comfort and luxury. It was a sickening thing to do, not to mention dangerous as hell. But Potemkin had put him in this situation, and what other choice did he have? Call the police?

"I can see why you enjoy flying," Witner said, his voice crisp through the intercom. "It's like being on a magic carpet."

Haines returned his full attention to flying. An engine failure at this altitude would require an instant autorotation to avoid slamming into the sea. Ordinarily, he wouldn't fly while surface-hugging at a high speed like this for such a long time. The need to avoid detection by air traffic control radar, however, overrode all other concerns now.

He must get Witner out to Potemkin's ship and then return without the bird displaying on any ATC database.

With the hospital deal done, he'd hoped to forever wash his hands of both Witner and Potemkin, but at dawn this morning he was utterly blindsided by an out-of-the-blue call from Witner. After escaping from the Patterson Institute last evening—an event Haines had heard nothing about yet—Witner sped south all night in a stolen vehicle, lurking in shadows less than a mile from Haines's house in Raleigh. Plans for the escape had been engineered by Potemkin, Witner told him. But things had gotten complicated, and Potemkin had instructed him to go directly to Haines, who would fly him personally to the ship.

Haines's first response was disbelief. To his immediate question of why Potemkin hadn't given him a warning, Witner had explained that the Russian believed his secure communication system may have suffered a breach in the process of arranging the escape. To protect everyone involved, Witner insisted, Haines should make no effort to contact the oligarch. No calls, no radio. Just fly Witner out to the ship. It would be a final favor. After that Haines would be free of further demands. No more contact with either of them. But Haines had meetings that morning that he couldn't avoid. No problem, Witner had assured him. Afternoon would be fine. Potemkin would understand and be waiting, and in the meantime, Witner would stay hidden until Haines was ready to fly.

So there they were, low-leveling toward Wiegatesland—the last time, God willing, that he'd ever see that damned floating den of corruption and insanity.

He glanced at Witner. "I still think I might ought to radio Potemkin and let him know."

Witner shrugged. "Do so if you insist, Lawrence. But I warn you, it's at your own risk. You know how angry he can get. If he says his communications were compromised, I suggest we believe him."

Haines swallowed. "All right, then. But tell me, how long was Potemkin planning to help you escape?"

"Since the beginning. I thought you knew."

Haines clenched his jaw. "I did not. I didn't know many things."

"I had to get something out of this, after all," Witner said. "When will we be there?"

Haines glanced at the GPS. "Twelve minutes. What's the matter? Feeling airsick?"

"Not in the slightest. I have a vestibular system of titanium. I used to drink you and Mikhail under the table, remember? Do you ever think of our Boston days?"

It was true that when the three of them would do a pub crawl after coin club meetings, Witner never seemed to loosen up, regardless how much alcohol he'd consumed. He would remain articulate and aloof, continued giving the impression he knew something no one else did. Every so often he would smile for no apparent reason and gaze at people in a way that made them feel uncomfortable.

Potemkin had liked to call him Dr. Witch, partly because it seemed to annoy Witner. Of course, this only encouraged the Russian. Sometimes in his cups, Potemkin would yell out, "And here's the infamous Dr. Witch," and he'd start singing the *Dr. Who* theme song. Weird. But the nickname fit. And, of course, Witner eventually had his breakdown and ended up in McLean for half a year, though that was after Haines had finished his training and moved on.

"I suppose I do think of those days from time to time," Haines said.

Witner chuckled. "And look how far we've come. You, the famous head of a massive doctoring company; Mikhail, an infamous master criminal who rules his own nation; and me . . . a recovering lunatic, whose help the both of you accepted. Aren't you glad we reconnected? Aren't you happy you considered my proposal?"

Haines gripped the cyclic stick more tightly and glanced at him again. As always—the inscrutable expression, the questions that may or may not be sarcastic. When Witner had reached out to him several years ago, saying he'd recovered from his psychosis, was lonely, and hoped that his dear friend would pay a visit for old time's sake, Haines had gone, partly out of morbid curiosity. But while they'd walked in the courtyard, Witner had revealed something astonishing. After all that had happened—the murders, Witner's arrest, him being locked away among the criminally insane—he could still log into the New Canterbury Medical Center's network, could update his password and browse the secure library. And he had a proposition for Haines. If Haines reached out to their old mutual friend, Mikhail, Witner could help the Russian computer genius bypass the firewall and enter the system. Given Mikhail's expertise, he could drill deep and surreptitiously surveil the medical center's accounts and business practices. It would facilitate Haines acquiring New Canterbury. Witner said he was certain that if Haines made the request, Mikhail would jump at the chance. As for Witner, he would be happy simply to help an old comrade expand his empire.

"The fact is, Witner," Haines said, leaning forward as he spotted something directly ahead, "I wish I'd never seen you again after I left Boston all those years ago."

"Despite what you've gained? More the pity."

It looked like a fishing boat returning from the Gulf Stream. He banked the bird to stay well away from it. His tail number must remain unseen. A few moments later, he spotted the superstructure of Potemkin's ship rising above the horizon. Ordinarily, he'd be in radio contact with it by now, but given the situation, radio silence it would be. It was disturbing, even surprising, that Potemkin had let his communications become compromised.

"So that's it," Witner said.

"That's it."

Witner laughed. "Well, well . . ."

As they neared, Haines pulled back the cyclic stick, climbed, and slowed to fifty knots to overfly the ship and set up for his approach. But as he passed over, it was clear that something was amiss on deck below. A tingle of alarm crawled up his neck. Armed Wiegatesland marines were spilling onto the deck, gesturing up at him.

"Did you not say Mikhail was expecting us?" Haines asked.

"Yes, I think I remember saying something like that."

"What do you mean, *think you remember*?"

"Don't worry. He just wasn't sure when we'd be here. My, what a big boat."

As Haines lined up into the wind and began his approach, it was increasingly obvious that many assault rifles were trained on him. By the time he brought the bird to a three-foot hover and lowered onto the helipad, his face was dripping sweat. He had no sooner than shut down the turbine when fifty or sixty of the marines coalesced around the aircraft, rifles aimed.

He slipped off his headset and glared at Witner. "What the *hell* is going on?"

"Very skillful landing," replied Witner.

Ducking under the rotor blades, Colonel Spavin yanked open Haines's door.

"Doctor, do you realize you almost got shot down? You're lucky we recognized your ID number before the lads blew you to pieces."

"There must have been a miscommunication, Colonel. I was told we were expected."

"Who the devil's that?" Spavin pointed at Witner.

"This is Dr. Bryson Witner. An old friend of the prime minister's."

"*Don't move.*" Spavin strode off and spoke into a walkie-talkie.

Haines fixed Witner with a stare. "What kind of game is this, you son of a bitch?"

"All will soon be clear. Be patient."

Spavin returned. "Come with me. I'll take you to the PM. Step out. Both of you."

As two burly marines aggressively frisked them, Haines caught Spavin's eyes. "Listen, Colonel, I came only to deliver Dr. Witner. I was told Potemkin wanted me to avoid radio contact. You know who I am. I have business back on the mainland and I'd like to fly out immediately and leave you in peace."

Spavin's nostrils flared. "Sorry, but the PM wants to see you both. He's the one you need to talk to. Let's go, gentlemen."

CHAPTER FIFTY-THREE

Jack listened as the footsteps continued up from the cellar, each footfall like a dagger stabbing his heart. They sounded heavy, too heavy to be the footfalls of his daughter. From where he sat in the living room, hands bound behind him, he could not see the basement door. But Liski was in his field of vision, standing with pistol pointed, waiting for the door to open. The light was fading outside. Tony sat on the far side of the living room, staring ahead blankly. Marianna lay on the couch. She looked asleep, her chest rising and falling.

Jack could visualize Zoë near the top of the stairs. She'd have been lulled by the fact that everything had seemed quiet for a while, Julia growing impatient. He could only hope that Julia was still hidden in the crawl space. The creak of the basement door opening sent a trickle of ice water down his back. He heard Zoë scream.

"Stay where you are," said Liski.

"Who are you?"

"Turn around and put your hands behind your back."

"Where's my nephew?"

Jack heard the outside door slam and heavy footsteps enter the kitchen. "Secure her wrists, Boris," said Liski.

"Where is my nephew?"

"Be still," Boris commanded.

"I'm in the living room, Zoë. Do as he asks."

"Now, tell me," said Liski. "Who else is downstairs?"

"No one."

"Don't lie. There are signs in the house of a little girl and a teenager. Are they down there?"

"There's no one else."

"I'll go see," said Boris.

"Hold on," said Liski. "What is your name?" he questioned Zoë.

"I am Zoë Andersen. Who are you?"

"I'm not interested in children. If you cooperate, I will leave them alone."

"What if they have a cell phone?" asked Boris.

"That's why we have the jamming device," Liski replied. "Block the door with something heavy like the refrigerator. That will give us time for what needs to be done."

Liski came back into Jack's field of vision, steering Zoë by her upper arm. Her face was flushed, her lips clamped shut. "Jack!" she exclaimed. "What is this all about? Vlada, are you hurt?"

Marianna stirred and opened her eyes. She drew in a shuddering breath and maneuvered into a sitting position. "I am very sorry. This is my fault. They are here because of me."

"A true statement," said Liski as he pushed Zoë onto the couch by Marianna. "Her name is not Vlada. It's Marianna. She is an escapee. She got away from me once, but she will not escape again."

"She's no criminal," said Zoë.

"I didn't say she was."

Boris came into the living room. "It's getting dark, Bodashka."

"I can see that."

"Is it time?"

"Yes."

With a flashlight in one hand and two shovels in the other, the older Ivan, the one with the mashed nose, led the way up the path behind the barn into the forest. He was followed by Zoë and Marianna, wrists bound behind their backs with zip ties. They were being prodded forward by the younger Ivan, the one with the snake tattoo. Tony came next, guarded by Boris. Not only were his wrists bound, but Boris held a rope that was tied around his neck. Last came Jack, also bound and roped around the neck, his rope held by Liski. Jack was frantically trying to think of some means of escape, ready to spring if an opening came, hoping these men might make some misstep he could take advantage of. He knew the odds were not good.

"Dr. Forester, you are limping," said Liski. "Why?"

"It's nothing."

The little man grunted. "What do you think of Marianna? Clever, isn't she? Too clever."

Jack turned his head to try catching Liski's eyes, the rope chafing his neck. "She doesn't deserve this. None of us do."

Liski grunted again. "Don't waste your breath, Doctor. I do what I must. I obey orders."

"Thank you for not sending your man down into the cellar. I see you have a streak of kindness," Jack added,

There was a pause. "Sometimes, yes."

"How about if you let my aunt and my brother go? They have no idea what's happening."

"I've already bent the rules once, Doctor. The person I work for would not approve."

"Is that Potemkin?" asked Jack.

"No more talk."

Boris slowed and turned back, causing Jack to stumble. The burly man cleared his throat. "Bodashka, I have a favor to ask. Before we kill the woman, could I spend some time with her?"

"Which woman?" Liski responded.

"Bodashka . . ." he said, his voice trailing off. "The younger, of course."

"We will see. Maybe."

Jack's heart plunged lower. They left the path and continued winding deeper into the forest. It was pitch-dark and the air was growing colder. After what felt like half an hour, they came to a small ridge and descended into a hollow. When they reached the bottom, they stopped. The older Ivan played the beam of light around. He called back to Liski. "This is it."

Boris and Liski led Tony and Jack forward into a small clearing. Liski ordered Marianna and Zoë to sit and Ivan Two to guard them. While the older Ivan and Boris kept pistols trained at Tony and Jack, Liski cut their zip ties, untied the ropes around their necks, and handed each a shovel. Producing another flashlight and using a stick, he scraped the outline of a square in the dead leaves. It was about six feet on either side. "Dig here," Liski said. "Take it down five feet. If one of you tries to make a break for it, the others get buried alive."

There was nothing to do but dig, so they dug. The older Ivan stood near the hole, a large stick in one hand, a pistol in the other. Liski lit a cigar, his lighter flaring in the gloom.

"Tony?" Jack whispered, his shovel cutting through the dead leaves into the soft earth. His brother gave no answer. Jack couldn't see his face, just heard his shovel scraping as it sank into the dirt. "Tony, I'm sorry for all of this."

"I'm sorry too, Jack."

"You don't need to be sorry."

"I'm sorry because I forgot something important," Tony said.

"What?"

Tony moved closer. "A CSI episode," he whispered, thrusting in his shovel and tossing aside a clump of dirt. "It showed how to get out of zip ties. You see, you make fists and put your hands together thumb side to thumb side. Then after the tie is on, you put your palms together like you're praying and there will be room to slip out. But I didn't think of it in time. Maybe I could have gotten one of my bows and shot them. I'm sorry."

"Hey," said the older Ivan, slamming the stick down on Tony's back, making him lurch.

"No more of the whispers. Just dig. Get this over with quick."

Off through the trees, Zoë sobbed softly and Marianna was talking to her. Marianna truly was a special person. A wave of scarifying sadness washed over Jack. He remembered the lullaby she'd sung, and its melody played inside his mind again. He was sick to his soul with regret and fear, made worse by imagining what the others must be feeling. But just outside this appalling fear, he felt another sensation lurking. It was a belief that perhaps the worst might not come to pass. It was telling him not to lose all hope. Not yet. Not ever. He realized he was observing the human capacity to deny the inevitable, to believe that death could be postponed or evaded. He kept digging slowly and steadily. There was almost a comfort in the rhythm of it.

When Zellie had died, she wouldn't have had much time to think. A few seconds maybe, as she'd lost control of the car. It was better that way. It was a dark and complex place, the vestibule of coming death. But, in truth, he had been in a dark place along with Zellie for a long time, not wanting to leave her alone during those last few seconds. He moved his digging closer to Tony again. Between scrapes of the shovel, he whispered, "I haven't been a good brother for some time."

The thug man brought his stick down on Jack's head this time, though not strong enough to knock him down. "*Dig*."

He fell back into the rhythm, thrusting in the shovel and lifting chunks of earth. Time passed. The air grew cooler. The pit sank deeper. Marianna and Zoë hadn't talked for a while. His arms and shoulders were aching. It was more of an effort now to toss out each shovelful of dirt. It was wet and heavy now, and water pooled in the bottom of the grave. They were sloshing in it. He felt grateful that neither Julia nor Kaitlyn were there. He could not have borne that.

Then the older Ivan swished his stick in the air and ordered them to stop. The moon was visible between the trees. Another man shone a flashlight into the hole. It was Liski. The big man, Boris, was beside him.

Ivan Two swished his stick again. "What do you think, Bodashka? Looks good enough to me."

"Not quite yet," Liski replied. "Another foot or two."

Then Jack heard something—a faint thudding, like a rapid heartbeat. Like a helicopter.

"Wait," said Liski. "Everyone be quiet."

The sound receded. Marianna said something quietly to Zoë. Maybe it was a truck passing far away. He shoved the blade into the sodden dirt.

"I said be quiet," Liski demanded.

The thudding noise returned and grew louder. It was a helicopter. It began to fade, but didn't disappear. Then it intensified once more, moving unmistakably toward them. Jack straightened. This was way out of the ordinary, a helicopter out here at night. It could be flying a search pattern, looking for them. He didn't dare hope.

"Get those two out of the hole," Liski barked. "Tie them up again, the doctor and his brother. Get under the trees with the women. We wait."

Jack and Tony dropped the shovels and clambered out, shoes sucking in the mud. The sound was growing rapidly more distinct. His clothes were soaked with sweat and muck. He shivered. They wrenched his arms behind his back and bound his wrists again. What was it Tony had said? Yes. He clenched his hands into fists and held them thumb to thumb as the thin plastic band tightened and clamped into place.

The chopper was closer still, almost upon them.

"Maybe they're hunting for deer," said Boris. "It's got a searchlight. Look, Bodashka."

Liski made a growling sound deep in his throat. "Be quiet. It's not for damn deer. Stay under the trees. Nobody move. Put out cigarettes. No lights."

A high-pitched ringing sound cut through the rotor noise. Jack felt his legs tense. It wasn't stopping. It could only be a phone. It was coming from Liski. The little man fumbled a device out of his pocket and put it to his ear. It was larger than the usual cell phone. Perhaps a satellite device.

"Yes, this is Bodaskha," Liski said, raising his voice. "Is that you, Colonel? This is not a good time. What is it you want?" The helicopter was almost over them now, flying low. Liski put a finger into his other ear. "What?" he shouted over the noise. "Tell me one more time!" Then Liski turned in a circle and made a sound halfway between a curse and a groan. "Mother of God. When did this happen?" The thudding grew thunderous. It would pass almost directly over them. "I understand, Colonel," yelled Liski. "Things are a little complicated, but we will be there as quickly as possible."

Jack stared up. The branches were so thick overhead they might never be seen. He put his palms together and tested the tie. Just as Tony had said, it was now looser, maybe loose enough to work his hands free. Liski jammed the phone into his pocket, muttering. The helicopter's searchlight lanced into the forest, silhouetting branches into a crazy stitching of black veins. The stream of air sent down by the rotor blades washed over his face. The helicopter came to a stop over the clearing, its searchlight hovering over the hole they had dug. His bones seemed to resonate with the vibration.

Liski cursed.

"Is it going to land?" shouted Boris.

"Not enough room," yelled one of the Ivans. "They'd be dead if they tried it."

The chopper turned and banked away, the searchlight winking off. It climbed away from them.

"Boys, listen up," said Liski. "Get ready to leave. We've been compromised. And there's something else . . ."

"What, Bodashka?" asked Boris. "What was that call about?"

The thudding continued to fade.

Liski sighed and shook his head. "It was Colonel Spavin. Something bad has happened at the ship. I will tell you more later.

But we must get back to Wiegatesland as fast as we can."

"What about them?" asked Boris. "Should we dump them in the hole before the helicopter comes back?"

"We will take Forester and Marianna with us. We may need hostages. Bring them over. Quickly!"

"And shoot the other two?" said the older Ivan.

"No. Shots might be heard far away. Leave them with wrists bound good. They won't be able to follow us in the dark. This was a stupid plan to begin with. I tried to tell Potemkin, but he never listened to me. It's too late now. Let's go. *Now*!"

FIFTY-FOUR

With Haines and Witner each flanked by two marines, Spavin marched them to the stern, into the tall atrium, and past the giant terrarium, halting in front of the metal detector. Another marine handed them plastic baskets. "Everything out of your pockets, please. And remove your belts." After they'd passed through, the guard didn't return the baskets, but gave them instead to Spavin, who commanded them to follow.

"Colonel," said Haines, grasping the waistband of his pants. "My belt."

Spavin tossed him the belt, and they set off down the corridor, Spavin carrying a basket in each hand like an usher after the offering. He opened the double doors and led Haines and Witner up into the cool, spacious office, the marines in tow. Potemkin was at his desk, half hidden by the monitors.

"They're here, Prime Minister," Spavin said.

"Goodness," Witner whispered to Haines. "Why not king?"

"Thank you, Colonel," Potemkin said. "Leave them with me."

"Shall I stay, sir?"

"Don't bother," Potemkin replied, striding over. He was dressed in a black T-shirt, khaki shorts, and leather sandals. He was also wearing a shoulder holster. The butt of a pistol protruded from under his armpit. "I'll call you when I need you. Just leave one of your men by the door. Armed. Anything of interest on their persons?"

"Nothing obvious, sir." Spavin held out the plastic baskets and gave them a shake.

"Set those on the coffee table." Potemkin pointed.

Spavin did so, then saluted and marched off, ordering one of his men to stay behind. The doors clicked shut. Haines had never seen him this tense looking. Potemkin had yet to make eye contact.

"Hello, Mikhail," said Witner. "Surprise."

The oligarch exhaled through his nose. "Hello, Dr. Witch."

"Listen here, Mikhail," said Haines. "I was given no foreknowledge of any escape plans, and I had no idea we weren't expected. He called me out of the blue this morning. Said you wanted radio silence."

"I believe you, Lawrence," Potemkin said. "I believe you. This is quite unexpected for me too. I have to give him credit for being full of resources."

Witner turned and spoke directly to Haines. "You see, Lawrence, I'm supposed to be dead. He betrayed me instead of helping me. But the tables turned. The best laid plans of mice and men."

"What the bloody *hell* is going on?" demanded Haines, blood rushing to his face. "You tricked me into bringing you out here and now you're saying Mikhail betrayed you."

"Mikhail tends not to keep his word," Witner said calmly. "But now that I'm here, a fait acompli, it will best serve us all for him to honor his original promise."

Potemkin sighed audibly and looked down at the plastic baskets. He lifted one and removed something. Haines could see it was a coin in a little plastic box. The Russian looked at Witner and chuckled. "Bryson, is this what I think it is?"

Witner's expression went blank. "Yes. Kindly leave it alone."

Taking the coin out of the plastic protector, Potemkin held it up to the light, rubbing it. Then he broke into a full-throated laugh and shook his head. "Yes! It's the one you outbid me for, Dr. Witch. I'm impressed you have kept it all these years..."

Winter's face darkened. "You couldn't have it then," he said, his voice deepening, "and you can't have it now."

"Oh really?" Potemkin replied, making an amused snort. "A brave statement, considering your position." The Russian turned to Haines. "This is no ordinary quarter, Lawrence. It's a 1970-D Washington Quarter that Dr. Witch outbid me for back in Boston. It was stamped upon a dime blank, see?" He held it up, then gave it a kiss and smiled.

"It's my lucky talisman," said Witner. "Hand it back."

Potemkin continued directing his attention at Haines. "It's touching, no? This is most likely his last item of value. He wants to hold it close. Bryson is right, of course, Lawrence. I tried to have him killed yesterday. My only question is why he comes here for me to finish the job? Maybe he has something up his sleeve." He turned to Witner. "What is up your sleeve, Dr. Witch? You think you have some power over me?"

"As a matter of fact, I do," said Witner.

"Something spooky, no doubt." The Russian chuckled. "Another spider?"

"I have planted an IEID."

"Ooooh . . . and what might be that?"

"An improvised exploding information device. I left behind a cache of compromising information. If I don't personally abort the process, in one week a great number of precise and well-documented facts will be released, detailing what you did at New Canterbury. I know that you're safe from prison out here in your little domain, but you'll lose all that work and destroy Lawrence and his company. And it'll help them catch up with you someday. I am the only one who can prevent this from happening. I will defuse the device on the condition that you set me up in comfort where I can't be harmed, as you once promised. Kill me instead and . . . *bang*."

Potemkin snorted again. "Bang? Why should I care? I might lose some investment, but just a drop. Lawrence is the person you'd destroy. You come invading my home and expect me to help you? No way, my friend. You are an illegal immigrant. Your time on Earth is over."

"Wait a goddamn minute, Mikhail," said Haines, straightening and pointing at the Russian. "Stop right there. I have a say in how this thing plays out."

"Then make your say," said Potemkin. "In the meantime, Dr. Witch can have his coin back. Let him enjoy it while he can. A single turd of mine is worth more than ten of these."

Potemkin tossed the rare quarter to Witner. It made an arc, twirling in the overhead lights. Witner, to Haines's astonishment, made not the slightest effort to catch it. He let it bounce off his chest and fall to the plush carpet. Witner folded his arms and grinned at the Russian.

Potemkin's smile slowly transmogrified into a puzzled frown, and his face appeared to grow pale.

A teasing smile played on Witner's lips. "How are you feeling, Mikhail? Maybe a little sick to your stomach? A little lightheaded?"

Indeed, the oligarch's face had gone gray, his forehead gleaming with sweat. Swaying slightly, Potemkin lowered himself onto the sofa and coughed, his neck reddening, his Adam's apple rising and falling.

"What's happening?" said Haines, glancing at Witner.

"Mikhail, tell Lawrence, *while you still can*, about the people you murdered as you helped him acquire New Canterbury."

Haines glared at Witner, then Potemkin. "What the devil are you talking about?"

Potemkin's face was now bathed in sweat. It was dripping off his chin. He opened his mouth to speak but groaned instead.

"I believe he's at a loss for words," said Witner, winking at Haines. "I'll tell the story for him. As far as murderers go, I'm a novice compared to him. One of Mikhail's techniques, you see, is to make people die in car accidents by hacking into their vehicles. That's what happened to the comptroller at New Canterbury and to my medical director at Patterson, may he rest in peace. And we can safely assume he was involved in the death of that fake Ukrainian journalist there, who was actually his niece."

"Good God," said Haines.

"And there's one other killing too, Lawrence. When I first

reached out to you, my primary motive was *not* to help you buy New Canterbury. That was just an incentive for you. What I wanted was for you to put me in touch with Mikhail so that he could conduct a little unfinished business for me—getting rid of Dr. Forester. Mikhail failed, though, and took care of his wife instead. But close enough."

"Both of you are disgusting bastards," Haines hissed.

Potemkin gagged and vomited.

Witner turned to the marine by the door, who had been edging closer, clearly concerned about Potemkin's condition. "Excuse me, young man," he said. "I think the PM needs some help."

"What's wrong with him?" asked the marine, striding toward them. "He looks sick."

"Very astute," Witner said. "I'm not sure what the problem is. I'm sure you have some first aid training; why don't you check him out while I call for help."

The oligarch swayed, saliva and more vomit oozing from his mouth. The marine dashed to his side, grabbed him by the shoulders and tried at first to steady him. "What's wrong, sir?" The Russian didn't answer. He was hyperventilating now, and sweat had begun dripping from his brow as if irrigation pipes were buried under the skin. Catching his breath, Potemkin tried to speak. He could only choke.

"We need help now," the marine said.

"You'd better lay him down, young man," Witner said.

Stepping aside to avoid another gush of vomit, the marine eased Potemkin to the floor and knelt next to him.

"Keep him on his side so he doesn't breathe in the puke," said Witner.

As the marine rolled him over, Witner suddenly reached down and pulled the marine's cap off. Haines stared. In his other hand, Witner raised up the large glass ashtray that had been on the nearby table. Haines hadn't seen him take it. Before the marine could express surprise, Witner brought the heavy piece down square on his head. It must have been made of tempered glass, because it didn't break as it slammed onto the young man's skull. The marine went rigid and slumped down next to Potemkin.

"Jesus Christ, Witner. What the hell are you doing? What's going on here?"

"Can you still hear me, Mikhail?" Witner asked.

The oligarch vomited again, groaned, rolling his eyes toward Witner.

Witner leaned closer. "It was the coin, Mikhail. I swabbed it with the Novichok that you had smeared on my reading device. I've got you to thank for my freedom after all."

Potemkin shuddered and began convulsing.

Witner turned to Haines and smiled. "I hope he heard me. It won't be long now."

"You really are a monster," Haines said, his throat tight. "You had this planned all along. You knew he'd take the coin."

Potemkin's seizure activity was already slowing, his face turning purple and bloated, his breathing erratic and raspy.

"I did, yes," Witner said, bending over and jerking the pistol from the oligarch's shoulder holster. "I wasn't sure whether there'd be a guard with us, but it was a scenario I'd thought about."

He turned and leveled the muzzle at Haines's head. Too stunned to speak, Haines stepped backward, nearly stumbling on the coffee table.

Witner laughed and lowered the pistol. "You are in no danger if you follow my lead. We must get to your helicopter."

"Why would I help you, Witner? I should just let them kill you."

"You will help me for two reasons. One is that you'll be seen as an accomplice, of course. We'd both be shot. And secondly, you won't want my information bomb to explode."

Potemkin was no longer moving or breathing. The marine, however, began to groan and attempt to roll over. Witner slammed the butt of the pistol against his temple, and all effort ceased.

Haines was speechless.

"We can't linger," Witner said. "I told Mikhail once that I didn't believe his ship was as big as he bragged, so he sent me a file containing the blueprints. There's a bathroom behind this desk that connects to his private stateroom. We can make our way to the helipad from there."

It took several minutes to reach an exit close to the helipad. It was already dark outside. Nobody was guarding the Jet Ranger, and they clambered aboard. Haines rushed through the starting sequence from memory. The engine whined to life and the blades began to spin faster and faster. He was almost ready to lift off when marines came running down the deck toward them. He saw bright muzzle flashes and the zip of green tracers.

"Make sure you're strapped in, Witner," he said. "This will be rough."

He lifted the bird in one swift movement, then hovered over the rail of the ship and made a turning dive. Switching on the landing light, he saw water in front of him and leveled off just above the surface, staying low and increasing the airspeed as quickly as the engine would allow. More AK-47 tracers zipped by like angry wasps, rounds hitting the fuselage with metallic thunks. He pulled power to the maximum, felt the turbine straining. They were at ninety-five knots now and past the bow of the ship. He pulled back the cyclic and they soared up, centrifugal force pushing him into the seat. No more tracers were visible now. They were out of range. He scanned the instruments and gauges. Everything was in the green and the controls felt normal, but every muscle in his body was trembling.

"We've made it," he said, then realized they didn't have headsets on. He turned on the interior lights and saw Witner leaning forward hugging his chest. Putting on his own headset, he jammed a pair on the other man's head.

"Witner, are you all right?"

Witner's face appeared ghostly pale. There was a dark patch of blood in the center of his chest.

"*Shit*," said Haines, turning off the overhead light to preserve his night vision. "*Shit*."

Witner made a sound like water gurgling down a drain, then managed to say, "Indeed."

"I'll figure something out," Haines said. "We'll get you some help."

"You always were such a boy scout, Larry."

Haines's face burned with frustration. "Level with me, Witner. This information bomb—is it real or something out of your imagination?"

"Oh, quite real," Witner said, shifting and moaning. "It hurts to breathe."

"Am I implicated?" asked Haines.

"Of course. Sorry about that."

"That's all you've got to say? *Sorry about that*? Is there any way to defuse it?"

"You mean if I'm dead? No."

Witner coughed. In the dim glow of the instrument lights, Haines could see blood oozing out of Witner's mouth, dripping from his chin. Witner groaned, gave a long sigh. Then nothing. As the helicopter bumped through a downdraft, Witner's head slumped forward and stayed there, lolling. Haines reached over and fumbled to find the man's carotid pulse. There was none. Witner was dead, his information bomb now ticking.

No longer caring about ATC radar, Haines climbed to twenty-five hundred feet. Far ahead he could see the lights of the first barrier island twinkling. His thoughts circled back to the agreements he'd made with Witner and Potemkin, and further back to the long-ago day he'd acquired his first hospital when the dream was fresh, and even further back to the summers working on the farm, his mother and father, his basketball days.

He undid Witner's restraining harness, reached over and unlatched Witner's door. Then he put the chopper into a steep right bank. He slowed to ten knots and added extra right pedal. The door opened, and he pushed Witner toward it until gravity took over and Witner's body slid awkwardly out into the night, the bird lurching with the loss of weight.

He leveled out and headed north toward Ocracoke Island, where he had a summer home. He should have enough fuel to make it, but what was he going to do afterward? An unaccustomed sense of fear invaded him. Like an unwholesome visitor, it rummaged the rooms, toppling furniture, yanking pictures off the walls, spitting on the carpet. The moon was a white smudge behind clouds that hid the stars, the sort of night that induces vertigo among inexperienced pilots. Half a mile below, the Atlantic was featureless. He slid on through the night. By the time he could see the scattered lights of Ocracoke ahead, it didn't seem worth it anymore.

He shut down the engine and dropped the collective pitch to autorotate, not sure when the air would give way to the sea.

CHAPTER FIFTY-FIVE

With Liski grabbing Jack's left arm and Boris his right, they steered him toward the path. One of the Ivans ranged ahead to guide, the beam of his light glancing off trees and undergrowth. Looking back, Jack could see Marianna being similarly manhandled.

As he walked, he maneuvered his wrists, bringing the palms together and testing how much slack was created. Bless Tony's heart. It genuinely felt like he might be able to get his hands loose. But the moment would have to be right. He needed a plan and his options were limited. Both Liski and Boris had their pistols out. The forest was thick with undergrowth. There were no longer any sounds of a helicopter, just the crashing of their movement.

"Bodashka," said Boris, "how did they know to look for us?"

"How should I know for certain? Somehow they were lucky. Now it is our turn to have some luck. When things seem bad, be confident."

"I will try, Bodashka. Tell me what bad thing happened at the ship that they call you."

Liski's voice fell to just above a whisper, enough so that Jack could just make it out. "I didn't want to tell the Ivans yet, but Potemkin is dead. The killers have escaped."

"That is terrible. I can't believe."

"Believe."

"Okay. So, if the police are there at the house, we use these two as hostages, right?"

"That's why they're with us. Our ticket to leave."

"Will we still kill them?"

Liski didn't answer immediately. He looked behind him. Then Jack heard him say, again in a lowered voice, "We will be taking them both to the ship. The doctor here, we can set free. But Marianna, no. How will it look if I release someone who escaped me once and wrote bad things about Mikhail, even if he is now dead? No, we will execute her in front of the crew. Perhaps both of us will have a little time with her first."

A blade of ice sank into Jack's chest. He stumbled.

"On your feet," Liski said. "Keep moving."

They finally came to the well-worn trail that ran from the cliff to his house. It seemed like an eternity ago that Julia had gotten lost here. He thought of Kaitlyn reading to Julia, of her proudly wearing the volunteer smock with the ID badge on a lanyard, of Jim Brady describing her schoolwork, of her courage when she'd been kidnapped. Zellie would have been immensely proud of her brother's daughter. He glanced back. The best he could tell in the shadows, Marianna was walking steadily between the two thugs. His breast swelled with rage and dismay as he thought of her being subjected to that animal Liski's abuses. It felt like broken glass was swirling inside his neck.

"Eyes ahead, Doctor," the little bastard said.

They were drawing close to the house now. They were still in the forest, but only a couple hundred yards ahead lay the yard. Through the trees he saw multiple lights. It looked like all the outside lights around the property were glowing. How had they found out? Was Frances Dirkens there? The barking of a dog filtered up to him.

"You were right, Bodashka," said Boris. "It looks like they are waiting."

"They are probably getting ready to search," said Liski. "It is good we came out now. Stop here." The sound of rustling feet ceased. "Boris, you will go forward and approach them. I am certain you will find police there. Ivan One, give Boris your flashlight. When you get close, Boris, raise your hands, shine the light on your face so they can see you, and call out to warn them you are coming. Say you are unarmed and want to talk. Can you do this?"

"I can." Boris released one of Jack's arms and stepped forward. Liski still held the other in a viselike grip. Liski's pistol pressed into his temple.

"Tell them that we have Dr. Forester and his lady friend, and that we will kill them unless they help us," Liski said.

"What if they shoot at me?"

"They won't. They will hold their fire. When they agree to talk, come back and we will all go down there to give them our demands."

"Okay. So, I raise my hands, light up my face, and say we have two people for hostage who we will kill if they don't help."

"Make sure you say that it's Dr. Forester and his lady friend. Tell them that the brother and the old lady are all right."

"We have Dr. Forester and his lady friend and will kill them. Got it. When I come back, will you still be here in the same place?"

"Of course. Get going."

Boris switched on the light, lifted his arms, shined it on his face, and set off. When he was out of earshot, one of the Ivans holding Marianna inquired, "Boss, was it wise to send him?"

"He'll do fine. Be quiet."

Jack checked the zip tie tension again. He believed that he could free himself at will. But not with a pistol to his head. Minutes went by and there were no gunshots.

"He's coming back, boss," said the younger Ivan. The beam of a flashlight came bobbing up the trail. Boris was running. He stopped, short of breath.

"Why are you running?" asked Liski.

"That was the most scary thing I ever do," Boris said, gasping for air. "But I did it. They will help us."

"Good," said Liski. "Easy, you see? You two Ivans stay on either side of Kovalenko. Hold her tightly and keep your pistols on her. Boris and I will hold Forester, and we will go first. Stay calm."

Thus formed, they emerged from the trees into the backyard and halted near the barn. The area was as well lit as a soccer field. A dozen police officers stood spaced out near the house and on the driveway, waiting for them. One of them held two German shepherds on short leashes. About half the officers were wearing black tactical uniforms with helmets and body armor, assault rifles pointed skyward. Jack could see an array of police vehicles parked near the garage, blocking in Liski's Suburban.

Liski commanded Boris to keep his pistol against Forester's head. "If anything goes wrong, kill them both." Then the little man let go of Jack's other arm and stepped forward two paces. Boris pressed the barrel painfully hard against his skull. One of the officers strode out of the shadows toward Liski. It was Dirkens. "That's close enough," said Liski.

She stopped about ten feet away and stretched out her arms to show she was unarmed.

"Jack, are you okay?" she called over.

"Yes."

"Both of you shut your mouths," said Liski. "I will do the talking now."

"And who are you?" asked Dirkens.

"My name is not important. If you want these two people to survive, you must do exactly as I say."

"Your man said the other two are unharmed. Is this true?"

"They are in the woods," said Liski. "Unhurt. You can find them after we leave. Now, I will tell you what we need."

"I'm listening."

"We will take our own cars to the airport. No one follows. You will fly us by jet to Wilmington, North Carolina, then you will take us in helicopter to my operations base, and then we will let these two go unharmed. If not, they will die."

"And where might that base be?"

"It's a ship in international waters off the coast."

"Ah, yes . . ." she said. "Mr. Potemkin's floating nation. I've been reading about it."

"How did you know to read about that?"

"Just a hunch. In any case, we can certainly consider your request."

"You had better. I give you five minutes to consider and one hour to arrange details."

"Can these two come back on the helicopter?"

"No. We put them on a small boat. No more discussion. You will make the call to superiors right here in front of me."

"Okay," she said. "I'm going to reach in my pocket to get my phone." She did so and placed it to her ear. "Get me the chief immediately. We've got a hostage situation." She listened. "No, I do not want additional personnel. Just get me the chief. Everything is under control. Quickly."

"One wrong move and you know what will happen," said Liski. "Many will die along with them."

Frankie Dirkens half turned away and continued speaking into the phone, occasionally glancing over at them. Jack's heart was pounding fast and steady. He wished he could send her his thoughts, let her know that Liski was lying about Marianna's release. He could shout over and tell her, but Liski would just deny it. Or it could trigger a reprisal. He had no leverage. Dirkens continued talking, nodding. Jack looked back at Marianna. She was standing straight, grasped by the two Ivans. Her hair was bedraggled, her face smudged with dirt, but her expression was strong and defiant. Their eyes locked for a moment and she tilted her head, made a slight nod as if saying goodbye. As he looked away from her, Jack thought he saw movement in one of the windows of Tony's apartment on the second floor of the barn off to his left. Perhaps they had stationed one of the officers up there. That could be good.

If only Liski would make a misstep. Jack closed his eyes and a thought bubbled up. Perhaps Liski had already made a critical misstep by letting Jack overhear his plans for killing Marianna. An idea began taking shape.

Dirkens finally lowered the phone and faced Liski. "We agree to your demands," she said. "Only one condition. Two of your people stay behind, to be released when our two are back in safety."

Liski nodded. "Reasonable," he said. "I accept. Ivan One and Two—you will stay behind. No protest. When is the plane ready?"

"About half an hour at the New Canterbury airport. It's five miles away."

"I know where it is."

"It'll take you to Wilmington, as you wanted. Once you're there, a state helicopter will fly you out to your . . . country."

"Very good. We will leave now in our vehicle. Move yours out of the way. No tricks."

"No tricks," said Dirkens. "You are free to go whenever you want. The plane will be ready, like I said, in half an hour."

"And no police at the airport."

"Right. No police at the airport. Officers, move your vehicles away from behind these folks. Give them free access out of here."

Liski's second mistake had been leaving only Boris to guard him.

It was now or never.

In one swift movement that he'd been rehearsing in his mind, Jack slipped his wrists out of the zip tie and grabbed hold of Boris's pistol with both of his hands. Then, swiveling his body violently, he twisted the weapon out of Boris's grip. The gun in his hands now, he dashed several steps forward, spun around, and faced Liski. Jack then raised the pistol to his own temple.

Liski bellowed a curse. "What the hell is this!"

Boris lumbered toward Jack, but Liski grabbed his coat and held him back. "Wait."

"Do I shoot the bastard?" said the mash-nosed Ivan.

"Not yet. Come back here, Doctor. Or I will personally kill Kovalenko in front of you. Give the gun back to Boris."

Keeping the pistol pressed against his temple, Jack directed his words at Dirkens. "Investigator, he intends to kill Marianna on their ship. I overheard the plan. She is not a hostage. I am the only real hostage."

"This is not true," said Liski. "Don't be stupid, Doctor. I know you want to live."

"He has a grudge against her, Investigator. I hate to say it, but she is already lost. And by the way, she is the real Marianna Kovalenko. She escaped him once."

Liski hissed. "You are a fool."

"Without me, Liski, you have no way out of here. I'm your only ticket, but I can make your avenue of escape vanish in a heartbeat. Don't think I won't. Let her go, and I'll hand this gun back to you and come with you."

The little man spat on the ground. "You wouldn't take your own life."

"Try me."

"Put the gun down," Liski said, his voice coarsening. "Our weapons are all pointed at you."

"You can take your revenge on her, Liski, or you can have your freedom. Take your pick. I've lost too much in my life already." He pressed the pistol hard against his skull and put his finger on the trigger. "I'll give you to the count of ten to let her go. Do it or none of you will walk out of here."

Would he really do it? Would he leave Julia fatherless? Would she understand someday why he was willing to take this gamble and make this sacrifice? It was an agonizing thought, but he believed she would. He took a deep breath. "One . . ."

When he got to eight, Liski gave off a stream of curses and spat again. "All right." He turned toward Boris and the Ivans. "She isn't worth it. Let her go. Now."

The thugs released Marianna's arms and she sagged. Jack took his finger off the trigger but kept the barrel pointed at his temple. She looked over at him, her eyes wide, an expression of blank shock. She shook her head.

Jack held her gaze. "Go with the investigator, Marianna."

She made a moaning sound but walked away from the thugs and didn't resist as Dirkens led her over to another officer. "Take her inside," Dirkens said.

"No," Marianna said, shivering. "I will stay here."

Jack faced Liski. "A deal's a deal." Switching on the safety, he tossed the pistol down at Boris's feet.

"Boris, pick it up and bring him back," ordered Liski. "Do a better job this time."

As Boris bent to retrieve the weapon, Jack heard a thud. Boris gasped and to Jack's astonishment, the huge man collapsed like a stringless marionette, falling forward. There was an arrow protruding from the back of his neck.

Tony, thought Jack.

"What the hell is this?" Liski growled, lifting his pistol toward Jack.

At that moment, an arrow sliced into Liski's shoulder. He spun around, dropping the pistol and crying out in pain. Jack dove and rolled away as gunshots erupted on both sides. The firing lasted less than a minute. Then silence. A pall of smoke shimmered in the light, and the only thing he could hear was his own ragged breathing.

Liski sat in the driveway, holding his arm, an arrow lodged in his shoulder. An officer stood over him, rifle leveled at the little man's startled face. The two Ivans and Boris lay motionless on the ground. There were bullet wounds and blood pooling. The younger Ivan, like Boris, also had an arrow protruding from his back. Looking around, still dazed, Jack saw with relief that none of the officers appeared to have been hit.

Leaping up, he yelled out, "Officers, that was my brother shooting the bow. Don't shoot anymore! Tony! Where are you?"

Tony walked out from behind the barn, holding his bow. He'd done it. Unbelievable. He'd gotten loose and made his way back to his apartment.

"Jesus Christ," one of the policemen said. "That was impressive."

A smattering of applause broke out among the officers.

"Let's go find Zoë," he heard Tony say. "I know where she is."

"Three of you please go with him," Dirkens ordered.

Jack wanted to run after his brother to thank him, but a wave of confusion engulfed him. Julia. He must find her. Marianna came striding toward him, rubbing her pale face, a dazed look on it. They came close and then embraced. Jack felt her shivering, her rapid breathing, her damp clothes. He smelled the musty odor of earth and leaves.

Dirkens strode over to them. "Dr. Forester, that was the craziest fucking thing I've ever seen anybody do in my life. I don't know whether to congratulate you or have you committed. We need to talk."

"Later," Jack said, filled with urgency. He took Marianna's hand. "Come with me."

They went inside and he pushed aside the refrigerator and rushed down the steps followed by Marianna. Crouching under the workbench, he slid away the plywood and clicked on a flashlight. Julia's hair caught the glow. She was lying on her side, motionless.

He called her name. The child stirred, squinted, and shaded her eyes. He pointed the beam at his own face. "It's just me, honey. All is okay. Let's get you out of there."

"Aunt Zoë didn't come back," Julia said, crawling toward him.

Jack lifted her out. "Aunt Zoë is fine. She'll be here soon. Uncle Tony's with her."

"I was quiet when they came, just like you told me," she said, hugging his neck. "Then I fell asleep. I'm hungry. You're wet, Daddy. Hi, Vlada. Where have you been?"

Carrying her, he and Marianna went back outside. Dirkens was waiting.

"How did you find out what was going on?" he asked her.

The investigator smiled. "You can thank your niece, Kaitlyn."

Julia lifted her head from his shoulder and said, "Kaitlyn? Is she okay?"

"She is, honey," Dirkens said. "She's with her friends now, Mr. and Mrs. VanDyke. You'll see her soon."

Jack straightened. "She's with the VanDykes?"

She nodded. "And you can thank them too. I'm sure you remember how kind they were to her the night of the kidnapping. Bea had given Kaitlyn her number and said to call if she ever needed help. Kaitlyn called and said she wanted to run away. Sounds like Bea tried to talk her out of it, and when that didn't work, old Ted drove over and picked her up."

"So it was him that morning," Jack said. "That's a relief."

"They're good people. They decided it wasn't right to keep you all worried, so they tried calling this afternoon to let you know she was safe. Kaitlyn had cooled down by then. But everyone's phones—Zoë's, yours, your brother's—kept going straight to voicemail. So they drove over and saw the strange vehicle, nobody around, doors unlocked, fridge moved, cigar smoke in the house. Kaitlyn still had my number, so she called. Like I said before, she's a smart kid. You'll be happy to know she's sorry she ran away and caused you distress."

"I think that was my fault," he said.

"In any case, we get here and find the cell phone jammer and we see signs of what looks like a group of people heading out into the woods. Given all that's been going on, I called for a helicopter and reinforcements."

"All I can say is thank you," Jack said, reaching out to shake her hand.

Jack looked at Marianna. Her eyes were moist. She nodded. "I thank you too," she said.

"So, this is the real Ms. Kovalenko," Dirkens said, looking at her and smiling. "Nice to make your acquaintance, and I look forward to hearing the whole weird story."

"Her name's not Ms. Kovalenko," Julia said. "She's Vlada. She and Daddy need a bath."

CHAPTER FIFTY-SIX

NEW YORK TIMES — MONDAY, NOVEMBER 1, 2018

US TROOPS RAID OLIGARCH'S OCEAN LAIR

Early on the morning of October 31, a joint task force of US Marines, Navy SEALs, and FBI special agents conducted an amphibious assault on the mega-yacht owned by the Russian billionaire, Mikhail Potemkin, a close associate of Russian president, Vladimir Putin, while the ship was anchored in international waters off the coast of North Carolina. The assault on Potemkin's ship, which is registered with the UN General Assembly as an independent state called "Wiegatesland," was carried out under a presidential emergency authorization for the use of military force.

According to a White House press release, the decision to attack arose when "overwhelming evidence gathered by the FBI implicated Potemkin in a cyberattack on the New Canterbury Medical Center in New York State that represented a vicious maneuver by a foreign power upon US home soil with the intent to damage the nation's health care system." Leaders in the House and Senate have demanded a "full investigation into this exercise of executive power."

Potemkin and his crew of nearly two hundred individuals from numerous nations were allegedly involved in an array of criminal activities including murder, extortion, corporate espionage, drug trafficking, human trafficking, prostitution, interference in the conduct of elections, securities fraud, forgery, tax evasion, insider trading, illegal arms dealing, counterfeiting, the facilitation of terrorist activity, bribery, grand larceny, artifact looting, and money laundering.

Troops ferried by stealth watercraft launched the assault at 3 a.m. Eastern Standard Time. Two US marines suffered minor injuries during the boarding. Expedition commander, Lieutenant Colonel James Corcoran, USMC, stated there were no casualties among Potemkin's crew thanks to an immediate surrender delivered by Wiegatesland's minister of security, Leonard Spavin. A former US Army ranger, Spavin is in federal custody along with 57 other Wiegatesland "citizens" with outstanding arrest warrants in the US, Mexico, Canada, Australia, France, Ukraine, Poland, Moldavia, Finland, and the United Kingdom. More arrests are expected to follow.

The corpse of Mikhail Potemkin, who had died several days before the attack, was discovered in the ship's cold-storage locker, along with that of another crew member who appears to have died from a head injury. Based upon the statements of witnesses aboard the ship, the authorities believe that Potemkin may have been exposed to a toxic nerve agent favored by Kremlin assassins. In a surprising twist to the story, the serial murderer Dr. Bryson Witner was on board at the time of Potemkin's death. Witner had escaped last Wednesday, October 27th, from the Patterson Psychiatric Institute.

According to anonymous sources in the Pentagon, Witner is believed to have been flown to the ship in a helicopter piloted by Dr. Lawrence Haines, president and CEO of Health Wealth Associates (HWA), a hospital consortium that owns and operates 38 hospitals in the Southeast and Southwest, and that had been in the process of acquiring the New Canterbury Medical Center, the target of the alleged cyberattack. Reports indicate that Haines, who had a previous social relationship with both Potemkin and Witner, flew off the ship with Witner on board shortly after Potemkin's death. Two days ago, the Coast

Guard recovered a helicopter registered to Haines in shallow waters near Ocracoke, North Carolina. The National Transportation Safety Board is investigating the cause of the crash. The bodies of Haines and Witner have not been recovered as of the time of this report. Shortly after this operation, the assets of HWA were frozen and its operations placed under federal oversight.

The Russian, Chinese, Iranian, and North Korean ambassadors have filed formal protests with the UN Security Council, declaring that "once again, the imperialist American government has staged an unprovoked attack upon the rights and property of a sovereign nation."

CHAPTER FIFTY-SEVEN

APRIL 5, 2020

It was late afternoon and Jack was finishing up in his office. His new administrative assistant, Joyce Demarco, had already gone for the day. Joyce didn't have quite the above-and-beyond work ethic that Tré had displayed, but she was working out well. Upon being awarded his MBA last spring, Tré was hired by the university's finance office and was enjoying his new responsibilities.

New Canterbury University had been rescued from its financial abyss by a federal grant that would be recovered through the sale of Potemkin's assets. As the stain on the medical center's reputation was erased, Damien Falconi returned to partner on the creation of a genomic research center. New construction was already underway.

He opened Marianna's email again. It had just arrived that morning and, though he had read it twice, he had not had time yet to write the response it deserved.

Dear Jack,

Along with all my best wishes, I write to give you some good news. My friend tells me that the chancellor at Kyiv University Medical School will soon confirm that he would like you to be a visiting professor of emergency medicine for a month this summer, as you and he had discussed! I'm all but 100% certain this will happen, and I am excited and happy to know we will have this opportunity to continue our friendship in person. There are so many things to talk about that are not easy by writing or by phone. When you came to Ukraine with Zoë, Kaitlyn, and Julia to see me last Easter, it was one of the best things in my life. It was wonderful to spend time with you all—and to be far away from the terrible things that happened to us the autumn before that. Olesia and her family are well. She asks me often how everyone is doing.

I am well and still enjoying my new job as the editor in chief of the Ukrainian Week. Our subscriptions continue to grow in number. The previous editor, whom I told you had disappeared, has now been seen in St. Petersburg working for a Russian newspaper there. There is not too much more to say about him. I think his spirit was broken by his contact with the men of Potemkin. I am myself working on another article about the growing military conflict with Russian-backed separatists in Eastern Ukraine, along with the threat of a possible general invasion of Ukraine by Russia. Most people in Ukraine do not believe this could happen, but we will see.

My anticipation runs high for your visit. After that it will be my turn to come and see you. I am glad for the work I do, and I am happy for the work that occupies you, but I sometimes can't help but feel the unfairness of our work being so far apart. But I will say no more. You are so often in my thoughts.

With affection, your friend,

Marianna

Jack read it one more time and hit reply.

Dear Marianna,

It is terrific to hear from you, as always. It sounds as though you are enjoying your new responsibilities. I'm not surprised. I can't think of a better person to be doing it. Thank you so much for passing on your intel about the visiting professorship! I will await final confirmation, but I've already cleared the way to take this coming July as a sabbatical. Operations are running smoothly here now and I'm sure they'll survive well without me for at least that long—and much longer, I'm sure.

Everyone sends you their kindest regards. Last weekend Tony and I built Julia a treehouse (not very high above the ground, I'd add). I will send you photos. She is enjoying kindergarten and has grown at least two inches since you saw her last. I don't know if I mentioned that Tony has begun studying for an online master's degree in computer science and plans on taking the business that he and Chad had started to a higher level. Zoë is well. She has started volunteering at an animal rescue shelter and just yesterday we discussed rearranging the barn and fencing in a field or two so that she can take in a few horses and maybe some goats and sheep in need of homes. It will be like returning this land back to when my grandparents had their farm. A nice feeling. The field where the wrecked vehicle sat rusting is now clear. I finally had it towed away (to the scrapyard south of New Canterbury, which is now under new management, not surprisingly). I often think of the day when I took a hammer to it, and you were so kind and understanding. I see that as a turning point in my life, to be honest.

Forgive the brevity of this message, but I am running out of time and must close for now if I'm going to make it to Kaitlyn's baseball game. It's the second game of the season, and she'll be the starting pitcher. We have a beautiful spring day for it. As I said in my last letter, she was named team captain this year. We learned last week that she is also in the final rounds of consideration for a baseball scholarship to Yale University. I couldn't be prouder of her. Her decision to stay with us has changed our lives for the better.

And everyone talks about you often. If all goes as planned for my visiting professorship in July, I would like to bring the whole crew with me. But sometime in the autumn, if all the stars line up, perhaps you and I could consider meeting in Italy for a holiday, just the two of us. I've always wanted to see the place.

Yours truly,

Jack

ACKNOWLEDGMENTS

I am deeply grateful to the many kind and talented folks who helped this story reach its current state, including early readers Eileen Forestell, Glen Cummings, Don Borland, and Susan Holmes. I received wonderful developmental editing help and encouragement from Christine Sneed and Elizabeth White. The Köehler Books editorial team of Hannah Tonsor and Becky Hilliker did brilliant work in the final stages, as did cover artist Lauren Sheldon. Last but not least, I would like to thank John Köehler and Joe Coccaro for bringing this project in out of the rain.

www.ingramcontent.com/pod-product-compliance
Lightning Source LLC
LaVergne TN
LVHW091621070526
838199LV00044B/886